PROMISERS BIG

Sandra Mann

Outskirts Press, Inc.
Denver, Colorado

Outskirts Press, Inc.
http://www.outskirtspress.com

ISBN: 978-1-4327-2225-8

PRINTED IN THE UNITED STATES OF AMERICA

Dedication

This book is dedicated to strong women everywhere, and in
particular to
my mother and her mother
my daughter and her daughters

Thanks
for sharing laughter and tears
for teaching what truly matters
for cherishing friends and family
for facing life with courage and grace
for being a part of my life.

Foreword

Dreamers envision the new, while doers create the practical. What was once innovative becomes ordinary; what was unique becomes commonplace; what was daring becomes the norm.

Past generations on both sides of my family came to the sandhills to live; and, in the process, established a legacy which I cherish. In spite of numerous tragedies and setbacks, they persevered so that I grew up on the very land which they homesteaded.

In the process of writing this book, I became aware of how little children truly know of their parents' growing-up years. Much of this book is based on actual events of my mother's life to which I have added my own details. This was necessary since Mom seldom spoke of her childhood, and we didn't ask about it very often since talking about the past seemed to upset her.

Mom and I were very close, and I was complacent when

she was just a phone call away. As I wrote this book, however, she was gone; and I found much that I didn't know. How I wish I had asked her when we still had time, but regret such as that accomplishes very little. Realizing that, my mission became to capture what I knew and to find answers to what I didn't know.

My goal is to celebrate the accomplishments of all prairie settlers while portraying the life of a particular family with realistic detail. All pioneers met the challenges of life, and those who stayed emerged in varying degrees of triumph. That is a story worth telling.

Thus it was with our pioneering fathers and mothers who came to a world largely untouched by civilization. Where some saw impossibilities, they saw potential; where some saw desolation and loneliness, they saw elbow room; where some saw difficulties, they saw opportunities.

They came; they saw; they conquered.

Chapter 1

She fidgeted beside the bed, hardly seeing the lace curtains blowing in the breeze as she gazed out the window. When she moved her eyes back into the room, she could see that Mama had finally drifted off to sleep. Now she could tiptoe around the bed and slip outside to play with Flaxie's new pups.

Quietly as an eight-year-old girl in an overfull room can move, she slipped around the end of the bed to make her way. The rustle of her movement apparently was enough to make her mother stir, and Maria shifted her head on the pillow to look at her daughter standing still and tall. She spoke with that familiar, breathless raspy sound, "Darlene, I was afraid you were gone and I was here all alone. It's good when you are here with me."

Darlene sat down, knowing her chance to slip out into the sunshine was gone for now, and waited as her mother gathered strength to resume the earlier conversation she had started.

It wasn't that Darlene was being naughty or neglectful;

she just had so much energy that it was hard for her to sit still. That fact really didn't matter. She was the youngest of the children, not truly big enough to pitch in and work, and Mama wanted someone with her. Darlene remembered all the times she had wished everyone else would just leave so she could have her mother all to herself. Now she had her wish, and it turned out to be much less satisfying than she had expected.

"I'd like to know just what is really going on around here," she mused to herself. "Everyone in the house is always whispering or they quit talking when I'm around. When I asked Theo why he was crying, he made up some stupid story about getting dirt in his eyes. They started this when Mama was gone for a while, and now that she's home, they're still acting the same. I'm going to ask her straight out what's going on since no one else will tell me. She'll tell me."

Maria pushed herself up on one elbow to look Darlene in the eye. "What is inside your head? I can see when you have ideas." The question came out in Maria's broken English heavily laced with a German accent.

The softness and concern in Maria's voice was Darlene's cue to demand her answers, and at first she found it hard to put her ideas in words. All of a sudden the gates opened and floods of words tumbled out, one after the other. "Why is everything upside down? Why won't anyone talk to me? Why did you have to go away? Why . . ."

Mother reached over and pulled Darlene tight to her chest. She smoothed back the auburn curls and softly caressed the lightly freckled cheeks, all the while saying, "Little Lena, Little Lena, please don't hurt."

Darlene noticed the tears in Maria's voice and instantly wished she hadn't started this. She burrowed her head more deeply into Maria's cotton gown and tried to stop the quivery feeling right above her belly button. More than anything, she was sorry for making Mama sad.

"I will talk because you need to know. This is a hard time and hard words, but you will need these words later on." Maria paused, and when she began again, she pulled Darlene up so they could look straight into each other's eyes. Both sets of hazel green eyes held tears ready to spill over, so Maria gently folded her frightened daughter to her once more and rocked back and forth, just as she had so often when nightmares or realities were too big for one little girl to face alone.

As they both relaxed into each other, Darlene sat up once again to look at her mother's face. Maria took a deep breath, spoke, and totally shattered Darlene's world. "I went away because I needed to talk to the doctor. I came back because my body is sick and he can't help me." Words came faster as Maria shared as much as her young daughter could comprehend. "I wanted to be here with my family, so I came home to stay."

Darlene listened but wasn't ready to know what she already knew. "We'll just have to take you to a doctor who can help you. Theo can find one." Reaching up to her mother's face, she smoothed Maria's hair as her mother had just done for her moments earlier.

Maria caught her by the wrist and held her at arm's length. Looking straight into Darlene's eyes, she shook her head and softly spoke, "Not this time, Little One. Your brother Theo can do much, but not this. No one can help me get better, so we all have to help each other."

"You can't leave me. You're my mother. I have to have a mother. Everyone knows a girl has to have a mother." Darlene kept repeating the phrases as if that would make them true. "Promise me you will stay here and be my mother."

Maria's answer was kind but true. "I will stay as long as I

can stay. Even when I have to go, I will still be your mother. I'll be gone, but you will find me in your heart."

"No, Mother, you have to promise not to leave me all alone. You're all I have."

"When a person makes a promise, it has to be kept, so I can't say what you want to hear. Even though I'll be gone, you're not alone. Your brothers and sisters love you, and Theodor will always look after you. He promised me so we know it's true. Let me hold you now, and later we will talk more."

Darlene needed to go talk to Theo, but she also needed her mother. They snuggled on the bed until Maria fell asleep soundly enough for Darlene to make her way out of the room and to the barn where she found her big brother sitting on a barrel, patching broken harness.

"Little Lena, come here." Ted could see that Darlene knew as much about the tragedy ahead as an eight year old could know, and he folded her in his huge arms. Wordlessly, the two auburn heads rested together, and the tears ran freely. "We can do this together, and we have to help Mama. We don't want her to worry about us, so let's make a deal. If we need to cry, let's come to this barrel in the barn. It's good to have a place to let sadness out."

Darlene nodded her head, and the two of them shook hands to make their agreement official. "But how can we help Mama, Theo? She said no one can help her now. What are we going to do?"

Theodor had been like a father to Darlene since Papa had died seven years ago. Maria was determined to hold on to the ranch that she and Ernest had worked so hard to build up, and she relied on Ted for advice on ranching business as well as for help with the family. Ted was the one who had started the nickname of Little Lena, and it just came out of his mouth naturally.

"We are going to be brave and strong and happy, Little Lena. As long as Mama is here, we can love her and she can love us. That is the best medicine she can have."

Darlene took time to think over his reply, and then solemnly shook her head. "Okay. I'll spend time every morning in her room and not leave when she falls asleep—not even to see old Flaxie's puppies. Maybe I can take one of them in her room every day so she can watch him grow. She loves baby animals. I can pick flowers every day from the hills for her so her room looks nice, and I won't fight with anyone ever again. Do you think all that would help Mama?"

Ted took time to consider Darlene's ideas before answering. "The puppies and the flowers sound just right, and she'd like it if we could all get along and not bicker, so I think you've got it figured out." That was what she liked so much about him—he treated her just like he treated real people. He never laughed at her when she shared her ideas or when she tried to work like the grown-ups all around her.

Darlene spent a restless night, excited about doing her part to make Mama smile. Right after breakfast, she scurried to the barn to pick out the just right puppy. Old Flaxie, Theo's favorite coyote hound, had four fat and furry babies at her side. Since Darlene spent so much time at the barn with her, the old dog looked at Darlene and wagged her tail without getting up. What a decision. Finally, Darlene put down the black one with the tip on its tail and chose the one that looked like a fuzzy snowball. Wrapping him in her apron, she hustled past all the kittens waiting for their usual rubbings and hurried to the edge of the corral where the dandelions were the thickest. Good as her word to Theo, she gathered a handful of bright yellow flowers to take into the house.

With her free hand, she grabbed the bean can that she

used for a vase, scooped it full of water from the bucket on the floor, and jammed in the flowers. Pausing at the bedroom door, she adjusted the flowers and shifted the bright-eyed white puppy on her arm for Mama's inspection.

Maria also had spent a restless night, concerned about her youngest daughter. Darlene would have to face all the upcoming events in life without either her mother or her father to help her through. Even though Darlene had wisdom beyond her years, she also had a generous spirit that made her sometimes do for others even when they were not people inclined to be generous in return.

When she saw Lena had brought gifts as a way to share with her, all of a sudden Maria knew Darlene's good heart would carry her through. She was anxious; however, for the little girl was so trusting and softhearted that unscrupulous people might exploit that loving nature. Maria set about preparing Darlene to be loving, yet levelheaded; trusting, yet tough when necessary.

Lena couldn't talk fast enough to keep her words from spilling over one another. "I'm going to make you happy. Look, Mama. I picked your favorite flowers for you like I always do. Do you love them? I'm putting them right by your bed so you can smell them whenever you want. Here is Flaxie's most handsome baby. I call him Potato cause he looks just like the bowl of mashed potatoes that you fix for us." With that, Darlene thrust the puppy into the air for her mother's approval.

They were both unprepared for what happened next. Mama reached out for the puppy, Lena pushed him toward her, and the puppy was so excited that he wet all over both of them. Shrieking, the startled mother and daughter caught their breath and collapsed into a giggling fit. Unable to catch their breath and unable to stop their laughter, they held on to the frightened, squirming pup while he tried to jump down and run under the bed.

Calming down gradually, they gently rubbed Potato until his little heart quit racing and he put his head down on Maria's arm. She gazed at him, and observed, as much to herself as to Darlene, "His hair is white and soft, just like Harry's." Then she gently stroked his head, closed her eyes, and let her head fall back against the pillow.

After she had lain there unmoving for what seemed an incredibly long time, she opened her eyes and looked directly at her daughter. "I loved him so much, and he left me too soon. He was such a good boy."

Maria did not cry this time at the mention of Harry's name, and Darlene sensed that she might finally hear what had happened to the brother who died long ago. Usually the entire family avoided subjects that made Maria cry, so Darlene knew a few details; but they all shushed her each time she asked a question about him. This time was different, though, because Maria felt driven by her desire to give Darlene a solid understanding of her own heritage. That link would soon be completely gone, so Maria had decided to spend her remaining time making sure that Darlene had a sense of who and what made family.

Little Lena felt confused about what had just happened. Even though she and Mama were spending time together because Maria was dying and that was sad, they had laughed the hardest she could ever remember. Even though it had felt right, she wondered how they could laugh at the same time they had such a hurt inside. She would have to remember to ask Theo if she had done something wrong.

Maria absent-mindedly scratched Potato's ear, and he drifted off to sleep. "I'm glad you brought me the flowers and the puppy. That's something just like what Harry might have done." With that the stories out of the past began.

Chapter 2

My little blond boy, my only blond boy, who never believed there was anything he couldn't do. And you know, he was most always right about that. Such stubbornness when he set his mind to do anything.

August is hard for me, ever since Harry. He came to me on the eighth of August, the hottest day I ever knew. Then he died one week after he turned ten years old. I still hate August.

What a boy—always knowing about animals. I could find him by looking for our dog because they went everywhere together. And you should have seen him ride. After Papa brought home a pony for his fourth birthday, Harry never wanted to walk anywhere.

When his legs grew so long they about scraped the ground on the pony, Papa traded for a big palomino horse with a white mane and tail. "How about a horse the same color as you, Son? I thought he looked like a match for you."

Harry grabbed Papa, squeezed him hard, and grabbed the outstretched halter rope. He and his new horse made a circle around the corral, Harry marching like the biggest rancher around, and the horse prancing right behind him. They were so beautiful, both with their bright blond hair, that I reached over and patted Ern's hand. He gave me that lop-sided grin of his that meant he was proud of himself, and said, "Guess this was a good deal, right, Mama?"

I'll never forget seeing Harry and Ernest saddling that horse, and Ernest giving Harry a leg up for his first ride. Harry circled the corral several times, and then he begged Ernest to let them go outside. "Please, Papa, let me show him where the tank is. He'll need a drink pretty quick. I'll be careful, I promise."

So Ernest opened the gate, and off they went. Soon Harry was trotting, and even sooner, he was loping around different places. When the horse glanced down and saw the overflow stream right in front of him, he gathered himself on his back legs, doubled up his front feet, and sailed over the water. He was so high in the air that I didn't think he would ever come back down!

That was when Harry fell in love forever. He ran the horse back to Ernest and me, laughing and waving his hat. "Did you see that? I never knew a horse could jump so high. I'm naming him Bullfrog."

Never a moment was he afraid, and that horse would jump any time Harry asked him to. No matter how many times they jumped, Harry would shout and wave his hat big in the sky, and Bullfrog would toss his head back and forth so his flaxen mane would flash in the sun. What times they had.

All the time we worked hard. Summer meant we would work in the fields, come to the house, unharness our teams, and then milk thirty or so cows. They were in the pasture east of the house, and always at the far end when we needed them. Harry figured that he could help by going after them a little while before we came in from the field, so he decided that his job was to get in the milk cows.

How often I would see him and Bullfrog zooming after the cows. Ernest would remind him to be careful in the prairie dog town by the north fence, and Harry would nod and say, "We're careful in that dog town 'cause Frog and I don't want to fall in those holes. That would hurt awful bad. Don't worry about us."

The summer was hot and Ernest tried to make it as easy as he could on us. Every day, he'd give us the signal to turn our teams around and call it a day. Fred, Alma, and I would take turns going early to the barn to start the milking. Ernest always stayed out longer in the hot, dusty days to get more fieldwork done.

That afternoon Ernest said, "Fred and Alma, all of you go in and let Maria go to the house to rest. I'll finish this field pretty soon and be there to help with the milking. Mama needs to cool off." What he didn't say was that the baby inside me was getting big enough that working in the sun made me very tired. He was a good man, your father.

We had grained the teams and turned them out to graze when we heard Papa shouting out in the cow pasture. Some of the cows were hard to drive in, so we thought Harry had trouble and Ernest was over there helping him move them along.

I came out of the barn to see the most horrible sight of my life. There was Ernest, carrying Harry like he was a baby. We rushed out and I could hear Ernest shouting, "Harness up the lumber wagon team right now." Fred and Alma ran to get the mules while I ran to see what was the matter. That was twenty-three years ago, and I can see it just like yesterday.

Poor Harry's face was bloody and bruised, and his eyes flickered as he mumbled, "Snake, hand, hurts." We looked where he was pointing and saw the two dots on the side of his wrist.

Ernest laid him in the wagon, telling me about how he had seen Bullfrog running wild, reins trailing and no rider in sight. The worst thing to see on these hills is a riderless horse since you never know where to go look. Ernest tied his team, jumped the fence, and found Harry in the dog town. Then he had scooped up his son and run the half-mile to the house, shouting all the way.

One of us had to stay home while the other went the forty miles to Ogallala to the doctor. We had two children at home, fieldwork to do, cows to milk, and all the other chores that never stopped, day after day, morning and night. Ernest was getting ready to climb in the wagon, and I shouted at him, "I will be the one to go. I'll not stay behind."

He knew I could make the trip by myself because my job was to go to Ogallala to get supplies, but never had I made such a trip as this.

I didn't think to grab anything for me, just a pillow and blankets for little Harry who was sprawled in the back. Ernest put his hands on my shoulder and shouted, "Find Dr. Schmidt. He'll fix him just like he fixed my hand."

I grabbed the lines, yelled at the mules, and took off at a high run. After a time, I realized the mules could not keep up like that, so I pulled them in and let them go slower until I couldn't stand it and then I pushed them hard again. It seemed like it took forever.

Our three children, especially Harry, had always begged to go on a freighting trip. It sounded so exciting to them, but to us grown-ups it was a different story. We would leave in the late afternoon, go about half way, and sleep in the wagon. By morning, the mules would have rested and be ready to go on. We'd get our lumber, fence posts, wire, and staples before we loaded the flour and coffee, then head back. Traveling in a lumber wagon isn't like riding in a buggy since there is nothing to make the ride smooth, and the jolting made our bodies hurt all over. When we would get home, we were tired, sore, and hungry so it was hard to imagine taking a young child on such a trip.

Harry had asked every day when he could go on a freighting trip, and finally I promised him I'd take him the next time I went. Here I was, good as my word, taking him to town with me right now. How I wished I had let him go when he asked before.

I don't remember much about the trip, but when people heard my team running into town, they rushed out to see why I was driving so wild. When they heard, they led me to the doctor's office and helped take Harry inside. Dr. Schmidt was gone to Omaha for the summer, so Dr. Norris was the man we saw. The doctor couldn't seem to understand me, and Harry had trouble talking.

We finally made him know, and when he heard how long since the accident had happened, I saw him turn away and shake his head. I held Harry while the doctor cut his hand to let the poison drain, and Harry and I cried together as the bandages went on.

Harry told me what he remembered. Bullfrog and he were picking their way through the dog town when a rattlesnake buzzed and struck at Frog. Harry made him jump, and when Frog landed, his front foot caved in a burrow. As they fell, Harry heard the rattle of a snake before his head hit the ground. He was still lying there, unconscious, when Ernest found him.

"How is Frog, Mama? Did you see him? Is he okay?" I told him how Papa had looked up to see Frog running as fast as he could, just like he was going for help. Harry smiled at the thought of Bullfrog flying past Papa and going to the barn, and then he told me, "When I get home, I have to take

Frog out for a ride so he knows I'm okay. He's probably worried about me. I hope Papa remembers to feed him every day."

When the doctor finished working on Harry, the Menters, a German family we had known back in Omaha, invited me to bring Harry there and stay while he was under the doctor's care. Harry had a room to himself, and I was close by so I could hear him when he needed help. I didn't think I would ever rest, but when I put my head down, I did sleep.

For two weeks, the doctor would come in the morning and look at Harry's arm. Everyday the swelling seemed more and the dark color spread everywhere on his body. Finally came the day when the doctor smiled at me as he checked Harry. "You know, today he seems better. His breathing is good and he seems comfortable. Let's have him sit up in a chair so he can get stronger."

Harry seemed tired to me, but he was so ready to get home to Papa and Frog that he sat right up and tried to move his legs all by himself. "Wait a minute, young man. We want you to be very careful. Take it easy at first."

We moved a chair in front of the window, and Harry was soon busy looking outside. For him to be shut up in the house for two weeks was hard. He loved the birds and the wind and the clouds, so this made him feel good. All morning he sat there, calling to me so often. "Mama, come look at this puppy. He tried to run and fell over his big feet. He's the kind I want for my next dog." Then he saw a tall man with auburn hair, and softly murmured, "That looks just like my papa. I wonder how he can get those cows in without me. I hope he is riding Bull Frog because he is such a good horse. Frog knows how to get those old cows moving, 'specially Rosie who likes to hang behind all the rest and try to sneak off into a washout so you can't see her. We know all her tricks."

Harry needed more water to drink, so I went out to the kitchen to get him some when I heard him cry out, "Mama, come quick!" I could tell by the sound of his voice that something was wrong, and by the time I got back into the room, he was so scared he couldn't even talk.

The poison had affected his entire body, and now he had a bloody nose that we couldn't stop. By the time the doctor got to the house, Harry was lying on the bed, so still that I was afraid no one could help him.

Dr. Norris held his ear to Harry's chest, felt for his heart, and then let his head drop before looking at me. "I'm sorry, Mrs. Soehl, but it was all too much for him. His heart just gave out. There's nothing more we could have done."

Can you imagine? One minute we were laughing and talking; the next he was gone. I sat by his bed so I could stroke that white hair and feel his soft brow while I rubbed it. He had always liked that. I sat there for a long time because I couldn't stand the idea of letting go.

When the Menters realized what happened and saw that I couldn't move, let alone know what to do next, they helped out. We washed him and laid him out in their parlor while we made funeral arrangements. I ran my fingers through his curls one last time, and then had to let him go. We found a German minister, and after he was done with his words, I was all alone.

Even as sick as he was, Harry had been excited about being in Ogallala. Now he would always be there.

No one at home had any idea what had happened, so after the service, I hitched the mules and headed out. I don't remember much about the trip home, except how I dreaded seeing their faces when they ran out to welcome us home. Ernest would rush out first, and the children would trail right behind him, looking for Harry to come back with me.

I was right. They saw the dust and rushed out along the

road to greet us, laughing and shouting. All of a sudden, they realized I was alone, and no one said anything.

Ernest helped me out of the wagon, and Fred and Alma took the team to the house. First he just held me, and then I could feel him shaking and his tears falling on my head. “Mama, I am so sorry not to be with you. How hard for you to be alone for so long.” What a good man, your father. Even though he was hurt, he cared for my sadness. That was the way he was.

Never did Ernest get upset at me, but he was still angry that his little boy was gone so Dr. Norris was the one to blame. Dr. Schmidt had helped him earlier when the corn picker mangled his hand. He had been able to save two fingers and kept the hand so it would work, so Ernest had great faith in him. “If a real German doctor would have been there, he could have understood you sooner and saved our Harry. Never again will we let some know-nothing touch our family.” From that day forward, Ern would only deal with German doctors.

We all went out the next morning because we had to get on with our lives. I hurried as fast as I could with the dishes so I could leave the quiet house, and I headed out to the barn where they were harnessing the teams to go to the field. Just as I got to the corral gate, Frog came up to me and nuzzled me like he was asking when Harry would come out. That was the time I cried the hardest.

Every time Frog came up to the barn, it was just like a cut in my heart. Ern saw how hard it was on all of us to see that horse; so later on, Ernest traded Bullfrog for a dark brown saddle horse. He made sure the horse with white hair would be far away so we wouldn’t have to see him. Not like that made the heart hurt go away, but it was better without seeing such a reminder.

It was the middle of August when he died, and working

outside was part of how we made it through such a hard time. Some things are too big to say in words, so each of us kept our hurt inside. I would rub Fred's forehead as he waited to go to sleep, and sometimes he would hold my hand over his eyes as the tears fell. A fifteen-year-old boy doesn't like to have anyone see him cry, so we never mentioned it when he did. When my tears would come, Fred would put his hand on my shoulder and squeeze. No words, but then, no words could say what was in our hearts.

Then in October, baby Elsie came and helped us all. Not that we ever stopped missing Harry, but having a baby around is good for everyone. Your father acted like no one had ever had such a fine family, and each new babe made him that much more proud. Being busy and having a baby to love is a good place in life to be.

With that, Maria and Darlene leaned back on the pillow while Potato slept beside them. Mama yawned and murmured, "Lena, why don't you run outside and play now and I will sleep. Tomorrow, we will talk again."

Darlene awakened the puppy and headed into the sunshine, pondering what she had learned and anticipating the next story her mother would share. She wanted to know everything about everyone, and Mama was ready to talk.

Early the next morning Darlene clambered up the hill behind the barn, determined to find the best wild rose bouquet ever. Even though the thorns were sharp, she kept pulling the spiny shoots until she was satisfied. Then she found some buttercups, wild sweet peas, and bluebells to go with the roses. Standing on top of the hill, she filled her lungs with her biggest breath, taking in the sweet odor all around her. Darlene loved this special time of the year and one time had asked Theo why it ever had to change. "I wonder why we can't have roses all summer long, just like we do sunflowers. Wouldn't that be better?"

Ted had nodded, rolled his lips together, and observed, "You know, Lena, if we had them all the time, maybe we wouldn't even notice. No one gets real excited about sunflowers, so I guess we like what we don't have. Suppose that's how people are about everything. When something is gone, we think more about it."

Darlene clutched her handful of treasures to take to her mother, careful to put the roses in the center and surround them with the softer stems. As she jumped down from one cat step to the next, her joyous laugh echoed down the hill. Breathless when she reached the bottom, Lena called to the pup who now knew the day's routine. "Tater, let's go. Mama is waiting and today I'm going to ask her all about Papa. I just know she will tell me everything."

Maria looked up and smiled when she saw the day's collection. "It must already be June since you found those roses and wild flowers. Such a wonderful time to climb on top of a hill to see so far and smell so good. Did Potato climb all the way with you? His little legs must have gotten very tired. I'll bet he goes right to sleep on his rug."

Darlene turned the vase so Mama could see every one of the blooms, and told her mother, "Tomorrow I'm bringing in some soap weeds. You always told me they were prairie bells, and they're ready now too. I couldn't carry everything today so I'll get more in the morning."

Maria reached out her arms, and her daughter lay down gently beside her. As Maria stroked her hair, Darlene took a deep breath, filling her nostrils with the familiar scent of clean sheets and rose sachet that her mother always placed in the chest of drawers. "Mama, do you remember when I was little and I talked about putting the rose sacks in Chester Drawers? That was what it sounded like to me when you talked about the dresser, and then everyone laughed at me except for Theo. He told me that would be a great name and now we all say that. Isn't that a funny story?"

Smiling through her teary eyes, Maria agreed. "You know, that's part of the fun of being family—all the little times we share and then remember later on. I want you to have lots of those to take with you when I'm gone."

Lena squeezed her mother and squeezed her eyes until she could sit up and smile. "You might not be gone. The doctors might be wrong this time."

"We'll see, Little One." Maria had felt the same hope earlier, but now she could tell the changes inside her. Still, it felt good to hear the optimism in her daughter's voice, and she decided to let Darlene have the momentary comfort such thoughts might bring.

"Mama, tell me about Papa. What did he look like when he was young? How did you meet each other? How did you know he was the right one for you?"

The questions tumbled out of her mouth and Maria laughed as she said, "Slow down, Lena, and I will tell you, starting from the first time I saw him and then what our life was like." Maria's eyes gazed into the air, and she mused, to herself as much as to her daughter, "He was everything to me."

Back in Germany, we lived in different towns. He was a university student with my cousin Peter, and I had become a tailor in my hometown. One weekend Peter brought Ernest to a family wedding celebration, and that was when we first met. If you want to know what he looked like, just take a good look at Theodor, tall and handsome with that wavy auburn hair. Ernest had broad shoulders that looked good in his suit. I noticed the clothes he wore since that was my business, and he obviously knew quality. That impressed me. His shoes were shining, his hat was cocked off to the side, and his shirt glowed pure white.

He always said the first thing he noticed about me was

that my hair was like his and that my green eyes were like no one's. When we would talk about how we first met, Ern would talk about my suit, and how it looked good on me.

Since I was in the dressmaking business, I had first chance at the fabrics that came into the shop. My suit was made from the most marvelous material I had ever seen, and it cost me three months' wages before I could afford to buy it. The cloth was soft black wool with small white and red threads running through it. My jacket was short and fastened with black braided loops, and the skirt was long with pleats on both sides. It made my waist look tiny and made me look taller than I really was. My blouse was the softest white silk ever with lots of lace at the neckline, and then I piled my hair in a twist before putting on my black hat with the veil that covered one eye. Quite a stylish look, I was sure, and Ernest agreed.

Ernest bowed and took my hand when Peter introduced us, "A fine lady such as you should always wear gloves. Then your hands will always be as soft as they are right now."

Of course I had heard other men say words to make believe they told the truth, but this time the words sounded like they were true. When he looked into my eyes, something clicked for both of us, and we spent long hours together that weekend. I talked to him about my dreams of having a new life somewhere else, even if my mother was not willing that I would go away from home. He told me of how he planned to go to America as soon as he was free which meant his mother also did not want to lose her son forever when he would go across the ocean. Since she was now very ill, he knew it was just a matter of time before all his ties in Germany would be gone.

All, that is, except for his brand new ties to me. By the time he left for the university, we had agreed that we would write letters and that we would have a life together in America. When I think of it now, I am so shocked at how I completely trusted everything he said. He promised to send money for me when he had made his way over, and I promised that I would come as soon as I could.

He did and I did, and that's how we got together. Isn't that a crazy thing?

Darlene nodded and pondered what her mother must have been like as a young girl. She had never realized that Mama could have been young and beautiful and in love. All she had ever seen was a woman who had weathered skin, grey hair, and a soft body that wrapped around a little girl. She'd have to think this one over.

"What did Papa do in Germany when he wasn't in school? Did he live in town or in the country? Did you ever meet his family? What did your mother say when you left?"

Maria laughed and filled in the blanks for her daughter.

Papa's family were landowners in Germany, but since he wasn't the oldest son, he never would have a chance to inherit the family home. Ernest was a farmer through and through who could figure out everything about animals and soil and crops. Everyone loved to be around him because his heart was big and his mind was clever.

When he got to America, he discovered that he was also a shrewd trader who could find a way to make money where others could not see it. Ernest had heard that Nebraska had lots of land and not many people, so the first chance he had, he left New York. Ern rode in a cattle car and looked after a family's stock they were sending to Omaha. The railroad crews were good to him, just like everyone was, so he knew where to get a room when he finished with the cattle. He spent the next year trading and saving his money until he had enough to send for me.

Can you imagine what my family said? They had been

telling me he was just a promiser big who never meant anything he said. I knew better, but I will tell you that year was a hard one for me. Other men would ask me to go with them, but I just shook my head and stayed home. My sewing was the only thing that gave me any comfort, and a job can just do so much. I was careful to keep my hands nice and soft so my Ern would be proud of the lady he married.

With that, Maria laughed and held up her hands so they could both examine them. Hard calluses on the palm of her hands remained even though she had not been well enough to be outside working for several months. The freckled, weathered and wrinkled hands had scars where the barbed wire had gouged her as they dug in new fences across the hills, knife marks where she had slipped when cleaning chickens and turkeys every year, and one thin band of gold on her left hand which she softly caressed.

"You know, Ernest bought this ring for me with the money he got from trapping badgers and coyotes. He had it with him when I got off the train, and after the judge married us, I never once took it off. When Ern put it on my hand, he said, "Now I have everything I ever wanted. Together, we will have the best life anyone could ever want."

I don't think either of us knew what we were in for; but he was right, we worked side by side for everything we got. And it was good.

"How did you get way out here from Omaha? Why didn't you stay there so you could be a dressmaker? What made you leave a town and go where there was nothing?"

It was kind of crazy how we got here. Two of Ernest's sisters were also in Omaha, and we had settled into a comfortable routine. It's always comforting to have family around, and I really thought we'd probably stay right there. Ernest's uncle was already out on the prairie, and he sent word that he needed help. Of course, that was all it took to give Ern a reason to set out for the sand hills. He had never given up on his dream of having a place of his own, and that sounded good to me. We loaded up on the train again, and Uncle Will met us at the station. After what seemed like hours in his wagon, we pulled up in front of the house he had been telling us about.

I have never been so shocked in my whole life. Instead of the wooden frame houses I knew about, here in front of me was a pile of earth with grass growing out of the top. He had used the word "soddie" but I thought it was just some strange American way of saying "house." Was I ever wrong. We were so tired that we just kind of fell inside and looked for some place to lie down. When I got inside and could see around, it really wasn't as bad as I expected. As a matter of fact, it felt cozy and safe inside. We snuggled under the quilts and fell right to sleep.

The next morning, Uncle Will carried in the cow chips to start the stove, and soon had fixed the best breakfast I have ever eaten. Hot coffee and biscuits on a blue enamel plate might not sound like much, but food was pretty skimpy on our trip out here. We rinsed off the plates and cups and headed outside to look at our new opportunity.

Daylight gave us a different look but I still couldn't believe my eyes. For as far as I could see, I could see what there was to see. There was not a tree in sight—just huge hills that seemed to go clear up to the sky, and then valleys that were long and straight until another set of hills started up again. Will had a huge grin as he asked, "So what do you think? Can you imagine us living someplace like this?"

Funny that I was ready to ask Ern the same question, "Can you imagine us living someplace like this?" I looked out the corner of my eye at him, expecting him to be polite as he explained to Will that we would be catching the first train back East, when he started talking the fastest I had ever heard.

"Why didn't you tell us how wonderful this was? I had no idea that our family had a chance to own land that never ends. Not only will we never leave here again, I'm writing my sisters to hurry out here so they can be here with us. I am so happy that I could dance a jig." With that, he grabbed me around the waist and whirled me so high that I got dizzy. So much for catching that next train back to Omaha.

We spent the next few months so busy that we hardly had time to sleep. Uncle Will had crops that needed work, and we had to have our own shelter before the winter set in. After helping him in the fields, we would go to flat places in the valley to cut the squares of sod to make our house. Ernest had learned how to lay bricks in the old country so he understood what needed done. He staggered the edges of the sod so it was like they locked together; and before we even knew it, we had walls. The roof had to have supports before they could put the sod on top, so that took a little while longer.

Ern knew that I would feel trapped if I had to be inside without any windows, so he traded his winter overcoat for a piece of glass to put into the wall. He was always like that, thinking how he could make our life better, even if it meant giving up something like his own coat. That windowpane went with us to all the soddies we built, and we still had it when we built our frame house. I do have to say that some of my best memories are of looking out that window to see the larks in the morning or the children playing or the huge pink sunsets. It seems like just yesterday that Ernest and I would stand there together and look quietly across the land that meant so much to us both."

"Mama, why did your family call Papa 'promiser big?' Didn't they like him? When you say that about someone, they usually are not very nice people."

"Sweetheart, you need to know there are all kinds of people in the world, and some can't be trusted. They sound like they can and they act like they can, but they talk more than they do. At home, we always said 'Promiser Big, Keeper Little' when someone would make big claims and then not be there to do what they said. You know how important it is to keep your promises? Some people just say the words and don't worry about carrying through. Be careful about believing everything you hear."

"Mama, how can I know the difference? How did you know that Papa meant it when he promised to send for you?"

"That is a hard question, and the best I can say is listen with your heart. If you feel uncomfortable when someone's talking, be careful. Promisers Big will have lots of reasons why they're not doing what they said. If you watch and listen close, you'll know what to do."

Darlene was tired of the serious talk and wanted to hear more about Papa and the olden days. "Why did you build so many soddies? Was it fun to have someplace new to live?"

Maria snorted, "Not hardly. It was hard work to cut and haul the sod, but sometimes the rain would wash out the corners so we didn't have a choice. The first time we built up high and far from the lake. We didn't understand why most soddies were in the wet valleys and often had to be abandoned when the water rose in the spring. By the time the sand fleas got done with us, we decided that dry houses in hills invited them, so the next spring we built by the sand hill lake on our claim. Sure enough, by the following spring, we were wading in water to our ankles in the kitchen and up to our waists in the living room. Needless to say, we found out that closer to the water can be too close. By the time we did our next one, we had our plans for this wooden house so we wouldn't have to move again. That was so exciting to talk over what we wanted and how to make it all happen."

Ernest was a natural designer, so he made up plans in his head all the time. Our dreams made all the work have a reason since we were aiming for something. One day he would ask me if we wanted a downstairs and an upstairs; the next he would ask me if I wanted dormers or high ceilings. Most of the time I didn't know what he was talking about, so I just said, "What do you think?" Then when he would say what he thought, I would say, "That's just exactly what I want." The only thing I knew was that more babies meant less room. I asked for places to put beds and space enough in the kitchen for us all to sit together. We had good times talking and planning. No matter what happened, we were in it together and side-by-side.

Your father loved children and every time we had a baby, you would think no one else had ever done as good of a job as he had. "Maria, look, he squeezes my finger to say he is happy to be here." Or he might say, "How pretty, this new daughter of ours. She will be as beautiful as her mother."

When he would come in the house, the first place he would go was to the baby's crib, lift out the baby, and go to the rocking chair he brought with us from Omaha. "Every baby needs a mother's hand and a father's shoulder" was his favorite way of explaining why he and the baby would fall asleep together every night. I loved to see his huge hands holding a tiny bundle. How tender he was, and how lucky I was that he cared so much.

He insisted that all of you children learn how to work and be honest, but he was such a tenderhearted man that he very seldom raised his voice. Instead, he would talk quietly and we all wanted to please him.

We would buy huge supplies of food in town and store our dried fruit and brown sugar in a chest with a huge domed lid. This special food was always a temptation when the children were in the house and there was no one watching.

Often he and I would go to the field and leave the older children at the house. One time when we got back to the house, the kids were inside and didn't hear us coming. The two older ones had held the lid while Emma, the smallest, climbed up on the stool and stretched as far as she could to reach inside. She had her fists full of fruit to share with the others as we walked in, and you can imagine their faces when they saw us. Ernest yelled, "Just shove her in!" and the kids all started screaming. He laughed so hard that he had to sit down before he could even hold the lid to get her out. Then they all sat there in the living room and ate their dried apples and apricots, Emma on his lap and the others with their arms on his shoulders. I can see that like it was yesterday.

Most of the time, he just shook his head when they were up to their tricks. Another time the little girls were in charge of keeping track of the hens and rooster so the coyotes couldn't come and slip off with them. The girls got bored and started plucking feathers off the rooster they called "Old Buff." They got carried away and didn't stop until he was completely naked. Then they decided they needed to hide their handiwork so they dug a hole big enough for him and some water and dragged some boards over the top. They would wait until we had gone to the field before letting him out for the day and would be sure to have him covered up by the time we got back. This went on for about three days, but then Old Buff started crowing before we left the yard. Ern investigated and just shook his head when he found his plucked rooster. You can imagine he teased the girls every time when chicken-picking time rolled around. The girls were so embarrassed when Aunt Minnie and Anna came to visit and that was one of the first stories he told them.

"I have so much trouble knowing who you are talking about when you tell of Will and Minnie and Anna. There is too much to keep straight. I don't even know who anyone is."

Maria patted Darlene on the head, and gave her a little shove. "Go over there on the Chester Drawers and get me the Bible. You know where it is."

Darlene used both hands to carry the Bible to the bed and laid it down beside her mother. "Why do you want this? We use it every Sunday morning but I don't think it's going to straighten out my brain."

"Lena, my mother gave me this when I left Germany. She wrote my own family's birthdays in it and told me to finish it when I had my own children. You will find all Ern's family and mine written here, along with your brothers and sisters. Always keep your connections to your family. That matters more than anything else."

Darlene looked where her mother was pointing. There was that familiar spidery writing which she couldn't read, but Mama acted like it was important. "This tells when we were married, when everyone was born, and when my babies died. Poor baby Freida and poor Harry. Ernest's name is right here. That was hard, to write those numbers." Maria dropped her head back on the pillow and stared at the ceiling.

"Mama, why do you and the older kids know German but I don't? I can't read this Bible and I always know when you have something scary to talk about because that's when you talk that way. When we have Sunday morning readings from this, I know the sounds but not what the words mean. Why didn't you want me to know what everyone else knows?"

Maria reached out to hold her baby. "When Ernest and I came over, we could use enough English to get by, but it was very hard for us. We got along and learned many words, but when Harry's doctor couldn't understand me, Ernest didn't want that kind of problem ever again. “From now on, our children will speak only English. We’re here to stay and they’ll be better off if they think and talk like others in America.”

From that time on, you children were expected to speak English even though he and I would use German when we were in a hurry or having a difficulty. His idea was to help his family to have a good life in the new country.”

“The reason we always use this Bible is for a connection with the people we left behind. It makes me think of when I was a little girl when I hear words from the old country. Ern always said that we might be far away from a preacher or a church but we didn’t have to be heathens. Ever since we came to these hills, we started our week by reading Ernest’s favorite psalm together.” Together, Maria and Darlene recited the familiar words:

Ich hebe meine augen auf zu den bergen,
von welchen mir Hulfe kommt.

“But what do those words mean? We all say them together, but I just do it because everyone else does. Why did Papa like them?”

Maria looked Darlene in the eye and translated, “ ‘I will lift up mine eyes to the hills’ is how the verse begins. Ern always laughed and said, “Who knew that David lived in Nebraska? All the time everyone thought he was over there in the Holy Land and he was really a sandhiller.”

“Is that true, Mama? Did those guys out of the Bible really live right here where we do?” Darlene’s eyes glistened at the thought.

“No, Sweetheart, they didn’t. Ernest just loved his hills so much that he liked to say that. He was so clever with his ideas and didn’t have many around him who could think like he could. You're like him with your questions and ideas."

Maria ran her hands over the worn black cover as she talked. "Lena, be sure to keep up all the family dates in here. It's important."

Darlene knew what her mother was thinking, and she didn't want to talk about who would write the next entry in the Bible. Instead, she brought the talk back to her father since her mother was in such a talkative mood.

"You said some doctor had to work on Papa's hand. What happened to it?"

"He got it caught in a corn sheller and crushed it so bad that one doctor wanted to cut it off at the wrist. Ern could not imagine life as a one-handed farmer, so he had me find a German doctor, Dr. Schmidt. Ernest thought that man was a genius because he found a way to keep all but the middle two fingers on that hand. It was hard for Ern to do many things, but he never complained because he knew how lucky he was. That was why he believed Harry maybe could have made it if the right doctor had been there."

Maria bit her lip and went on. "Then when you were one year old, Ernest came in from checking the cows with such pain in his stomach that he could hardly move. Right away I said I was taking him to Ogallala. When he never even argued, I knew he was bad off.

He just said, "Whatever you think, Mama." That trip was so hard, just like with little Harry. Ern never complained, but every now and then he would make a grunting sound when we hit a big bump.

I pulled up in front of Dr. Schmidt's office and went in to ask for help. Dr. Norris was there and told me that Dr. Schmidt didn't do any work in Ogallala any more but he would be glad to try to help out.

I felt so sick when I went back down those stairs to tell Ernest the news, and he said just what I expected. So sick that he could hardly talk, he just shook his head and said, "Never. Let's go back home. He's the one who took Harry from me and I'll never let him touch me." Once Ern's mind was made up, he never changed it so I didn't argue with him. We both knew this was not good, but we didn't ever say the words.

The Menters were still in town, and they had heard about our trouble. They took us in again, and Ernest lay in Harry's room for two days, moaning and thrashing around in the bed. Early in the morning of the third day, he reached out his hand to take mine, and said, "Maria, you are my lady." Then he slowly became more quiet and finally didn't take the next breath. We buried him beside his little Harry, just where he would have wanted to be.

This ride home was even longer than going home after we lost Harry. I had lost the man who promised we'd spend our lives together. Guess this time he was a Promiser Big, because he didn't stay with me as long as I thought he would.

I had plenty of time to think about how we would get by, and I knew that Fred and Theo were old enough to help me hold it all together. When I pulled into the yard, there was Ted, holding you and looking after you just like he always has. The boys helped me into the house and we all sat together at the table. Theo left after a few minutes and brought out our Bible. It fell open to the 121st Psalm, just like always, and we all said it at the same time. We cried and talked and sat together as a family, even if Ernest was not there. No one sat in his chair for a long time, and it felt like he was still there, looking after us.

Finally, Ted spoke up and said, "Mama, would you write in the Bible for us? Papa would have wanted us to keep it up just right. You know how particular he was about doing things when they needed done."

So I wrote the day he died after his name, and then I let Fred hold me while I sobbed just like a little baby.

All of us just sat there, not knowing what to do, but all of a sudden, you gave out your little sound that meant supper better be served pretty soon. Even though our hearts were heavy, we were glad that something good was right there in front of us. "Little Lena, you are big enough to help us all, aren't you?" Ted swung you up to the ceiling and laughed with you as you gave out that big giggle he loved so much. And our life went on without Papa.

Fred was twenty-six and Theo was fourteen when Ernest died. They had worked side by side with us all their lives, and I knew we could keep the ranch going. Ern had been so good to tell the boys and me what needed done that we didn't miss a lick. At first when we were married, we would sit around the table and dream about what we wanted. After we moved to the hills and had children, we all talked about our plans for what we wanted to do and how we would get more land so everyone could have a good life. It wasn't the same without him, but he had us ready to go on anyway.

Lena pondered her mother's information, and decided to ask a question that had been on her mind. "Mama, why is it that Theo is the one who does the most? He's the little brother but he always decides what needs done and how to do everything. Fred never seems to have ideas, but he never seems to like Ted's ideas either. Why do they fight so much?"

Maria sighed as her daughter described the situation that had developed on the ranch. Fred did what needed done when someone else told him, but Theo saw what needed done and pitched right in because he loved everything about ranching. Raising cattle and horses and working the land was so satisfying to him that he was always busy making things better. If he weren't in the barn getting the tack ready for the next day, he was breaking the new colts to drive or ride or putting in more fence. All Maria had to do was mention something she would like, such as a fence around her garden, and as soon as he had a bit of time, Ted would take care of it. At the end of every day, he would head to the house, but always stop before he opened the door. He would turn around and gaze over the entire meadow, looking at the cattle grazing on the hillsides, the clouds of each season, and listen to the birds as they settled in for the night. Then with what seemed like reluctance to leave what he loved so much, Theo would turn the knob and walk into the home to relax with the family.

"Lena, people do what they can do. Ted is good at making plans to keep us growing like Papa wanted, and Fred likes to stay with what has been started. They are just different in the way they look at what needs done. Your Theo is a dreamer, and Fred wants to have his life good right now rather than waiting for something a long way off. Neither way is right or wrong, but it is hard for them to put up with each other's way of doing things. It does upset me when they argue, but they both have good ideas that we need to hear. That is a part of being in a family, disagreeing but still working together to get what you want."

Satisfied with her mother's answer, Darlene went on to her question. "If Papa only had one good hand, how did he do the work? Could he still milk or shoot a gun or fasten his pants? I think it would be hard to get along with just one hand."

Maria laughed and started with the last part first. "Ern figured out a way to shut his pants by himself. He didn't ever want to ask for help, and especially not for something so private. After he lost those two middle fingers, his hand was so swollen and stiff that he couldn't move it. After it healed, every morning he would sit on the edge of the bed, rub his hand, bend his fingers, and stretch it until he would have tears in his eyes. He never said a word, but pretty soon he started doing more and more with his hand until one morning he sneaked out to the barn before we were even out of bed. When we got up, we heard him yelling at us from the barn. We were so scared he was maybe hurt that we ran as fast as we could go. When we rushed in all out of breath and wide-eyed, he showed us the milk pail, foaming and filled up to the brim, just like a little boy wanting everyone to be proud of him. From that time on, he did everything just like before, except that he didn't want to shoot a gun."

"Why would that stop him, Mama, if he could use his hand to do everything else?"

"Actually, it had more to do with what he needed to shoot at than with his poor hand. We used to be bothered by a wolf that really had gotten bold. He would come right up to the barn to steal our chickens or bucket calves, and later on would jump on a yearling out in the pasture and start eating around its tail while it was still alive. It was a horrible thing to go out in the morning and find a half-eaten animal and think how terrible it must have been for the calf.

This wolf would follow the hay sled when Papa would go out to hay the cows, staying back just far enough to be out of range but close enough that everyone was on pins and needles. Ernest always had a pitchfork handy, even though the wolf was not crazy enough to get that close. People always asked why Ern didn't shoot the wolf, but he was afraid his aim would not be true and that a wounded wolf might be even more dangerous."

Lena knew this story, but she loved to hear it time and again. "What happened to the wolf, Mama? How did you get rid of him? Did Papa have to shoot after all?"

"No, Little One, he didn't. One night our dog set up a terrible ruckus outside. When I went to the door, that poor dog yelped and bolted right in past me. He was so scared that he ran under the bed, whining and shaking. Ern said, 'Let him stay inside this once. Any dog so crazy scared has to have some help.'"

We all put in a really bad night, and when morning came, we walked outside. There right beside the house we saw huge paw prints where the wolf had chased the poor dog right up to the door. Ernest decided that was the last straw, so he asked Uncle Bill to come out and stay however long it would take to get that wolf.

It really didn't take long before Bill had his shot since the wolf was so brazen. On the third day, the men had loaded the haystack and were headed out to feed the cattle. Before they left the yard that day, they had shot a rabbit and hung it on the back of the sled. Bill had burrowed deep enough into the haystack that he couldn't be seen, and Papa headed the team to the pasture. He had Molly and Jeff walking slow; and when Bill said to stop, he did.

Sure enough, just like always, the wolf was in sight, trotting far enough back that he was out of shooting range but close enough to keep an eye on the action. When the team stopped, so did the wolf; but then he kept coming, probably because he could smell the rabbit's fresh blood.

Bill let him get close enough for a sure shot, and then stood up and fired. BOOM!! The wolf rolled twice and never moved after that. Bill's shot had hit him right in front of the shoulder and went straight through the heart. It took both of the men to load the carcass on the sled so they could bring it back home.

Ern was still laughing when they pulled in the yard. "I looked back and all I could see was this huge clump of hay with fire shooting out of it. The wolf fell and Bill started jumping up and down. When he finally stopped, he had hay sticking out of his cap, his collar, and his pants, and the biggest grin I've ever seen. Not a bad shot for a hayseed." And then Ern would shake his head and laugh again, partly because he had been there for the action, but mostly out of relief because he knew his family and stock were safe, for the time being at least.

Bill had a taxidermist mount the wolf, lips pulled back in a snarl, and all of us were kind of scared and fascinated at the same time. Every time we went to Ogallala, we would stop in at Bill and Nettie's for coffee and a look at the wolf. I guess all the kids in the neighborhood love to hear Bill's story and touch the head. Then they go home, have nightmares, and come back for more. Crazy how we like to scare ourselves, isn't it?

Darlene could see her mother needed to rest, even though she was impatient to hear more stories about Mama and Papa and the older kids. "I think I'll go put Potato outside so he can play with the other puppies. Did you see how much he has grown since the first time he came to visit?"

With that, Lena scooped up the pup and held him in her arms. "This time I'll be careful not to let him wet on the bed. Good idea, don't you think?" She and her mother laughed at the memory of how their strolls down memory lane had begun, and Maria's eyes were closed by the time Darlene got to the doorway and turned around. "Sleep well, Mama. I love you."

"Love you, too, Lena," came the soft reply from the quilts behind her.

All night long, Darlene struggled with questions that she couldn't sort out for herself. When morning finally came, she groggily swung out of bed and trudged down the hall to the breakfast table. Theo had come back in from the barn and tousled her hair as he walked by her chair. "Looks like you and the bed bugs were fighting all night and they won. What's the problem?"

Darlene mumbled, “Nothing,” while thinking how amazing it was that he could read her feelings without a word on her part. “I just had some weird dreams that made a mess of my night.”

Ted leaned over, laid his cheek on her red hair, and gave her a big hug. “I know, Sweetie. That happens to me sometimes, too.” Then he sat up and stood up in one motion, shoved the chair under the table, and put both hands on his hips. “I need to replace leather on Jed’s harness and you’re really good help. Want to come with me?”

With a big sigh and shrug of her shoulders, Darlene nodded. Might as well go with Theo. Maybe he could help her figure out how things worked because she wasn’t having much luck at it.

Walking into the barn, Darlene waited for her eyes to adjust to the darkness inside. While she stood there beside the grain box, she took a deep breath. Sure enough, the familiar smells of leather, sweaty horses, and dried manure worked their magic to settle her down and give her a sense of ease. She heard the workhorses stomping in their stalls, chewing grain and rubbing against the worn wooden supports where their long halter ropes were fastened. Even though her gray cat rubbed against her leg, Darlene remained still for several minutes. Since this place held many good memories for her, she always liked the barn.

She remembered being confused as a little girl hearing Ted talk about single trees and double trees. For days she looked everywhere in the barn to find out where they were growing, and finally asked him if he would please show her the trees.

Ted tousled her hair, led her where the team was harnessed, and explained how to hook up each part. From the hames to the collar to the crupper, he told her what each was called and how they all fit together. Never once did he laugh at her or make fun of her when they all sat down at the supper table. No wonder she loved him so much. Now that she was older, she knew the name of every piece of tack, where it was all kept, and how to fix most of it.

After a time, she headed to the tack room where Ted was already laying out the pieces of Jed's headstall. Sweat and time had weakened the leather strap which was inserted into the buckle, and it had broken when the big black draft horse had rubbed on a post in the corral. Ted had carved a new leather end that he handed to Darlene. "Here, if you want to hang on to this, I'll get the rivets and we'll be back in business in no time. Old Jed'll learn that he can't get out of work even if the equipment does break down. He has such a soft mouth that I wouldn't even need a bridle or a bit to work him. I could put a spider web in his mouth and we could drive a sparrow up a drain pipe."

Darlene let out a giggle, imagining a snaffle bit made of a spider webs and the big black horse scooting around to stay ahead of a flitting sparrow. All of a sudden, the morning felt better. She reached out for the leather ends and held them square so Ted could finish his job. Ted was so particular that he preferred to do his leather work by himself if she couldn't help with it.

The two of them could work side by side for hours, enjoying being together even if they were quiet most of the time. This time, though, Ted knew she needed words, so he opened the conversation. "So, Lena, anything on your mind you want to talk about? It's kind of hard to sleep when the dreams keep you awake, isn't it?" Then he let out a chuckle in wheezy gusts.

"I don't get this marriage thing. Mama told me about how happy she and Papa were even when they came here with nothing and how they really had a good life. So that's one way to be married. Then I hear Fred and his wife Ruth arguing all the time about never having enough money. They have lots more than Mama and Papa ever had, and yet it's not enough. They never seem to be happy, no matter what. And that's another way to be married. Then I see how Alma never knows when her husband will be home or where he will be; and every time he comes back, he fills her full of stories that make her excited. Then one morning, he's gone again and she's sad. Mama talks about a Promiser Big. Is that what he is? He's so full of hot air that he makes me mad. Why would she want anything to do with him? I'm going to be just like you. I'll never get married."

"Hold it, Little One. No wonder you can't sleep with that much whirling around inside your head. You're right about one thing—that there are lots of ways to be married. Just because two people are together doesn't mean they're good for each other or to each other. Mama and Papa loved each other and worked hard for what they both wanted. They didn't think it was anyone else's job to make them happy, so they felt good when they did things for each other and for themselves.

We do hear Fred and Ruth argue and complain, but sometimes people just get in the habit of growling about what's wrong rather than being glad about what's right. Maybe they are happy together because they see things the same way. As for Alma and James, he's a good feeler who talks big, but she is so softhearted that she can't stay mad at him. Maybe she likes the good times so much that she will put up with the hard times. Until she decides enough is enough, he'll probably come and go. That's up to her.

As for me getting married, I might just fool you sometime. Wouldn't you be surprised if I went out coyote hunting one day and came home with my new wife riding behind me on the saddle?"

Darlene giggled at the thought. She could see Theo

galloping up to the barn in a swirl of dust with a woman hanging on to his waist—hair, skirt, and hounds trailing behind. "What kind of a wife would you bring home? Would she be tall and thin or short and round? Would she let you bring your dogs inside the house or make them stay in the barn? Would she. . ."

"Whoa, Lena, I didn't mean to get you started. When I find a special girl, I'd want your approval before I'd do anything, so you can relax for now. I have too much leather to fix to have time to go out wife shopping for quite a while." With that, Theo stood up and fastened the bridle parts together. "Perfect fit. Jed and I thank you, little lady, and now we are off to mow the rest of the alfalfa field. Give Mama a hug from me when you go see her."

Darlene nodded, called for the pup, and headed to the house. "Come on, Tater, Mama likes to see us in the mornings when she wakes up. That's when she feels the best."

Darlene stopped and pulled some tiny purple flowers along the side of the barn, then skipped to the house. She slowed down at the door, but was still breathless by the time she sat beside the bed. "Here, Mama, I've never brought you these before, have I? Is it okay to have them in here or do you want me to get rid of them?"

Maria took the flowers and motioned Darlene to come close so they could look deeply into the delicate blossoms. "Put them right there so I can see them all day long. You know, I think these look just like the fancy Venetian lace we used on ladies' blouses in the shop in Germany. So soft and delicate that we had to be extra careful when we sewed it along the sleeves and collars. I never understood why anyone would call them 'stinkweeds' when they are so wonderful. Do you remember last summer when you would pick all the tiny seed pods and call them your string beans? You cooked so many of them that you tried to feed your cats and dolls that they wouldn't even come after awhile."

Darlene laughed and shook her head, "That was when I was much younger, of course, but I sure did like to pretend I was cooking a big dinner, just like you. I tasted them once, and they really aren't very good. No wonder my cats wouldn't eat them." With that, they both laughed and Tater knew it was time to settle in for another long, lazy morning. Soon he was snoring and yipping as he chased rabbits in his dreams.

Maria studied her daughter's face and remarked, "You look a bit off this morning. Is it well with you?"

Hesitating just a bit before answering, Darlene decided that she could open the same subject with her mother as she had with Ted earlier. She hadn't told him everything that was troubling her since she didn't know exactly how to talk about such matters with her big brother. "Mama, I was dreaming last night, and I woke up with a not good feeling this morning. So many things make my head hurt from trying to figure it all out."

"Lena, would it help if you and I thought about the same thing and told each other what is in our head? I always feel better when I talk about what whirls around inside my mind, especially if I have someone else to listen. Otherwise I just talk to myself and don't ever seem to get an answer. Lie down here beside me while we talk. You go first."

With a sigh that came from deep inside, Darlene began. "Alma is so nice, Mama, and she is married to someone who isn't nice. Why does he make her so sad when she makes everyone else feel happy? Did she look in her heart like you did when you found Papa? Why is everyone so nice to him when he does show up here after taking off and leaving her and the kids all alone? I don't ever want some man to make me that unhappy. Do you think it would be okay if Ted and I just decided not to ever marry and stay here on the ranch to take care of each other? That would be better than so much sadness."

Maria had seen the same situation as Darlene and had asked herself the same questions. Now she was faced with being truthful and at the same time not leaving a bad feeling about marriage in the mind of her youngest. "Lena, you know how you pick out favorite puppies and they are the same ones that your sister Eva can't stand. Why do you like some and she likes others?"

"I don't know. I just know what I like and don't like. She sure makes some dumb picks, but I guess she can have her own ideas."

"Picking who you want to marry is kind of like that. Even if you and I might not want to be with James, there's something about him that makes Alma happy enough that she will overlook the sadness that he brings with it. Staying away from that kind of trouble sounds good now, but you and Ted will both find someone who is just right for you. Then you'll go and make a life of your own, just like Papa and I did. We both waited until we were sure, and you and Ted will, too."

Darlene pondered her mother's words, nodded her head, and decided to ask about the rest of what had been puzzling her. "Mama, after James came back this last time, later on Alma's tummy got big and then she had a baby. Is that kind of like how cows and cats and dogs get really big before they have their babies?"

Maria's and Lena's eyes met and Maria felt a surge of pride at how naturally observant this young girl was. "That is exactly how new life happens, and it basically doesn't matter what mother it is. You're really good at noticing everything around you. I like that."

Now Darlene was encouraged to go on to the next question. "Mama, are you going to have another baby? I don't know how that can be since Papa has been gone for so long, but your tummy is growing and looks kind of like Alma's did the last time before her baby came."

Maria laid her head back on the pillow, placed her hands on her rounded stomach, and thought again about how her daughter saw every detail around her. "Little One, you are seeing right. My tummy is getting bigger, but sometimes there are other reasons than a baby. Do you remember I told you the doctor couldn't do anything more for me? What's wrong inside of me is growing and that makes my tummy look round. There's no baby inside me. You're my last baby."

All of the tiredness and hurt of the past weeks welled up inside Darlene, and she clung silently to her mother while the tears ran down her cheeks. With her face buried in the covers and shaking with sorrow, Darlene let slip the brave front she had put on every morning before coming into Maria's room. Now she had been caught off guard and cried in front of her mother, no matter how much she had tried not to.

Maria stroked Darlene's hair and let the little girl cry. Gradually, the shaking of her shoulders eased, the jerky breaths smoothed out, and Little Lena slept in her mother's arms.

Waking up with a start, Darlene carefully shifted so she could see her sleeping mother's face. Sliding out the side of the bed, she patted her leg softly so Tater and she could go find Theo.

Walking across the yard the next morning, Darlene stopped to shoo the chickens out of the way and dodged the turkey gobbler that chased after her. Breathless as she went into the bedroom, she gasped, "Why do you love turkeys so much? I think they are a real pain, especially the way that old gobbler gets after anyone who gets in his way. I think they are disgusting and stinky and dumb."

"Whoa there, girl, you make my head spin when you whirl in here like that," Maria laughed. "You'd better take your time and catch your breath."

Darlene rubbed the back of her hand across her forehead to wipe away the sweat and then moved her fingers above her lips, moving the beads that had formed there. "It's bad enough when I have to gather the eggs and the hens peck at me, but at least I know what to do about them. Do you remember when I was a little girl and so afraid of the setting hens? I always felt like they were going to peck out my eyes when I had to move them off the nests. That was a neat trick you showed me about grabbing their tails and throwing them down before they knew what I was going to do. I still was scared but never got hurt. Did you always love hens and turkeys, even when you were a little girl in Germany?"

Maria patted beside her on the bed to signal Darlene to have a seat, and surprised her little girl when she spoke. "I still hate those feathered things just as bad as I did way back when I was a little girl just like you."

"No, Mama, that can't be true. You always looked after the babies the old hens would hatch out and made us kids carry corn and clabbered milk and boiled eggs out to them. Not only that, I remember the time you cried just like a baby after the weasel got into the chicken house. If you didn't like them, why'd you care what happened to them?"

Maria caught her breath at the memory of walking inside the shed to find two hundred half-grown chickens lying dead all around. Weasels slaughter every animal, apparently for the enjoyment rather than for the hunger since they don't eat what they kill. "Oh, yes, I remember that too. Those chickens were the only thing we had raised that summer that even had a chance of working out for us. Grasshoppers had devoured our crops and hill hay, and anything that survived the hoppers had dried out completely by July. What I saw lying there when I walked in was money from the eggs we wouldn't have to sell, and the empty table from the chickens we wouldn't have to eat. You're right, I did cry hard, but mostly out of disappointment for the family. Not only that, I don't like to see any animal suffer."

Darlene paused and thought over the new information, then continued, "I can't remember how many times I had to go out all day long and watch the turkeys while they picked at bugs and grasshoppers. I loved being on my horse and eating my lunch whenever I wanted, but those ugly old turkeys were so stupid that they made me mad. Remember the time it rained and they just stood there getting wet and holding their heads up to let the rain run in? We had to make them move or they would have drowned. And you're telling me that we did all that for animals you hated? I just don't get it."

"Lena, we all have things we don't like to do; and if they're important, it doesn't matter how we feel. Even though it wasn't fun to raise chickens, having eggs and fried chicken to eat felt pretty good. Turkeys are all you said and even more, but they made us lots of money that helped pay for our land and what we needed around the ranch."

Maria looked off into the distance while she remembered her children going out on horseback to herd flocks of turkeys on the broad treeless flats where grasshoppers and bugs were abundant. Natural predators like coyotes or skunks or hawks would make short work of animals that truly were as dumb as Darlene had described, so the job of the younger children was to go on horseback and spend the days drifting with the turkeys. At evening, kids and birds would make their way back to the homestead so the turkeys could be shut up into a safe enclosure, spend the night, and head out the next morning to start all over again.

This went on until early November when the entire ranch would stop to butcher the turkeys, stuff the carcasses into barrels, salt them down, and ship them by rail to Omaha for the Thanksgiving market. Hard and tedious work, but work that Ern and she had discovered would make land payments and a bit of extra for other necessities.

"Mama, do you remember the time we laughed so hard at the turkeys when I got back and we were letting them go into their roosts? They had eaten so many grasshoppers all day long that when one fat hopper landed right in front of that big old tom, he just looked at it, stepped over it and went to his roost."

Maria laughed with her. "He was just like a kid who ate too much candy and didn't want another bite. That hopper didn't know how lucky he really was, did he?"

"All this time I thought you liked them and you really didn't. That's just crazy. Next you'll probably tell me the same thing about the milk cows. You never would let us run them in from the pasture, and we had to grain them morning and night. When you would catch us kids riding them, it made you mad even if we were just having a little bit of fun. Tell me the truth. Do you like milk cows or not?"

Responding to the intensity of her little girl, Maria very seriously said, "Honey, it's kind of the same thing. The cows and their milk were important to us, so we had to have rules. It makes cows give less milk when they are jostled around, so running them or riding them never seemed like a good idea to us, even if it was fun for you kids. In answer to your question, cows have been good to us, and I like that part of it. Having to milk them morning and night every day of the year was tiresome but just had to be done. I guess we never thought about whether we liked them or not; we did what we had to do.

I did have a favorite cow, old Blossom. Every year, she

had a big heifer calf and she gave a lot of milk. She was easy to milk, and never kicked or swished me with her tail, even if the flies were biting something awful. Ern always said I spoiled her because I'd give her an extra bite of grain and scratch her ears before I'd turn her out. I did like her."

Darlene chimed in with her memories of Blossom. "She was the first one I ever milked, and I thought every cow milked that easy. Boy, did I find out different when I tied into others. It took me forever to get done when I moved on to Soapy. Why in the world did you ever name her Soapy anyway?"

"Her mother got out of the corral in a big snow storm when it was her time to calve, headed up the biggest sand hill she could find, and had her baby. Ern rode all morning before he found her, and just about missed the calf where she was all tucked in beside a huge soap weed. Ern came bringing the calf slung over the front of his saddle, with the cow trailing along behind. When he got to the barn, he shouted out, 'Hey, you guys inside, open the door. Soapy and I need to come inside.' And her name stuck from then on."

"How did you and Papa learn so much about taking care of animals? You'd never even worked outside before coming to the sandhills, and Papa had lived on a farm, not a ranch like where we are. You can do anything."

Maria snorted at the idea of being smart since it seemed she was always playing catch-up. Because Ernest truly was a visionary, he plunged them into projects that few others had undertaken. That meant the two of them had to learn as they went. The good thing about his approach was that he not only had the ideas but the determination and energy to put forward to make things happen. He had seen people who were dreamers but who never became doers, so he was particularly careful not to fall into the trap of starting exciting new ventures only to abandon them when the newness wore off.

"It may seem like I know about many things, but that's just because I've been around quite a while. We had lots to learn when we came here, but Uncle Will helped out, we watched what others did, and we figured out what we wanted and the best way to get there. What I do know is that a girl like you can do anything you decide to do. You'll remember what you've learned here and add to it along the way. Hens and cows and turkeys all teach their own lessons, mostly that doing a job right is more important than what the job is."

Darlene could see Maria needed to rest, so she gently kissed her cheek and went out into the bright sunshine, shooing the turkeys away with a new awareness.

Hot July days ran from one into another with just a sweaty sleep break between. Maria's room had windows on the east and the north where she would ordinarily be sheltered from the fierce afternoon sun, but her room was always warm since these hot days continued into hot nights with little relief. Each hot day started out the same for Darlene. She enjoyed her routine of breakfast, a leisurely stroll to the barn for kitten time, then with a slap of her hand to her leg, she signaled Potato to come along for their grand entry to Maria's room.

Darlene saw at a glance that Maria was still asleep as she now was so often, so Lena and Tater silently slipped into their places. Darlene leaned against the back of the chair and let her gaze wander to all Maria's needlework. She checked out the open cutwork dresser scarf, shifted her eyes to the embroidered pillow shams, and on to the quilt with its elaborate appliquéd blocks. Maria had pieced the squares from Ernest's and her wool suits, and then covered each square with whimsical fabric flowers encircled with elaborate green vines.

Even though she knew the answers, Darlene often asked Maria about each piece so she could hear again the familiar stories. Light gray pin-striped squares were from Maria's wedding suit she had stitched in Germany, charcoal gray pieces were from the suit that Papa had bought in Omaha before they came West, the narrow black border came from a doctor's topcoat Ern got in a horse trade, and the middle squares were from the wool blanket found in the abandoned house on a section he had bought from a settler who gave up on his ranching venture.

Maria stirred and felt Darlene sitting quietly beside the bed. "Oh, Sweetheart, I'm glad to see you. Already a beastly hot morning. What is going on today?"

"Mama, tell me how you could make up all these flowers without anyone drawing them for you. I think they are all beautiful, and the yellow ones look just like the sunflowers outside by the lake. Who showed you how to do this?"

Maria reached out her hand to stroke Darlene's cheek and thought about how she had sewed every night beside her own mother in Germany. "When I was about your age, Mama showed me how to do fancy work, and every time I put in a stitch, it is like I'm with her in a small way. She would have liked how this quilt turned out."

With that, Maria rubbed her hand across the top of the quilt and laughed as her work-roughened hand snagged the surface. "Ern probably would shake his head and tell me, 'Maria, why haven't you been wearing your gloves? A lady's hands should be protected.' Then we'd laugh about how our lives changed from when we first met."

"Mama, am I old enough to do some fancy stitches? I could make a blanket for my doll if you'd help me."

"Little One, go over there below the dresser and get my sewing bag. We'll see what we can get done."

Hanging in the air was the unspoken reality that time would be a factor in how much Maria could share with her young daughter. Maria's condition had worsened to the point that she was now eating nothing and seldom left her bed.

Darlene proudly brought the hoop to Maria. "Look at how pretty this bird is. You just showed me once how to make the lines, and I made all these around him. Now I want to do some of those long loops and big lumps like you do."

Maria laughed and told her daughter, "Those long loops you like are called 'lazy daisies' and the big lumps are 'French knots'. Your baby will be so happy to snuggle under a cover you made for her. Let's get started."

For the next hour, Darlene worked to master the stitches with her head bowed over the needlework. Needle up through the material, two wraps around the needle with the thread held tight, then down beside the first stitch. Maria's patient instruction helped her through the tangled thread, empty needles, and misplaced stitches. Each time Darlene would see a mistake in her work, Maria would encourage her to take it out. "Little One, don't settle for less than your best. When you look at your work, you want it to be right. It's always easier to fix a small bobble than to take on a huge mess. Take your time and do it right."

Darlene would let out a huge sigh, drop her shoulders, and pick out the mistakes.

Maria lay on her pillow and watched her daughter at work. Darlene would squint her eyes, wrinkle her brows, and stick the tip of her tongue out the side of her mouth.

All of a sudden, Darlene put the hoop on her lap and started crying. "I'll never get it right. Yours is so nice and mine is just wrong. I may as well just quit right now."

Maria reached over and pulled her daughter to her as she had so many times before. She waited until the sobs slowed down, and then gently urged her daughter up so they could be eye to eye. "I used to be so discouraged that I'd cry to my mother, and she told me this verse. *When you sew, I'm there with you. Helping out with all you do.* Look at these flowers you just made. Did you know that my mother was right here, helping me just like I helped you? I know that because she promised that's what she would do. I promise I'll always be there with you, even after I'm gone."

Darlene looked long at Maria through wet lashes over hazel eyes. "Mama, when I have a daughter, I promise I'll do that for her too."

Strangely enough, this did not bring forth the usual tears from Maria. "Darlene, I know you will because we Soehl women are not Promisers Big. We do what we say."

With that, Darlene folded up the cloth and put away the sewing bag. "I think you need to rest now so Tater and I'll leave. I'll get back to this sewing later."

Maria smiled and patted her daughter's hand. "You are a special girl. Thanks for being so good."

As Darlene walked out of the house, she looked over to the barn and saw Ted beside the mower. He waved and hollered to her, "Are you busy right now? I could sure use a hand." With one motion he slid his straw hat off his head and rubbed his forearm across the sweat rivulets running down his face. His light blue denim work shirt, now completely sweat soaked, was a deep indigo tone, and his face seemed even more ruddy than usual.

Darlene had left her shoes beside Maria's bed where she always kicked them off, and she didn't want to go back and disturb her mother. Pleased to have an opportunity to help Theo, she took off running across the sand to where he stood. No more than three steps into her sprint, her feet were seared by the hot sand. Skipping and hopping from one foot to the other, she made it to his side and made sure to stand where the mowing machine cast its shadow and kept the sand cool.

She wriggled her toes and buried both feet in the soft white sand to cool off while Ted let out that hearty laugh she loved so much. "That was the fanciest foot work I've ever seen. No wonder you always want to go to the dances with me. You can dip and dive and glide with the best of the girls."

Darlene giggled and said, "Do you remember when I was little and you would whirl around while I stood on your shoes? We got really good together after you showed me how to move my own feet. When is the next dance we can go to?"

"I don't know, but if we don't get this hay up we aren't going to have to worry about having any time for dancing. Are you ready to pitch in?"

"Just watch me move this time. I'd better run back to the house to get my shoes from Mother's room if you want me to work on the sickle. Tell me when to start and I'll show you how fast I can go."

"Ready. Set. Go." Skipping across the yard she went, jumping from one foot to the other in quick movements to escape the hot stinging sand underfoot. Once there, she quietly slipped into her mother's room.

Darlene heard Maria's loud, labored breathing and glanced at her mother's thin face. Maria didn't stir when Darlene entered the room, so the daughter stood quietly, noticing for the first time how her mother's skin had taken on a yellowish tone during the past weeks. Maria's wispy grey hair spread over the white pillowcase covered with white doves and roses she had stitched last summer. Darlene remembered how puzzled she had been when Maria began sewing with the white floss on the white material. "Why are you using thread that no one can see? You might as well not do it as use that stuff."

Maria had given her a smile before she replied, "Sometimes simple is good when shape is important. We'll see how this turns out. If I don't like it, I can always change it later." The simplicity and elegance of the white on white design impressed everyone, especially Darlene the skeptic.

Darlene leaned over to brush a hair back from her mother's forehead, reached under the bed to grab her shoes, and tiptoed out without waking her.

The trip across the sand was much more leisurely this time, and she sauntered over to Theo. "Have you ever wondered how Mama can know so much? She can milk a cow and clean a chicken and build a fence, even though she was raised in town and never wanted to go outside and play while she was a little girl. She knows everything."

Ted nodded in agreement. "She's the best, and we're lucky to have her. I can remember being a little boy and wanting to be strong enough to carry pails of milk like she could. I'd wait till the milk pail was full, and then I'd grab it with both hands. Of course I spilled more than I saved, but she never scolded me. All she ever said was, 'Soon enough you'll be a man and then will come the big loads. Don't be in such a hurry. Grown up is forever.'"

"That's what she told me when I asked why I couldn't work in the hay field with a team of horses like everyone else did. Isn't it better to be grown up? Then you can do what you want to without everyone telling you what to do."

Ted laughed, "I had it figured the same way, but somehow it doesn't seem to work out like that. There is always someone taking care of your business, even if they don't know much about what is going on."

"No one can tell you what to do. You're the biggest and the smartest, just like I want to be." With that, Darlene grabbed the wrench and loosened the nut on the closest bolt.

"You keep working at it like that, and you'll get there

before you know it. I like having you here to help me because you pay attention to what needs done, and I don't have to tell you the same thing every time. You're a good worker."

With that, the two auburn heads leaned wordlessly over the mower bar, took out the sickle, replaced the missing sections, and slid the sickle in so Ted could get back out to the field to mow more meadow hay. "Thanks. We got that sickle fixed faster than ever before. How about heading back to the kitchen for a quick drink before I head out?"

As the brother and sister made their way back to the house, their sister Alma who came over every day to help out, stepped to the porch and hollered, "If you two are interested, I have some apple dumplings I just took out of the oven."

"Thanks, Sis, that sounds great. You are just about as good of a cook as Mama, and you always make my favorites." Ted touched her on the shoulder as they went into the house. "Wow, it is even hotter in here than out in the sun, especially when you have to fire up that cook stove. I wish it would cool off just a little so Mother could rest better. How's she doing today?"

Alma handed him the cream to pour over his pie and gave him a warning look along with a nod of her head at Darlene. Their little sister, leaning over to take off her shoes, picked up on Alma's pause and quickly looked up.

"Mama was doing all right when I sat with her this morning. She taught me how to do some fancy stitches and she's going to show me how to make a doll quilt just like hers. I had to go back to get my shoes, and I was careful not to wake her up cause she was sound asleep."

Alma came to Darlene's chair, lifted her little sister on to her own lap, and softly asked, "Honey, have you noticed that Mama hasn't left her room for the last two weeks? She's been sleeping more and not eating very much. Mama's getting very weak."

Darlene whirled around so she could hide her face in Alma's apron front before the tears began. All of a sudden, the unspoken fear she had been holding inside had now been put into words. She had noticed all that Alma mentioned and much more. The clammy feel of Maria's skin, the exhaustion from simple movements, and the long periods of deep sleep had been apparent to Darlene. Although she didn't know exactly what the changes meant, she did know that her mother was weaker with each day that passed.

Making the instinctive movement of rocking back and forth, Alma let her sister cry. Darlene had decided that making Maria's days pleasant meant there was no place for sadness or talking about what would happen when her mother died. Now there was no denying that the time was near.

Ted and Alma sat in silence, tears running down their faces at what lay ahead. Ted stroked Darlene's head with his huge hand, letting it trail down the long auburn curls. As he laid his other hand on Alma's shoulder and squeezed it, she reached with her free hand and clung to him silently since no words were big enough to say what each was feeling. For a moment, the current that flowed through the three united and comforted them before they had to face what was coming.

"Do you think it hurts to die?" This question had been in Darlene's mind since the first day Maria told her about her sickness.

Theo looked her in the eye and said, "Honey, none of us can know for sure, but I don't think so. Mama seems quiet and calm now, almost like she's decided she doesn't need to worry about us. She can let go and let us take over. She told me that even if she isn't here with us, she'll be looking out for us, so I don't think she will hurt. It seems like she hurt the most when she first realized she had to leave before finishing everything she wanted to do for us."

"Mama is ready to see Papa again. I know because she told me that the other day. We were sitting together, and she reached out to take my hand. Then she said, 'Alma, I like knowing you're here so I don't have to worry. I will see Ernest soon, and that is good. Take care of my babies, will you?' When I said I would, Mama closed her eyes and smiled. I don't think dying will hurt her nearly as much as it hurts the rest of us."

Darlene clung tight to her brother and sister. She had decided pretty much the same thing, mostly because she thought about watching animals die. She remembered earlier that spring when she had cradled the littlest kitten that was so weak. After Darlene wrapped a handkerchief around it and warmed its tiny body, the kitten quit trembling, relaxed against her for a time, and then stopped breathing. Darlene knew instinctively when the life went out, even though the kitten had been lying there the same quiet way all the time. It wasn't a horrid, shrieking moment in any way; instead, it was a peaceful way for a life to end.

After everyone was done with their dumplings, Ted put down his fork and laid his palms on the oak table. He pushed himself up, tousled his little sister's hair, and stretched his lanky arms over his head. "Guess I'd better make hay since the sun sure enough is shining." With that, he put on his hat, pushed open the wooden screen door, and started across the yard where Darlene had danced her way across the burning sand.

Just then, Emma came trotting up on her horse that had sweat dripping from his neck and flank. She had left early to ride around all the pastures to be sure the windmills were working and the tanks were full. With this kind of heat, cattle would die if they were without water for very long. "Ted, we have to do something about the cows and calves in the south pasture. The cattle are all standing around a bone-dry tank. The pump rod is broken plus the wind hasn't blown for two days so they are in bad trouble."

Ted sighed and turned back to the porch where Darlene now stood. "Guess that hay will have to wait. Lena, how about getting changed into your trousers and saddling up that wonder horse of yours? Emma can go on to check the other pastures and I'll bet the two of us can move that herd to the next pasture with that spring-fed pond. Even though the grass is short since we had them in it earlier, we can move them back once we get the well work done."

Darlene had already headed in to get ready as soon as Emma gave her report. Throwing down her cotton dress in the corner, she grabbed her pants and shirt and shimmied into them. Looking back at her room, she stopped long enough to snatch up the dress and fold it neatly on the bed. The gesture was a tribute to Maria's insistence that everything be put in its proper place, not later, but right now. Lena knew Mama wouldn't be in her room to see a mess, but it felt right to do what would make Maria proud.

"Okay, Theo, we're lucky. I locked the horses in this morning when I fed them. Your Cheyenne and my Dime are out there in the corral so we can get there in a hurry. It's a good thing Dime and I can help you out. Otherwise you and that slowpoke of yours would take all day and half the night."

With that, she took off on a run for the barn with Ted close at her heels. "What kind of a remark is that about the best horse on the place? Cheyenne and I'll probably have to sit on the top of every hill and wait for you and that plug you ride to catch up." She giggled as he caught hold of her waist and swung her around once before they both went into the tack room to get their bridles and saddles. "Now look what you went and did to me. I'm sweating and haven't done a lick of work yet."

The easy companionship between brother and sister was something they both took for granted. The pasture was four miles away; and by the time they moved the cattle and rode back home, they would have spent hours together. Riding along, they often spent miles just listening to the saddles creak and the larks sing. Other times, they talked over whatever happened to come up in the conversation. Today was one of the quiet times since Maria was on both their minds.

Reluctant to move and yet restless, the cows and calves hadn't cooperated. "Are you glad Dime and I came along to help out? You and Cheyenne might've had a devil of a day doing this alone."

"Yeah, I have to say the two of you were handy to have around. You're really quite a pair. Now did you want to apologize to Cheyenne for calling him a slowpoke? That really hurt his feelings."

Darlene and Ted were sitting on a hillside watching the cows and calves pair up. She leaned over and stroked the big black's mane. "Don't be sad, fella. You did a pretty good job today and I was just teasing. I'll even give you an extra bite of grain when we get back home." When they had gotten the herd in sight of the pond, the cattle took off on a run even though both riders had done their best to keep them in check. To the cows, quenching their thirst was even more important than keeping track of their calves so the pairs had been separated. After the turmoil and a deep drink for all, the mothers started milling around and bawling for their babies.

Gradually, the matching process was completed to Ted's satisfaction so the riders could head back home. "Let's go, Lena. We're done here until the mill is fixed and we can move them back to the summer range. By the time we get back, most of the day will be shot; but maybe I can get in a little bit of haying." With that, they turned their horses back to the ranch.

"How are you going to get the well fixed and the haying done? It seems like everything piles up at once." Darlene had that deep crease between her brows she always had when she was thinking over something that bothered her.

"I guess Fred will have to come out here and work on the well while I do the haying. This well has been pumping slow, so we might as well re-leather it and fix it up right when we're doing it."

"Remember the last time you worked on that well on the Smith section? It took us most of the day and we didn't even pack a lunch to take along. Man, was I hungry." She rubbed her stomach and wrinkled her nose at the thought of so many hours without food.

Ted threw back his head and laughed, "Yeah, everything that could go wrong that time did. Since we couldn't just take the team and wagon five miles home for lunch and turn around and go back, we were glad when we finally got back home."

He continued with a sigh, "Guess we'll have to ask Fred to come out here tomorrow and get this fixed so we can move the cattle back. Grass is too short to leave them very long. That way I can get back to the hayfield."

Since it was so hot, they let the horses set a leisurely pace on the way home. The minute they rode up to the barn, Alma met them. "Darlene, how about if you unsaddle the horses. Ted, I need to see you right now." It was so unusual to hear her give orders that both of them nodded their heads and did as she asked.

Gesturing and speaking intently, Alma immediately engaged Ted in conversation as they made their way across the sand to the house. "You won't believe what Fred has decided to do. He wants to move Mama to Ogallala right now; says it will be 'easier' on everyone. He had the car right up to the front gate and was ready to haul her out while you were gone. I stood up to him and said he couldn't do a thing until you got back. He's hopping mad."

Ted let out a deep sigh and put his hand on the door just as Fred jerked it open from inside. "It's about time you got here so we can get some things settled once and for all. You know I'm the oldest and I've been the head of the house since Papa died. At least that's the way it's supposed to be. Every time I try to do something, everyone runs to you to see what dear old Ted thinks is right. I'm sick and tired of hearing about what you want or think or do." By now, Fred was shouting and waving his arms.

Ted interrupted with a low voice. "Let's see if we can talk about this without Mama hearing us. She doesn't need this added to what she's going through. How about us stepping outside--"

"See, you're doing it again. Always taking over like you're the big shot. Okay, buster, we will step outside, but just remember you asked for it."

Closing the door quietly behind him, Theo followed Fred and Alma outside where Fred started in again. "All I'm trying to do is make it easier on us all. A doctor could help Mama and we wouldn't have to ask Alma to come over and pitch in so often. It just makes sense to me."

Ted had listened calmly, waiting until Fred had run out of bluster. Now it was his turn. "For one thing, the doctor already told us there is nothing he can do. I'm guessing that Alma wants to spend all the time she can with Mother, and that looks to be pretty short. I guess the last thing is that making it easier for us would mean making it harder on Mama. What is the big deal with you anyway? The most you do is peek your head in her room and say 'How's it going?'

before you hightail it out of the house. Easier for you just means her not being here so you don't feel guilty about avoiding her. It's okay with me if you never set foot inside her room again, but I'll tell you this. No one moves Mama, period."

By now, Ted was face-to-face with his older brother and speaking with a controlled but deadly serious tone. Fred whirled and stomped off the porch just as Darlene rushed up and grabbed Alma around the waist. After taking care of the horses, she had gotten to the house just as the conversation had moved outside. She had heard it all and was in tears.

"Please don't let him take Mama away. She's all I've got and I need her so bad. Oh, please promise me she won't have to go."

With one movement, Ted knelt in front of her and took her in his arms. "Little One, I promise you that Mama will stay right where she is. That's where she wants to be and that's where she'll stay."

Darlene took him at his word and relaxed her grip around his neck. "Why is he so selfish? Mama always tells us to care for one another, and it doesn't seem like he listens to a thing she says."

"This is a tough time on us all, Lena, and the only thing we have to do is make sure we do what Mama wants. Right now, that means not squabbling so she's unhappy. I think she probably was asleep and didn't hear this ruckus, so let's not mention it to her at all, okay? Fred finds it hard to show how much he cares, so sometimes he does things that we can't figure out. I don't think he intends to hurt anyone, but he has a different way of looking at things. He'll be okay after he has time to cool off." With that, the three of them opened the door and walked into their home, troubled yet together.

Ted was right, as usual. Maria's time was getting short,

and her days were mostly spent in a deep sleep from which she seldom roused.

Darlene would tiptoe into the room each morning, sit beside the bed, and stroke her mother's brow. "Mama, good morning. Tater and I are here right beside you." After that, Darlene would take up her sewing and stitch contentedly while sitting with her mother.

By now, Darlene was used to Maria's staying asleep when she and the pup came in, so she was surprised when Maria blinked her eyes, stretched out her hand, and whispered, "Well, hello, Little Lena." Darlene squeezed back, then Maria let her pale, cool hand lie on Darlene's palm.

Alma and Ted looked in at the two of them, and then went back to talk while drinking their coffee at the kitchen table. Pleased that her mother had roused enough to speak to her, Darlene sat stroking Maria's hand when, all of a sudden, she let out a pathetic shriek.

Alma and Ted rushed to the bedroom where Darlene was desperately grasping her mother's hand and sobbing. "No, Mama, no. Don't leave me like this. I'm not ready. I don't have your blanket done yet. Please stay here with me. Oh, please don't go."

Ted sat on the chair so he could hold Darlene as they cried together. Alma put her hands over her face and didn't make a sound. After her shoulders quit shaking, she bent down beside Darlene and they sat there, knowing it was over but not exactly knowing what to do next.

Finally, Ted stood up and said, "I'll go tell the others. We need to send someone to tell the neighbors. I'll see if Fred will go." With that, he moved out of the room.

"Oh, Alma. One minute she was here with me and then she was gone. I could tell when the life wasn't in her anymore. I didn't know she would go so soon. There are so many things I wanted her to know, but I didn't tell her. Now she'll never know."

"Sweetie, Mother knew what was in your heart even if you didn't say it. Don't be sad about what you didn't do, but always treasure the times you had together. She often told me how much she wished she could stay around longer to be with us, so you gave her joy right up to the end. I'm sorry you were in here alone."

"No, Alma, that was okay. I wouldn't have wanted to be anywhere else when it happened. At least I know it didn't hurt her to die. She was taking those little breaths, and then she just stopped and kind of folded back into the pillow."

One by one, Maria's children came in to sit by her bed and say their own good-byes. Darlene and Alma moved back to the wall to let the others have a chance to stroke Maria's face and let out their grief in their own private ways.

Fred came in and stood at the doorway, tears running down his face. He stood quietly, then said, "I guess I'd better be on my way. Bye, Mama." He whirled and made his way out of the house into the Model A, started it up, and headed out.

Emma, Elsie, Clara, Eva, and Millie filed into the room. They had been in the garden working in the ease of the morning, so they blinked as they came into the cool, dimly lit room. Each of them spent time beside the still, slight form in the bed, then headed to the kitchen table where the family always gathered in difficult times.

Looking to Alma, Clara asked, "Who's going to get word to everyone so they'll know about Mama?"

"Fred will go to a couple of the closest ones, and they will spread the word. We'll stick with what people around here have gotten used to. They'll come visit as soon as they hear, then we'll have service for Mama at the house tomorrow. That new undertaker in Arthur will come out to take care of the burial."

"Will he take her to Ogallala to be with Papa and Harry? It seems like that would be right." Darlene knew where her mother would want to be, even though it was many miles away from home.

Alma nodded her head, "She just whispered to me yesterday to please take her there, so I'm sure that's what we'll do."

All of the sisters but Darlene and Eva were old enough to know what needed done. Alma poured water into a basin, reached into the cupboard for a cloth, and sighed, "I dreaded this, but I'm glad we can get Mama ready for her last trip to town. You know how particular she was."

With that, the girls went back into the room and bathed their mother. Rather than being squeamish about touching Maria's body, every action was one of love and respect as they undertook the final act they could ever do for her.

By the time the girls had finished with their preparations, Ted came back in the house. "Walnut was Mama's favorite wood for furniture, so I picked up some the last time I went to Ogallala. I wanted her to have a beautiful place to rest in, and I'm glad I got it done in time." With that, he placed the gleaming wooden casket on the floor. "Guess we need to arrange the furniture so we can set it up in the living room. Mama had lots of friends who will come to pay their respects."

"Theo, I can see myself in the wood. How did you do that?" Darlene ran her hand down the wood and felt the silky finish.

"When Uncle Will was out here one time, he talked about using Swedish oil as a finish instead of using varnish. I've given it lots of coats to get it to look like this." Ted answered while moving the pieces so the casket could sit on chairs in the middle of the room and yet leave space for people to move around. "There. I think that's just about right." Ted had quickly organized the room with an eye for what needed done.

All of a sudden Darlene understood what Ted had been doing every night after supper. When the rest of the family would play cards or read beside the lamp, he would stretch and say, "Guess I'll go out to the barn for a little while." No one thought it was unusual since he was always checking to see everything was okay.

"So that is why you've been staying out at the barn. I heard a bunch of hammering and saw the lantern when I would go to bed, but I guessed you were overhauling haying equipment. This is so pretty that it would make Mama cry."

With that, Darlene went into the bedroom and brought out her sewing. "Could this be Mama's pillow? It's not near as nice as what you did, Ted, but I'd like for her to have it with her even if it's not quite done."

Gently, Ted took the blanket and held Darlene to his side. "Sweetheart, this is perfect. How about if you put it in the way you want it? Then we'll be sure it's done just right."

Darlene folded the square perfectly and put it where Maria's head would rest. She adjusted the material and straightened up. "Do you know the one good thing about this, Theo? Mama told me she hated August since Harry and Papa died, and she won't have to face another one. Funny how that worked out, isn't it?"

"God let her go so she didn't have to face any more hard times, so you're right, that is one good thing that happened for her. Hard for us but good for her."

Right then the girls came out of Maria's room and saw the coffin set up in the living room. "Should we bring it into the bedroom so you can put her in it?"

Ted shook his head and wiped his eyes. "That won't be necessary. I'll be honored to carry her one last time. That's the least I can do." With that, he took the few steps into the bedroom and scooped up the slight form on the bed. Cradling her in his huge arms, he buried his face in her hair and carefully deposited the body into the casket. After he had her situated, he nodded to Darlene and together they laid Maria's head on the tiny embroidered pillow.

"There, Mama, rest well. We'll miss you."

One by one the sisters came by and reached in to give the finishing touches. Eva straightened her mother's collar. Emma moved Maria's hands so the right one was over the left one the way she held her hands when she would finally sit down in the rocking chair. Alma arranged her mother's gray hair so it was smooth and waved back at the temples. Clara pinned on Maria's favorite brooch. Finally Millie made them all laugh through their tears as she tucked white gloves into Maria's left hand, "Here, Mama, maybe you can put them on before Papa gets a look at you. He'll be proud of you looking so fine in your gloves and dress."

Each person performed the ritual as a way of letting go; and when they were all done, they became aware of the total silence in the room. Alma was the one who guided them to the kitchen where they all sat down for the first time since they realized their mother was gone. What amazed each of them was how empty the house felt even though Maria had been silent for the past few days. Her sheer presence was so powerful that once it was removed, each person started feeling isolated and alone. No matter how many were in the room, the one link that bound them together was gone.

Not knowing what else to do, Emma pushed back her chair as she spoke, "Guess I'll get out there and pick those beans. Maybe we can have them for dinner."

When she left, the other girls followed her out to pick up where they had started earlier in the day. It was almost as if they tried to resume their natural existence even though their life had been irrevocably altered at the moment of Maria's death.

As expected, the neighbors poured into the yard as soon as they heard. Some came in cars, some in buggies, and some on horseback. Each new visitor brought funeral food; and before long, the kitchen table seemed to sag under its huge load. Alma had made a big pot of coffee, and people were everywhere. With much hugging and crying, the guests would speak to each of the family members, then go in and stand quietly beside Maria's casket.

Then they would go back to the kitchen where they would tell stories. They laughed about how Maria would describe her first impression of the hills she had come to love. "For as far as I could see, I could see what there was to see. There was not a tree in sight—just huge hills that seemed to go clear up to the sky, and then valleys that were long and straight until another set of hills started up again." And then she would let out that deep laugh of hers and shake her head. "Who knew?"

Stories abounded about what a hard worker she was, about how Maria would work in the field until a week or so before she would have her next baby. Since she was too short to harness the teams, Ernest had built her a box to stand on. Only when she was so big she couldn't balance on the box would she let him give her a hand harnessing her team.

Shrieks of laughter followed after Reichenbergs talked about how they came over the hill just in time to see her spanking the hens and throwing them out of her garden. When Maria had gotten to the end of the row, she turned around and saw that the hens had followed right behind her and scratched out every kernel of sweet corn she had planted. "Wow. We knew right then and there never to cross her. She could explode bigger than any little German lady we ever saw."

Of course, no gathering about the Soehls was complete

until the wolf story was told. No matter how old, it seemed exciting, especially the part about how Maria would tell Ernest not to scare the children with his stories of the glowing red eyes and huge teeth. He would just pat her shoulder and say, "Now, Mama, they need to know how things really are."

Others spoke of how deeply she felt the loss of little Harry and how Ernest was such a shrewd trader, but he could never pull one over on Maria. She would turn her head to the right, cock an eyebrow, and he would come clean. It was comforting for the Soehl children to hear these stories, some familiar and some totally new. As the community came together in the kitchen, it felt right to have so many people share their loss.

The next morning was the first cool morning in three weeks. After chores, Maria's family cleaned up and put on their best clothes, ready for the minister to come at ten o'clock as he had promised. Maria had instilled in her children the importance of dressing well, and she would have been proud to see how good they looked. Waiting for the undertaker and the minister was difficult for them all because they knew when the words were spoken and the casket was loaded, it was all over.

Darlene walked out to the sadness barrel in the barn where she was sure Ted was waiting. Sure enough, she came around the corner to find him looking off in the distance while he fingered a piece of leather. "I thought I'd probably find you here. What do you think?"

"Not much, I guess. It's kinda hard to wait. We can't get dirty, but it's sure hard to just sit around. How are you doing?"

"Theo, I'm surprised at how much it hurts to think Mama is gone. We've known for a long time this was going to happen, so why isn't it easier? Sometimes I start crying now over the dumbest things. Isn't that kind of crazy?"

Ted clinched his jaw to keep back his tears before he answered. "You know, Little One, I don't know that we're ever ready to let go. No matter if it is sudden or if we know it's coming, saying good-bye is one of the toughest things to do."

"We're really lucky that we got to spend time with Mama before she died, but it was hard to wake up every morning and know about it. I think I'd rather not know what's ahead. It made my stomach feel funny and now my head hurts. Why did this have to happen? Is God mad at us or did Mama do something really bad that we didn't know about?"

Ted grabbed Darlene fiercely to his chest, "Never think that, Sweetheart. Our mother didn't do anything to cause this. Sometimes a body just quits working like it should and then it breaks down. When bad things come into our lives, it isn't because God got mad and decided to zap us. Do you remember when that big wind blew over the cottonwood tree and pinned those cows underneath the branches? God didn't decide they should die and throw the tree on them. It just happened. It wouldn't make much sense for me to be mad at God."

Ted took off on another part of his explanation. "Did Mama ever tell you why Papa died?"

Darlene nodded her head, "He was really sick and didn't trust that doctor."

"That's right. I never heard Mama say she was mad at God, so I don't blame Him either. My idea is that whatever is meant to be is meant to be. I can't change what happens so I take the time to hurt and then get back to taking care of my part."

"That seems to make sense but I'm going to have to think that over a little bit. I hear some more cars coming so I guess we'd better get back to the house.

He bowed and swept his arm toward the door. "After you, my dear."

Darlene had never been to a funeral before, and she didn't know what to expect. The minister read some Psalms, and talked about Maria's life, both in Germany and in Nebraska. Sitting up late the night before, the older brothers and sisters had written down what they knew of her past. Now that part was over, and the minister was talking about how Maria had gone home to be with Jesus, Ernest, and Harry.

Darlene leaned over to whisper to Ted, "How is that supposed to make us feel better? We're here without her, and I don't really think she was ready to leave."

Ted whispered back, "Remember what I told you—some things we just have to accept. This time God had a different plan than we did."

All of a sudden she heard the familiar words of Psalm 121, and the whole family recited-it together. Darlene knew that Maria and Ernest both would have liked that sound.

Ich hebe meine augen auf zu den bergen,
*Von welchen mir Hulfe komm*t

Too soon the service was finished, the top screwed on the casket, and the mourners carried it to the undertaker's vehicle. The family had agreed that Maria should be in Ogallala, and they also agreed to say their farewells in the home rather than driving the forty miles of sandhill trail to get to the cemetery only to turn around and return. While they all knew it was practical, watching the dust of the retreating car made them all want to jump in and follow.

Emma was the one who found her voice first. "Now I guess it's time to go in and write in the Bible. How about it,

Alma, would you take care of that for Mama?"

"Sure. I think Mama would want us to all be together when we write in it. Let's do it right now."

All the brothers and sisters gathered around the oak table, and Alma opened the Bible to the center where all the births and deaths had been recorded in Maria's spidery script.

Marie Meyberg Soehl Died July 9, 1924

When she put the final touches on the entry, Alma closed the Bible and handed it to Darlene. "How about putting this in Mama's room in the Chester Drawers? She always liked everything in its right place, so that's the last thing we can do for her."

Chapter 3

It was over. The time they had all been dreading and expecting had come and gone, and now the family had to go on without Maria at the center.

Realistically, the days didn't change all that much. Maria had been ailing for so long that everyone had settled into a routine that revolved around her illness, yet one that focused on taking care of the business of ranching. As a practical person who had put her entire being into creating a ranch from what had been just wide-open spaces, Maria wouldn't have had it any other way.

What Darlene noticed was that everything was the same, yet nothing was the same. When she had first heard about her mother's illness, she had told Theo that she would spend time every morning with Maria. Darlene was as good as her word, and this promise took up a major part of her day. After her morning visit, then Darlene would spend the rest of the day pondering about little surprises to take to Mother the next time she saw her.

One day she had grabbed a tablespoon from the kitchen,

climbed the big hill just north of the barn, and found a barrel cactus in bloom. Even though Darlene was careful, she still rubbed against the spines which stuck in the side of her hand. They itched and burned, but she didn't stop until she had the round cactus in a ball of dirt. She filled a pint Mason jar nearly full of sand, shoved the cactus in, and poured more sand around it. When she was done, the deep pink star-like flower peeked above the top, and Darlene was satisfied. She stood up, dusted off her hands by striking them together with an up and down motion, and ran down the hill, jumping from one ridge to another. From a distance, these were paths that looked like steps running across the entire length of the huge hills that rose straight up from the meadow.

Darlene had told Maria about her adventure, and ended it with something that had been puzzling her. "I get such a flighty feeling in my tummy when I jump down the 'can't steps.' It makes me feel like I can fly when I give a huge jump from one ledge and then float down to land on the next. I know they're steps, but why don't people call them 'can steps'?"

Maria had reached out to smooth the curls that were bouncing all around Darlene's face, then smiled and said, "You know what, Lena, I like the words of that. I think you'll find 'can steps' lots of places. Most people around here say 'cat steps,' but maybe they never took the time to think for themselves."

Darlene had cocked her head off to the side and looked up at the ceiling before answering. "Can you imagine a cat big enough to use those steps to walk right up a hill? If I ever saw one like that, I'd make him my pet and name him Look Out. I bet all the coyotes and wolves would run away when they'd hear me say, 'Look Out, here we come!'"

Maria and Lena had leaned into each other and shared one of those private giggling moments that no one else would ever understand. Darlene had so many times like that in her memories, and suddenly it hit her that there would be no more. Everything she had shared with her mother had transformed into solitary, silent sounds in her mind; and she instinctively knew these moments were uniquely hers. Rather than comforting her, however, this knowledge produced an overwhelming feeling of isolation. She realized it wasn't just the events that made a moment special; it was everything combined. It was a feeling that defied description, no matter how many words she would string together. If she ever tried, she knew that Theo would listen to her, but even he was an outsider. It felt like being all alone.

When Darlene awakened the first morning after the funeral, she simply lay in bed and thought. After months of finding ways to brighten Maria's days and silently hoping her mother would get better, she truly did not have any idea of what to do with herself. Deciding she couldn't stay in bed for the entire day, she slowly sat up and dangled her legs over the edge of the bed, let out a big sigh, and slipped into her clothes.

As Darlene buttoned the white blouse, she was surprised to find it ended above her waist rather than going past the top of her britches. Cocking her head, she slipped into her work pants, only to find the same sudden stop as she put them on. Darlene wasn't used to bare skin showing, and she wondered what had gone wrong with her clothes.

Making her way out to the kitchen table where Ted and Emma sat with their huge hands circling the heavy porcelain coffee cups, she asked, "Emma, did you do something different last time you did the washing? I don't remember having trouble with this stuff before and now nothing feels right."

Tugging at her blouse and rubbing a foot above her stocking top, she reminded Ted of the colts out on the meadow. They had a kind of awkward grace about them as their long, gangly legs held up a body that grew in different stages. For a time everything worked well together; and they would burst into action, running straight away from their mothers and, all of a sudden, switch direction to run right back at her, veering at the last moment. They would circle around and nuzzle her as if to double check that she was still there, and then the adventure was on again.

All of a sudden, the colts would hit a growth spurt and nothing worked right. Their legs would get tangled up so they would stumble, and often a colt would stop and look down between his front legs as if puzzled why they didn't do what he expected. Tossing his head as if to shake off the momentary setback, off again he would speed, figuring out very quickly how to make the parts work right.

"Lena, when was the last time you wore that? I don't remember seeing you in those clothes lately." Darlene had inched over to Ted's chair, and he circled her waist with his arm as she stood there. With one slight motion, he drew her down to sit on his leg where she relaxed against him.

Squinting one eye and turning her head slightly to the side as she always did when deep in thought, Darlene pursed her lips before she answered. "You know, I guess I haven't really worn these since I got out of school. Most days this summer I wore dresses to visit Mama, but I grabbed these 'cause I want to go along and help you."

Emma let out her deep chuckle as she gazed at Darlene. "It's kind of funny how I've seen you every day and didn't notice how much you've grown. Guess I'll have to check on what fits and get rid of the rest. We surely have some outgrown pieces around here that you can wear, so I'll take care of that today. You really are growing like a weed."

Though unspoken, each person shared the awareness that this was one more task that Maria had taken care of, never making an issue of it, just keeping life organized and tidy. Their new life without Maria would undoubtedly reveal many more tasks she had done that, although small, all created their sense of home.

Ted took hold of Darlene's waist, stood her up, and announced, "Lena, I've got lots of work to get done, and you know you're always welcome to come sweat with me." With that, he rose, put on his hat, turned back to the table, and continued. "You get some breakfast in your gullet and then we'll take off. See you at the barn."

All of a sudden the room felt empty to the sisters, so Darlene perched on her chair, grabbed the pitcher of heavy cream, and flooded her bowl of oatmeal. She loved the way Emma fixed the cereal, and one time she asked, "How do you make this taste so good? No one else's even comes close to yours." Emma had let her watch as she stirred in generous amounts of brown sugar and a generous pinch of salt while it was cooking. The heavy, sweet concoction was one of the family's favorite ways to start the day since it tasted so good and held them until the next meal.

Done with her breakfast, Darlene grabbed her dishes, shoved the chair under the table, and headed to the sink. Working the pump handle up and down until the water splashed out, she rinsed off the dishes and put them in Emma's dishpan with the others. "See you when we get back, Em. Thanks for breakfast." With that, she pushed open the screen door and was half way to the barn before it slammed shut. Emma watched through the window and waved back when Darlene turned around at the barn and flung her hand in the air.

Going into the barn was always her favorite feeling. Just moving in from the outside meant an immediate difference of temperature. The dark, cool interior held a combination of smells which she inhaled deeply as she stepped inside the door. Closing her eyes, she could identify the smells of clover, grain, well-oiled leather, and sweaty horses. Draft horses in their stalls made the familiar chomping sound as they chewed their grain, the cats came up to rub and purr, and the chickens scolded her as they scooted around her and headed outside.

Ted was inside getting the harness ready, and she ran into the tack room to grab the bridles for Molly and Jeff. As they headed for the stalls, Fred appeared in the doorway and asked, "So what do you think we need to do now?"

Never missing a step, Ted went beside the big black mare and threw the harness over Molly's back. "Well, I guess haying the meadow is the most important thing right now. We mowed some of that before Mama died, so we need to get it raked and stacked. Then we can probably get to some of that lower grass where it's usually too wet. With the dry summer, I think we can hay more than we ever did before."

Fred shook his head impatiently, "No, that's not what I'm talking about and you know it. Now that it's just us two men running the ranch without Mama to make decisions, we need to come to some kind of an agreement. Who's going to be in charge? Someone has to be, and since I'm the oldest, it seems like I'd be the one."

Darlene heard Ted let out a weary sigh, buckle on the harness, and stand up to look at Fred. "You know, I knew this was coming, but I guess I thought you'd wait a little longer before trying to bull your way around. Yeah, you may be the oldest, but I don't know that we really need to change things all that much. I think we can just keep doing what needs done, and when something comes up, we'll deal with it later."

"No. I'm tired of you acting like you own this place. You and Mama sat and talked all the time and never bothered to let me in on your precious plans. Now that she's gone, things are going to be different around here. Starting right now, I say we do need to change things all that much, and the first thing is that we are going to buy some tractors and machinery. Everyone else does, but it's like we're so stuck in the past that we use horses for everything on the place. It's not like we can't afford it."

Darlene saw the glint in Ted's eye before she heard the harsh tone of his words. "Fred, you don't give a hang about land or animals or ranching, and that's okay. We all have our own interests and way of looking at the world, but I'll tell you this. There is no way I'm going to stand for you squandering what Mama and Papa worked so hard to put together. The reason we have some money is that we've always been careful to make do with what we have until we had a good reason to change. You know that we all agreed that buying a car would make it easier for us to get back and forth, so we did it. Maybe we do need to talk about buying a tractor for some of our work, but you're not just taking a blank check to town so you can buy every new-fangled thing you see. What we're doing is working just fine for the most part."

With that, Fred whirled and stomped to his house.

"I hate it when you guys yell at each other. It makes my stomach twist up inside and I get scared. Why isn't he happy with things the way they are?" Darlene clutched her stomach and twitched her chin to keep from crying. "I bet Mama wouldn't have liked this."

Ted grabbed a nail keg lying by the wall, sat down on it, and pulled Darlene on his lap. Smoothing her hair with his freckled hand, he let out his breath. "You're right about that, Little One. Whenever Fred and I would start to squabble, she would just give us that look and say, 'A little kindness please' and that would end it. Only we both know nothing ended; it just got put off until now. You don't have to be scared of anything. Fred and I can work this out, but right now things are a little bit tough between us. I'll make sure everything's all right, I promise."

Darlene buried her face in his neck, and just as fast jerked it back. "Ouch! That hurt. I'll bet you haven't even shaved yet today, have you?" Rubbing her whisker-burned cheek, she gave him her best glare.

Laughing while he stood up, he agreed, "You called that one right. I guess my most important job isn't looking pretty; it's getting this hay all stacked up. How about us saddling Eagle so you can come along with me? I'm working at the end of the meadow, and you can play around the cottonwood tree you like so much."

What a wonderful invitation. It meant Darlene had something to do with the time she had been spending with Maria, and it also meant she would be spending her day with three of her favorites—Ted, Eagle, and Tater. She ran to get a halter while Ted loosened the rope that had been half-hitched around her saddle horn to keep it suspended from the tack room ceiling.

When Ted finally had the gear on all the animals, he gave Darlene the signal to get mounted on the tall sorrel gelding. Eagle was a perfect kid's horse. Willing to go as fast as Darlene could handle, he looked out for her. Now he patiently waited while she pulled herself up. Wrapping her hands around the back saddle strings, she stood back and kicked high enough to catch her toe in the stirrup. She dangled back momentarily until she could gain momentum and leverage herself to the front where she would grab the front strings. Unwinding the back strings, she then clutched the cantle and vaulted into her seat.

Once seated, off they would go in pursuit of adventure. Sometimes she would urge Eagle to run across the end of the pond, each time trying to splash water farther than before. Other times they would pick their way up the blow-outs and cat steps until they reached the top of the biggest hill around. With hills and sky that seemed never-ending, Darlene and Eagle sat so still that they blended right into the landscape.

When it was time to go down that same hill, she would let the reins feed through her hand until Eagle was in full control. He would pick his way down, rear end nearly touching the hillside while he would zigzag to find the best footing. Darlene would brace her arm on the saddle horn and lean back as far as she could go. Never once did she doubt that he would get her down safely, and never once did he disappoint her. By the time Eagle had her to the lower slope, she would gather the slack and kick him so they could zoom down the rest of the way, giggling as she felt the wind blowing the hair straight back from her face.

Darlene would stop Eagle and let him catch his breath while she stroked his neck and looked back up the huge hill. Sometimes as they sat, she would see the sand lizards running around his hooves on their way to a soap weed, and ants would drag their tiny meals along the sand. She was at peace.

Before they set out on this outing, Darlene stopped at the house to grab the lunch Emma had ready for them, and Ted had grabbed the filled crock jug wrapped in a gunnysack that had been soaked in water. Working in the hay field meant hot, sweaty hours spent long distances from a water source, so they always carried their own supply. Even though they started with cool water, by the end of the afternoon, the water in the jug was lukewarm at best.

Ted would pull his team up beside the stack where the jug was tucked into the hay on the shady side. Wrapping the lines beside the seat, he would gingerly step down, stretch his back, and stroll over to the jug while he took off his hat and wiped his brow on his sleeve. Pushing his index finger into the circle beside the spout, he would remove the stopper and hoist the jug until it rested atop his elbow. Lifting his arm, he could then take deep drinks of water, occasionally allowing the liquid to dribble down his front to saturate his shirt. When done, he would close the jug, most of the time using the end of a corncob since the original cork had long since disappeared. As he would re-mount the seat and take off across the field, the air would move across the dampened fabric and give a sensation of coolness until all the moisture was gone. Brief as it was, the relief was welcome.

Imitating Ted in every way she could, Darlene also would take deep drinks from the jug. When it was full, she had trouble lifting it with both hands. Later in the afternoon after enough water had been chugged down, she would finally succeed in lifting the crock with one hand. Even then, she still hadn't developed the knack of throwing it over her arm to take a drink. Letting the water trickle down her blouse, she gulped huge mouthfuls and headed into the breeze to welcome the momentary coolness.

Summer passed in days that were remarkably the same even though the jobs might be different each day. With unspoken understanding, she and Ted headed out every morning to take care of business. Darlene was running behind one day after sleeping later than usual, and as she ran to the barn, once again she heard the familiar angry voices.

"I told you we needed to wait until we spent that much money. Why do you always have to jump in without thinking anything through? It's not like you didn't know where to find me so we could have talked about this." With fists clenched at his side, Ted loomed over his brother and glowered down into a scowling face. Fred stood defiantly, feet planted solidly and shoulders squared while he glared back with hostile eyes. Both men had the same stubborn set of jaw and bright red, angry face.

"Who do you think you are anyway, my lord and master? I don't have to get permission from you for every move I make and wait for your final say-so on what goes on around here. If I want to buy machinery to make it a little easier around here, that's just what I'll do. You'll just have to learn to deal with it because that's the way it is from now on." With that final remark and a jab of his index finger into Ted's chest, Fred made a quick exit to get out of harm's way.

Ted let rise a guttural sound from deep in his throat, whirled around, and launched his fist into a bag of grain sitting on a barrel. All at once his boots were engulfed in the shower of oats that gushed forth from the split in the cloth. Stomping his feet and scattering the grain, he charged into the tack room, grabbed the harness, and thrust it at the big gelding's back. As if sensing his anger, the horse shied away and whirled to the far corner of the stall.

Almost at once Ted came to his senses, eased over to the horse to pet him, then crouched down on his haunches outside the stall. He dropped his head on his crossed arms, and let out a huge moan. "Nice mess you left me in, Ma. How in the world can I make any sense out of this?"

Walking in softly, Darlene reached out to hold him, almost as if their roles had reversed.

"I know you can do it, Theo. You can fix anything and I can help, too." Then she smoothed back his hair to give him time just like a mother soothing a sad child.

"Lena, you are the darnedest one to show up right when I need help the most. I don't know what's going to happen, but we'll work our way through it together. Sometimes I miss Mama so much that I just feel lost."

"Me, too. And you know what? For a minute there, you WERE lost in all that oats that was flying around."

Her droll sense of humor made Ted laugh, and he tousled

her hair. "You and I make a pretty good team, all right, and this day already feels better. Guess we'd better head out to the field so we get something done before noon."

"Theo, why is Fred so mean to you? We didn't even need that stupid tractor that he brought home. And I don't like it when he yells at you and then just runs away so you can't even answer."

Ted rubbed the stubble on his chin, twisted his lips over to the side just as he did when concentrating on a tough situation, and let out a big breath. "Lena, just because he and I are grown-up doesn't mean we don't act like children. From the earliest time I can remember, we never got along. He didn't like the slow pace and hard work of ranching, and I never liked the way he looked for the easy way out. We argued and bickered when we were little just like we do now. The biggest difference is that Mama was there to keep us in line, and we weren't the ones responsible for deciding what to do. Now we're both trying to be in charge, and we keep butting heads. He isn't being mean; he's just being the way he's always been."

"But I don't like it. When you guys yell, I'm afraid one of you will hurt the other one. Why can't he just straighten up? What's going to happen here? If he keeps spending money, he'll make us really poor and we'll lose everything. He needs to straighten up." With that, she planted her hands squarely on her hips to make her point just as she had seen Maria do so often.

Ted recognized the gesture and knelt down in front of her. "Little One, it's okay. Actually, buying the tractor was probably a really good idea for the ranch, even if I did get mad about the way Fred did it. It'll help us get more work done so we can make more money in the long run. You've heard us yelling at each other for a long time, but it's all just loud sounds and big talk. No one is going to get hurt, that's for sure. You have my word on that."

Big tears shone in Darlene's eyes as she gazed unblinkingly into Ted's eyes. "I get so scared that something might happen to you that I get all shaky inside. Will you promise nothing will ever happen to you? What would I do all alone?" With that, she flung herself into Ted's arms where her shoulders jerked with the quiet sobbing of a hurt child.

"Little Lena, don't be afraid. You have all of us so you'll never be alone. I promise to take care of you as long as you need me, no matter what. You know someday you'll grow up and leave the ranch; and even then, I'll still be your big brother."

"But promise me that nothing will ever happen to you. Please, Theo. You have to say it."

Ted held her out at arm's length and spoke to her in his open, honest way. "Darlene, none of us knows what's going to happen. I can promise to never let you down. I can promise to love you with my whole heart. I can promise that I will protect you, but I can't make a promise that says nothing will ever happen. That wouldn't be honest, and you know what Mama would say about that kind of windy talk."

Darlene laughed as she wiped her nose on her sleeve. "She'd say, 'Shame on you, Theodor. I didn't raise you to be no Promiser Big. Don't fill that girl's head with mush. Shame on you!'"

"Right you are, Little One, and I won't do something that would have made Mama sad.

How about if we both promise each other to be good and do what would make her proud? Deal?"

"Deal." With that, the tall, lanky brother and the slight, auburn-haired sister solemnly shook hands to seal their bargain.

"Now I'd better go in and sweet talk my horse so we can

get out to the field to get some corn picked. Suppose he'll let me bridle him now that I've cooled off?" Picking up the headstall, Ted eased into the stall beside Jeff.

The horse turned his head and stood patiently while Ted slipped the snaffle bit into his mouth. Once the leather straps were over the ears and adjusted, Theo led Jeff outside and hitched him to the double tree alongside Molly. Theo always took time to gaze at the matched team of blacks while they were hitched, and today was no exception. "You guys may have a little easier time of it once we get into the habit of firing up the tractor. Maybe you can just stand around all day and graze while we're out in the field slaving away."

Imagining Ted bouncing around the field on a tractor seat in the smoke and noise while his horses stood and watched over the fence was an idea that made Darlene laugh out loud. "I can just hear them now. Jeff would say, 'Hey, Molly, take a gander at what that crazy Ted is up to now.' And she'd say, 'Yeah, Jeff. I wonder how long before he'll come back and beg us to take over and do it right.' They'd probably be happy at first and then sad if they couldn't help."

"When you see me using a tractor full time and letting my good team go to waste in the pasture is when you'll know I've lost my mind. I can't imagine a good ranch running very well without good horses."

With that, he flicked the lines and the team took off toward the cornfield where Ted planned to spend the day picking. Darlene had crawled on Eagle's back and went galloping past Ted and the briskly-stepping blacks. Waving to him, she let the wind blow through her hair while she left the worries of the morning behind.

With fall came school once again. Losing the liberty of the summer was hard, but finding the routine of school and spending time with classmates made up for the loss. Darlene had started school early and had been skipped ahead a grade, so she was the youngest in her class. Some of the boys would stay out in the fall to help finish the harvest and leave early in the spring to start the planting, so they would be placed in different grades as needed. Because they were so much older than she and because she was so willing to help them with their lessons, it was as if she always had a big brother at school looking after her.

Darlene liked nearly everything about school, whether it was penmanship with its push-pulls, or recess with games of pump-pump-pull away, or getting to ride in the car with her sisters on the really cold days instead of riding her horse.

Her least favorite part was lunch. Packing food was a real challenge. Every noon when she would use her fingernails to pry off the lid from the lard can, she would hope for a surprise. She knew it wasn't likely since she was the one who packed it every morning, but she kept hoping. The sandwiches she assembled of homemade bread were crumbly and soggy after an entire morning of the filling soaking through. Sometimes it was a fried egg filling, while other times it might be homemade jam or clover honey they robbed when they could find bee hives. The apples were juicy in the fall but wrinkled and soft later on, and desserts were unheard of.

No wonder all the students would wolf down their food and run out to play. Cactus and sandburs made it dangerous to fall down, but games of tag and baseball were played with reckless speed and all-out effort. When teacher would ring the bell, puffing and sweating children filed into the schoolhouse to line up at the bucket for a drink before they would take out their work and return to the business of education.

Winter brought a different kind of delight for the students. Cold weather meant the teacher would get to school ahead of time to fire up the coal stove and carry in the water from the pump. By the time school started, the sharp cold was gone, and students would come in and huddle around the stove. The smell of wet wool and warm bodies went throughout the room, along with the giggles of children as they shared spaces and shoved each other around the stove. Almost in unison, they would change positions so cold backsides faced the fire and hot sides turned away to gradually cool off. Gathering together provided the opening exercises, and lesson recitations by class then took up the morning.

Darlene walked into the one-room building each morning glad to be there. Whether it was books to read or friends to enjoy, school was a good place where her world was complete. While there she didn't worry about what was going on with Fred and Theo, nor did she have the empty feeling that came from being in a motherless house.

Miss Edgars, the new teacher, had gone through state normal training while in high school. This curriculum had allowed her to teach the next fall immediately after her own high school graduation in the spring. As a result, she had started teaching in her first school when she was barely 16 and many of the boys in the upper grades had been nearly the same age as she. Now she was a veteran and ready for this new school.

When the students of District 16 came for the first day of school, they were busy noticing how much they had grown and changed over the summer. The boys ranged from tiny first graders with scared eyes and tiny hands to lanky seventh graders who looked like a mismatched collection of elbows and ankles to older eighth graders who had shot up in height and also had a telltale squeak when their voices would shift right in the middle of a word. Girls giggled about new ways to wear braids and shared fun stories from the four months since they had seen their classmates.

It was this motley crew that looked up to see their new teacher and pegged her as an easy target for practical jokes and misery. When stretching to her full height, she could just about claim to be five feet tall. Her easy smile and soft voice contributed to their estimation of her as their newest victim.

Before Miss Edgars rang the first bell signaling time to go in for opening exercises, Robert Reichers had already slipped into the schoolhouse. His lucky catch of the day was a huge bull snake that had been moving slowly in the coolness of the morning. Robert quickly opened the book case door and draped the snake in a circle atop the fifth grade McGuffy readers. Closing the door, he rejoined the crowd outside, anticipating the screaming and panic that was to come.

After the bell rang, students knew it was time to say the pledge, sit quietly in their seats, and wait for the new teacher to give orders. "Students, I want to get to know you better, so please be ready to tell me your favorite animal and why." Looking at her student roster, Miss Edgars chose the first name she saw. "Robert, please begin."

Robert sucked in a guilty breath, then realized he had been chosen at random, and stood up to recite. "Well, Miss Edgars, it's kinda hard for me to decide. I like my dogs a lot 'cause they're the fastest coyote hounds you ever seen, and my horse can outrun every horse around. I like both of 'em the same 'cause they're the best and they're mine." With that, he gave a smirk to the entire classroom and sat down with a swagger.

Darlene and her best friend Amy looked at each other, rolled their eyes, and slightly shook their heads. Every child in the room who knew him was familiar with his brags and insolent air. Whatever he had was the fastest, the biggest, the strongest, just simply the best. Any unfortunate student who dared have anything better than Robert became an immediate target for taunting in the classroom and for bullying on the playground. He took special pleasure in intimidating the smaller boys, nearly all of whom were better coordinated and more clever than he.

Picking up on the glances and nods, Miss Edgars filed away the knowledge for later use. Continuing around the room, she gave each student time to share, and then announced, "I know we will have a delightful year, and I want to get started right away." With that, she whirled around and marched over to the bookcase. "Reading is most important so I'll start out by handing out the books. You may keep these in your desks, and I know you will take good care of them." Firmly clasping the book case handle, she pulled open the huge door.

Robert could scarcely contain his anticipation as she made her way to the case, then he could hardly conceal his disappointment with her total non-reaction. He nonchalantly accepted the reading book that she handed him and slumped back against his bench seat.

"Will you please print your name in the front of the book, and then carefully and quietly place it into your desk? When you're done, it will be recess time." Miss Edgars gazed all around the room and smiled at the delighted students.

Grabbing his book, Robert shoved it into the front opening of his desk. Clunk. Too soon the book stopped, and no matter how hard he pushed, it wouldn't budge. In disgust, Robert slammed the book on the desk behind him, shoved his chair back so he could get level with his desk, and bent over to stare into the cubbyhole.

Staring right back was the unblinking, huge bull snake that had warmed up and crawled out of its original resting place.

Screaming, lunging, knocking over his chair and

charging out of the room, Robert left complete disarray in his path. Knocking aside students and rushing past the teacher, his frenzied escape route took him across the yard to the outhouse where he slammed the door and bolted himself in. Leaning against the door, Robert gradually regained his breath and contemplated what had happened. Hearing the chorus of cheers outside, he peeked through a knothole and saw Miss Edgars wielding a shovel. She gently carried the snake beyond the fence where she deposited it and signaled the children to go back to the yard.

"Let's give this big boy some room now. He's probably just as surprised as we are, and all he wants to do is find a nice quiet hole." With that, she delicately lifted her skirt to walk back towards the school. " Okay, how about a game of Pump, Pump, Pullaway? The students with birthdays in August can be It." The teacher stood and watched until the children's game was underway, and then she casually strolled over and knocked on the outhouse door.

"Robert, are you calmed down so you can join the rest of us? I don't blame you for being startled, but I just can't imagine how that snake got inside the room. Since your father is the president of the school board, maybe we can ask him to check the doors and windowsills. Do you suppose that would be a good idea?"

Sheepishly, Robert opened the door a crack and looked over at the game in progress before answering. "Yes, ma'am, that'd probably be all right."

Miss Edgars smiled at Robert and continued, "Not everyone likes snakes, but my brother Joe and I used to catch bull snakes and haul them away. Mama was afraid of them and always wanted Papa to kill them. Once in a while they get on the fight and try to act like they are really tough, but we knew they wouldn't hurt us. Mostly they try to get away." She chuckled and added, "Kind of like you just wanted to get away. Right?"

Hanging his head and wondering how he could ever face his classmates again, Robert was surprised to feel Miss Edgars put her hand on his elbow. "Come on, let's go over and see how the game's coming." With no way to refuse, he reluctantly trudged alongside her to the playground.

One reason he hesitated to make the long walk to join the others hinged on his own behavior. If he ever had an opportunity to make fun of another, Robert never wasted it. His voice would be the loudest, his mockery the cruelest, and his memory the longest. Seldom did he get a dose of his own medicine, and he dreaded what he faced.

Darlene looked up and said, "Robert, that must have been too scary. Here, you can be on our side." She scooted over and motioned for him to be a part of the group. Even knowing how mean Robert could be, Darlene couldn't enjoy watching him feel so miserable. She glanced over at Amy and knew what was coming. Sure enough, Amy's brown eyes glistened with anger and disgust as she gave a slight impatient shake of her head to let Darlene know this was totally wrong.

Robert pushed himself into the space which Darlene had created, and very shortly recovered his usual bluster. "You know, I really wasn't scared. All of a sudden I had to use the outhouse and that's why I ran. No dumb ole snake can make me afraid."

Instantly Darlene regretted her kindness, but she just turned her back to him and rolled her eyes at Amy. Other students didn't hold back and the tallest eighth grader Joe piped up, "Nice try, Windbag." Then Joe reached out to pat Robert on the head as he continued, "Yeah, Bobby-Boy, one look at that snake and you probably had to head outside before you messed your pants. Everyone here knows what happened so just give it a rest."

"Get your hands off me, Joe. You'd better watch out or. . ."

"Or what, Bobby? Are you going to run home and tell Daddy what happened here at school to his iddy-biddy baby boy? When you're tattling to him, I hope you remember all the story, like maybe how the snake caught a ride so he could get inside the school to begin with. Do you get my drift?"

Robert blinked several times so he could choke back his tears. "I don't even know what you're talking about, you beanpole. You act like you're cock of the walk around here, but you're not the boss of me. Leave me alone." With that, Robert stalked off the playground and spent the rest of recess throwing clods at a soap weed and mumbling to himself.

"See what happens when you try to be nice to such a jerk? Why did you even think about it?" Amy's voice was indignant and her eyes danced with anger.

Darlene shrugged and answered with a soft voice, "I know better, but it makes me sad to see anyone all alone, even if it is just nasty Robert. I thought maybe he'd be nicer after knowing how bad it feels to make a fool of himself, but that didn't happen, did it? I don't ever want to be as mean as he is, so I'm not sorry I gave him a chance." She took hold of Amy's arm and draped it over her own shoulder, "Let's just be glad we have each other for friends and ignore him for the rest of the day. Okay with you?"

"I still think he got what he had coming, and I don't feel a bit sorry for him. You're such a softie that I'll bet you're speaking to him before the day is over, but I'm not going to." Amy grabbed hold of Darlene's waist and squeezed. "Best friends like always, even if once in a while you really make me mad. Let's go play before teacher rings the bell. Race you to the step."

School was restored to its usual rhythm with Amy and Darlene running and laughing, Robert pouting, and Joe watching out of the corner of his eye to make sure all the kids were good sports. Miss Edgars had seen and heard it all and understood that the natural order had resolved the situation without any action from her.

After lunch, activities on Fridays included spelling bees which Darlene inevitably won, math contests at the slate board which were not quite so much fun for her, and art class which she loved. Supplies were limited so often the teacher would let them go to the slate board to practice drawing people or animals. When November came, Miss Edgars announced the plans for Christmas. Friday afternoons would be spent drawing designs on a feed sack, then students would build a picture frame with left over barn siding, and each one would have a gift to take home.

Different activities were fun for different students, and Miss Edgars encouraged those with special talents in one direction to help those with abilities in other areas. Darlene was surrounded by students who wanted her to show them how to draw a horse or dog or flower, and Joe was busy cutting the wood so it was the right size for a picture. Robert sneaked over to Amy's desk and put a tack on the seat, but Joe saw him and slipped it back over to Robert's chair as they went out for recess.

"Ouch! Who did this?" Robert screeched when he plunked himself down after being outside. Jumping up, he pointed at Amy and shouted, "Why would you put this on my chair? I wasn't the one who set it for you. Why would you think I'm the one? Everyone picks on me and that's not right." Looking around, he discovered every student in the room had turned away so they wouldn't be laughing in his face, and this enraged him even more. "I hate you all. You'll think this is funny when my dad hears about it!" With this parting shot, he stalked out of the school.

Robert's biggest problem at this point was that he had no

place to go. School wouldn't be out for over an hour and his father always was just on time to pick him up. Robert also knew he didn't plan to share any of the details about this miserable day with anyone, least of all his father. His greatest fear was that some of the kids would be outside when the car pulled up, and they would be sure to drop hints so Dad would pry the whole ordeal out of him. So long as Robert was alone, he could manufacture a plausible story about how Joe bullied him and Amy was spiteful and the teacher just let it all happen. The worst thing that could happen would be for his father and Miss Edgars to have time to talk.

"Robert. You will come back in the school right now." Too well he knew that tone of her voice, and he knew better than to ignore her. Miss Edgars stood in the doorway with her hands on her hips and didn't move. She never entered into a physical confrontation with her students, but the sheer force of her personality was enough to command respect and obedience.

"Yes, ma'am. I did what you said to do when I get mad. I came out here to get some fresh air and cool off. I feel better now." He glanced sideways to see if this approach was going to work with her, but she was shaking her head and let out a sigh of exasperation.

"You exploded because you got caught at your own game, and you ran out because you couldn't face what your own actions had caused. Every one of the students would give you a chance, but you seem determined to make your own way very lonely. I will definitely have a talk with your father after school today. I hope you find a way to rein in your temper and work at being decent because I will tolerate no more bad manners. I've had enough of your shenanigans and they will stop as of now. For right now, since you want to be out here, you can stay out here and dust the erasers while the rest of us are finishing our art projects. When you are done, you will come back in and apologize to the rest of the students for your outburst. Do I make myself clear?"

Tears gushed down Robert's face as his entire body appeared to collapse. "Please, Teacher, don't tell my dad. He promised me a terrible whipping with the razor strap the next time I got in trouble here in school, and I don't think I can take another beating." With that, Robert twisted around and lifted his shirt high on his back.

After one look, Miss Edgars gasped, whirled him around, and pulled his head onto her shoulder. All the way from his shoulder blades to his waist were angry welts of different colors. Some were fresh and angry red, while some were old enough to have turned various shades of yellow and green. Under it all lay several old scars.

While the two leaned into each other, Darlene could do nothing but look on in amazement. Miss Edgars had asked her to go pump some fresh water for the room as soon as she had finished her art, and that had put her on the scene. She had been there just long enough to see Robert's back and realized the best action for all concerned was for her to retreat. Quietly, she closed the door and went back into the classroom.

"What's up with you? Our water is gone and you know teacher told you to take care of it. Do you want me to do it?" Amy started talking before she had looked at Darlene's face, and all at once, she saw how distressed her friend was. "Oh, never mind. It's just about time for recess and we can do it together." Then quietly she asked, "Are you all right? You don't look so good."

Genuinely feeling sick to her stomach, Darlene had folded her arms across her belly. "I'm okay. You know how I sometimes get a side ache when I go too fast. I guess that's what happened. I'll be okay in a minute." Darlene needed time to digest what she had seen and couldn't even speak about it to her best friend.

When she finally got home, she rushed out to the barn where Ted was working on a broken harness. "Theo, I'm having a tough time. I just don't know what to think."

"Little One, have a seat right here and we'll see if we can hash it out together." He motioned to the small nail keg beside him and leaned back against the wall. "You seem to be pretty stirred up about something."

"I don't even know what I need to know, but something I saw today really confuses me. Remember how many times I've told you about Robert and the nasty, mean things he does to all of us? Today he was SO bad, and I was so fed up that I really hated him. The only thing I could do was wish someone would do something so he'd understand how much he always hurts us. I could hear Mama saying 'He needs a taste of his own goings on' and I was ready to be the one to give it to him. I know that makes me bad too, but I just couldn't help it."

Ted started to interrupt her, but her words came spilling out. "Then I started outside and saw sores and bruises all over his back and heard him tell teacher that his dad beat him. Do you think he's lying? At first I thought it would be just like Robert to make up some story like that. But I can't even tell you how awful his back looked. Robert couldn't do that to himself, but who else would? Do you think his dad is like that?"

Darlene gulped before she could go on, "And then I started thinking about Robert's family, and his mom is so pretty but she never talks. Would she let Ben do something like that to her own boy? I know Mama never would have let anyone hurt me, no matter what."

Drawing a deep breath and carefully choosing his words, Ted pulled her over to him and stroked her tangled curls.

"Honey, you can't know what people are like if the only time you see them is when others are around. Ben's mom and dad were good people who worked hard so he could go away to business school. He never liked it around here, even when he was a boy. Then his dad fell off a windmill tower and Ben had to come home to run the place. He never seemed to get over that."

"When he came back to the home place, he bid on the post office and got it moved to his place. Then he put in a mercantile store in the back and ran them both. He sold the cows and let us lease the land since it wasn't what he wanted to do. He was engaged to Susan so they got married before he came back here. She was a city girl and never has quite fit in here. They had a baby girl, but when she was about two years old, her mother was hanging out the wash and the little girl wandered off and fell in the tank. Susan never seemed quite right after that, and everyone said Ben blamed her."

Darlene leaned back and rubbed her eyes. "That is so sad. Can you imagine how bad that would be? So do you think that is why Ben is the one who always takes Robert everywhere and stands up for him even when he's just plain nasty? But then why would he hurt him on purpose? This must be some kind of a mistake, cause Ben's so big in the church that he surely wouldn't be like that."

Ted fell back on his favorite way of helping Darlene sort out facts. "I wonder if you remember Mama's rule about who could go to the post office?"

"Sure, I remember. She always said it was a guy's job to take care of the mail, and she never let any of us girls go there. That meant we never could go to his store either."

"Okay, now I want you to think of the last dance we went to. Do you remember what you said when you watched the three of them walk in?"

"I do know what I said. Ben walked in first, and Robert

and his mother came in behind him. I said it looked like he didn't have time for them. She's pretty but I've never seen her smile. If she does talk to someone, she acts as scared as a rabbit ready to run away. But he's not like that. He talks loud and slaps the guys on their shoulders like he's their best friend. Maybe that's how he got elected to the school board."

Ted nodded. "Now tell me about when he comes to school. Do you think Miss Edgars enjoys talking to him?"

"Nope. She rings the bell early if he's there, and she keeps us late if he's there. It's like she knew Mama's rule and doesn't want any of us girls where he is. I've never told her this, but I don't like it when he comes to school either. He stands way too close and puts his arm around me every time he comes in. He does it to Amy and all the girls. You know what else—when he smiles, his eyes don't smile."

Darlene wasn't looking at Ted; but if she had been, she would have recognized signs of trouble brewing. His eyes narrowed to slits, the muscle along his jaw bulged, and his hand tightened on the harness. "Does he come in very often?"

"Not so much as he used to. When school first started, he was there about every night after school, but for some reason he doesn't drop in very much anymore."

"Lena, this is hard to understand, but I think you have it sorted out about right. Robert sounds like one of those people who try to hurt others because he's been hurt himself. That doesn't make it right, but it won't be the only time you run into someone like him."

"What about Ben? Do you think he hurts Robert?" All of a sudden she sucked in her breath, "He surely wouldn't hurt Susan, would he? You always said a man never hurts a woman, child, or a helpless animal. That would be so terrible I can't even think of it."

"Honey, I don't know what goes on in their house so I

wouldn't say yes or no. What I will say is that some men can't be trusted, but your heart always can. Anytime you have bad feelings about someone, get as far away as you can and let me know. I'll take care of everything for you.

Darlene leaned her head on his knee and let out her breath. "Ever since Mama— " then she choked and tears ran down her cheeks.

"I know, Little One. Sometimes I need to talk to her so much that I can't even catch my breath. It's a good thing she took the time to talk to us before we lost her, or we'd really be in bad shape."

"Why do we say 'lost her' when we know where she is? My little green ring is lost and no one can tell me where to look. You said Mama is in heaven with Papa and Harry, so why do we say that?"

Ted threw back his head and laughed with the sound that Darlene loved to hear. "Right you are, my dear, as usual. She's not gone like your ring; she's just where we can't see her for a while. Do you have any idea how great it will be when we can get together again? No matter how long it is, I'll bet she's the first one we see. She'll be blowing away that little piece of hair that always hung down in her eyes, no matter how hard she tried to make it stay in a bun."

"Yeah, and I'll bet Harry's on one side and Papa's on the other side and lots of sunshine is everywhere. Do you think there's a place for Boomer there? He always trotted right at her heels when she left the house, and he'd sit and whine until we cracked open the door so he could slip in and lay down on the rug. She acted like she didn't see us, but when we went to bed; he'd creep over and snooze at her feet. I kinda like the idea of them being together again."

Ted took a bit of time before he gave his answer. "You know, I really hadn't thought about him for a long time, but for what he put up with from you little girls, he probably earned a place up there in the sky."

"We did pull on his ears at first, but then we treated him really nice when we got older. Those long ears and short legs made him look funny but he was so sweet. Do you remember how Mama wrapped him in that rug when we buried him? She said he always liked to sleep on it so it seemed right for him to take it with him. If he's there, I'll bet there are tons of rabbits running all over so he can wuff and snuffle and race around like crazy and then curl up at Mama's feet for a big nap." Darlene gradually sat up straighter and clapped her hands at the thought.

Ted helped her up and gave her a quick squeeze. "Now you'd better go help Emma with supper before she gets on a rampage with both of us and puts us on bread and water."

Skipping out of the barn, Darlene yelled over her shoulder, "Okay, Theo, I'll make sure we at least have some jam to put on the bread." After her talk with Ted, she had sorted out her confusion and felt ready to tackle whatever came next.

If she had stayed behind in the tack room, Darlene would have been surprised to see the tension erupt in his body. The very thought that arrogant Ben Reichers might have touched his little sister was so repulsive that Ted reached for something to do. Grabbing a piece of leather, he grabbed his knife and cut it into tiny shreds. By the time he was done, he had relieved his immediate anger and formulated a plan for the next day. Going to the post office the next morning would definitely be a man's job.

Chapter 4

Finally the last day of school came. Students had jabbered for the past two weeks about how great it would be, but they all knew it was mostly bluster. Even though they all had little spats and disagreements, spending time together was a highlight of the school term. With the summer break, all that came to an end; and students would spend weeks at a time without seeing anyone outside the family. Even so, the students were in a holiday mood.

Part of the reason for their excitement was the community picnic taking place at the school. Last day of school ceremonies included eighth grade graduation, perfect attendance medals, and recognition ribbons for outstanding students. Miss Edgars insisted the students clean everywhere and put all the books in the cupboard. Only then did she allow the boys to carry in the planks and saw horses to set up the tables.

As each family arrived, they set their picnic baskets on the floor and made a production of arranging their food. Soon the tables appeared to sway under the weight of potato salads, baked beans, fried chicken, fresh rolls, cakes and pies.

Darlene had been nervously watching for Emma and Theo, and when they pulled up, she ran outside and took them both by the hand. "Hurry up, you guys. I didn't think you were ever going to get here. What took you so long? Did you remember to bring the apple butter like I asked? That fried chicken smells so good I don't think I can stand it. Let's hurry in so we aren't the last ones there."

Emma laughed at her impetuous little sister, "Hold on. Take a breath and slow down. I'll get the food over there right now, and you can run along."

"Come on, Theo. You never did get here to school and I want you to meet my teacher." By then Darlene had dragged Ted over to the side of the room. "Miss Edgars, I want you to meet my brother. You know all about him, right? And Ted, this is my teacher. Isn't she just as pretty as I said?"

With that, Miss Edgars and Ted exchanged embarrassed glances above Darlene's head. "Yes, Lena, she is pretty; and I hear pretty handy when it comes to snakes, too." His remark broke the awkward moment and they laughed together.

"Oh, there's Amy and her dad. I've gotta go." Darlene rushed over to spend what little time they had left together.

"So Darlene tells me you are from Omaha. Is that where you plan to spend your summer?" Ted had heard about the wonderful Miss Edgars all year long, but he was accustomed to Darlene's enthusiasm about school and chalked her reports up to how much she loved school. Now that he was face to face with her, he was amazed at how well his sister had done in conveying her teacher's charm.

"Actually, no. I didn't tell anyone this before, but Amy's mother is not doing well since the last baby was born, so I'm going to be staying with her family while she regains her strength. It just seemed easier to keep their attention on schoolwork if they didn't know I'd be around. The doctor said that rest will be what helps her the most, but with four young children, it's hard to do that. Her husband is my cousin so I'll be glad to help out." Miss Edgars smiled at Ted. "Since the girls are such good friends, maybe you can bring your sister over to visit once in a while."

"Yes, ma'am. That sounds like something that would tickle Lena and Amy. Maybe I could find a way to get over there so the girls can get their visit out." With that, Miss Edgars held out her hand and Ted gently touched her fingertips. "I truly am happy to meet you, and we'll probably be seeing more of each other as the summer goes on."

A loud bustle at the door naturally made everyone pause where they were. "Yep, folks, sorry we're late but the mail has to go. Right?" And in bustled Ben Reichers followed by Robert and Susan who obviously were uncomfortable with all eyes on them. Catching sight of Miss Edgars, Ben smiled and started over to where she stood. "I hope you didn't start any of the ceremonies without me since I feel it's important for the president of the board to hand out the honors." Then imperceptibly, his back stiffened and his step became a bit shorter as he looked to her right and caught a glimpse of Ted standing beside her.

Ted had felt her hand tighten momentarily when she caught sight of Ben, and then she smiled graciously as she nodded to him and turned to include all in her welcoming gesture. "We are certainly pleased to have so many gathered here for the students, and I think we'd better announce the awards so we can eat this food that is so inviting. Students, please line up by grade and we will recognize your accomplishments."

Ted remained where he was, and Ben appeared at a loss as to where to stand since students spanned the entire front of the room. Finally he stepped in front of the first graders who looked up at him as if he had crowded to the front of the line.

"Children, shall we move over a bit so Mr. Reichers can join us?" Miss Edgars motioned the students to shift to the left, a move which allowed Ben a place in line but which also made it impossible for him to step forward and make a big show of congratulating the students as he had planned.

Darlene had earned several honors and ran over to hug Ted when the program ended. "Miss Edgars, could you sit with us for lunch? Amy and I talked it over and we think it'd be really neat. Would that be okay with you, Theo?"

"Sure enough, Lena. I think it would be mighty pleasant if Miss Edgars doesn't have other plans." Ted had sensed Ben moving over to join them, so he turned slightly which set his broad shoulders squarely in Ben's path. "Let's go get our plates from Emma and we can let you girls have one last visit before we all go home for summer." Skillfully, Ted held Miss Edgars' elbow and guided her so that he placed himself between Ben and the girls. Looking over their heads, he gazed directly into Ben's eyes and silently reinforced the message delivered at the post office several weeks earlier.

Ben never missed a step but moved on past, wordlessly grabbed his plate from Susan, and got in line ahead of both her and Robert.

Miss Edgars let out her breath and mouthed a quiet "Thank you" to Ted. "What are you two girls discussing so seriously?" she asked Amy and Darlene.

"We don't know how if we can stand it apart all summer long. That's forever!" Amy tugged at Darlene's hand as they contemplated weeks on end without each other.

"It'll be really hard, even harder than over Christmas and that was too tough. Please don't laugh. It's not funny," begged Darlene. "Best friends need each other." She shook her head as Ted and her teacher laughed. She didn't understand this cruelty on his part and wanted to pull away when Ted put his arm around her. Instead she buried her face in his shirt and felt the tears running down her cheeks.

"Little One, we're not laughing about you having to be apart, but laughing because we had already figured out a way you might get to see each other a few times. Do you want to hear about it?" Ted could feel Darlene sit up straighter and try to cover the tears she had shed.

"I know her mom can't come visit, and I probably can't ride my horse that far, and you work so hard all summer that it's like there's no hope. How can you fix all that?" Darlene's eyes shone with excitement, but Ted could also sense her hesitation.

"Why don't you ask Miss Edgars? She might have something to say you'll like to hear." With that, he turned to her and nodded.

Nodding back at Ted, she replied, "First of all, after we're done here at school today, I'd like it if you would call me 'Beth' like my family does. Everyone, that is, except my mother who insists 'Elizabeth Anne' is my name and never shortens it at all. Secondly, I'm going to be at Amy's house all summer so I can help out. Your brother Mr. Soehl—"

"Now fair is fair. How about you using my name too? Most everyone calls me Ted, everyone, that is, but Sis here. When she was a baby, she'd try to say 'Theodor' like Mama but couldn't get any more than 'Theo' out. Take your pick."

Beth smiled, "As I was saying, Theo and I had already decided good friends like you should have a chance to see each other once in a while. Since Darlene's birthday is the end of May, we thought that—"

She never had a chance to finish. Darlene and Amy were squeezing and hugging and laughing with relief and anticipation. "Oh, this is the perfect ending to a school year. Now I'm glad we can go home because we won't have to wait until next school year to visit." Darlene let go of Amy and hugged Ted and then Beth. "You are the best brother ever, and you are the best teacher ever," grabbing Amy," and you are the best friend ever. I'm the luckiest girl in the whole wide world, other than you." With that, the girls went dancing outside to share their good fortune with their schoolmates.

"If I had to guess, I'd say we did a pretty good job of giving them a fine send-off into summer," laughed Ted. "We'll both hear a countdown until the big day so we don't dare change our minds on this deal."

Beth smiled as she watched the girls jumping around outside. "Both of them deserve some good times. They've had some hard times to go through, but they're still sweet little girls who don't complain."

"Would it be all right if we would come calling sometime before Lena's birthday?" He cleared his throat and went on, "I think the girls would like that."

Beth returned his look and gave her answer, "Yes, Theo, and I think I would like that too." Even Ben's stepping over to their table wasn't enough to make Ted stop smiling.

Ted was right. The six week countdown had started the very next morning when Darlene came out of her bedroom and plopped herself down at the kitchen table. "Forty-one days until my big day. Last night I counted up the days and I think I'll write the new number every morning so I don't lose count. I still can't believe I'll get to see Amy that soon. What are you headed out to do today?" With that abrupt change, Darlene adjusted to ranch life and fell into the pattern of accompanying Ted whenever possible.

"Actually, Lena, I have some pairs to drive to pasture and I could sure use your help. Since I want to ride the colt I started this winter, I wondered if you'd like to ride Cheyenne. He needs to do something other than just stand and eat. He'll get so big it'll take a work horse harness to go around him if we're not careful."

Darlene ran over to Ted and jumped on his lap. "Are you serious? You never would let me ride him before, and now you say I can? This is the neatest thing ever. What's the deal? Why'd you change your mind?"

"Well, I've noticed how much you've grown and I think you can handle him now that you're older. He's a good horse with quite a bit of spirit but a whole lot of common sense. I think you'll be a great pair. Just remember, he's still MY special horse even if you do get to use him."

"You don't have to worry. I'll ride him for you so he can learn how to do things right, and I'll let you have him sometimes to see how much better he is." She twisted off Ted's lap before she made her remark. "You'll be glad when he turns into the best horse you ever rode." Laughing and ducking the hat Ted tossed at her, Darlene hustled into her room and put on her riding clothes.

"Let's go, Slowpoke. I'm ready and you haven't even finished your breakfast." Darlene skipped into the kitchen and reached out to stroke Ted's cheek.

He grasped her wrist and turned her over his knee as if he were going to spank her. She squealed and he spun her around for a quick hug before he set her on her feet. "Glad you're feeling so lively. Guess we'll have to see if you're this spunky after we get done with all our work."

With that, the tall, lanky man and the tiny, slender girl matched steps out of the house and all the way to the barn.

The day was all that Ted had promised. Cheyenne was ready for some action and the colt Boxer had much to learn about driving cows and calves. By the time they were finished driving the second bunch, Cheyenne had settled into an easy stride, and Boxer had figured out how to rate cattle.

Ted and Darlene stopped under a lone cottonwood tree

to eat the lunch Em had packed for them. "Whoa, Boxer. Let's take a break here before we go get the bulls from the Dawson Quarter. We've been in the saddle quite a while by now." Ted loosened the cinch and looked over at his little sister. "How's it going, Lena? Think you can make it a while longer?"

Stepping onto a log lying close by, Darlene was grateful for his concern. "It's crazy, but I am kinda stiff. Last summer I rode lots longer and further than this and it never even bothered me. It'll feel good to sit here and eat a bite before we take out again, but I'm not about to quit."

"You've spent most of your time working hard at your studies, so I'd expect it may take a little while to get your riding legs back."

Darlene giggled, "I don't think it's my legs that are the problem. I may need to get my riding bottom back."

Patting the ground beside him, Ted motioned for her to lean against the log and handed her a jelly sandwich. "One good thing about being gone all day long is how good a hot supper tastes when we get back home. It looked to me like Em was fixing to make a special treat for you when we left."

"Really, Theo? What do you think we'll be having? I love it when she bakes bread, but her pies are the best. Oh, and how about those sugar cookies with frosting? Maybe it's about time for an angel food cake since the hens started laying again." The images of favorite foods seemed to appear to Darlene faster than she could say the words. "After a whole year of lunches, it's great to be home for dinner and supper." Looking at the sandwich in her hand, she continued. "You know, this tastes a whole lot better outside than it does at my desk." With that, she lay against his shoulder and watched the clouds overhead.

"I don't rightly think she'd have time to do all that baking, but I did see her boiling the water and getting ready

to clean some of those young chickens when we rode out."
Ted noticed how Darlene's eyelids were closing, so he shifted to let her lie down with her head on his arm. In no time, she snuggled closer to him and began taking the regular breaths that signaled a deep sleep. He smiled, dropped his hat over his eyes, and followed her example.

"Theo, what in the world do we do now?" She squeaked out as alarm made her voice climb higher than usual.

Startled, he jerked his head up and looked around him. "What the—? Well, I guess we'll crawl back on and—"

"No, Ted, our horses took off while we were snoozing. It must be six miles back to the house and now we'll have to walk all that way. I hope Em doesn't see the horses and get worried. You remember that Mama said that a riderless horse is the worst sign—"

Now it was his turn to interrupt her. "Just a darned minute, Little One. Your imagination's running away with you and there's no need to worry. Watch this." With that, he put two fingers into his mouth and blasted the shrill whistle that Darlene wanted so badly to master.

"What good will that do? We're so far away that no one will hear it and come get us." She stood up, dusted off her jeans, and sighed. "We might as well start walking so we're home before it gets dark."

Just then, Cheyenne and Boxer popped into view at the top of the hill. "I guess I forgot to tell you that I played around with them this winter and got them both whistle broke. If you want them to come, all you have to do is give them a blast and there they are." Ted was as proud as a little kid showing off a new trick, and Darlene didn't disappoint him.

"That's the neatest thing I've ever seen. How long did it take you to teach them? Will they come to me if I can make the same sound? How did you know they wouldn't run away?" Questions rolled out of her at the same time as she clapped her hands and jumped up and down.

"Now, maybe you ought to calm down a bit until we get our hands on them. They may be whistle broke, but they haven't seen too many girls dancing a jig out on the prairie." Ted squeezed her shoulder and then reached out to catch the reins of both horses. "Let's head over to the bull pasture and put today's work behind us."

In amiable silence, the two riders mounted up, pointed their horses north, and took off at a jog trot. During the entire trip home, Darlene sat on her saddle, fingers in her mouth trying to copy Ted's whistle.

"Lena, if I didn't know better, from what I've heard so far, I'd say there was a windstorm sitting on old Cheyenne. You've got a lot of air but mostly it's coming out like a breeze. Let me see how you're holding your fingers."

Darlene wrapped the reins around the horn and raised her hands toward her face. With that, Ted reached over and took hold of the right rein lying on the horse's neck. "Honey, no horse is ever so broke and nothing's ever so big that you take a chance like that. Cheyenne may be the best horse in the whole world, but a grouse could fly up from the grass or a bee might sting him and he'd take off. Where'd you be then? Never put yourself in a bad situation when you can avoid it. Here, let me lead him and you can work on your whistle."

"He's never even spooked all the time I've been riding him, so I guess I thought he never would. It'd take a lot to make him scared, but I guess it could happen even to him. I won't do that again, I promise."

Leaning over to tousle her curls, Ted grinned, "When you make a promise, I know you mean it. I feel good knowing you'll respect your horse and do what's right. That's why I decided it was time for you to move up to

Cheyenne. You two are quite a team. Now, let's figure out how you can let him know when it's time to come."

After several miles, Darlene suddenly let out a giggle. "My fingers are dripping wet with my spit and I'm getting closer every time I blow. I've heard Fred say 'Wet your whistle' to his friends when they're heading off to town. Suppose this is what they are up to? "

Taking time to stop laughing and to wipe the tears from his eyes, Ted replied, "Most of those guys have given up on riding horses and take their jitneys when they head out, so I doubt that's what they're up to. Have you ever been around when he gets home?"

"Yeah, and he usually acts so dumb then I don't even like to be around. He stinks, too, so I just stay away from him and his buddies. One time I asked him where they went, and he told to some parlor in town. I'm guessing that parlor isn't the same as Mama's."

"You've got it figured out about right, and staying out of their way is the best way to handle it. Sometimes when guys talk about a parlor, that's their way of saying a tavern where they go to drink. Not much good comes from those deals." Ted worked hard at finding a way to balance telling his sister the truth she needed to know without shading his brother in a negative way. Even though the two brothers had their differences, the bond of family was still important to Ted.

"Wheet—eet!" All of a sudden, Darlene found the right combination of air, fingers, and lips and let out an abrupt burst of sound. "Theo, I did it! I did it! Did you hear me? I just whistled! Right now I did it—I promise I did!"

"Did I hear it? Here I am, right beside you and you let loose with a sound like that practically inside my ear. My hearing'll never be the same, but now I know you can whistle in your horse anytime you want to catch him. Try it again before you forget how you did it."

The rest of the way home was punctuated by short shrill blasts interrupted by dry rustling sounds when the combination wasn't just right. By the time they rode into the yard, Darlene could let out a whistle any time she wanted. Riding up to the gatepost, she let out a blast.

"Ted, what in the world do you want now? I'm right in the middle of baking an apple crisp for supper so this better be important." Hands on hips, Emma stood in the doorway with flour on her face and wearing a serious scowl.

"No, no, Em. Don't look at him. Look at me. I'm the one who did it. Can you believe it? I can do it just like Theo. Isn't that just the best news?"

"Hmm. Let me see. Now I have a brother and a sister who can BOTH make the loudest sound known to mankind. Do I think that's the best news ever? I guess you'd have to tell me why that's such a good thing." Pleased to see the sparkle in Darlene's usually serious eyes, Emma leaned on the post and waited.

"Now I can whistle and Cheyenne'll come running. I can get your attention when we're away from the house and want you to come see what we're doing. When I'm at school, I'll be the one who can call the boys back when they're sledding on the far hills. It just took me this afternoon to figure it out. I'll be so excited to tell Amy and everyone else. What a good deal."

"Yeah, it just took one afternoon, five miles, and the loss of my left ear. Other than that, no big deal." Ted and Emma exchanged glances as they headed the two horses to the barn. "We'll be in and wash up for supper as soon as we get the chores done. Be back real quick."

The next morning, Darlene was out of the house before Ted and out to the barn so she could try out her new trick. Looking east, she sighted the grazing horses. Raising her fingers to her mouth and stretching her bottom lip tight, she let out a blast of air, only to come up with a whoosh of wind and no sound. Darlene adjusted her lip and gave it another try. This time Cheyenne pricked up his ears, looked toward the barn, and came at a trot, followed closely by Boxer. Darlene giggled and ran to the grain bin to get the scoops of grain for the horses. She filled the feed box in each stall, stood back so the horses could get in, and had haltered Cheyenne by the time Ted sauntered in.

"Morning, Sleepyhead. You might want to get a move on so you don't let the whole day get away from you." Darlene teased her brother while standing beside the big horse and currying him. "Thought we might need them to-day so I got them in for you."

Ted could see how proud Darlene was, and he tousled her hair as he reached out and stroked the big horse's nose. "You probably don't know this, but you're the only other person who has ever caught this big boy. He must really like you if he let that happen. I've been thinking about how well you two got along yesterday, and I've decided that he's yours. No need for me to wonder what horse to catch from now on. I'll use Boxer and you can use Cheyenne—that is, if that sounds okay to you."

He had hardly finished speaking before Darlene launched herself into his arms and squeezed him with all her strength. A muffled sound came from where her face was buried in his shirt, so he took hold of her shoulders and held her out at arm's length. "I didn't exactly hear what you said, but I'm guessing you aren't arguing with me. Am I right?"

"Oh, Ted, you don't know how long I've wanted a horse to call my very own. No one's ever given me such a special present. He'll have the best life ever 'cause I'll brush him and feed him and put lots of hay in his stall every day. He's the best ever and you're the best ever and I'm the luckiest girl in the whole wide world. There's no way this day could get any better, no matter what you say."

"Well, I guess I won't bother with what I had in mind when I walked in the barn. You probably wouldn't have liked it anyway." Ted shrugged and walked over to give Boxer a quick pat on his rump.

"Wait a minute, Theo. If there's something I need to know, please tell me and I promise to listen, even if I can't imagine anything bigger than this."

By this time, Ted had made his way to the tack room where he pulled up his customary nail keg. "We got so much done yesterday that all our cattle work's done for the time being. That means we don't really need the horses for a couple of days, so I thought we'd take the car and run into town. I need to go to the courthouse about some taxes, and I need to talk to the guy at the lumberyard about getting a load of posts hauled out here so we can put in some fence on that new quarter we bought. Think you'd like to come along?"

"Wow, Theo. It's never been just you and me going to town because you always had to go when I was in school. That would be so neat. Can we go right now?"

"I imagine the cows need milked and the calves would appreciate being fed before we take off; but when the chores are done, it'd be time to take off. We maybe need to check with Em to see if she needs any supplies. We darned sure don't want the cook to run out of baking stuff— right?"

Ted pushed himself up and reached for his milk pail. By the time he reached the door, Darlene had already run out to the corral and had the cows in the barn. She had let each one into its stanchion and grabbed her milk stool from the wall. "Come on, Slowpoke. This is the second time today I've had to wait for you. What's the deal? You must be getting old."

"Lena, you're the one with the next birthday, so I'm thinking you're the one showing some age. As a matter of fact, you might be so old and slow that a trip to see Amy will be too much for you. Suppose we'll need to call off our trip to see her?"

"You know better than that, Ted. Besides, that'd mean you wouldn't get to see your Elizabeth Anne either, and I think you're sweet on her. I think she's sweet on you, too, so I'm pretty sure we'll be taking the trip over the hills."

About then, Darlene felt the warm sticky pelt on her arm as Ted unloaded a squirt of milk in her direction. "What makes you say something like that? I didn't meet her until the school picnic, and we didn't have a minute alone without all you noisy kids running around."

"Well, Theo, since you asked, I'll be glad to tell you. She had a funny sound to her voice when she called you 'Theo' and you got that squishy smile when she said it. You shook her hand and didn't let go near as fast as you do when you meet some guy for the first time, and the two of you came up with a way to see each other again. That's what makes me say something like that. Besides, it's not my fault you didn't meet her earlier. Didn't I tell you all year long that she was someone you'd like to know? I guess you'll learn to listen to me."

"You've got me dead to rights, Sis, so from now on, I'll let you make all my social arrangements. Do you have any suggestions for what I need to do next?"

"I think you need to ask her to go with you to the box social at the school. She's new here and if you don't get with it, someone else will beat you to it. Then you'd be sorry to have to sit and eat all alone."

"You know, I had given that a little thought even before you told me, so we might have to drop in on them this afternoon on our way home. Do you think that'd be okay with you? You could visit with Amy and I could ask Beth if she'd be interested."

Darlene jumped up so fast that her head hit the cow's

flank. "Can you milk any faster? We've got so much to get done that I can't believe we're out here messing around. I'll let the horses out and feed the bucket calves while you pitch them some hay. That way we'll both be done and head to the house to get ready."

By the time everything was done and they were cleaned up for town, Em had given them her list and stood on the porch to wave at them. Reaching the one-time icehouse that had been converted to a garage, Ted swung open the doors and signaled Darlene to stand back while he cranked the car.

Never one to accept an action without a reason, Darlene had a question for Ted. "Why do you always tell me the same thing when you start the car? It doesn't go until you get in and run all the pedals inside, does it?"

"You know, that's the way it's supposed to be, but these newfangled machines sometimes have a mind of their own. Once in a while they will creep ahead even if no one tells them to. I guess it's easier to be safe than to take a chance when you don't know what could go wrong."

"Is that why you're so careful to check out everything before you turn the crank? I've seen people just walk up and turn it and nothing happens."

Ted stood up to look her in the eye. "Yes, I've seen lots of people do it that way, and I've even seen a few of them sorry they didn't take the time to be sure everything was right."

Darlene's eyes got big as it dawned on her what he had said. "You mean like when we first got the car and Fred said he knew all about how it ran since he was the one who picked it out?"

"Yep. And do you remember how that worked out?"

Darlene twisted her mouth to keep from smiling. "He wasn't such a big shot after the crank whirled back and did him in, was he?"

Ted smiled at her and said, "That broken arm kind of seemed to take the wind out of his sails about how much he knew about machines, that's for sure. It took me quite a while to get the hang of running it, but it is handy to have when we need to get around in a hurry, even if the roads aren't very good."

As he started the car and drove out of the garage, Darlene jumped in and shouted, "Take off for the city, Theo. We have a big mission today and no time to lose!"

Driving west on the sand hill trail, Ted glanced at his sister to find her staring at him. "What's going on in that little head of yours? I can always tell when you have some kind of a plan by the way you cock your head to the side and wrinkle your nose."

"Well, Theo, I was just thinking how much fun we have no matter what we're doing. Even last winter when I went with you in that blizzard felt good. I really liked how you let me help. You said I was the best help on the place when it came to getting the cows out of those drifts."

"There's no way I could have done it alone, I'll tell you. With deep snow like that, those cows just couldn't get out by themselves, so you saved the ranch a bunch of money by helping out."

Darlene smiled at his compliment. "You know, it scared me to have you go right up to those cows and put the chain around them so we could pull them out. Lots of those old cows were really on the fight and didn't know we were just trying to help. I knew I was all right sitting up there so I could drive the team, but you were right there where you could've gotten hurt."

"Actually, Lena, most of them were so worn out from climbing through the snow that they didn't have enough strength to come at me very fast. The ones who had calves close by were just worried about getting to their babies, so as long as I didn't get between them, I was okay."

Giggling, Darlene mentioned the one cow that didn't fit his theory. "That old brockle-faced cow had a different idea, didn't she? I was so afraid when she took a run at you, but you made it back to the sled just in time. It looked like she was coming right up there to hit you, but her calf bawled just then and she forgot about you. Lucky for you, I'd say."

Ted shifted in the seat before he answered, "Oh, you know, I'm so quick she never had a chance."

"Yeah, I guess that's the reason her horn ripped a hole in your pants, right?"

"You've got me there, Missy. She darned sure put a mark on me, but the good thing is that it's not where anyone will ever see it."

Darlene put her hands over her face when he said that, and then continued, "It doesn't matter if we're saving cattle, riding horses, putting up hay or driving to town on errands. We are a pretty good pair, if I do say so."

"Little One, everything you said is sure the truth, but I still think I see some ideas rambling around in that pretty brain of yours." Ted grinned as she blurted out what was on her mind.

"I've been thinking how great it will be when you and Beth get together and Amy and I will get to spend time together and we'll all go to town for the Chautauqua gathering and—"

"Whoa, there, girl. You may just be getting the cart before the horse. What if Beth has other plans than to hang out with me? What if she's planning to go back East instead of staying out here? Maybe she's tired of the prairie and needs to spend time with lots of other people her own age. You best not get your hopes up and then have a big let down. Better be happy that you and Amy will be together sooner than you expected and let everything else fall however it will."

"You know what, Ted? I think you're a big chicken and afraid that she won't want to go with you. I don't think you're as worried about me as you are worried about you. How about a little bet between the two of us? I'll bet she agrees to go to the box social and the Chautauqua with you, and if she does, I win Cheyenne to be mine forever. If she doesn't, I lose and I'll let you keep Cheyenne. How about it?"

"Mmm. Why does it seem I'm the only one risking anything in this bet? If I lose, I lose my horse. If I win, I get to keep my horse. Doesn't seem like you can do anything but come out on top, but you know what? I'll just take that bet, but you can't do any talking or try to push Beth into going with me. You just have to stand back and see how it plays out. Deal?"

"Deal." With that, Darlene had other ideas to discuss. "Whenever we go to town, we have five wire gates to open. Some of the kids at school say there is a way to let cars go through a fence without having to stop to open gates. We have three gates on our road, so why don't we have something like that? Maybe I'll be the first one on this ranch to have an opening that lets us through but keeps cows out. Would that be a great thing to have?"

After getting in and out for the fourth time, her idea sounded good to Ted. "That would be absolutely the best invention I could ever imagine. Until you get that built, I guess we're stuck with doing the gate thing. Maybe when you get old enough to drive, you'll have everything fixed up."

"When will I be old enough? It looks like so much fun to be the one running all the hand and foot stuff, but right now I have trouble reaching everything and being able to see over the steering wheel. Do you think I can drive when I'm, say, ten years old?" Darlene peered directly into Ted's eyes with such a serious expression that he knew she'd remember his answer exactly and bring it up precisely on her tenth birthday.

"I guess I'd have to say when you're tall enough that your feet reach the pedals and you can see over the wheel at the same time, you're ready. You just let me know and we'll go have a driving lesson. Fair enough?"

"Perfect." Darlene imagined herself piloting the car with Theo in the passenger seat. In her mind's eye, they drove right up to a gate that automatically opened before them and closed behind them. As they drove through, passenger Ted looked at her and said, "Nice job on that gate, Lena. So much easier now that you can drive and I don't have to do anything."

As Ted stopped the car at the next gate, she came back to reality and watched him lean into the wire gate latch. "If you'd just fix those gates so I could open them, I'd do that and you wouldn't have to get in and out so often. Why do you make them so darned hard?"

"Well, you've seen how cows rub on posts and lean on wires to scratch themselves. First thing you know our cattle would be out on the neighbors, and we'd have even more work to do. I guess it's better if I have to work a little harder to open them than to chase cows all over tarnation."

Darlene could appreciate his reasoning, so she sat back and enjoyed the rest of the ride. As they approached town, her inquisitiveness took over again. "What's so important that you have to get to the bank today? Most of the time you stay at home, and Fred or Emma come in to take care of business, but not this time. Must be a big deal to get you off the ranch."

Taking a breath before he answered, Ted let it out and turned slightly to her. "Honey, you know how serious Mama was about getting more land if it joined us and had good water? When that section west of us came up for sale, Fred decided we had enough land and he didn't want to tie up any family money. I talked it over with him and Emma, and they both said it was okay with them if I bought it on my own. I've always kept my share of the money when we sold our calves, so I can swing this on my own. The banker holds the paper on it, and I need to meet with him today so he can make out the deed in my name. After today, I'll have the beginning of my own spread."

Darlene jumped up and down in her seat, "Theo, that's the best news I've ever heard. How could you be so calm when that is so exciting? I'd be telling anyone who would listen and even those who wouldn't. I can't wait until I can get some land of my own. If I had money, I'd be your partner. Do you think I could buy some of your land later on? Have you told Beth about this? She'll think you're really smart, I bet."

"Little One, sometimes you say so many things that it's hard for me to keep up. I'm calm because it's something I've planned on for a long time. I haven't told anyone because I've found out that the more you can keep your business to yourself, the fewer problems you seem to have. When you get money, I promise you I'll be proud to be your partner, and Beth probably thinks I'm the smartest guy around already, don't you think?"

Darlene lightly punched him in the arm, "You're pretty sure of yourself, aren't you? Let's see if you feel that good when I'm riding on my new horse Cheyenne and you're feeling all droopy because I won the bet."

Just then they pulled up in front of the bank, and Ted winked at her as he shut off the engine. "If you'd like, you can come in and listen while we get the papers signed. I figure it'll take about forty-five minutes to get everything done. You understand you'd need to be quiet and not ask any questions, right?"

Darlene rolled her eyes. "That sounds like the worst way I can imagine to spend my time. How about if you give me Em's list and I go to the store? Mrs. Dolph is good about telling me what Emma usually buys, and I like to visit with her. Maybe she got in some new yard goods and I can pick out the material for my new school dresses while you take care of your business. How's that for a plan?"

"Yep, you're a good one to have a plan, and this one sounds about right. Be sure to stay there and I'll come get you as soon as we're done. Tell Mrs. Dolph that I'm sure Em forgot to mention picking up a pound of horehound candy and a handful of licorice sticks, so you'll need to add that to the list."

Swinging out of the car, he and Lena met on the sidewalk where she grabbed him with a huge hug. With that, Ted turned to head up the steps to the bank when a man called out to him from the other direction. "Well, Mr. Soehl, as I live and breathe. This is indeed your lucky day."

The suddenness of the familiar voice stopped Darlene from crossing the street to the mercantile, and she whirled around to check if she had heard correctly. Just as she thought, there was the man known as Trader Keith who made his living buying and selling stock in the area. He stopped often at the Soehl homestead because of Ted's reputation as a horse breeder. Anyone who had a chance to buy a work horse or a saddle horse from Soehls would jump at the chance since Ted broke all his own stock with a level head and a quiet hand. He was never in a hurry to move a horse until he was sure it was the right match between horse and new owner.

When Darlene was younger, she would hear Ted come in to mention that the trader would be joining them for dinner, and she misheard the man's real name. "Guess what, Mama," he'd say. "Trader Keith is here today and he'll probably be here for dinner."

Maria saw Darlene run for her bedroom and shut the door, so she followed her and knocked. "Honey, what's wrong? You always have fun listening to Trader's stories, and he's got better manners than some of the hooligans that come traipsing in here to visit Fred. Why are you so upset?"

"What does Trader Thief want from us? Will he steal everything when we're not looking? Mama, you always said that anyone who takes stuff from someone else is bad so why does Ted stand around and laugh and talk with him?" Five-year-old Darlene flopped down on her bed and buried her head in the pillow. The bed shook from her quivering and sobbing.

"Sweetie, come here." Maria sat on the bed and picked up Darlene so she could hold her in her arms. "You're right about bad guys, but you know what? He's a good guy. When you think you hear us say 'Thief' we're actually calling him by his name 'Keith.' The words do sound the same, but trust me, he's an honest man who keeps his word. Ted doesn't like to have many horse dealings with him because he trades so many animals, and you never know where your horse will end up with him. You know how Ted is about his horses, so he's too particular to let Trader get a hold of them. You don't need to worry about a thing with Ted taking care of business. Now come on out and help me in the kitchen so we're sure dinner's on at noon." Maria led Darlene to the kitchen where the two of them worked together to get the fried chicken, mashed potatoes, and fresh bread ready right on time.

"Wow, this smells wonderful. You have no idea what it's like to sit down to a meal like this when I'm used to my own fixings. I'm no good in the kitchen so this is a real treat." Trader had taken off his hat, washed up on the porch, and sat down to wait while everyone else got situated. "Maria, I'd like to show how much I appreciate your hospitality so I'm willing to move some of those horses out there in the corral for you."

Maria felt Darlene tense up beside her, and before she could stop her, the words poured out of her daughter's mouth. "No way, Mr. Trader Thief. Those horses stay here because Mama said they could. It wouldn't be right for Theo to be sad. He'd miss them and so would I."

After a shocked silence, Mama reached over and patted Darlene's shoulder. "Trader, she--"

Trader Keith's face showed several different expressions before he spoke, starting with surprise and finally moving on to amusement. The rest of the family sat in embarrassed silence and waited to see what he had to say. "You know what, Little Lady? I like a woman with spunk and fire, and you seem to have enough of both to get you through. I have to admit I've never had anyone use that name to my face, but there are probably lots of people who may think it fits. I do drive a hard bargain, but I do my best to make sure it's an honest one. If you'll ask Ted here, I bet he'll tell you sometimes he comes out on top and sometimes I do; but at the end of each deal, we shake hands and leave as friends. I'd like it if you'd give me a chance to be your friend, too. When you're ready, maybe we can shake hands and agree to be honest with each other."

Trader leaned on his elbow and rested his chin on his hand while he used a soft voice and gentle words. It was as if the only ones present were a little redheaded girl and a tall red-faced man looking at each other across the table.

Darlene turned her head to see Ted's eyes, and he gave her the tiny nod that always meant everything was all right. "Yes, Sir, I'd like that. And I'm sorry I messed up your name but I promise I won't do that again. If you're Ted's friend, you can be my friend too."

The tiny girl stood on her tiptoes and the lanky horse trader leaned over and reached across the table so they could shake hands. "I'm proud to be numbered with those you like, and I promise you I'll deal fair and square with you and your brother Ted. Now that we have that taken care of, I can't wait any longer for a bite of that chicken leg."

After dinner, Maria and Darlene did the dishes while Ted and Trader went back to the barn. "Thanks for being so nice to Sis, Trader. She hears everything we talk about, and sometimes we forget she's a little girl who might not know when we're joking." Ted jostled the man beside him and went on, "You have to admit, though, that name is kinda funny. I can just hear the first person who sees you coming from a distance turning around and warning everyone. 'Hide the good stuff 'cause here comes Trader Thief.'"

A man with a keen sense of humor, Trader nearly collapsed with laughter. "You know, Ted, it was all I could do to keep from busting a gut right then and there. She's a keeper, that's for sure."

From then on, Darlene would run over to shake Trader's hand every time they ran into each other. Glad to see her friend, Darlene strung together greetings with questions. "Hi, Mr. Keith. How did you know this was Ted's lucky day? I only found out a few minutes ago. Is there something else going on that I didn't hear about yet?"

"What little girls are made of, made of, made of? My mother used to say that poem to us kids, but she'd have made up a new ending if she'd had a chance to know you. I think you, little lady, are completely made of questions. There can't be any room for the sugar and spice, even if you are really nice." He slid his hands down to his knees and looked her in the eye. "I think you've grown since I was out your way last month. Have you convinced Ted to let go of any of those broomtails yet?"

"Nah, Trader, we talked it over and decided they like it where they're at right now. Besides, I've moved up to the big horses, and now I need something to ride when we work cattle." Darlene looked right back at him and stood up her straightest. "When I grow just a little bit more, Theo is going to teach me to drive. All I have to do is get so I can see over the steering wheel."

"Don't forget, Lena, I also mentioned reaching the foot pedals at the same time." Ted reached out to shake Trader's hand as they met on the sidewalk. "What kind of mischief are you peddling now? Don't get thrown in the hoosegow because Sis and I are on a tight schedule. We've got lots to do and it all has to get done before tonight."

"Okay, I won't keep you from whatever is so important, but I'll just tell you I got wind you're the buyer of that Logan section west of your place. Never mind how I know it, I just do. As a good friend, I wondered if you needed some cash so I thought I'd make you an offer on that black horse you ride. Seems like you call him Omaha or Denver or Ogallala—something like that. I've got a buyer that your horse would just fit."

Darlene piped up and said, "Cheyenne, Trader. Cheyenne's his name. Too late, though, I've already started riding him and may even own him by nightfall. Ted's in a horse deal with me, and I'm sure to come out on top this time."

"Drat it, Ted, I've always asked you to give me first chance and now a new trader has moved in on my territory. Did you think you ought to give me a break, considering how long I've tried to do business with you on that big black bruiser? Looks like it's too late now, right, Darlene?"

"Yep." Darlene loved to try to sound like the guys when they were doing business together. "Too bad, Trader, but I'll let you know if I come across any deals you might like."

The three friends nodded at each other and went their separate ways—Trader on down the sidewalk, Ted to the bank, and Darlene skipping into the mercantile.

Pausing at the door, she took a moment to take in the odors of her favorite place in town. Inhaling, she could pick out freshly ground coffee beans, peppermints, and leather, along with something she hadn't noticed before. "Mrs. Dolph, what is that I smell? You've added something new since I was here last. I love it even if I don't know what it is."

Tracy laughed and said, "Darlene, I've been so excited to have you come in because I know how you like surprises. Come on over here and close your eyes." Darlene hurried to the back shelf and did as she was told. "Now hold out your hands." Obediently, Darlene stuck her hands straight out. "No, silly girl. That always means to hold your palms up, like this." With that, Tracy turned Darlene's palms so they were facing the ceiling and then poured a small amount of a liquid out of a fancy bottle.

"What is that—ice water?" Darlene jumped back and looked at her hands, then raised them cautiously to her nose. "What is that? I've never smelled anything like that except when the wild roses are in bloom. How could you catch that in a bottle? And where in the world did you ever find such a fancy glass shape? This is all so exciting that I can't believe it."

"I knew you were the one who'd understand how special this is. It's glycerin and rose water that I ordered from Omaha, and it has a fancy name I can't even pronounce. It's supposed to keep your skin soft, even if you're outside lots of the time. What do you think?"

"I think it's the best ever. If they can do that with roses, do you suppose they can do the same thing with apple pie or spring rain? Maybe the men would like new leather or clover or fresh bread. Does it come in any other smells?" Darlene continued to rub her hands together and then raise them to her nose to take huge gulps of air. “My hands feel just as soft as when I use Bag Balm when we’re milking.”

“If that isn’t the surest sign this is good stuff, I don’t know what else would be. Bag Balm is the trick for nice skin, but if your cows dry up, maybe this would be a close second.” Tracy laughed so hard she had to hold her stomach, delighted in Darlene’s reaction to her surprise. “Now I know you didn’t come in here just to sniff around, so what do we need to round up so Emma can keep putting good grub on the table?” She reached out to take Darlene’s list so they could start shopping in earnest.

“Ted said Em forgot to write down horehound and licorice candy so he wants to make sure we get home with that. I can play shopkeeper, and you can take a break since you’re in here all day long without anyone to pitch in. Maybe I can sweep for you if we have time before Theo gets done at the bank.”

Tracy had a soft heart and no children of her own, so she loved it when Darlene would come in. “Do you know that is the nicest thing anyone has said to me today; and as quick as we are, I’ll bet we have time to sweep and then look at the new material that just came in. How does that sound?”

“If Trader came in now, he’d say you ask as many questions as I do, but I don’t know how I’ll ever get any smarter if I don’t ask, do you?” When she realized she had tacked on a question at the end of her remark, Darlene giggled at herself. “There I go again, but it’s hard not to do it, isn’t it?” This time she and Tracy had such a spasm of laughter that they didn’t hear the next customer come in. Looking up, they both saw Ben at the same time, and it was amazing how quickly the fun evaporated and the caution set in.

“Well, if it isn’t two of the finest ladies in the entire town.

How could a man be so fortunate as to find two such beauties under the same roof?" As he headed toward the back of the store, their quickness in moving behind the counter was astonishing.

Wordlessly, they became very formal and serious. "Mr. Reichers, its always a pleasure to have you in our store. I'll call Edgar since I'm sure you'd appreciate having him wait on you."

Before Ben could protest, Tracy maneuvered Darlene through the back door that led to her living room. "That man. No way I'll stay in the same room with him, and I want you to promise you'll do whatever it takes to never be alone with him. Do I have your word?"

This time there was no laughter at Tracy's question, but there was a sincere reply, "I promise you, Tracy. Wherever he is, I don't ever want to be. He's got a mossy smile that makes my skin feel funny, so you can bet I'll keep my word. Shake on it?" Darlene extended her hand to meet Tracy's, and they both felt safe and warm in their shared embrace. Darlene slipped her hand up to her nose, and they both laughed as she sniffed the rose water fragrance.

Stepping outside the door, Tracy spoke firmly. "Edgar, you need to do some store tending. You've got a customer that needs the kind of attention you can hand out." Tracy called out to the blacksmith shop where Edgar was busy forging horseshoes. "I know you'd rather not stop, but trust me, I need you right now."

Very few situations made Tracy ask for help so he had an inkling of why she had insisted. Hearing the urgency in her voice, Edgar didn't stop to ask any questions but left his task and strode into the store. "Well, well, Ben, what can we do for you today?"

"I tried to tell Tr—your wife that she needn't bother you. My wife has been ailing and asked me to pick up some salve for sore muscles so here I am. What do you think might help?"

Edgar had his suspicions as to the origin of the soreness, so he casually asked, "What seems to be the matter? It'd help to know what's bothering her—open sores or more bruises? The last time I saw her she had that black eye from falling down the cellar steps. Can you tell me what we're trying to relieve? Maybe you should bring her in to see Doc Weiler so he can help her."

"Nah, that's not necessary. Thanks for being concerned, but the poor dear just happens to be one of those fetching females inclined to clumsiness. She falls a lot and has bruises most of the time. I just thought another woman might have some suggestions so I stopped in."

Giving him a hard look, Edgar spoke in a firm and low tone. "You know what, Ben? Tracy isn't in the habit of giving men advice, so I don't think it's a good idea for you to come in here for conversation with her. After this, I'd appreciate it if you'd check in the shop out back to see if that's where I am. If I'm not there or in the store, it would be best if you'd come back another time. Understand?"

Edgar's gaze along with his direct orders set limits that Ben understood, so he nodded his head and worked at finding a way to cover up. "Sure, Ed, I was hoping you'd be here so you could help me find the right fittings for my well. We both know how women are in that department, right?" His usual bluff manner had returned, but instead of making Edgar warm up and joke about how women didn't know as much as men, Ben's remark had the opposite effect.

"Oh, I don't know that I'd say that exactly," Edgar replied. "Most women are pretty quick to catch on about how things work. I'll say it again. You find me if you want to shop in our store. Otherwise come back later. Let's get your fittings so we can both get back to work." He motioned for

Ben to move to the hardware section, and the rest of their business was conducted in total silence.

Ben paid for his supplies and headed out the door, feeling Edgar's glare all the way out.

Back in the living room, Tracy and Darlene were waiting for the sound of the door's closing so they could get back to the ranch shopping. "Honey, I have a question for you—there we go again with the questions—but I didn't really understand what you meant when you said Ben had a mossy smile. Tell me about that."

Darlene shrugged her shoulders and started, "I didn't mean it was green or anything like that, but this is how he makes me feel. I don't know if you've ever been by a tank that has moss around the side, but it has a really neat fuzzy color. Then when you reach in and run your hand over the moss, it's slick and slimy and makes your skin feel funny. His smile is like that—good looking at first, but then it makes my skin feel all creepy. Does that make sense to you?"

"I don't think I've ever thought of a better word for his smile. Now every time I see him, I'll probably smile because I'll think of what you said. Too bad we have to put up with someone like that, but you know what to do if he's around, right?"

"Oh, boy, do I. I'll high tail it right out of there, no matter where we are. Mrs. Dolph, I love having you for a friend." With that, Darlene squeezed the woman's shoulder and headed to the store. "We need to get our stuff so that when Theo comes, we can get on the road. Did you know we're going out to Amy's this afternoon? I'm so excited."

Moving around the store to collect the staples Emma had ordered, Tracy paused and asked Darlene a question. "What in the world possessed Ted to take an entire day away from the ranch? He's such a home-body that we never see him here during the day, so this must be a big deal."

Darlene held her finger up to her lips and whispered confidentially, "It's hard for me not to jump out of my skin so it'll feel good to tell someone what's going on. Ted is buying land today; and when I get some money saved, he said I could be his partner. Then after he's done at the bank, we're going out to Amy's. I didn't think I'd see her until my birthday, but Ted has something to ask Miss Edgars. She's staying at Amy's this summer, did you know that?"

"Really, honey? I didn't. How in the world did Ted ever get off the place long enough to meet her, let alone decide to go see her today? She's been in here and seems to be a down-to-earth gal with good sense and lots of spunk. Do you know what he's going to ask?"

Giggling, Darlene was eager to share her news. "You know about the box social at the school next week and then the Chautauqua gathering in July? He's going to ask her to go with him, and we have a huge bet about what she'll say. If she says yes, I get Cheyenne to be all mine. The only thing is that I have to keep completely quiet while he's asking. I don't even know if I can stand it, but maybe Amy and I'll have enough to talk about that I can make it. Isn't that the most exciting day ever? Almost as exciting as my birthday when Ted promised we'd get to spend it together."

Only because Tracy knew how Darlene's mind jumped from one idea to another was she able to keep up with the rush of words. "Whoa for just a minute, Lena. You've filled the air with lots of news, and I need a bit of time to sort all this out. First of all, where did they meet? Second, that box social is next week, and third, I think your birthday's in about three weeks, isn't it?"

Sighing with the effort of slowing down and filling in the gaps, Darlene started at the first question. "The first time they met was when Ted came for the last day of school picnic, even though I'd told him all year long that he needed to meet her. He always said he had too much work to do to come over the hill to school—you know how men are. To make a long story short, they both tumbled for each other and she's spending the summer at Amy's and they said we could spend my birthday together but I think it might have been for them as much as for us. And yes, it is the last day of May so getting to go over there this soon is just the best. Anything else?"

"Nope. I think that took care of everything I wanted to know. Now why don't you go and check out the new yard goods while I get all this ready for Ted. He'll be in an buzz when he gets here so we want everything ready." As Darlene moved to the back of the store, Tracy double checked the list and the supplies, then looked to see that Darlene was occupied in the back. Seeing it was safe, she wrapped the fancy bottle and packed it securely in the bag of coffee beans.

Just as she finished, the board beside the door creaked and she looked up to see Ted standing there. "You haven't gotten Ed to fix that squeaky floor yet, Tracy. Is that in your plans?"

"You know, that's as good as a bell to let me know when I have a customer, so Ed's off the hook on that deal. I'll find something else to occupy him when he gets a minute to do some improvements in here." She motioned Ted to the counter. "Here you are, Sir, everything Emma ordered, along with the added goodies you requested. Have a look."

Tracy was so thorough that Ted had never checked his order before, so he did as she said. When he was close enough, she showed him the delicate bottle tucked in the coffee beans and whispered instructions to be sure Emma hid it until Darlene's big day. Loud enough for Darlene to hear, she commented, "Sounds like you have a big day ahead of you, so maybe the two of you can come to town again so

Darlene can do some material shopping. We didn't have enough time this trip to get everything done."

"How much time do a pair of women need in a store? It seemed like I was in the bank all morning, and you still didn't get everything done?" Shaking his head, he grinned, "I guess I don't get it, but maybe someone else will be back in town one of these days. I sure don't think it'll be me, but you never know."

Darlene had sidled up to Ted by this time, and she tugged on his sleeve. "I'll tell you all about it when we're on our way. If we don't get started, Amy and I won't even get to visit, and you may not have enough time to get Beth's answer. I can carry this coffee and you can get the rest." With that, she hoisted the bag up and headed out the door.

Hurrying to the door, Tracy took hold of the bag. "Lena, why don't I carry this and you get the doors for Ted and me? You're such a big help that it's no wonder Ted likes to have you around."

Passing the heavy bag over, Darlene nodded and skipped out to the car which Ted had pulled up right in front of the store. "Whew, that was close, Mr. Soehl. I hope those bouncy roads don't ruin her surprise, but I know you'll take care of it for me."

Bowing as he passed her, Ted replied, "I thank you kindly, Mrs. Dolph, and when Lena gets her present, you'll probably hear her all the way in here. We appreciate your kindness."

Being careful to pack the groceries and supplies so the bumpy roads wouldn't cause a problem, Ted waved to Tracy and let himself in the car. Darlene was bouncing in the seat and wound up with excitement. "Finally, we're on the way. Did you tell the banker that someday I'd be in to give him money so we could be partners? How do people know you own the land? Do you get papers that say it or is it something that people just have to know?"

"One thing about it, Little One, I won't have to worry about trying to remember stuff with you along. First, we record the deed at the court house so it's a matter of public record. Word seems to get out and people know, but I did get the deed and had the banker put it in the bank safety deposit box. That way I won't have to try to keep track of it because it'll always be in a safe place." Reaching over to pat her shoulder, Ted headed out of town. "By the way, what took you and Tracy so long? I didn't think the list was that long."

"Oh, Ted, I just get so mad. What gives Ben Reichers the right to go wherever he wants and make everyone miserable? He came in and we hightailed it for the back. Tracy got Edgar to handle him, and all of a sudden, Ben took off. She told me the same thing you did. I'm never to be with him, but what happens if I can't get out the door or there isn't anyone else there and he comes in when I don't even know it? What would I do then?"

Ted's instant fury made it necessary for him to calm down before he gave his suggestion. "Tracy is right, and I'm glad you asked. If there isn't any way to avoid him and you're scared, I'm telling you to let out the biggest whistle you ever made. That should shock him and let someone know you need help. He's a bully, but I think he's also a big chicken who doesn't want anyone to know what he's up to. If you send out your biggest blast, someone'll come running and scare him off. Are you okay with that?" While Ted was giving advice to Darlene, he was also making plans for another visit to Ben. When he had visited him at the post office earlier, Ben acted like he got the message, but dropping in once more might just be the way to make him understand how serious Ted was.

Driving on the winding roads took Ted's concentration, and he smiled as Darlene snuggled in and took a nap when they were a few miles out of town. As keyed up as she had been, he knew the rest would do her good. As he pulled up to the last gate before Amy's place, Ted reached over to rouse her. "Lena, honey, you might want to wake up so you're ready for your visit. We're almost there." Looking sideways, he could see her blink her eyes in the bright sunlight, yawn, and stretch out both arms as she let out a big sigh. "If you want to go back to sleep, I'll tell Amy not to bother you. She's a good enough friend that she'd understand."

Bolting upright, Darlene was quick to respond, "Theo, how you do talk. What sense would it make to be here and sleep when I can do that every night at home?" Seeing his grin, she caught on to his teasing and said, "Now you're in for it, mister. You'll never know when I'll get you back for that one." Then she laughed out loud and urged him, "Can't you make this car go any faster? I've never seen anyone who is quicker with a joke or slower on the move. I'll bet I could get there faster if I got out and walked."

"Easy, girly-girl, easy. I'm trying to keep from breaking a spring on these deep ruts so we can get around some other time. I'll be as good as my word and get you to your friend's house lickety-split." Turning the curve, they could see Beth and Amy hanging out jeans on the clothesline behind the house.

At first, the two girls looked up with curiosity to see who was driving in the yard. The longer they looked, the more surprised they were to see who it was. "Darlene! We're over here! What's going on? It's not your birthday yet." Then with a serious tone, Amy stopped suddenly, "Has something happened? Is anything wrong?"

By then she had scampered to where Ted had parked the car and jumped on the running board. She reached in to grab her friend's hand just as Darlene pushed herself up and out the window. A chin collided with the top of a head, and the two friends dropped back, one inside the car and one outside. As they recovered, predictably, the two eight year olds dissolved into spasms of giggles. Darlene moaned and rubbed the top of her head while Amy checked her chin and teeth.

Ted and Beth had heard the crunch and waited to determine if the wounds were serious. After a few moments, the girls started laughing, and the adults exchanged glances and shook their heads. Giggling continued, and its sound was so infectious that the four of them broke into chimes of laughter.

By the time they all caught their breath, Darlene provided the answer to Amy's questions. "Nothing's wrong, as a matter of fact, I think everything's just right. We're here to visit for just a little bit before we have to go home and do the chores. Let's go in so I can see your mom and the new baby. I'll bet he's really grown a lot already."

Darlene and Amy had their arms around each other as they skipped toward the house, leaving Ted and Beth alone. "This is a pleasant surprise. How nice you could spare an afternoon to let the girls be together. That is very thoughtful." Beth smiled with her eyes and let her fingers linger on Ted's sleeve as she made her observation.

"Actually, Beth, you're the reason I'm here. I wanted to ask you something and now's the best time with the girls out of earshot. You know how they are." Ted leaned back against the back of the car and stopped talking. He had blurted out what was on his mind, but then didn't how to get to the next part.

Beth could see his discomfort, so she moved over to stand beside him and echo his leaning on the car. "If you have anything to say, it might be a good idea to hurry since they won't stay away very long. You know how they are." With that encouragement, she eased the way for Ted to continue.

"I was wondering if you'd be interested in going to the box social with me next week end. If you don't want to, I understand, and I'll not bother you again. Shucks, while I'm at it, I may as well ask about Chautauqua in July too. Since I won't see you very many times before then, I thought I'd get it all over with at once. If you don't want to, it won't make a bit of difference about the plans we've made for the girls. We can still let them have their fun just like we said— "

Beth softly put her finger on Ted's lips. "Hold it, Theo. You've bundled a whole bunch of questions and answers and decisions without even giving me a chance to get a word in. Am I a part of this conversation or not?" With that, she pushed herself away from the car and turned to face him. "It will be easiest for us if I deal with your questions in two parts. First, about the box social. I'm going to have to turn down your request," seeing the blush crawl up his neck, she was quick to continue, "because my brother is coming to visit that week end and he has plans for what he wants to do. I already told him we'd spend time together because he's moving to St. Louis in August so I won't see him again for a long time."

Sensing there was more to come, Ted hazarded a glance at her to see if it were good or bad upcoming news. "That's okay, Miss Edgars. I understand how it is."

"Oh, you do, do you? And would you like to tell me how it is? What exactly do you mean by that? One thing you need to get straight is that I am perfectly capable of telling you how it is, and unless you read minds, you might not know as much as you think." She fired off this round of information and saw him bat his eyes a couple of times as if he were trying to follow her drift. "As for July and Chautauqua, I can't think of a more pleasant way to attend the festivities. Now, do you still understand how it is?" Smiling to lessen the sting of her words, she could see a hint of a smile appear.

"So you think something is funny about this?"

"Not really funny, I guess, but I was just thinking that you can shift direction quicker than a coyote tracking a bunny. We'll have time to talk over our plans when we come over for Lena's birthday, so I thank you for your reply, even if it is about halfway disappointing. It's important for a brother and sister to be together as much as they can, so I admire you for the choices you made. Just in time. Look who's coming back from the barn."

"Theo, you won't believe all the new kitties they have. Some of them are black, some are white and some are pure gray. They don't have a single calico cat, and we don't have any that aren't spotted. Maybe we can trade some cats so we can all have lots of colors." Darlene opened up her arms and showed Ted the gray kitten snuggled there. This one is ready to be weaned and Amy said I could have it if you don't care. What about it? Can John come home with us?"

Beth laid her hand on Ted's arm to stop him. "Where did you come up with that name, Darlene? It's kind of unusual."

"You remember when you told the eighth graders about the guys in that big war where they wore blue and gray? When I saw this one, it made me think of the boy in the poem you read to us. Remember the words to it?

Johnny Reb was dressed in grey
When he left his home that day.
To his mother he did smile and wave
As he marched off so handsome and brave.

This kitty is young and might miss his mother at first, but he'll have a good home with me even if he does have to move away. What do you say, Theo?"

"I like the idea of some different colored cats in the barn, and I think you'll help Johnny feel right at home." He and

Beth moved toward the house as he continued, "I want to go in and say hello to Amy's mom and visit the baby, and then we'd probably better head out. You girls decide if you want to spend your birthday here or at our place, and let Beth and me know so we can make plans." Ted looked over Beth's head and caught Darlene's eye. Shaking his head ever so slightly, he motioned Beth to lead the way to the house.

Later, after farewells had been said and the cat snuggled down on Darlene's lap, they turned the car around and headed home. "Ted, what did that head shake mean? I can't believe Beth said no. She had that fuzzy smile, and you two sure spent a lot of time talking. Tell me the truth, she didn't really turn you down, did she?"

"Yep. Flatter than a pancake."

Darlene persisted, "Theo, you've got to be joking. Why in the world would she act so nice and then be so mean?" All of a sudden, she realized there might be an unpleasant reason for Beth not to accept Ted's offer. "Oh, no. Did someone else ask her first? I told you all along that you should come to school to meet her, but you said you were too busy. I can't believe this. This isn't how I had it all planned out."

"I know this may be hard for you to understand, but sometimes people have other things going on that you may not know about." When he saw Darlene was close to tears, Ted relented and gave her the whole story.

Darlene cocked her head to the side and took a moment to think before she reacted to his news. "So who wins the bet? She's kind of going with you and kind of not. Who gets Cheyenne since this is entirely different than what we had talked about? I suppose it'd be fairest if I took him as my horse to ride but let you keep him as yours. What do you think?"

As Ted got out to open the gate, he called over his shoulder, "I can live with that. At least this way I still have something to call my own. For a while there, I thought I was going to be completely afoot. Guess I should be glad Beth likes her brother that much."

"You know what, Theo? When I'm a teacher and you want to come visit, I'll be just like her. That box social was probably going to be boring anyway, and besides, you'll still see her a couple of times this summer." Never one to dwell on disappointments, Darlene was busy planning the fun she and Amy would have the next time they met. They had agreed it would be best to spend their time at the Soehls so they didn't disturb Amy's mother. Beth had volunteered to have Amy there by mid morning so they could have most of the day to celebrate.

Although she was sure the time would creep by until her birthday, Ted needed help getting the fencing done after the winter's blizzard had flattened miles of fence, so Darlene hardly had time to be impatient. Each evening, Ted would load the posts and wire onto the sled so they were ready to head out bright and early. While Darlene finished feeding the bucket calves, he would hitch up the team and they would take off. Since fencing was hard physical labor, Ted liked to get a good start before the day became too hot. When they found a stretch of fence that needed repaired, each one followed a set routine. Ted would grab the posthole diggers and remove the dirt for the new post. By the time he had the hole deep enough, Darlene would hand him the post to drop in the ground. Using the side of his foot, Ted would scrape part of the dirt back into the hole and reach out for the tamping rod which she had ready. Pounding the sand to pack it in firmly, he would continue scraping and pounding until the post stood as straight as a hedge post could stand.

Taking a break after replacing five posts in a row, Ted puffed out, "I think we've planted enough osage orange here to make a forest." Ted plopped down on the sled and whipped out his red handkerchief to mop up the sweat running down his face. Exertion had given his face a reddish color, and he heard a small amused sound as he reached for the crock jug. "What's the joke, Missy? Did I miss something?"

"Of all the forest pictures in our books, I never did see one that went straight out for miles, one tree at a time. Maybe someday kids in school will see pictures of a fence line forest in their books. Wouldn't that be fun?"

"I can see you standing in front of the classroom telling them about how hard you worked to get that done, so I'd better get back to it so you won't tell your students that all I did was sit and watch."

Darlene scampered over and stretched her arm all the way across his shoulders, "No way I'd ever tell anyone, Theo, so your secret is safe with me." Spinning out of his grasp, she spun away so his grab at her wrist left him with nothing but air.

Slowly unfolding until he stood his full height, he ambled over to the next broken post. "Nothing left for me to do but try to save my reputation, so here we go again." Soon he had resumed the steady rhythm of dropping the diggers straight down, pulling the two handles apart to get a bite of dirt, lifting the diggers above ground, pushing the handles together to empty the dirt beside the hole, and repeating the steps. "At the rate you're pushing me, we'll be done with this quicker than a flash and have time to sleep in till noon."

"That'll be the day, Theodor Soehl. Even when you don't have work to do, you're outside before the birds even get up. Really, what would you do if you ever had all your work done and could do whatever you wanted?"

Ted contemplated her question while he tamped in the final post of the day. "You know, I've thought about that a time or two, and it'd depend on when I had all that time. If it happened in the winter, I'd take my hounds and Cheyenne—that is, if you didn't need him—and go coyote hunting. I don't really care if we catch any coyotes as long as we get a good run. Sometimes when I'm headed home and the boys haven't had a chance at a good all-out run, I swing by that pond at the end of the meadow. One old female always has a litter of pups there, and she's good for a chase. I haven't ever had a set of hounds cagey enough to catch her, but we've had a whole lot of fun matching wits. After that, I'd go in and tool a fancy headstall to put on that new bit I traded for, and then—"

"Ted, listen to you. Even if you had all the time in the world, you'd just be doing what you're doing right now. Don't you want to travel to the city or go stay at a fancy hotel or find something exciting to do?"

Ted wrinkled his brows together as he looked out of the top of his eyes. "Nah, Lena, none of that sounds like what I'd do with my time or my money. I guess you could say I'm doing what I want to do right now, so even if I never get all my work done, I like what goes on right here. I'll leave the travel and adventure to you, and you can write back home and tell me all about it. We can still be a team, even if you're off seeing the world and I'm perched right here. Deal?"

"That sounds just about right so long as you promise to come see me where I'm teaching just like Beth's brother is. If you'll do that once in a while, we can still be partners when I have the fun and write home to let you know what it's like."

Birthday time finally came, and Darlene was up even earlier than Ted. She went down to the kitchen and was surprised to find an angel food cake sitting on the counter. Emma had saved up the eggs and must have baked it after everyone else was in bed. Darlene hugged herself and whirled around in the middle of the kitchen. "Wowee! Amy and Beth will be here soon and I'm so happy I could just bust."

"Well, if you want to do that, it'd be best if you'd step outside and not make a mess in my kitchen," came a deep voice from behind the pantry door. Emma stepped out and squeezed her sister. "You are one big nine year old, and I think you might even be too big for a spanking. How about nine hugs instead?"

Giggling, Darlene pretended to lose her breath as Emma made good on her remark. "I'll never forget this one, Sis. What a way to start out my day." Turning around swiftly and grabbing Emma's waist, she blurted out, "This is my first birthday without Mama, and I was afraid I would cry all day long. Now I don't think I will."

Ted's booming voice erupted from the porch, "Lena, are you ready to get the milking done? I hear the cows bawling and the calves mooing and the horses tromping around waiting for us. Let's get a move on, okay?" With that, he walked inside the kitchen wearing his most intense working expression only to duck as a potholder come sailing past his head.

"You can't fool me, Theodor Soehl. You know darned good and well this isn't just any day. It's my birthday and you're just as excited as I am. You'll probably want me to do the chores so you can be out at the corner waiting for them to get here. I'm on to your little game, and it won't work on me." Darlene had spun away from Emma and into Ted's arms while she was teasing him.

All three laughed together and sat down to eat breakfast. When Ted had finished his second cup of coffee, he glanced at Emma and said, "It seems like this coffee tastes a little different than what you usually make. Did Lena and Tracy get mixed up on what kind of coffee beans you asked for?"

"I wondered the same thing when I ground that first

batch. Darlene, would you mind jumping up and looking at that sack of coffee beans? Maybe there's something about them that I didn't notice." Emma turned in her chair to point at the pantry cabinet where she kept the beans, and Darlene scooted back, pushed herself up, and marched to the bag of coffee.

"Leave it to Ted to know when some little thing isn't just like it was before. I'm just sure Mrs. Dolph and I double checked to make sure we had the right ones." By the time she was finished speaking, Darlene's hands were on the outside of the burlap holding the beans. All of a sudden, she gasped and said, "Something's wrong here. There's something else in here with the coffee." Carefully reaching inside, she caught hold of and removed the delicate bottle of rosewater and glycerin that Tracy had so lovingly tucked inside. Her yelp of astonishment and her huge startled eyes were enough for Ted and Emma to burst into laughter.

"Do you remember how much the car bounced on the way to Amy's that day? I was nervous that we'd be drinking rose-flavored coffee for weeks," Ted leaned back in his chair and opened his arms so his little sister could slide into her favorite resting place. "Guess we pulled one on you that time, right?"

For once, Darlene didn't have any questions to ask or comments to make. Her birthday had started out with one gigantic shock, and she just sat and stroked the cut glass bottle. "I'll always keep this. It's the most beautiful thing I've ever seen, and I never would have dreamed I could own something like it. I can't wait to see Tracy so I can tell her how much I love this. I am the luckiest girl ever. Amy won't believe it either." With that, she sat up and turned to look Ted in the eye. "We'd better get out there so we can get our barn chores done and clean up before company gets here. I don't want to smell like a milk house, and now I have just the thing to take care of that. Actually, Ted, if you play your cards just right, I might even let you put a dab behind your ears before your honey gets here."

"Yeah, Ted, by the time you're this sweet, Beth might just be sweet on you. This birthday could work out pretty well for both of you." By this time, Emma and Darlene stood together with arms around each other's waist while they teased their brother.

He rolled his eyes, sighed, and shook his head, "There truly is no rest from you two women when you get on a kick, is there? I've taken all the abuse I can stand, so I'm out of here." Pausing with his hand on the doorknob, he continued, "That is, unless there's something you need done before company gets here. Em, how about it? Any orders before I head to the barn?"

"You know, Darlene here was good enough to remind me every day that we had a big shindig coming up, so I've had plenty of time to get ready. I'm in good shape here, so the two of you might as well hop to it so you're ready to visit when they come." Emma tousled Darlene's curls while she grinned at Ted. "I wasn't sure if you had time to stick around here today or if you planned to work on that well over on the eighty. Did you plan to put new leathers on it today or can that wait?"

"Em, you're heartless. I guess it won't be enough for you two until I say it out loud. Yes, work can wait today. Yes, I'm looking forward to a visit from our friends. Yes, I'm out of here before you cause me any more embarrassment." Ted plopped his hat on his head at a rakish angle, and winked at her while he held the door open for Darlene.

The happy talk in the kitchen was reminiscent of earlier times when Maria was in charge of birthday celebrations. Although it wasn't her habit to give store-bought gifts, Maria had created her own form of giving. She made enough of a fuss over the birthday person that everyone looked forward to the special dinners complete with favorite food, good china, and hand embroidered tablecloths. The whole family knew how much she had loved preparing a surprise, so they had all given her uninterrupted time to whip up her concoctions. Even though they never knew what to expect, they did know it would be magnificent. Now the tradition she had established was continuing, and her three children reflected wordlessly on their private memories while they went about their business.

Barn chores were usually done in companionable silence, but this morning had Darlene so keyed up that she talked nonstop. First she chatted with the dogs and cats, next she had a conversation with the horses as she scooped up their grain, and then even the cows came in for their share. "Hold still, Ada. If you'd just give your milk down, we could be done with this and I'd be on my way to the house. That's it, old girl. Keep up the good work." As her hands found the rhythm of stripping out the milk, she looked over at Ted as he plopped himself down on the stool to finish the last cow.

"You know what, Lena, since this is your special day, I'll give you a break and take care of the bucket calves by myself. That way you can head to the house and get ready. I wouldn't guess the girls will be here right away, but if Amy is acting like you, Beth might just have decided it's easier to be on the road than putting up with Amy's twitching. Maybe you ought to be cleaned up and smelling good just in case." Ted knew his little sister well enough that he had braced himself on the one-legged stool to withstand her excitement.

Darlene launched herself at him and squeezed his neck so tight that he gave out a choking sound and untangled her arms. "You're the best brother in the whole wide world and this has already been my best birthday ever. I can't imagine how it could get any more better."

"I just know one thing, Little One," Ted laughed, "if you say 'more better' in front of Miss Edgars, she'll probably want to start school right away. You might be careful if you want a few more weeks of freedom."

"Sometimes my tongue lets words out even if that's not the way I plan to say them. I don't like to say things wrong 'cause it sounds like I don't know very much. You can bet I'll slow down when my teacher is here because she might think you're a bad influence on me. Then where would you be?" With that, Darlene spun out of Ted's reach and ran to the barn door. Pausing in the sunlight, she turned her head over her shoulder and yelled, "Thanks again, Ted. I'm on my way to get ready."

Watching her silhouette as she scampered across the yard, Ted smiled and stroked the cow's flank. "You got to admit, Rosa, she keeps it from getting dull around here. What a girl." As he muttered to the cow, his mixed feelings for the day surfaced. He had dreaded Darlene's birthday because he thought of how Maria had been gone nearly a year by now, leaving them all behind. At the same time, he also had anticipated the day since it was a rare occurrence on the far-flung ranches of the sandhills for good friends to have time together.

Just as Ted squirted the last of Rosa's milk into the bucket, he heard the roar of an auto coming in the gate. Beth waved at him over the steering wheel as the engine hiccupped once, backfired, and then chugged to a stop. Darlene's squeal and Amy's high pitched giggle echoed through the yard, Tater howled, and the chickens squawked as they headed for cover. Ted stood up, slapped Rosa on the rump, and headed out to feed the bucket calves with the girls scampering behind him.

"Theo, can Amy ride on Jet while he drinks? I do it every morning and it's lots of fun. He's the tamest calf we have and he doesn't mind at all. He even stays close to the fence so I can climb off when he's done." Darlene and Amy skipped beside him, swinging their clasped hands back and forth as high as they could go. All of a sudden they broke into giggles that made their bodies shake all over and they simultaneously turned to each other and leaned together to touch their foreheads.

By now, Beth had followed the sounds to the barn and peeked around the corner, "Just wondering what's so funny that I could hear you two girls all the way to the porch. Is it that exciting out here in the corral?"

Her appearance was enough to set the girls off to new chortles and to allow Beth and Ted the chance to exchange glances above the two curly heads. "You know, Beth, I think we'll just let these girls finish feeding the calves so they can get all this silliness out of their systems. If you'd want, you could help me with the list of chores Emma gave me early this morning. I've found out it's never a good idea to get crossways with the cook, if you know what I mean."

"Glad to pitch in and even more glad to let these girls have some space. I don't know how your house has been, but ours has been topsy-turvy, what with Amy making all her plans for what they'd do when they finally got together." With that, Beth and Ted turned towards the house and walked in easy silence to do Em's bidding.

When they were about halfway along, Ted touched her arm and motioned for her to stop. "I can't thank you enough for bringing Amy here. It's been rough on Darlene since Mama died, but she hasn't complained a bit. Mama always made such a big deal about birthdays that this will help us all get through without quite so much sadness. This means a lot to Lena to have you here."

Beth waited until the quiver in her voice was gone before she answered, "Ted, you know I'd do anything to make it a bit easier for Darlene. You're right; she's strong enough to get through hard times so I'm glad to help out. Just wondering if that's the only reason you're so glad to have us here? I thought about sending Amy's dad and staying home to get some laundry done—"

Ted shook his head and let out a huge sigh, "You know what? You're just about as tough as the women here about making me 'fess up. Okay, Amy and Lena are happy and I'm happy for them; but honestly, I'm even happier for me. I've been a little topsy-turvy inside too, and now that you're here, this feels just right." As their hands joined, they headed across the yard, swinging hands back and forth. They were so entranced with one another that they made their way, oblivious to Em peeking out the kitchen window and the two giggling girls peering around the corner of the barn.

As they stepped onto the porch, they wordlessly dropped each other's hands and shifted their shoulders before walking into the kitchen. Emma was rolling out pie dough with her back to them, and she turned around in mock surprise. "Oh, I had no idea you two were anywhere close. I'm really not needing any help just yet, so why don't you show Beth around the place? She's never been here, but I'm sure she's heard plenty about it from Darlene." With that, Em dusted the flour off her hands, expertly flipped the crust into the pie pan, and put it aside. "I'll make the chocolate filling later; and maybe around eleven thirty or so, you can come in and set the table. Otherwise, everything is pretty well taken care of." She smiled at the backs of the young couple as they had whirled out the door with her first suggestion. "Guess that was the right thing to say."

"Oh, Ted, how beautiful. I had no idea that it would look like this. When Darlene said the hills came right up the back of the barn, I didn't have a clue how big they were. Do you suppose we could climb up to the top? It looks like we'd be able to see forever from there." Beth had dressed quite sensibly for her outing, so it was easy for her to wrap the skirt around her legs and take off for the nearest gate.

"Hold up there, girl, that view isn't going anywhere, and you may need your air before you get all the way to the top." Ted quickened his step to keep up with the agile frame already going up the first part of the steep climb. "Not only that, I may need MY air before I get all the way to the top." His long legs easily caught up to Beth, and they took their time moving back and forth in the crisscrossing cow paths they followed up the hill.

Halfway up, they were both puffing with exertion, and Beth nodded her approval when Ted signaled her to stop where the paths crossed and formed an open place between two soap weed plants. "I see what you mean about needing my air. I can't imagine I'm so out of shape; but I guess staying in the house to help with a baby might not qualify as exercise, even if it can make me very tired at times." With that, she plopped down in the soft, white sand and looked at the valley for the first time.

What she saw was an entire vista of a wet meadow laid out before her. To the northeast of the house was the tall red barn with its hayloft and corrals filled with bucket calves and workhorse colts. Extending in front of the cozy house was the natural bluegrass that had crept up from the wet valley, and the shop and Fred's house followed the natural contour of the hill further east. Shimmering in the sunlight, the lake's surface reflected cattails and rushes around the shore; and Beth saw the ripples where a fish had jumped moments before.

"Oh, Ted, no wonder you never want to leave home. I've never seen such a sight in my entire life. Look at how many green colors there are in one place. The willow trees beside the water are light green, the meadow looks like emerald, and there are some really dark places there in that alfalfa field. Why is that?" Beth was totally enthralled by the variegated scene before her, yet she found it difficult to put her reaction into words.

Ted was pleased to see how moved she was by the land he loved. "You have a good eye, Beth. Those dark spots in that field are where I clean out the stalls and dump the loads in the spring. When you think how light and fluffy hay is when you pitch it into the mangers, it's amazing what happens after the horses get ahold of it." They both chuckled and he continued, "The folks came here and homesteaded a place with nothing on it and this is what they built. It feels good to be a part of what they started, and I just bought that section to the west that ties in with our land."

She turned to look where he was pointing and leaned back into the curve of his shoulder. They naturally turned toward each other and had just leaned their heads forward when soft giggles erupted above them. Ted shook his head, and Beth called out, "Listen here, young ladies, if you know what's good for you, you'll show yourselves within the next ten seconds."

Above them loomed a huge washout with a wall that angled sharply to the left. Out of the shadows popped one blond head followed by an auburn clump of curls. "Oh, come on, Beth, we were just having some fun. Besides, everyone knows you're sweet on each other so it's no big deal. Guess we'll go on to the top and let you two catch your breath. See you there." With that, the girls zigzagged up the cat steps out of reach.

"Seems like we'd better head up or we'll never hear the end of this. We may not anyway, you know." Ted extended his hand to steady Beth as she regained her feet. She took his left hand in her right hand to stand up, then quickly stood on her tiptoes to plant a soft kiss on his cheek. Before he recovered from his surprise, she had a gigantic head start on him. "Race you to the top, Ted. Loser has to do the dishes!"

Never one to back down from a challenge, Ted lunged forward, only to stumble and fall back down to the resting place. Slowly he dusted himself off and hollered up the hill, "Okay, you girls, I give up. Now I'll race you to the bottom, and the loser has to clean out the chicken house."

Shifting to go downhill, he acted as if he were heading down the cow path but ducked into the same washout where the girls had hidden.

Screaming and laughing, a flurry of motion came from the top of the hill as all three girls rushed toward the bottom. When they were even with him, Ted stepped out of the shadow and grabbed the little girls by their waists. "You should know it's dangerous to pull a trick on me. I usually come out on top." He held them by their belts to keep them from escaping and laughed as their legs churned in one spot. "What do you think now, girls? Anything you'd like to say?"

By the time they caught their breath to talk, the four of them were huddled together on the small flat spot where he and Beth had first sat down. "Ted, you've got to admit that it was kinda funny when we popped up. We slipped up the hill and hid, and you didn't even know it. How about if you watch us go down so you know where we are, and you and Beth can go on doing whatever it was you were doing?" With that, the girls broke into fresh peals of laughter as Ted released them and gave them a gentle shove.

"Then be on your way and don't make a false move. We're watching from here." Ted and Beth stood side by side while the girls scooted down the hill much faster than they went up. "And you, my dear, must believe in the element of surprise. Did you figure that was the only way you could win the race up the hill?" By this time, the young couple had turned to face one another and had totally forgotten about the girls scrambling below them.

"The look on your face was priceless, Ted, I have to admit that much. I also have to say the race wasn't even on my mind when I gave you that kiss. It just felt right." Beth stroked the side of his jaw while speaking in the direct way he had come to cherish. "If it were all wrong, maybe you could give it back, and we'd be even then. If it were all right, maybe you could give it back and we'd be even further ahead than we are right now. I guess it's up to you." Unblinking, she gazed into his eyes so it felt to Ted as if she had penetrated his soul.

Gently sliding his arm around her waist, he lowered his head and pressed his lips full on hers. "There, I gave it back with interest, and I hope this is a habit I never break."

"Wowee! Will you look at that! Kissee! Kissee! Just wait till we tell Em." Unnoticed by the pair, the girls had circled back and were absolutely elated that they had succeeded in sneaking up the draw. "When you're married, Amy and I can be together forever." Words tumbled out of Darlene's thoughts faster than her tongue could keep up with them. Looking at Ted and Beth, she realized it was truly time to go. "Okay, okay, we'll clear out. See you at the bottom." With that, the girls launched themselves from one cat step to another as the adults watched them all the way down the hill.

Embarrassed, Ted began to apologize for the situation he had created. "Beth, I'm sorry—"

She put her finger on his lips and smiled, "For what, Ted? Sorry you kissed me? Sorry the girls saw? Sorry we got caught caring about each other? From where I stand, I'm not sorry for any of this. It's easier when everyone is honest with each other, especially about feelings. I do care for you, and I think you care or this wouldn't have happened. The question now is what we do next, and we need to think seriously about what's best for us all."

Ted was so relieved that he let out a huge sigh. "Oh, Beth, I've never cared about anyone like this. If my actions made you uncomfortable, that's the only thing I'd care about. Lena jumped the gun about where this is headed, but she just said out loud what I've been hoping for. I don't expect you to know if you want to marry an old bachelor who might drive you crazy when you get better acquainted, but we've got time to find out—that is, if you want to." His hand still rested on Beth's back, and they moved in unison to share a quick embrace before facing each other.

"We might not be able to guess where we'll end up, but let's enjoy getting to know one another. I probably have an advantage since Darlene told me all about her big brother. She thinks the world of you, and it seems as if she's a pretty good judge of character. The first thing we have to do is go down there and face the music. You can bet we're in for our share of teasing, so let's get it over with."

As Beth smiled at her companion, the sun glistened on her hair as it blew in the gentle breeze. She turned her head to shake the chestnut brown strands away from her face, and all of a sudden caught a whiff on the wind. "Ted, I have never smelled anything so sweet. I'll bet that's the wild roses Darlene was talking about. She said they always came out in time for her birthday, and here they are, right on time." Looking to her left, Beth caught sight of a huge patch of wild rose bushes. Edging her way to the flowers, she simply stood and breathed deeply of the aroma. "What a perfect morning this has been. I can't imagine how it could have been any better."

Ted had never shared his world with anyone outside of his family, and he didn't want to interrupt the moment. Beth's obvious appreciation of the beauty of the land and simple treasures of the hills moved him in a completely new way. "What I know is that those roses don't last very long. If you're not here at the right time, you'd miss one of the best parts of springtime. I'm so glad you like what you've seen—and smelled, too, for that matter."

They smiled at each other as people do when they share special moments, let their hands naturally intertwine, and left the heights for the valley below. Even though they knew they faced some immediate good-natured joshing, they were looking forward to future discoveries about one another.

Walking quietly into the kitchen, they found the girls and Emma stirring up a concoction for lunch so engrossed that they didn't notice the couple's entrance. Giggling and licking batter-covered spoons, Darlene and Amy jostled each other for a spot in front of the bowl, then grabbed each other's waist so they could both be in front of the goodies. "Too bad Ted and Beth don't get to taste this before lunch. Bet they'd want to shove right in and grab a spoon, too." Amy laughed as she hoisted the spoon high in the air, tipping her head back so she was ready to slurp the golden batter.

Shrieking with amazement as the couple slipped up behind them, Beth felt Amy's hand on her waist and the other on the spoon. Beth guided the spoon into her own mouth and consumed the bite with savor and a huge sigh of satisfaction. Simultaneously, Ted had grasped Darlene's spoon and finished off her dollop. "Thanks for saving the last bite for us, girls. We do appreciate it more than you know." With a great deal of laughter and hugging, they all ended in a group embrace with Ted and Amy while Emma leaned on the counter.

"All right, you people, if you're done making my kitchen into Grand Central Station, you can all clear out and I'll finish this in peace and quiet," Emma herded the group to the porch and ended with her ultimatum. "If anyone ends up underfoot before I'm done cooking, that person'll be the one doing all the dishes while the rest of us sit and watch. See you at twelve noon. Now go find somewhere else to spend your time."

As the foursome strolled across the yard, Darlene's incessant chatter resumed. "Guess what, Beth. I just got the best surprise ever. Tracy sent it out with Ted and I've never had anything so sweet. I'd get it for you but you heard Em. No way I'm crossing her before lunch."

"That's okay, Darlene. I can wait till we all have permission to go back in. While we were up in the hills, I found out why you get so excited when you talk about the wild roses. There was a huge patch of them beside the trail and I agree there's nothing quite like that smell in the whole world." Beth leaned over and lightly tapped Darlene's nose. "You've got a good smeller there, girl."

Darlene grabbed Beth's hand and drew her close. "Put your nose beside my neck and get a deep whiff of that. What does that remind you of?" She stood momentarily still so Beth could take a deep breath.

"My goodness, that's what I smelled up there. What did you do, roll in the rose bushes?" Beth held Darlene's shoulders as they gazed into each other's eyes.

"No, silly, those roses are too pokey to do that. That's what I told you about. Tracy found some stuff that smells like roses and she sent it out so I could have it on my birthday. Isn't that just the most amazing thing ever? I told you it was the biggest surprise ever. Do you believe me now?"

Beth fervently nodded her head up and down as she spoke, "That probably edges out the surprise I had planned for you. Since you've had such a big one, we'd better not spoil you by giving you anything else. I guess I can just take this one back to our house until you're ready for it."

Before she had finished with her last word, Darlene had jumped into her waiting arms and squealed, "Beth, how can you think that? I can have more than one thing today without turning into some rotten child. Besides, how would I ever let you know the right time to bring it back and that would make an extra trip for you and I'd just die wondering what it was." Darlene's words came spilling over one another so rapidly that it was almost as if the air in a balloon had escaped in a big whoosh.

Seeing she hadn't taken time for a breath, Beth took her by the shoulders and looked deeply into her eyes, "Well, Darlene, sounds like you're ready for a bit more on your special day, so I guess this is as good of a time as any. Do you remember that I was busy on the box social weekend so I told Ted I couldn't go with him?"

"Oh, boy, do I! I lost a big bet with him that day—oops, I bet I wasn't supposed to say that either, was I?" Looking at her brother, Darlene had such a sorrowful expression that Ted reached out to reassure her.

He tousled her hair and comforted her, "That's okay, Lena. I already told Beth about our little wager—after she had turned me down—so you didn't give away any deep dark secret." He draped his arm around her shoulder and gave her a friendly squeeze.

"If you remember, my brother had planned to come out here and visit me, which is exactly what he did. Big brothers must be kind of alike, because he's always one to keep me guessing, just like Ted does for you." She took a moment to gaze above Darlene's head at Ted who had started to turn red. "Imagine how excited I was when he told me to close my eyes and hold out my hands. I did what I was told, but when he put it in my hands, I was so startled that I nearly dropped his gift. Thank heavens he was there to catch it so nothing bad happened."

By now, Darlene had caught her breath and launched into another series of gulps. "But what in the world was it and why were you so shocked and did it hurt you and when will you show it to us? Big brothers are the best, even if they are the biggest teases in the whole wide world."

"Okay, little miss, I think you're ready for this, so we can go to the barn where your newest gift is stashed. While you girls were planning your mischief in the hills, Ted and I were hatching our own plans for you. Let's go, and while we're on the way, you have three guesses. Make them count. By the way, no fair asking Amy to help since she knows all about it."

"Oh, my gosh. How can I figure it out without some kind of a hint? I don't even know your brother so that makes it hard. Is it big or little, fast or slow, hard or soft?" Without waiting for an answer, she chattered nonstop all the way to the barn.

In front of the huge sliding door, Beth paused and put on her serious look as she delivered her instructions, "Now, Darlene, please listen while I give you directions."

With that, Darlene let out a huge giggle, "That is your school teacher voice, Miss Edgars." Mimicking Beth's tone and posture, Darlene gave her best imitation, "First, we'll have a look and see if there is anything unfamiliar, and then we'll—"

By this time, all four of them were holding their stomachs and wiping the tears from their eyes. Finally, Beth caught her breath and gasped out, "I had that one coming, didn't I, Darlene? Okay, here's the deal. You'll have to do just what my brother made me do, so shut your eyes and hold out your hands. No matter what, hang on tight so it doesn't slip through your fingers."

Ted had slid the door open and they all stood for a moment, letting their eyes adjust to the dim interior. "Not too many surprises out here in this old barn, are there, Lena? Most of the time, we can pretty much guess what's going to happen, but this is a whole lot different. Got your eyes shut tight now? Let me have your hand and I'll lead you a little ways, then you're on your own."

While he was talking, Beth had slipped to the side and knelt over a box in the manger. Reaching inside, she pulled out a half-grown Siamese kitten which she gently deposited in Darlene's outstretched hands.

Instinctively, the little girl grasped the warm kitten and snuggled him in the hollow of her neck. In the dim light, she could make out the whiteness of his coat. "Oh, do you hear him? He's already happy here. I'd better take him around and introduce him to all the other cats so he knows this is where he belongs." As she emerged into the sunlight, she let out all her breath in a low whistle, "I've never seen anything like this in my whole life. What in the world do you call a cat like this? Ice blue eyes and light little gray ears and the most beautiful body I ever saw. I can't believe my eyes."

Beth and Ted had noiselessly moved toward one another, and they shared a knowing smile at her obvious pleasure. "Honey, that's known as a Siamese cat and that's what they all look like. My brother works for some people who raise cats like this, and they gave him these kittens when their mother got run over. He didn't want them but knew they'd have a good home with me. When I saw them, I wanted to share with you, so there you are. Now, how does that work for a birthday surprise?"

For once, Darlene was wordless. She would alternate between holding the kitten to her face so she could stroke and love him and then holding him at arm's length so she could stare at him. The kitten patiently tolerated having its nap interrupted and would snuggle into her warm neck each time it had a chance, purring loudly.

Softly, Beth inquired, "It looks like he's found a home here, so do you have any idea what you might want to name him? Maybe you need a little more time to get to know him before you can answer that."

Almost immediately came Darlene's reply, "Jitney. That's his name forever."

Furrowing her brow, Beth finally asked, "Where in the world did that come from? I don't think I've ever heard of a cat with a name like that."

Darlene held out the kitten that was purring loudly enough that they could all hear. "Whenever Ted starts the car so we can go somewhere, he shoves his hat to the back of his head and says, 'Don't you love that sound? This jitney purrs just like a kitten.' Then he cinches his hat down like he does when he heads out for a wild horseback ride and climbs in."

With three pairs of feminine eyes on him, Ted could feel the blush creeping up his neck once again. "Well, enough about me for a while. Would you like to see how well Johnny Reb has done since we brought him home from your house?" With that remark, Ted was able to direct attention away from himself long enough to regain his composure.

"That's the best idea yet. Now we can both have a baby kitten to play with. Come on, Amy, let's get Johnny so he and Jitney can be best friends just like we are. The funnest thing is that Em gave me some baby clothes for my dolls, and they're just right for a kitten. We can play dress-up and pretend we have a real live baby to play with. Let's go find him." With that, the girls scampered up the hayloft ladder to find the barn cats that had burrowed into the hay for a snooze after lapping up their morning pan of milk.

Ted and Beth found themselves largely forgotten and took advantage of the peaceful moments to have a serious conversation. "I'd have to say you outdid yourself with that kitten. Since we don't know if we'll ever have another quiet moment today, I'd better work this in while the girls are busy. I have something I've been wanting to ask you for a long time. I'd be honored if you've decided to accompany me to the Chautauqua gathering in July. I know it's a long ways off, but I might not get over to visit before then and I don't want to miss out on another time with you." The more he talked, the faster he talked, almost as if he could prevent bad news by filling the air with his words. Looking at Beth and not finding encouragement in her eyes, he continued, "I understand if you don't want to make plans like that, and I really hope I haven't made you uncomfortable. It's just that—"

With her finger on his lips, Beth softly shushed him. "Stop right there, Silly. If I looked sad, it was because we won't get to spend time together for so many weeks. I understand that you're busy with the ranch, and I'm busy helping out with Amy's family, but it makes me sad to think of being so far apart for so long. I'd love to go with you, and I'm excited about having a whole day to spend with you."

Ted cleared his throat and let out a big sigh. "You really had me worried there for a minute, and now you've made me the happiest guy in this whole county. I just wish we could be together, but you know how it is with all the work we have to get done. Too bad we can't move the ranches closer together, but I don't see that happening."

"Even if we have to be apart, there is one thing that'll help me get through—that is, if you'll agree to it," Beth's voice dropped as she lowered her gaze.

Ted attempted to speak several times before he could make a sound. Although he had experienced a wide range of emotions throughout his lifetime, this was totally new and unexpected. Not having words big enough to capture his feelings, he swallowed deeply and let out a tiny squeak before his voice kicked in. "Beth, you may not know it, but I'd do anything in the world you asked of me. All you have to do is tell me and you can consider it done." Reaching down to lift her chin, Ted ended his remark with a straightforward look into her eyes.

"Oh, Ted, you're different than anyone I ever met before. Every day when the mail comes, I'll be so excited that I can't wait to get the letter you wrote that day, and you'll know a day won't go by without hearing from me. Isn't that the most romantic thing ever?" Beth squeezed both his hands and swung them back and forth just like an enthusiastic toddler.

Once again, Ted attempted to speak several times before he could make a sound, but this time there was an edge of desperation when he began. "Beth, you know I'd do anything for you, but you don't know what you're asking. It's hard enough for me to talk when you're right in front of me, but putting words on a piece of paper is well nigh impossible for me. I'm ashamed to say I never went to school and I don't know any fancy words. Papa insisted we all learned to read and write, but that was before we had neighbors around here. Mama showed all of us older kids the letters and then she'd have us practice reading when we came in for supper. I can see her stirring our supper and listening with me sitting at the table and sounding out the words. It was torture for me and probably not much better for her, so we came up with a deal. When I got so I could read one whole chapter out of the Bible without any mistakes, my school days could end. I had Emma find the shortest chapter for me, and we practiced until I knew it by heart. Mama probably knew what I was up to, but we both were relieved when it was over. I'm not very smart, Beth, and I guess it's a good thing you found out right now."

While Ted was confessing his embarrassment, it was Beth's turn to be overcome by a totally new emotion. Reaching out to comfort him, she drew him to her just as a mother would hold a hurting child. He leaned his head against her, and she stroked his hair. "Ted, there are so many ways to be smart, and most of the ones that truly matter don't have anything to do with a book. It breaks my heart to hear you say you're ashamed of who you are. What I see in front of me is a man holding a ranch together, one who can read people and cattle and horses better than I ever dreamed anyone could, and a person who knows a whole lot about how the world works. Most of what you know can't be found in any book I've ever read, and I think you're the smartest person I've ever known. Please don't be sad."

Ted shrugged his shoulders and continued, "Part of the problem was that my lessons were in German, so now I have to stop and think about every word before I go to the next one. It's not easy for me to read a whole string of English words, but I can make do when it comes to bills from the lumberyard or hardware store. Numbers are easy but those letters just seem to swarm like bees and fuzz up my mind. Maybe it would be better for you to find a man who can read books with you and write you pretty letters. That's just not me, and I'll understand if you turn away now that you know what kind of a deal you'd be getting into."

"Theo Soehl, do you think I'd let a little thing like words on paper get in the way of caring about you? If you think I'm such a snob, I guess it is a good thing for me to know what you truly think. What gave you the idea I was looking for someone to sit beside the fire and read words? I can do plenty of that for both of us. What I'm looking for is a man who wants to hold me and take away the hurt of the day; a man who loves babies and puppies and the smell of wild roses; a man who can laugh with me and cry with me and be excited to see me no matter what or when. If that sounds like you, then we're in fine shape. If not, I need to know right now."

Seeing how agitated Beth had become, Ted realized how precarious his situation had become. One false word and he faced the prospect of continuing his long, lonely bachelorhood. Gently taking hold of her chin, he softly replied, "Beth, I want to be the man in your life. I just don't want you ashamed of me. If you settle for someone less than the man of your dreams, it's a long life of regret. If you want to do the reading for both of us, I'll be more than glad to do the numbers. Would that be a fair deal?"

Moments after sharing a long direct look, the two melted into each other's arms. "Would you be willing to teach me German, Ted? I'd love to know it, but I never had a chance to learn a different language. When I have babies, I want them to start right out hearing German lullabies and stories. What do you say about that?" Beth had shared her private dreams with Ted, and she was shocked and instantly furious at his reaction.

Letting out a huge burst of laughter, Ted held tight to Beth as she struggled to escape and stomp off. "No, you don't understand, Beth. How funny is it that now we're talking about home and children and lullabies when we started out talking about how to get through a few weeks of being apart? I think this day has been very good for us, and I think we've realized this is serious. We're both old enough to know what we want to do, and we don't have to ask anyone else for permission. Let's take the next few weeks to think long and hard about our plans, and when we get together the end of July, we can compare answers and ideas. I know right now what I want, but I want you to have time to consider what you're getting into."

Gradually her struggles had eased and Beth once again leaned against him. Turning to face each other, their arms naturally slid around each other, she stood on her toes and he bent his neck so they could share a kiss in the dim coolness of his barn.

"Wowwee! Kissee! Kissee! Don't you guys ever get

tired of that silly stuff? Give us a minute so we can get outta here so we don't get sick. Should we tell Em you're too busy out here and she might need to pack you a lunch?" Amy and Darlene had finished playing with their kitties and were on the way to the house when they stumbled onto the couple's embrace. "Em said you guys needed time to get to know each other, and it looks like that sure happened!" Darlene danced outside Ted's grasp and Amy ignored Beth's scowl and shaking head. Giggling and skipping, they headed to the house for dinner.

"Oh, no. Do you think we'll ever live this down?" Beth laughed and reached out for Ted's hand. "I think the best way now is to face them and let them know we aren't embarrassed about what they saw. With kids, the direct way is usually the best. Are you ready?"

Ted had sat down on the sadness barrel, rubbing his forehead and rolling his eyes, "That's easy enough for you to say, Beth, but do you realize I have to live with these women here? They're unmerciful when they get a guy on the run." Sighing, he continued, "I know you're right, and we might as well hit the teasing head on. The sooner, the better." Pushing up, he grasped Beth's outstretched hand and stood. "Into the lion's den we go."

What they didn't know about was the scene that was simultaneously taking place in Em's kitchen. When the girls had burst in giggling and chattering, she had let them talk until there was a momentary lull in the air; then it was her turn. "Okay, girls. You've had your fun, and now I'm laying down the law. Those two out there care about one another, and it is hard to be so far apart for so long. What we're going to do is give them peace and privacy so they can figure out what to do next. Under no circumstance are you to pester them, and I don't want to hear a giggle or see even a hint of a sideways look. Do you understand?"

Dropping their heads as they realized their fun was over, the girls softly muttered, "Yes, ma'am. We understand," then almost in unison, they went into a siege of laughter and shouted, "but it was probably the funniest thing we've ever seen. You should've seen them jump backwards when we sneaked up on them, like they had a hold of hot coals and couldn't get away soon enough. We didn't know old folks could move so fast."

Shooing them out of her way so they couldn't see her smiling face, Em warned, "You have until they get over here from the barn to finish up your giggling, and then you'll act like perfect ladies. If not, you know the consequence?"

All of a sudden, Darlene was all business, "Yes, Em, I do. I sure don't want to have to do the dishes for a week all by myself, so you can bet I'll obey." One final smile crossed her face, and she turned to her friend, "We're on our best behavior. Right, Amy?"

"Right, Darlene." Amy paused while she considered the situation, "But it might be kinda fun if you had dishpan hands for a solid week." She twisted quickly enough that her friend missed grabbing her sleeve, and they scooted out of the house yelling and sprinting across the yard.

"Whoa, girls, you'd better look out or we're all going to be in a huge crash and miss lunch. I don't know about you, but I'd hate that more than anything." Ted moved in front of Beth and held out his huge hand to keep the girls from a direct collision with her. "You two are about as keyed up as a pair of coyotes in the middle of a covey of quail. What in the world set you off this time?" Beth and he exchanged glances, ready for the teasing they were sure to come.

"Oh, nothing, Big Brother. I just needed to set Amy straight, only she wasn't ready for her lesson." By this time, the girls had their arms around each other's shoulders and were breathless from their excursion. "Let's head in 'cause it looks like Em has the grub ready, and I can't wait to see my cake. Do you suppose she knows how many candles I need? I'd hate to stay eight years old just because she forgot."

"With as many reminders as you've given us this last month, there's no way she could make a mistake on that deal. Trust me, we all know what we've been told." Ted tousled Darlene's hair as they eased into the kitchen where Emma was waiting.

"It looked like I was going to have to eat this all by myself, and then I'd have to sleep for a week. Glad you spared me that. After you wash, grab a chair and let's get started." Emma motioned the girls to the basin and dipper where they dipped their fingers and wiped their hands on their pants. Emma shook her head and smiled, "Hope you won't keel over from whatever was on your hands since I think most of it's probably still there. Beth and Ted, it's your turn now."

After Darlene had directed each one to an assigned seat, she sat down and they all waited to hear who would say grace. "Lena, since it's your big day, how about you doing the honors? I'll bet you have lots to give thanks for."

With eyes glistening, Darlene softly began, "Father, thanks for all my family and friends and puppies and kittens and horses. Please help me to grow up big and strong and do what is right. Oh, and 'specially thank you for birthdays that are so much fun." She whooshed out her breath as Ted smiled and nodded to her. "It's not like last year when Mama was still here, but it's still okay, isn't it?"

Everyone felt the sadness in the room, and Darlene broke the tension when she said, "I'll bet I get the gizzard this time, even if it isn't my turn, right, Em?" She twisted in her chair to tell Amy how the most delectable parts of a fried chicken are the giblets and the golden-brown crunchies left on the platter. "We had such fierce fork fights trying to stab the goodies that Mama laid down a rule. Every time a different person got the liver, heart, gizzard, and crumbs. You can bet we knew when it was our turn, and we never had fork marks on our hands. Dinner wasn't so wild after that, and things have worked out all right since then unless someone is gone for a day. Then we have to sort what happens the next day. We're pretty careful not to have very big arguments 'cause Em settles them by eating the pieces before we even sit down to eat."

"Glad you told us about that so we don't interfere with the usual order of events," Amy threw her head back and let out a snort. "I had spied a liver underneath the chicken pieces and thought about maneuvering it out. I surely wouldn't want wounded over a chunk of meat." She held up her left hand and said, "If I lost this, I'd miss being able to write letters to my friends," and looked meaningfully at Ted who nodded back.

Darlene missed the glance and interjected, "Do you remember when I came home and told you my teacher was one of those 'left writers' just like Em? I can't even get a fork up to my mouth using my left hand, let alone write a letter anyone could figure out. Is it hard for you to use your right hand?" Out of the corner of her eye, Darlene giggled as she caught a glimpse of Ted quickly letting go of Beth's right hand. "Guess you're pretty handy with that left hand of yours, aren't you, Theo?"

No one else had seen the brief flurry of activity going on between them, and Darlene's natural protectiveness of her brother and special teacher kept her from revealing their secret. Ted winked at his little sister and shrugged, "A man's gotta do what a man's gotta do." While the others looked quizzically at what was going on, Ted scooted his chair back and let out a contented sigh. "Did you have time to fix us one of your famous birthday cakes, Em, or we going to have to go away hungry?"

Emma gave him a sideways glance and shook her head. "No, Ted, I don't want you getting weak on my watch, so I found time for the cake. And might I say, I do believe this might just be one of my very best. The eggs whipped up like they knew how special today is. Lena, how about you and Amy clearing the table while I fetch the dessert? I don't want my masterpiece sitting in the middle of a messy table. Moving quickly so they could see what Emma had created, Darlene and Amy made short work of the dirty dishes.

"I'd say that table's slicker than a pond in January, Em, and the table is fit for whatever you fashioned back there in the pantry." Ted leaned back on his chair and winked at his big sister. "Who gets the honor of showing it to us all?"

Emma rested her right elbow on her left wrist at her waist. Lifting her hand to her face, she stroked her chin in deep concentration. "You know, Ted, I've been trying to figure that out. Is there anyone here too excited to wait a minute longer? If there is, I'd guess that's who needs to scamper around the corner to pick up the cake—VERY carefully, might I add."

No sooner had she finished than Darlene leaped out of her chair and bounded to the pantry. "Oh, Em, you know I've been so keyed up for weeks that I couldn't even stand it. Now the big day's here, and so are our friends, and I finally get to see the big mystery."

As she rounded the corner, Darlene caught sight of the cake which Em had set out on the pantry counter. "I can't believe it. I don't even know what to say. I've never seen anything like this in my entire life. Where did you ever get an idea like this? How did you do this? Oh, my, Amy, I can't wait for you to see this. You won't believe it. This is so amazing—"

"Lena! Enough already of the jabbering. Maybe you

could bring it out here so all of us could have a look," Ted nudged Beth while he spoke. "After all, how much different can one cake be from another? Bring it out here, and I'll be glad to sample it for you."

Emerging from the pantry with the cake held high as if it were a precious offering, Darlene glared at Ted. "One look at this and I'll bet you change your tune. This is the most beautiful thing I've ever seen, and I don't think we can cut into this. I want to keep it forever." Gently placing the cake in the middle of the table, she whirled to grasp Em in a fierce embrace. "You're the best sister in the whole world."

Even Ted who had pretended to be so calloused about the fancy cake was completely silenced, as was each person gathered around as they viewed the creation that had momentarily taken Darlene's words away. Emma had kept her eye out for what she would need to create Darlene's cake; and when a traveling salesman stopped at the Soehl household, she immediately spotted the tiny doll with real hair that she had kept hidden for months.

She had mixed up one of her famous angel food cakes; then after it was cool, stood over the wood stove and whipped the fluffy white frosting until it was perfect. In honor of the day, she even used some precious drops of her genuine vanilla flavoring. Placing the doll in the center hole, Emma created a fairy tale delight, precisely fashioning a gown with row upon row of swirls and peaks. Nine candles, each in its own miniature cupcake, completed the birthday scene. "Honey, I'm glad you are so taken by it, but it really has to be eaten today or it'll go to waste. How about you getting out the first piece so the rest of us can join in?"

Darlene found herself in the situation of wanting to hold on to the moment and, at the same time, desiring a taste of the scrumptious cake. "You know what, Em? This is the first time you've let me be the one who cuts the cake. I really must be getting older if you think I'm responsible enough to run one of your knives. I promise I'll be careful." The sharpness of Emma's knives was legendary in the neighborhood, so Darlene's remark acknowledged what everyone at the table knew.

She began pushing the blade straight down as if she were cutting a fresh apple. "Oh, Honey, let me show you how to do that. This cake isn't so tough you need to attack it, so be soft. Pretend you're sawing through a pile of feathers and go back and forth." Darlene offered to hand the knife to Emma who held up her hand and shook her head. "Oh, no, Hon, I didn't mean I wanted to do it. Now that you're nine years old, it's time for you to take over some of the kitchen chores. Go ahead and try it like I said."

"Wow! Emma, I can't believe how this absolutely glides through the fluff and the cake. You're right. I don't need to use all my strength to get this done." With that, Darlene finished her first slice and turned the cake a bit to carve the second side. Slipping the broad cake server under her piece, she eased it out and let out a huge shriek. "Emma, how in the world? Where did you ever find this? This is too much." Plopping herself down into her chair so she could lower her head and peer directly at the cake, she continued. "No one will ever believe this. Amy, you'll need to tell the kids at school that I'm not making up a story about my cake. They'll never believe this."

Sitting on the saucer was a slice of cake with swirls of red, green, and yellow. Not only had Emma decorated the outside of the cake, she also had bought tiny bottles of food coloring from the Watkins man when he had dropped in. "Do you like it, Honey? I had such a hard time not telling you, but sometimes keeping a secret is worth it at the end. You know how I always tell everything I know? This time I held out."

Darlene was speechless. She took a few breaths, and then slowly picked up her fork. Tears coursed down her cheeks as she nibbled on the first bite of her cake. "You really did it this time, Em. I'll never have a better day. Never ever."

"Not even your wedding day? Bet that'll make your husband sad when you get married, " Amy giggled while Darlene poked at her with her elbow. "Do we have to watch you eat and hear about how good it is, or do we get a taste of that fancy-dancy cake?"

Emma grasped the knife, "Go ahead, Lena. Next time you can do the carving honors, but this time I'll serve everyone. Raise your hand if you want to try this." Hands shot up all around the table, and she served them all in short order. Comparing the colors and designs of each piece kept them busy until the concoction disappeared.

When they were all finished and so stuffed that they could hardly move, Emma fired out the orders for the afternoon. "The girls and I will do the dishes, and you two can stroll around and check out the rest of the ranch. This is such a mild day for the end of May that you might want to take a walk down by the lake and get the cool breeze. We'll be done here in no time, and you girls can run off and play in the barn with Johnny and Jitney before it's time for to head out. I really don't think it's fun trying to make it home after dark on these roads."

Darlene and Amy made fake moaning sounds, and then jumped right up to get to work. Emma had the hot water in the reservoir so they washed, dried, and put away the dishes while they laughed and jostled one another. With one final snap of the dish towel as they finished, they headed for the door as Emma issued her ultimatum, "If I hear one more crack out of a dish towel, you'll both march right in and take a nap—no arguments; no discussion. Understood?"

Saluting her and ducking away so she ended up with a handful of air, Darlene and Amy were quick to circle back when she wasn't looking and plant a loud kiss on each cheek. Running out the door, they shouted back over their shoulders, "Thanks for everything, Emma. We love you." Grabbing on to each other's hands, they skipped across the yard to the barn to spend the afternoon dressing the kittens.

South of the homestead, Ted and Beth were on a leisurely walk around the lake. Blackbirds twittered, frogs croaked, and a few early swamp bugs skittered on the water's surface. "Ted, I can't imagine how still it is. If I didn't know better, I might think that's actually a mirror sitting in the middle of your meadow. Whoops, I guess I spoke too soon." As they looked across the water, a turtle's head came lazily into view from the rushes. His movement sent ripples to the pond's edge while a swish came from the other side. "Oh my gosh. If we had fishing poles, I'll bet we could catch a nice mess of fish for your supper. Do you know what kind are in here?" Beth leaned forward to catch a better view of the action.

"Do I ever—bullheads, lots of bullheads. We've got cane poles with double hooks in the barn; and when they're biting, you can pull in two bullheads at a time. It might look like a lot of fun to you, but I don't have any fond feeling for fishing. We just about lived on fish once when we lost all our chickens. Fred and I were little boys, so Mama would hand us the poles and send us out here. We'd bring a gunny sack to throw in the water to keep the fish alive while we worked, and then we'd have to haul them to the house where we'd clean them. Until you've cleaned a sack full of fish every day before dinner, you really haven't lived. Not only that, I couldn't get the fishy smell off my hands, no matter how hard I scrubbed them. Even though we were all glad to have food on the table, it got so I couldn't choke down another bite of fish, no matter what. To this day, it turns my stomach when I smell it cooking."

"Well, I guess I won't invite you over for a mess of fish for supper anytime soon. Fish are such a treat to my family that it surprises me to hear anyone not like them." Beth paused and gently laid her hand on Ted's arm. "Do you realize how little we know about each other? And yet, instead of scaring me off, it makes me wish we could spend every day together exploring old memories and making new ones." She moved closer to Ted at the precise moment that he sucked in a huge gasp of air and extended his arm in an attempt to dislodge the deerfly which had just stung him. Beth and Ted's combined movements put him in the unenviable position of pushing her away, and her in the precarious position of nearly being flung into the water. She was so startled that she made no sound while holding tightly to the same arm which nearly dislodged her.

Reaching out, Ted encircled her waist and drew him to her, safely away from the water and held her close. "Beth, I wouldn't hurt you for the world. That consarned deerfly sure put the bite on me, and I guess I kind of did the same thing to you. All I can say is that I'm truly sorry. Will you forgive me?" In suspense, he waited for her and all he found in return was a long drawn-out silence. Looking down at her, Ted was mortified to see her whole body quaking. "My dear Beth, please look at me. I'll not be able to stand it if I hurt you."

Beth finally gained her composure enough that she could return his gaze, and it was Ted's turn to be instantly angry. "If you're going to laugh at me when I'm worried about you, I don't think that's—"

She firmly grasped both his biceps in her delicate fingers and gave him a playful shake. "Ted, is this the way our life together would be? Every time we about get to the point of making some serious statement, something happens. If it isn't a pair of third graders jumping out from a blowout, it's the same pair of girls dropping out of the hayloft. As if that weren't enough, here we are talking about making memories, and that deerfly sure enough gave us another wild moment. If we get together, I'll bet we have lots of times like this to look back on and have a good laugh about. Tell me the truth—have you ever had quite such an event-filled visit with anyone else? I know I've never been through anything like this, and it makes me excited to find out what's ahead for us. I don't know about you, but I think this day's been filled with plenty of good signs."

This time as she approached her man, he shifted to face her at the same time. As their lips tentatively met, each one firmly expected an outcry from somewhere. When they realized they were truly sharing a moment's privacy, each was overcome by an intense yearning, fervently wishing for more uninterrupted time to continue their journey of discovery while dreading the upcoming separation they would endure. Clinging to each other for a few private moments, they moved imperceptibly apart in an attempt to regain their composure. "I darned sure know what Darlene meant by days that crawl by. These weeks until Chautauqua will feel like a year, and there's not much we can do about it, is there?" Ted finally knew the comfort of finding someone to care about deeply, and he was reluctant to have the day end. Stroking Beth's hair, he whispered softly, "I wish Mama could have met you. She'd always say, 'Theodor, some woman will have your heart in her hands before you even know it. I want for you the right one, so please to wait for her.' I know she's smiling now and saying, 'See, Theo. Waiting is worth it. Your heart is in good hands.'" Placing Beth's two tiny hands on his broad chest, he pleaded, "Beth, will you be careful of my heart? Mama was right—this happened before I even knew what hit me, and now there's no way I can feel right without you."

Two tears coursed down her cheeks as she gave her answer, "Ted, I'm glad you waited for me, and I'm honored to be the keeper of your heart. I promise to look after your heart, and I can't wait until we have time together again." As a way of lightening the moment, she continued, "I imagine all of us will be ready to meet in Arthur for the Chautauqua celebration. Would you like it if I bring a lunch and plan to meet at noon in the park? That way Emma can take a break from fixing meals, and you can all be my guests this time."

Ted hugged her and let out a chuckle, "I think that sounds great, but I'm guessing Em would choke at the idea of going somewhere without fixing food. Maybe you could convince her to bring the dessert since that's really her specialty. We probably had better get back to the house so you and Amy can get on the road." They shared one final embrace before leaving the tranquility of the lake.

"Oh, no, it's not time yet. You just barely got here. How can you even think of leaving so soon?" Amy and Darlene were grasping each other with the intensity of desperate children, and Beth put a hand on each shoulder to comfort them.

"Girls, I know the day slipped away from us, but we really do have to get back. Your mom and dad will worry if we aren't home by dark; and I don't know the roads well enough to be comfortable starting any later. Have you made plans for where you're going to meet when we get together in Arthur? Even though it's not a very big town, by the time everyone gets there for the program, it'll be full of all kinds of people. Take a few minutes to make your plans while I thank Emma, and then it's time to load up."

Excitedly, the girls began chattering about their next adventure while the adults stepped back to make their own plans. "Emma, I'd be honored if you'd let me bring the lunch for the gathering. I'll have time since Amy's mama is much stronger and doesn't need me nearly like she did before. I've heard so many stories about your famous pies and cookies that maybe you could bring something special for after dinner. How's that sound to you?"

Emma blushed at Beth's remark and shrugged, "Ted's got such a sweet tooth that I suppose he's the one making all those brags. I'd be glad to rig up something for dessert and sit back and enjoy whatever you make for us. A few more times of someone else doing the cooking, and I'll just want to sit around and get fat. Are you sure there's nothing else you want me to bring?"

Reaching out to give Emma a soft hug, Beth shook her head, "Not a chance, Emma. You've shown us such wonderful hospitality today that I want you to have a break from cooking and be our guest. Thank you for a very special outing that's been far better than Amy or I ever dreamed." Bending down to hug Darlene, she continued, "You've been a sweet birthday girl, and I'm proud to have been here for this special day. This might be the start of a tradition, so when it's Amy's turn in October, we'd better plan on another get-together. You take good care of Jitney and Johnny, and we'll be back to visit them sometime." Awkwardly, she turned to Ted, not sure of the best way to part from him.

Ted solved her quandary by reaching out to take her hand. He then bent down and placed a gentlemanly kiss just behind her knuckles. "Papa was right, you know. He always said a lady has soft hands that have a strong hold, just like yours. Thank you for a wonderful time, and we look forward to seeing you in late July." He straightened up to his full height, and turned to the little girls. "Okay, Lassies, you've been peeking around washouts and barn doors, so how about this?" More quickly than anyone could believe it, he circled Beth's waist with his arms, pulled her to him, and planted a loud smack on her lips.

Amy and Darlene erupted into spasms of giggles, Emma chuckled deep in her throat, and Beth turned her head away in embarrassment and pleasure. Ted leaned over to open the car door so Beth could slide in under the steering wheel. "Now I think the day's officially over. This car needs to get headed home, and Darlene and I have some chores to take care of. Good to see you and hurry back." He squeezed the door shut, tapped on the car's top, and gave a smart salute.

Beth started the engine, cocked her head, and called out the window, "Listen to that jitney, purring like a kitten." Then she revved up the motor, let out the clutch, and headed for home in a cloud of dust and smoke.

The Soehls watched until the dust cloud disappeared, and then they wordlessly fell back into the usual routine of ranch life. Emma stepped into the house while Ted and Darlene trudged out to the barn. Force of habit led them where they needed to be, but each one was quietly mulling over the events of the day.

Ted absent-mindedly picked up a piece of leather to fix while Darlene scampered up the hayloft ladder. "I just want to make sure Jitney and Johnny are settled in before I help you feed the calves and horses. Is that okay, Theo?"

At the mention of his name, Ted emerged from his reverie to answer, "Sure, Little One, we're not in a great big hurry now, are we? Nothing else going on today, for sure." He plopped down on the sadness barrel and ran the leather through his fingers. Tipping the barrel backwards so his head rested on the wooden wall, Ted pulled his hat down to cover his eyes.

Satisfied that the kitties were content, Darlene came bounding down, and then suddenly halted when she saw how Ted was sitting. "Are you all right, Theo? Is anything wrong? Do you want me to get Emma? What's going on anyway?"

Casually bumping his hat to the back of his head, he signaled Darlene to his side. "Not a thing is wrong, Honey. This has been quite a day for me, just like it has for you, and I need a bit of time to sort out some things."

"Can I help, Ted? You always say that I'm a good thinker, and you know I'd do anything in the world for you." Words spilled out as she shared both her concern and willingness to pitch in when needed. "Are you unhappy about something that happened today? I'm sorry if Amy and I made you sad. We were just having fun, but it wasn't fun if it made you feel bad. Can you forgive me for being naughty? I promise we'll be good next time."

"You sure say lots of things at the same time, and sometimes it's hard to know which part to answer first. Yes, I'd like it if you'd help. No, I'm not unhappy about the way things went today. No, I didn't think you girls were naughty; and no, I don't need to forgive you for anything. What I need to sort out is how I can be so taken by Beth and not even know her very well. It makes me sick to think I have to wait two whole months before I get to see her again, and I don't know how I can go from being the most satisfied man on earth like I was yesterday to the most stirred up man in the county today. Now how about that for a wad to chew on?"

Darlene cocked her head to the side, and pondered for a few minutes. "You know what, Ted? It sounds to me like this visit was a good one for us both. I had my best friend here with me, and you found a best friend you didn't even know you had. Seems like we both came out smelling like roses. I'll tell you what you told me when I didn't think my birthday would ever come. 'The best way to get time to hurry is to hurry up and keep busy.' You did a darned good job of keeping me hustling so I wasn't fussing about how many days I had left, so I guess we'll have to do the same for you. Crack of dawn tomorrow, and we're on the move."

"Wow, that's a plan in a hurry. You're right, Lena, the best thing I can do is get to work and figure that every time I put my head on the pillow is one less day to worry about. First thing tomorrow we'd better get around and do some fencing so we can turn out to summer pasture. Then we'll have first cutting of alfalfa to put up; and before you know it, it'll be the Fourth of July when we start haying the meadow. Maybe we'll see if we can have all the sloughs cut out and stacked by the end of July so we're ready to go to town and have a whee of a time." Shoving himself up tall, he dusted off his pants, hung up the leather strap, and took three big strides toward the horse stalls. Suddenly he turned and said, "Well, what're you waiting for? We've got lots of work to do."

With that, Darlene scooted up to him and the two of them fell into step as they gathered up the pails and halters. "I'll catch Cheyenne and Boxer while you get the cows ready. Sometimes I think these old milk cows own us. We can't ever be gone because they need milked morning and night. Do you ever get tired of this and want to go do something else? If you moved to town and did leather work or blacksmith work, you'd have lots of business and still be able to do what you wanted."

"You know something, Lena? The good thing is that I'm doing exactly what I want to right here. You're right about the chores getting tiresome, but the cream and eggs help pay the bills. Besides, if I started doing leather work as a business, I'd lose it as a something to do to relax. I'll leave the leaving to you, and I'll stay here to wait for you to come back and report on your adventures. That way we'll both be right where we're the happiest."

Darlene stopped dead in her tracks. "Don't you remember, Theo? I'm staying here with you forever. We're a good team and I don't want to be anywhere else. This ranch is good enough for me."

Loosely draping his arm over her shoulder, Ted patted his sister before answering. "You know, Lena, we do make a great team. The biggest difference between us is that I'm here because I decided long ago that ranching is what I want to do. You're here because you haven't had the time to check out other things to do. For the time being, nothing is going to split us up; and right now we don't have to deal with anything more serious than these empty milk pails and bawling bucket calves. Lead the way, my fine milkmaid."

Throughout the summer, the family members followed the rhythm of the seasons. Cattle work took up early June; and one day after moving pairs to summer range, Ted went to pick up the mail. Pleased with the way the cattle and horses had worked, as well as with the increase in the cow herd, Ted was deep in thought as he drove up in front of the post office. As he untangled his legs and crawled out, he looked up to see Ben leaning on the doorjamb with a knowing smirk.

"Funny thing about being in charge of the mail. It seems like I'm often in the know before anyone else. A fancy envelope came for you, and from the looks of it, I'd guess it's not a bill. I thought you'd be hotfooting it over here to pick up the mail. In all the time I've been postmaster here, this is the first personal letter I remember coming to you. Could it be you have a secret admirer, or could it be you're embarrassed to say who's chasing you? Oh, yeah, I had a nice chat the other day with your brother Fred about some fine visitors at your ranch, and he said you put on quite a show. Did I hear it about right?"

Ted climbed the steps, put his hand on the rail at the top, and squared up his shoulders in front of the postmaster. "You know, Ben, there's a whole lot of conversation wrapped up in those words of yours, and it's hard for me to know where to start. As postmaster, you're sure enough in a perfect place to snoop into everyone's business, and as a storekeep, you're sure enough in a perfect place to broadcast whatever stories you can make up. It doesn't surprise me that you take pleasure in being the biggest gossip in the county, but it kinda does surprise me you'd be so bold as to say anything to my face. That's definitely not your usual way."

Red-faced and blustering, Ben bristled up and sneered at Ted, "What're you getting at, Soehl? If you have anything to say to me, spit it right out." Noticing Ted's silence and thinking he was cowed by his presence, Ben charged on, "You swagger around like you think you're too good for everyone else, and that little school marm comes in, wiggles in your direction, and you make a total fool of yourself. Next thing we know, you'll be going to school every day to try to teach her a thing or two. Guess as school board member, I'd better be there in case she needs some one to turn to when she's tired of some seedy rancher. Too bad, but I guess that's just a part of my civic duty."

"Is beating your wife and kid what 'civic duty' means to you? Or does 'civic duty' mean forcing your attention on any female unlucky enough to be in the vicinity? I might not have gone off to school for any high-falutin' lessons, but what I did learn at home is to respect ladies and to work for a living. From what I hear, you're pretty fierce when it comes to scaring kids and women, but I never did hear anyone accuse you of mixing it up with a man. This might just be the chance you've been waiting for. I have one thing to say to you, and I hope I make myself clear. If I ever hear of you speaking disrespectfully of Miss Edgars or forcing any kind of attentions on her or any other lady, it won't be up to you to decide if you want to mix it up with me. You might start it but I guarantee you, I'll be the one to finish it. Understood?"

Looking around and realizing no one would rescue him this time, Ben began to babble. "What's the deal with you, Ted? I was just joshing with you. No need for you to have such a thin hide. It seems like you don't understand that it's just my way to make conversation. I certainly didn't mean anything by it, and it don't sound neighborly when you take off talking about wanting to 'mix it up' with me. I don't think I ever made any threats against you, so why would you talk like that?"

Ted gave a sardonic smile as he let Ben string together a series of denials and apologies before speaking. "I guess I'd just find it unfortunate for you if some customer took exception to your talking and decided to make it hard for that jaw of yours to keep flapping. It might be a good practice for you to cut back on the idle conversation and keep your vile imagination under control—just so there's no misunderstanding, don't you know?" After delivering his veiled warning, Ted motioned Ben into the post office. "Now, if it's not too much bother, how about handing over the ranch mail so I can be on my way."

Ben knew when he'd been bested, and he wordlessly handed over the mail, fancy envelope and all. As Ted was on his way out the door, he heard Ben slam the door into his living quarters behind the post office, and wasn't surprised when Robert came bursting out. Surprised that anyone was present, Robert stopped and tried to nonchalantly walk to the door. "I'm tired of being cooped up in the house today so I think I'll go climb around in the hills. It's lots nicer there."

"Sometimes it feels good to get away and have a little time to yourself, doesn't it?" Ted spoke sympathetically to the young boy who had traces of tears on his face and a wariness in his eyes.

"You've got that right. Hanging out in the hills may be a little lonely, but at least no one can bother you out there. See you later, Mr. Soehl." With that, Robert hurried down the stairs and followed the trail that led to the hills behind.

When he started the car, Ted took the time to glance at the letter which had started the entire incident. He recognized the writing from Darlene's report cards, and he put the car in gear and drove out of the yard without taking the time to open it. No way would he give Ben the satisfaction of knowing how much the letter meant to him, so he traveled until he was around the bend and secure from any prying eyes. Then he braked the car and slid his index finger along the closure. Inside he found two fine sheets of vellum covered with the most breath-taking script he had ever seen.

Dear Theo,

I'm hoping this letter finds you well. We had an uneventful trip home, other than the large bull that claimed his territory by making his stand right in the middle of the road. Neither honking nor shouting could convince him to relinquish his position, so finally Amy and I climbed out of the vehicle, being certain to remain beside it at all times. Finally, we decided to ignore him and talk over the outstanding day which we spent with your family. To all appearances, Mr. Bull had every intention of remaining planted where he was, and we were not going to chance an encounter with him out on the prairie. It wasn't until we came to the part about the birthday dinner that we hit upon an effective tactic. We burst into the 'Happy Birthday' song, and it was as if he could not stand our particular brand of culture.

Without a backward glance, he lumbered off to the west. When he was far enough away, I started the engine and put it into gear. With a final swish of his tail, he disappeared down a hill and we motored on home. As you can imagine, Amy and I found it quite amusing that he was so distressed by our singing, but were very relieved that we could resume our journey.

Our time together was brief, but every day I relive each moment, recall each word, and remember the joy of our embraces. I also have moments when I laugh aloud considering the humorous moments with the girls and their antics.

I do have to say, Mr. Soehl, that all the times they startled us were nothing compared to how unprepared I was for your farewell gesture. Never have I been so surprised in my life! If I close my eyes, I can feel the power of your embrace and the boldness with which you declared our relationship to the world. Although I know a respectable woman should be mortified at the public display, I have to confess that I truly cherished every moment.

Do you think that makes me sound like a frightful and forward woman? I do hope not. I hope you think it makes me sound like a caring and fortunate woman who has found her soul mate, for that is how I feel.

Yes, my dear, I do remember how you stated your reluctance about our correspondence, but I feel so full of emotions that I must share them with someone. So that is why you are receiving this letter although we agreed that letter writing was not what we planned to do. My feelings are so private and so delicious that I can feel closer to you by putting these words on paper. The words are not big enough to capture my swelling heart, but they must do until July 28.

Even if you do not care to decipher my words, perhaps you can be content to hold this letter in your hands in the same way that you also hold my heart.

I am planning our feast, deciding what to wear, and generally finding various ways to make the days pass faster. Please know I am taking good care of your heart, just as your mother would have wanted.

With sincere affection,
Beth

Deciphering the words, as Beth put it, took Ted a great deal of effort, but the thought of leaving one precious syllable unscanned was not an option he considered. Stumbling over the longer words and savoring the shorter ones took the better part of an hour, and when he finished, he leaned back and closed his eyes. Not a man inclined to impetuous decisions, he had spent each day pondering his future. In spite of her statements about how much she loved the ranch, he knew isolation and loneliness could wreak havoc on relationships that might have survived in other locations.

Those who felt trapped tended to lash out, and the immediately available victims were family members. His brother was a perfect example. Fred's true interests lay in mechanical devices; and the only time he appeared content was when he was surrounded by people, not ordinarily the case on the ranch. The sense of obligation to finish what their parents had started produced completely opposite responses on the part of the brothers. Fred truly preferred the action and large numbers of people to be found in town. Because he needed the approval of others, he was too insecure to cut his ties to the ranch for what people would think if he walked away from a large spread. Instead of fulfilling his dreams, he stayed on the ranch and cursed everything and everyone with whom he had contact.

Ted, on the other hand, could not imagine a lifestyle better suited to his interests. His greatest satisfaction came from the very elements which frustrated Fred—spending his days in solitude working with horses and cattle. During Ted's leisure time, he contemplated how he could enhance breeding programs and increase the ranch's income. He was concerned that Beth's limited exposure to ranch life did not equip her to make an informed decision, so he concentrated on how he could present the somewhat harsh reality to her so she would not resent his bringing her into a situation for which she was not prepared.

Now that he had her declaration in his hand, he was certain of his course of action. With all the openness of his nature, he would set out the benefits and drawbacks and wait for her answer. As she deliberated, he would be fervently praying for the right outcome. If she wanted to be with him forever, that would be the best news he could ever hope to hear. If she wanted to live in the city, that would be bitter news but better to know it early rather than late. The arrival of her letter was a well-timed event that cemented his decision. He would write a letter.

Dear Beth,

I am well. I like your letter and carry it with me always. Thanks. I want to talk to you about what we do next. If you feel ranch life is good, maybe we can make plans. If you don't want ranch life, I'll be sorry but know we will both go on. Days go slow and I miss you.

Theodor Soehl

Writing the letter made him sweat. He didn't want Beth to think badly of him, but he did want to communicate with her. When he had finished writing at the kitchen table late in the evening, Emma looked up from her tatting. "Em, do you have to go to town for supplies anytime soon?"

"Actually, I do. I need some flour and some new material for Darlene's school dresses. Why, do you need me to pick up something?" She stood behind his chair and rubbed his shoulders.

"If you have an envelope around here, I just finished a letter that I'd like mailed in town. If you don't mind, I'd sure appreciate it." By this time, Ted had folded the page and held it out to his sister.

Ted had not told anyone about the scene with Ben, other than growling to Fred about his choice of friends. Even though he said not a word, Emma and Darlene had noticed the letter which he started to keep in his shirt pocket. They also were aware that Ted made sure to be too busy when it was time to go to the country post office and let Fred be the one who traveled in that direction.

"Theo, I have an envelope right here, and I'd be glad to address it for you if you'd like. I'm guessing it goes to Beth because I don't know of another soul in the world who could make you put words on paper. I'll go in tomorrow and she'll have it inside of a week." Emma eased the page into the envelope and sealed it before addressing it to Beth.

Grateful for no questions on her part and relieved that his words would soon be on the way, he motioned to a chair. "Em, how about helping me sort out some of what's spinning in my head? I need someone to help me think."

Emma let out her characteristic snort, and plopped down beside him, "I'm always glad to talk, Ted, you know that. As for the helping you to think, I've not seen many times you needed much help in that direction. You look a bit frazzled, so let's do have a bit of a confab."

Reaching out to pat her arm, he softly shook his head from side, "Emma, everyone knows you're one of the most important reasons we've been able to make this work without the folks. When Mother died, you stepped right up and gave us a mighty nice home. I feel bad about your having to give up your plans to go back East and work, but you've never let out a peep about your disappointment."

Emma nodded her head and smiled, "You know, Theo, it did look like I was going out in the wide world to make my way, but there's not a force on earth that could have made me go once things turned out bad for Mama. Sure as the world, once you make a plan, you'd better look over your shoulder and over your head and over the next hill 'cause there's usually some spoiling in the works. I'm okay with this for now, and maybe later on will bring a different chance." Looking directly into her brother's eyes, she assumed control of the conversation. "But, Ted, I don't think this is about me. I'm thinking it's maybe about how your world has changed this summer. Am I right?"

Ted chuckled, "Now see, Em, that's what I'm talking about. You know what's going on and cut right to the heart of it. Yeah, nothing is the same as it was a few weeks ago, and I'm grateful for that. But now I need to figure out what to do next. If Beth will have me, I've made up my mind to ask her to marry me. Now I know it's quick and we haven't spent much time together, but I firmly believe this is what I want. On the off-hand chance she'd say 'Yes' to me, then I'd have some serious planning to take care of. Where would we live? Would she be able to stay out here where it sometimes gets mighty lonely? Is it right to Lena to throw her world into another spin so soon after Mama's passing? Is it right to Beth to ask her to take on a nine-year-old girl when she's first married? I can't imagine a life without Beth or Darlene or you, but that's a whole lot of females to put into one household." Resting his head on his hands, Ted let out a huge sigh before looking up. "That's what I've got spinning in my head."

Emma took one of his hands and nodded, "Ted, I've seen this coming, and I understand why you are so up in the air. I guess I'd just have to say this. First of all, you're borrowing a whole bunch of trouble because you're trying to sort out all this before you even have talked to Beth about it. From what I saw of the two of you together, I'd guess she's puzzling out these exact same questions. What you need is an unraveling of this when you're both in town. Now, I'll tell you where I fit in. You're right, I did have some plans for going to York to work. Even though I'm glad I could help out, I'm ready to try my hand at something else so long as I know you and Lena are settled in. Your Beth has a good heart and knows you and Darlene are a package deal. So far it hasn't made her back away, so it looks like she is good with that. So far as where you'd live, I'd think right here where you've always lived. It's your home and that's where a husband usually takes his new wife. You bet I'll mail this envelope, and I'm probably just about as nervous and excited as you are. Guess we'll have to wait and see."

Ted hugged his sister before he replied, "I know I can't make any plans until Beth and I talk, but I still mull it over in my head. Neither of us is a kid, so when we make up our minds, I don't see we'd need to wait a long time. So then does that mean we could get married right away or does it mean we'd have to wait for school to be out? It's not fair to go ahead with this until you've figured out your next move, but you might not want to move if Beth turns me down. This makes my head hurt."

"Okay, Theo, I might as well level with you. I've been doing the same kind of looking ahead and trying to find the best way for all of us. You know we own that little house in town where the kids have stayed when it's time for high school. I'd probably move there and get a job helping Tracy Dolph at the store. She's often said it's hard to find anyone willing to work, and that would give you and Beth some privacy and me some time to check out where I want to go next. We just need the end of July to hurry up and get here, so you can bet I'll see this gets to Beth so she knows you're still thinking of her." Emma tucked the letter into her purse and went on, "Maybe you can help me load the eggs and cream early in the morning so I can make good time. I've still got lots to do around here, but I think a run to town is the first order of the day."

"Thanks, Sis. You're so much like Mom in so many ways. I do appreciate you even if I might not mention it very often," Ted squeezed Emma's arm as they both turned towards their bedrooms.

Haying took up most of July, and it felt as if the final week of the month had taken its time arriving. "Ted, do you know what today is? It's the day before our big day. We need to figure out our plans for tomorrow." Coming back in after finishing the milking, Darlene had gone to the calendar where she had marked off each day after her birthday, and she turned around triumphantly to face Emma and Ted, "Wow! We're finally about to get to have some fun. Can we get some stuff done today so we can head out bright and early tomorrow?"

Ted had a solemn expression as he shook his head, "That really sounds like a good plan, but we might have some problems getting away from here very early. Any other time of the summer, we'd have had wind that blew a gale about every day. Now that we have something to do, we're right smack in the calmest summer I've ever seen. If the wind doesn't blow today and fill some tanks, tomorrow I'm going to have to move those pairs from the Harris section to the north where that stock dam still has a little bit of water in it."

"Okay, Ted, let's just do it today and have it taken care of. Wouldn't that work?" Darlene was quick to see the advantages of moving the cattle quickly so nothing interfered with their summer-long plans.

"Sounds good, but we've got to check the other pastures today to be sure nothing goes wrong there. With it this hot, we don't dare take a chance that they'll be okay. I thought we'd take a big circle and look at all the cattle today, and then move the others early in the morning when it's cool. I don't dare risk cattle being without water in this terrible heat. What we need is a good rain to take the pressure off all of us." Ted stood up and moved toward the door, "If we get a good start now, maybe we can be back before it gets so burning hot this afternoon."

Darlene reached the door before her brother, and she called back over her shoulder, “I’ll catch the horses and saddle them while you feed the bucket calves.” She was hardly out the door before she let out her ear-piercing whistle.

“If nothing else happened this summer, she sure enough learned how to make a sound that could wake the dead,” Emma stood at the kitchen window and traced Darlene’s progress to the barn. “Mama would be proud of how she’s turned out, and I know she’d pat you on the back and say, ‘My big boy helping my little girl. You have the kind heart like Papa did.’”

Ted paused at the window and rested his hand on Emma’s shoulder, “It’s nice to see her so happy, isn’t it? We’re lucky things have worked out this way, aren’t we?”

“Well, I don’t know that it’s all blind, dumb luck. Could be that you’ve had a hand in making things turn out like they have. Glad we’ve muddled along so far without any major problems. It could have been a lot worse than this.” Emma turned to the sink to finish drying the breakfast dishes. “You’d better quit thinking and get to moving before I put a dish towel in your hands and put you to work in here.”

Ted stuck his hat on his head and quickly made his exit, “Love to help out, Sis, but looks like Lena has my horse caught. I’d better be ready when she is or I’ll never hear the end of it. She’s so excited about tomorrow that she’s pushing pretty hard to get our work done today. I’d bet she doesn’t sleep a wink tonight.”

“Theo, do you know anyone else who’s a-tingle about tomorrow? Seems like she might not be the only one on pins and needles.” Emma wasn’t about to let him act all calm and collected when she had seen how antsy he had been for the past few days.

“Too many women spying on a good hard-working man;

that's all I have to say. Don't look for us back by noon. We've got a bunch of miles to cover, and it's too hot to hurry. Be back as soon as we can."

When Darlene and Ted were mounted on their horses, Emma appeared at the barn door with a bulging sack. "Thought you might get a little hungry before you get back, so I wrapped up a couple of buns and apples. Not enough for a real meal, but could keep your stomach from scraping your backbone before you get back."

Ted took the sack and tied it behind his saddle, "Em, this makes what was going to be a good day into a glorious one. Good horses, good company, and good food. What could possibly be missing?"

"Thanks, Emma. I'm the luckiest girl in the world—two good days in a row. See you later."

With that, Cheyenne and Boxer found themselves pointed south on what would be a long but uneventful trek. Ted was relieved that each pasture had enough water in the tanks or dams to keep the cattle watered for a couple of days at least, and Darlene was thrilled that no ranch emergency would prevent their taking in the celebration.

"What time do we need to get up in the morning to move those cattle, Theo? It gets light about 5:30 and takes about an hour to get all the way there. I hope those critters know we've got something better to do than to wait for them to mother up and get their calves on the move. Too bad they're in such a big pasture. It seems to take forever to round up the whole section." Back at the barn, Darlene was still busy making plans for the next day, and they certainly didn't include patiently waiting in a pasture.

"Honey, I've been mulling this over, and this is what I think we need to do. If you'll stay home and do all the barn chores, Boxer and I'll take out at the crack of dawn and move the cattle. That way, you girls can clean up, pack the lunch, and get to town in good time. When I get home, I'll clean up and throw my saddle on Cheyenne. He'll be fresh, and he's been to town enough times that the crowd and the noise won't bother him. I'll be there just as soon as I can; but this way, Beth won't have to worry like she would if we're all late. Does that make sense to you?"

Darlene glanced out of the corner of her eye to see if he were making fun of her impatience, "Theo, that doesn't seem right for us to leave you home without any help. I know how long it takes to ride that pasture, and it's darned sure nicer with two than with just one. How about if we both go and then we can get it done that much faster so we can meet Emma and Beth in town?"

"I sure do appreciate your offer, Lena, but there's just one problem with it. If we both ride, then we don't have any fresh horses to ride to town. Those cows are hanging around the tank the way it is, so they won't be scattered all over the pasture. They'll work really easy and I'll be there for sure by dinnertime. Just be sure to save me a plate and a place, okay?"

Reluctantly, Darlene nodded, "You're not just saying that so I'll go on ahead, are you? 'Cause if you are, I don't want to leave you behind. Tell me the truth, Theo."

"I've thought it through and this is the best way for all of us, I promise. If I needed help, you know I'd ask you. We're the best pair ever for getting things done, and by you doing the chores at home and me doing the work away from home, we can all have some fun. Shake on it?" Ted and Darlene solemnly shook hands and started toward the house. "Hold it. If we want Em to send us lunch again, we'd better return her flour sack. She's kinda partial to her belongings." Ted untied the empty sack and tossed it over his shoulder. "Do you suppose she has anything left for a pair of cowpunchers coming in off the range?"

"Here, I can check for us." With that, Darlene let out her now famous whistle and waited. "Bet that gets her attention."

The door opened and Emma peeked around the corner, "It's not like I have to wonder who's there when I hear that sound, is it? You two made good time, and the rolls aren't even cold yet. Grab a seat, and I'll fill your plates so you can fill your bellies. You must be ravenous."

"Not really, Emma. That lunch staved off starvation and saved us so we can dig in. It didn't take long for us to put it to good use, so it's been a while since we ate but we're not desperate."

As they sat down to a meal of cold roast beef and warm cinnamon rolls, Ted and Darlene shared their decision as to how the next morning would go. "Emma, I know you haven't had the time to help with the milking, what with your cooking for us all, but we were wondering if you'd be able to help me with the barn chores while Ted leaves early to get the cattle juggled around. Then you and I will pack everything in the car, and Ted will ride Cheyenne to town as soon as he gets home. How about it? Does that sound all right?"

"All but the part where he rides into town as soon as he gets home. I think it might be in his best interest if he'd make a stop at the bathtub before he joins us. Beth might be a little hesitant about dancing with some sticky, smelly guy fresh off the range." With that, Emma and Darlene glided together as if they were dancing, then Darlene stopped and pinched her nose as if she had caught a whiff of something very unpleasant.

"Oh, I do declare," Darlene uttered with a high tone, "whatever could that most foul odor be? I must find some fresh air." She and Emma collapsed into the closest chair and laughed until tears rolled down their faces.

Ted stood patiently until they had recovered a degree of

calmness, and smiled at them both, "You know, I've heard there are men in this world who do not have the advantage of a sister to look after them. I am truly charmed that I have not only one, but two, caring sisters who will let me know the best way to succeed in the feminine world. Yes, ladies, I will be visiting the soapsuds before I join you in town. Do you, by chance, have any other last minute instructions for this old country boy?"

By this time, Darlene had slipped under his arm where she gave him a huge squeeze, "Theo, I think Beth's lucky to have you, stinky or not." With that, she whirled away and gave him a mischievous grin. "You've never embarrassed me yet when you've been in town, so I'm not nervous this time, especially since you're going to meet your special girl. Isn't this the most exciting thing ever?"

"No doubt about it, Lena, this is exciting. Now we'd all better get organized so we can get out of here in the morning. I think we can double hay the calves tonight so we just need to milk and separate. Do we need to carry anything to the car so we have it tomorrow, Em? Could I help with blankets or coats or anything?"

Darlene broke into peals of laughter, "Theo, why would we take coats to town when all we want to do is wear the lightest clothes we own? It is so hot the birds take turns fanning each other, and you want us to drag out our coats? Why in the world did you say that?"

Ted smiled at his little sister, and then exchanged a knowing glance with his big sister, "Right now, it's kind of hard to imagine needing a coat, but things change so fast that it never hurts to have one tucked in the car. I've found it's easier to drag along an extra jacket than to wish I had the one I left at home. It's the same reason Em shuts the windows whenever she leaves home even though we haven't had any rain since right after your birthday. I guess she'd rather come home to a stuffy house than to a wet one. Suit yourself, but I plan to stash a coat in the car tomorrow morning on my way to move cattle."

Darlene skipped to the coat hooks and grabbed a coat for herself, Ted, and Emma. "How about if I take care of this for everyone? They'll be right here by the door so we can load them with everything else."

"That's a wonderful start, Darlene, and we might as well gather everything we need in a pile so we're sure not to forget anything. Let's start by packing our picnic basket so we can eat. I'd hate to miss out on that." Emma pointed to the entryway where she had hung curtains to conceal the storage area behind them, "Ted, if you'd want to get the basket from back there, Darlene and I'll start loading the enamel plates and cups. We'll need silverware, too, and this would be a good time to grab that. Let's put in enough for Beth and her crew, even though she'll probably have plenty with her. I never want to come up short when it concerns food business."

Ted looked over his shoulder and snorted, "Emma, the day you come up short in the food department will be the day. No matter how many sit at your table, it's like you're cooking for a threshing crew. I don't think I'll get nervous any time soon about food with you around." Lifting the basket from behind the curtain, he eased it down in front of the cupboards so the girls could get to work.

"I'll be out as soon as we get this all together, and maybe we can do the chores early tonight so we can get to bed early. I want to be ready to see the sights and have some fun." Darlene was handing plates and cups to Emma while making her plans. "One thing puzzles me, though, and I haven't been able to figure it out on my own."

Emma, never one to leave a question hanging, spoke up, "Well, honey, you've got two of the strongest minds on the ranch standing here with you, so why don't you quiz us to see if we know straight up." Laughing at her own joke, she straightened up to face Darlene.

"What I don't get is why the three of us are the only ones responsible for getting everything done before we can leave the ranch. Why can't Fred do something around here? The only time I ever see him is when he's tinkering with the tractor or when it's time to run to town on some errand. Otherwise, he's pretty much missing in action while we do all the work and he hangs out with his buddies that're always at his house. Is that right?"

Immediately, the kitchen was transformed from a chattering scene of laughter and comradeship to one of awkward silence. The situation as described by Darlene was totally accurate and one which had been discussed in depth by the older siblings. Ted worked hard at not making nasty comments about his brother and wife who lived in the little house around the curve but who didn't participate in any of the real everyday ranch work. The two brothers had no common ground on which to meet, so the easiest course of action seemed to be total avoidance of each other. Ted made sure the work was done, and Fred made sure to collect money anytime crops or cattle were sold. Otherwise, he was, as Darlene described him, the invisible brother.

"I guess the easiest way to explain our dealings is that we agreed to disagree. Fred is so filled with bitterness that I'd rather do everything than ask him to help out. It would be nice if we could work together like we did when Mama was still here, but she was the one who kept us all under control. I admit I get feisty when he gets cocky, so there's probably enough blame to go around. We've gotten everything done without him, so I guess I'd rather work longer and harder than beg him to do what he knows he should be doing. It doesn't make me proud to admit that I'm as stubborn as he is, but that's the lay of the land." Ted had spent hours contemplating how to make things work, so he was able to deliver his honest appraisal without asking Darlene to take sides. "He's still your brother, and Mama wouldn't like it if we were hateful to him even if he's not pulling his own weight. She made it look easy to keep him on track, but he darned sure won't take any suggestions from me, so I just leave him alone. I figure he's got to know what's right even if he takes the easy way out."

"That's a good enough answer for me. He'd probably get in the way if he came along with us. Remember the time we were branding and he jumped in the middle of the sorting crew? He was so busy shouting instructions to all the neighbors that he never even saw that old Hereford bull heading for him. I'll never forget the look on his face when he finally turned around and was face to face with him right before the bull ran the whole length of him." Darlene had been sure to report the wreck to Emma when she came back from the branding corral.

Ted looked at Emma as he embellished the story, "There's more to it, you know. He didn't take it kindly when Trader Keith helped him up and said, 'Now that's what I call being on the horns of a dilemma.' Fred couldn't blow up at anyone since it was his own darned fault, but he was hot. He acted like he was counting how many calves we had left to brand and came up missing shortly after that. He didn't show up until we all came in for dinner. A few of the guys ribbed him about needing a longer sorting stick, but they could see he was in no mood to laugh. I think that was the last time the cows had the pleasure of his company."

"I say we're getting along fine the way it is, so let's shake a leg and get ready for tomorrow," Emma gently shoved Darlene out the door. "You go on along and help outside. I've got everything about done here so you can go make yourself useful with Theo. Most people polish and shine their vehicles, but he's so hung up on that horse of his that he'll probably spend half the night brushing him and polishing all his riding stuff."

"Hold it, Em. Don't forget Cheyenne's my horse now, and Ted's borrowing him just for the day, but you're right about how particular he is. Too bad he doesn't sit around the house and clean like he does in the barn. That'd make our job lots easier, wouldn't it?" Darlene stopped at the door and laughed, "Can you see him wearing an apron and running a feather duster? That'd be a sight to behold."

Emma chuckled and shooed the two of them out of her domain and watched as they scuffled and shoved all the way to the barn.

With the dawn came three people bustling around the ranch, intent on their assigned tasks. When Darlene had come into the kitchen, Ted and Emma were already on their last cup of coffee and pushing back from the table. Ted signaled his little sister to take her usual perch on his lap, and she stifled a yawn as she snuggled into his shoulder. "You know what, Little One, you'd better slow down so you don't outgrow your spot. Look how long your legs are by now. Pretty soon you'll be looking me in the eye."

Darlene gave a sleepy smile and burrowed in a bit deeper, "Sure seems like morning came awful quick. It feels like I just barely crawled in bed and here we are again."

"Lena, maybe you should try sleeping faster next time. Then you'd be rearing to go sooner than the rest of us." Ted jiggled his sister who sat up and gave him a quizzical look before breaking into a giggle. "Why don't you go on back to bed; and when you're done being Sleeping Beauty, we'll decide what we want to do today? Seem fair enough?" He was alert to the change in her posture; but even so, the sudden transformation to an upright and wide-eyed young lady took him by surprise.

"Theo Soehl, how can you joke about such a serious day? I don't know why we're sitting in the house when we have business to take care of." By now she had pulled on her trousers and blouse and slipped into her shoes. "It's a good thing I've got a good horse I'm willing to loan to you, otherwise I don't know if you'd have a chance of joining us later." She hit the door at the same time as her brother, and they struggled to see which one could get out first. Darlene wriggled her hips one last time and shot through. "I may be a slow sleeper, Theo, but it looks like I'm ahead of you." With that they both took off for the barn at a high run.

Ted slowed his pace so the pair arrived at the door at the same time. "Give me a quick hug, Lena, and I'm off to the wide open spaces. The next time I see you, you'll be all decked out and I'll be slicked up, and the whole world will wonder at the Soehl kids, I promise you that."

Darlene was in high gear by now, and by the time Boxer was saddled, the first cow was in the stanchion and half milked.

Emma called to Darlene as she strolled in from the house, "You got my milk stool in there or do I need to find one? You've been taking my place for so long out here that I kinda lost track of where we keep things."

"I laid one by the wall so you can find it easy. The next thing I know, you'll be telling me you lost track of how to milk a cow." Darlene's good nature emerged in the midst of the work as she joked with Emma. "If that's the problem, I give good lessons and I'd be willing to let you have the extra cow so you can have a bit more practice."

"Honey, please don't put yourself out to be so good to me. You're about to smother me in kindness." Emma put the kickers on the heifer, settled on the stool, and clamped the pail between her knees. "The one thing I've learned is that you never forget how to milk a cow. No matter where you may go or what you may do, it comes back the minute you slide under her belly. Oh, yeah, how she slaps with her tail never changes, either." Emma had established her milking rhythm and soon had a head of foam in her bucket. "Race you to see who gets a full pail first."

With that, the contest was on. Although Darlene had gotten a head start, Emma wasn't as far out of practice as she had made it sound. Just as they both finished, Emma's heifer gave a big jump and knocked the pail out of Emma's legs. Although the pail landed right side up, it sloshed onto the inside of both of Emma's legs. "Save some for the calves, Em. They'll be sorry if they have to go hungry this morning."

Darlene had hurried over to her sister to take the pail as Emma stood up and shuddered, "Yuck. Nothing stickier in the world than this nasty milk. Let's hurry up and get this done so I can crawl in the tub and find some clean duds. How many more do we have?"

"Em, let me finish. We've only got two more since those others went dry last week, and they're easy milkers. You go on ahead, get cleaned up, and start loading our stuff. I'll be there before you know it." Darlene was already half through with her next cow. "You did that young heifer I'm kind of scared of, so the rest of this is plumb easy. You go on and maybe you can have the tub ready for me by the time I'm done here."

Emma saw that her sister had the barn chores under control, so she replaced the milk stool in the wall brace, and trudged to the door. "Honey, for this, I'll buy you a candy bar when we get to town. You're a sweetie. I'll have everything done in the house so as soon as you're ready, we're out of here."

True to her habits, Darlene was finicky with the balance

of the chores. On her way to the calf pen, she took a moment to fill the cat dish. "Dig in, fellas. I squeezed this with my own delicate hands just for you." This time she was focused on doing the chores as quickly as possible, but she did take the time to pick up Jitney and Johnny. "Just wondering if you guys had your motors running this early in the morning, and it sounds like you do." Moving her face from one kitten to the other, she rubbed her nose against the soft fur and gently squatted down to give them a place at their breakfast table. "Eat up so you can grow up. That's what good little kitties do."

Picking up the full pails, Darlene made her way to the shed. Picking up the buckets hanging inside, she found the measuring can on its hook inside. Pouring the right amount into each pail, she stepped into the pen and separated two calves to start out. When those were done, it was time to get ready for the next pair. She fed each of the bucket calves, even though they butted and shoved while they sucked each other's ears. "You guys, what's the deal with you? Can't you wait your turn?"

Then she laughed as she kicked away the one that had latched on to the end of her shirt. "Charlie, you're so greedy I think you'd drink plain old water if that's what I put in your bucket. Take it easy, Dusty, there's more where that came from." As each calf finished, she shoved him into the next pen where the grain in the pan was waiting. It kept them away from the gate so she could move the next bunch when they finished drinking. "That's it for now. We gave you extra hay last night, and Ted told me we'd probably skip the evening chores since we'd be getting home late tonight. Bet you'll have a huge appetite by the next time I see you."

Darlene held the milk pails to catch the fresh water pumped by the windmill beside the barn. Swishing the water around the edge, she had them slicked up in no time and hung upside down on posts to stay clean for the next time. Taking one last look at all the gates to see they were securely latched, she closed the barn door and took off at her fastest for the house. Leaping up the steps two at a time, she grabbed for the door as Emma jerked it open from inside. The two sisters collided, hugged each other, and moved aside so one could spring inside and the other could continue carrying supplies to the car parked beside the gate.

Darlene shed her clothes on a path through the house, starting with shoes and socks at the door, shirt draped over the corner of a kitchen chair, and pants on the doorknob of her bedroom. Grabbing the clothes she had laid out the night before, she made a beeline for the tub which Emma had ready for her. Not even taking the time to test the water with her toe, she plunged in, shampooed her hair, swished soap all over, rinsed her limbs, and stood straight up. Plucking the towel from the chair shoved beside the tub, she quickly rubbed it all over her arms and legs. Pulling her blouse over her head, she shook her hair forward and wrapped the towel around it. "At least that'll keep the biggest drips off me while I get everything else done. A lick and a promise is all I've got time for right now, so on go my skirt and shoes and I'm out of here. Oh, guess I'd better do something with all these tangles before I head out." Talking to herself as she completed each step, Darlene removed the soaked towel and brushed through her hair. "Ouch. I can't believe how tough this is. If I had straight hair like Amy, I could be done in no time. One thing I know is I'd rather do this than let Em have a shot at my head. She's ferocious when it comes to snarls."

While she was engrossed in preparations, Emma had stepped back in the kitchen. "Oh, really, Missy? I may be ferocious, but you always look pretty as a picture by the time I'm done." Moving over to where Darlene was struggling with the back section of hair, Emma eased the brush from her hand and took over. "Can you believe how long your hair is getting? How do you want this fixed today? Maybe we could pull the top back and let some curls fall around your shoulders. That way it'll be out of your eyes and still stay neat. Okay with you?"

"Em, whatever you can do the fastest is what I want today. I'm not arguing or complaining or wishing or whining. Let's just get it done and get the heck out of here." Darlene sat uncharacteristically still and never made a sound even when her sister found a particularly stubborn tangle. "That's okay. Just get it straightened out and do what you have to do. I promise I'll be the best customer you ever had."

Giving a quick pat to the top of Darlene's head after all the combing and twisting was done, Emma gave the go-ahead. "The only thing that's holding up this parade is you, my dear, so as soon as you get one leg in the car, we're gone." Seeing how quickly the small girl covered the distance from sitting in a chair to sitting in a car, Emma shook her head as she opened her own car door. "Guess I was wrong this time. The driver's the one holding up the parade, but that's behind us now." She started the engine, pulled it into gear, and eased onto the sand hill trail that led away from the ranch.

Looking backward, Darlene mused, "I hope those cows cooperated with Ted this morning so he doesn't miss any of the fun. Maybe I should have gone with him to be sure."

"Honey, it wouldn't make a lot of sense for you to have worn out his good town horse. Then it'd take even longer for him to get around. He'll be fine and join us sooner than you can imagine. Let's go make sure Beth doesn't turn around and go home because she thinks he stood her up. That'd really be a sad thing."

With that, the sisters drove out of the yard in a huge cloud of dust as Ted popped up on the horizon several miles away. He saluted as he said, "See you soon, girls" and urged Boxer into a fast trot on the way home.

Even though he was impatient to be in town for the day, Ted was glad for his long morning ride. It gave him uninterrupted time to plan his words once he was in town with Beth. It may have surprised an observer to see the lone man earnestly gesturing, talking softly, smiling at nothing in particular, and nodding his head emphatically. His private rehearsal always ended the same with Beth's throwing her arms around his neck and saying, "Yes, Ted, yes. Of course I'll marry you. How about as soon as my family can meet you?" It didn't matter whether he said "Beth, are you sure you want to marry me and live out here so far away from your family?" or if he said, "I'd be honored if you'd consent to be my wife," or "I don't have much to offer you in marriage but a home in the wide-open spaces and a snug little home." Regardless of what he said, she was exuberant in her acceptance. "That must be a good sign," he told himself as he stopped Boxer in front of the barn door.

He jerked the saddle off the sweaty horse and rubbed his forehead before he turned him out to pasture. "Won't be needing you for a day or two, old boy, so get out there and fill up on green grass. You've darned sure earned it today." With a spring in his step, he slid open the door and approached Cheyenne in the box stall. Darlene had taken the time to slip the halter on and brush him so his coat had an absolute sheen. She had also combed his foretop and tail so they were sleek enough to satisfy even Ted's particular eye. "You ready for a jaunt today? She's got you so slicked up that you could be a one-horse parade. Maybe Beth'll see how fine you are and beg to come live on the same ranch as you. Work your magic is all I can say to that."

Leading the shiny black horse to the hitching rail by the front door, Ted looped the reins and entered the house where he was greeted with a neatly folded pile of clothes and steam rising from the warm water on top of the cook stove. His black boots, with a shine so deep he could see himself, were standing on the floor beside the kitchen chair holding his freshly ironed shirt; and his good Stetson hat was brushed and hanging on the hat rack. "Girls, girls, girls. You'll spoil me yet."

Pulling off his right boot and then his left, he shucked out of his socks which he placed inside his boots. "Didn't even wear these long enough to get them dirty so might as well be ready for tomorrow." Ted was appreciative of all Emma's housework, but especially of her laundry duties, so he was careful not to make her any extra work. He carefully put his clothes in the entry way closet, hung his work hat on the wall rack, and undertook his cleansing routine.

"Aah, nothing like a good hot bath and a close shave to make a new man out of me," Ted mused as he examined his image in the mirror. "Don't hardly see how that woman could resist me, but there's no sure thing on this old earth. Surely Emma and Darlene have softened her up so she's rearing to see me. Cheyenne, you'd better be hitched up and ready to fly." With that, Ted tucked his shirt into his pants, tightened his belt, and heard the 'whump' of his heels as he pulled on his boots, "Nothing better than a boot that fits like a glove." Laughing at his own remark, he continued, "Better get a move on or I could be in deep trouble," as he closed the door behind him.

Swinging on his saddle without bothering to use a stirrup, Ted was soon a speck on the same horizon where his sisters had traveled a few hours earlier.

"Oh, I can't believe it! I've never seen so many people in my whole life. Who would have thought this little old place could get so big overnight? No matter where you look, there's not a lick of open space. Where did everyone come from?" Darlene's eyes were huge with wonder. "Emma, don't let go of my hand. How in the world would I ever find you again? This is kind of scary—in a kind of fun way. Does that make any sense?"

Emma chuckled at her sister's amazement, "Honey, you just have to remember how this place looks every other time we come to town. We parked our car on the north side of the square right across from Dolph's store. If we ever get separated, let's plan to go back to the car and wait until the other one comes to meet us. That way we shouldn't have any kind of misunderstanding. Is that a deal?"

"Deal, Em, but I can't imagine I'll ever let go," Darlene squeezed Emma's hand so hard that her palms soon became sticky and sweaty. "Well, maybe we could let go for a minute but be sure to walk really close." No sooner had the words come from her lips than she let out an ear piercing scream and took off at a high run. "Amy! Amy! Amy! Beth! Amy! Here we are, over here by the lemonade stand. Come over this way, hurrrry, please." Without a backward glance, she took off in a direct line through the huge crowd where she had glimpsed Amy's yellow and white sundress.

Stopping abruptly as she had lost sight of both the dress and her own sister, Darlene felt a momentary sense of panic. All of a sudden, she remembered Emma's words and, like magic, she relaxed and headed back for the car.

"Darlene! Darlene! Lena! Wait for me." Appearing out of the faceless throng, Amy grabbed her friend from behind. "Aren't you going to wait for me? Where are Emma and Ted? Are they lost?"

By this time, Beth had caught up with the two chums and heard Darlene's explanation, "Ted had to stay behind and move cattle so they'd have water, so he sent Em and me ahead. We're supposed to tell his sweetie-pie that he's burning up the road and hurrying to come see her. He was so nervous that she'd be mad that I don't think he slept a wink. Where is she, anyway? I need to let her know 'cause I promised Ted I'd tell her as soon as I saw her."

"I'm right here, Darlene, and I'm pleased your brother is so concerned about my peace of mind. We got here early and laid out our things so we have a nice place on the east side of the park. That way we won't be in the sun this afternoon, and we're close enough to the road that we can get out when we want to go home. Do you think Emma would want to drive the car over close to where we are?"

Emma had come up from the other direction and was quick to see the advantage of Beth's plan. "Sure enough, Beth. I'll go move it right now so we have everything together. I'd guess Lena already delivered Ted's message to you since she was so fidgety all the way to town I thought the trip would never end. Between the two of them, trust me, this has been a tough July to get through. If Darlene wasn't checking the calendar, Ted was deciding the best way to get the cattle situated so we could let the chores go for one day. I tell you I'm glad this day finally got here."

"I have to confess, Emma, Amy and I have been about the same way. We're so excited to be here, and now we'll have double reason to celebrate once Ted joins us." Impetuously, Beth hugged Emma and then recovered her composure. "We'll help you get your things out so we're all settled and then the girls can go out and explore. I told Amy that she's not to go anywhere alone, and I don't think there's much chance the two of them will split up, do you?"

Shaking her head, Emma answered, "No, Beth, I'd bet the hardest part of today is when we tell them they have to split up to go home. Maybe they'll be so tired after all the festivities that they crawl into the car and go right to sleep tonight. Probably don't need to worry about that till the time comes. Right?"

With everyone pitching in, their place was readied; and the girls were off to check out the sights. Different booths of all kinds had been set up where vendors were hawking their wares. Some had food, some had trinkets, and the bigger ones had the entertainment.

Reading the day's schedule, Darlene and Amy had decided which shows sounded like must-sees, and which ones sounded like should-sees. The must-sees offered various acts such as magical events, musical performances, and exotic adventures recounted by pirates and swashbucklers. Amy guessed that Beth would say, "Oh, girls, I do believe you should see the reenactment of Jonathan Edwards delivering his famous Sinners sermon" while Darlene's hunch was she would direct them to the Temperance piece of William Jennings Bryan. "Oh, dear, can you imagine we have a chance to hear such a famous man right here? You must go hear him."

As they fell giggling across each other's arms, they made a pact to be scarce if it looked as if the adults were about to hand out suggestions. A teary-eyed woman came out and wrote "Cancelled" across the Jennings session, then fixed her gaze on the girls. "You know, young ladies, this is a most tragic time for us all. We just received word that the illustrious Mr. Jennings was taken to his heavenly home two days ago. We are just devastated."

As quickly as it had started, the laughing fit subsided, and they were respectful and somber. "Oh, ma'm, we're sorry for your loss; that is, sorry for our loss; that is, we are truly sorry." With somber faces, they wended their way back through the crowd to deliver the sorrowful news to Beth. As they approached their base, they caught sight of her reclining on a quilt, apparently waiting for Ted's arrival before she went out exploring.

"Beth, you know what? That lady over there told us that

William Jennings Bryan died two days ago. Isn't it too bad he couldn't have spoken here before he died?" Amy realized that didn't sound right, so Darlene jumped in, "What we mean is that you've been so busy talking about him that we wanted to be the ones who told you about his death." Again, the girls were discomfited by how harsh their words sounded and tried once more. "We're mighty sorry to be the bearers of such tragical news, Beth," and both plopped down beside her.

She surprised them with her calm acceptance of the news, "Girls, I appreciate your thinking of me at a time like this. I had been informed of Mr. Jennings' death by the lady at the water bucket, so this is not a shock to me, although it is very upsetting." She hurriedly gathered her skirt and rolled over so she could modestly go to her knees on the way to standing upright, and the girls did the same. "Perhaps you could go see if they know who will substitute for him. Unfortunately it may mean an entertainer rather than an educator, I'd predict."

Darlene nodded her head and put her most serious countenance, "Yes, Ma'am, that would be unfortunate, indeed." She winked at Amy and continued, "We're on our way to find out right now. Come on, Amy. How about us checking out some of the other tents so we can let you know what else is going on? Would that be all right?"

"Yes, girls, that would be perfect. In the meantime, I'll start getting our picnic lunch ready. It's nearly noon and I'm about famished. How about you?" Beth began rustling around in her basket as she spoke.

In unison, the girls gave their enthusiastic response, "Yes, ma'am! Let's eat." Darlene continued, "You know, I couldn't even think about breakfast so early this morning, and now I'm absolutely starved. I might eat it all before anyone else even gets a chance at it."

Beth smiled as she hugged her, "This day's been a long time coming, hasn't it? I think we're all pretty keyed up and relieved that it's here so we have an entire day to spend together. You girls run along, and I'll have everything ready so we can eat as soon as Ted makes his appearance."

"And we all hope that is very, very soon. Right, Miss Edgars?" Darlene nudged Beth with her elbow and scampered out of her reach. "He'll be here quick 'cause I loaned him the best horse on the place. Old Cheyenne and Theo will come blazing in here sooner than you can imagine, and I bet he'll have a powerful hunger too. He was gone before daybreak, and it's a good thing he knew where he was going with it being so dark and all."

"Well, I guess I'd better have something to feed an entire starving family, so you run along and I'll take care of this end. You might want to ask Emma if she needs any help with her basket. Tell her I'll be glad to pitch in if she wants me to." By this time, Beth had placed all her containers on the table cloth which she had spread under the tree and was moving the basket back out of the way.

"We're off to see what adventures we can find, and we'll report back as soon as we know something you need to know." No sooner had Amy finished than the girls grabbed hands and sped off seeking excitement and information.

As they made their way into the throng, they slowed down to look at each of the activities. Artists had posted signs offering to do five-minute pen and ink sketches for a nickel, and both girls agreed that would be a good way to spend the coins which they had brought with them. "Look there, Darlene, he's not busy right now, and we could surprise everyone when we come back. We'd remember this day forever every time we see the picture."

Darlene laughed, "Even when we're old like Theo and Beth, we'd know what we looked like as kids. Let's do it."

Moving forward, she made the arrangements with the artist, and both girls soon walked away with their treasures rolled up under their arms.

Pausing in front of the tent to study all the performances and times, Darlene sensed a male presence standing close enough that she could feel his warmth and hear his breathing. Darlene's face brightened and she whirled around with her arms extended. Just as quickly, she seized Amy's hand and jerked her so they could melt into the crowd.

"What in the world came over you, Darlene? One minute we're figuring out when and where, and the next we're tearing off like the world's on fire. What's going on?" Breathless and totally puzzled, Amy had planted her feet and stood with her hands on her hips. "I'm not going another step until I find out what's going on."

Darlene's eyes filled with tears as the words spilled out, "I thought it was Ted and it was that awful man. I came so close to hugging him that I feel like I'm going to throw up." Realizing Amy would not be content without more information, and realizing she herself needed to share her own discoveries and fears, Darlene pulled Amy over to a huge cottonwood tree and leaned towards her. "Do you remember the day Robert ran out of the school and I went to get the water but came back without it?"

"Do I ever? That was another time you were really weird but wouldn't tell me what was going on. You've got to tell me 'cause that's what friends do." Amy gazed into Darlene's eyes and could see how upset she was. "They tell each other everything, no matter what."

Darlene sucked in a deep breath, then released it with a huge sigh. "Okay, but you've got to promise you won't tell the other kids at school. This is really terrible. Do I have your word on it?"

"Cross my heart and hope to die; stick a needle in my

eye," Amy recited the familiar oath and made the motions over her heart. "Now you know the secret is safe with me."

"That day back at school, you know, when I didn't get the water, that was when Miss Edgars followed him outside to straighten him out. When she threatened to talk to his dad, Robert pulled up his shirt so she could see the terrible marks on his back. He cried and begged her not to go to Ben, and then I ran back into the schoolhouse. That got me to thinking about times I'd been around Ben when he didn't act very nice. I talked it over with Theo, and we agreed it's not safe for us girls to be alone with Ben. You know how he stands really close and always puts his hands on our shoulders and acts like he's our best friend."

Amy looked both ways before nodding, "Yeah, Beth told me to be sure to have someone with me whenever I see him, and I know she doesn't like it when he stops in after school. We talked it over, and I'm going to stay in my seat so she's not alone when he's there. He's creepy."

"Tracy Dolph and I were in the store when he came in, and she shoved me into the back room while she got Ed to come and wait on him. I overheard Ed yelling at him, and Tracy made me promise to get the heck out of any place where he is. I get sick to my stomach when he acts like he's such a nice guy when I know different," Darlene kicked at a clump of grass where the gnarled trunk emerged from the ground. "He's so bad."

Amy was still puzzled, "You know, I think just about everyone's got him figured out, so why is this bothering you so much right now?"

"You know how you can feel someone watching you? I knew a man had moved up behind us, and I was so sure it was Ted that I whirled around to hug him. Instead, it was that snaky Ben and when he gave me that creepy smile of his, I took off. Why doesn't someone do something about him?

It's not right."

So engrossed in conversation that they didn't notice the shadow looming over them, both girls let out shrieks as each one felt a huge arm encircle her waist. "Let us go! Let us go!" Kicking and yelling, the girls fought desperately until Ted's familiar voice finally broke through.

"Lena, Lena, get hold of yourself. Amy, what's the matter? I'm sorry I scared you, but this is way crazy. Stop this, right now. I'll let go if you'll talk to me." Suddenly he had an armful of sobbing girls clutching at his shoulders and clinging so fiercely he could hardly pry them off. "What in the world brought this on? I've never seen anyone so scared in my life. Can you tell me what happened?"

Shaking her head, Darlene buried her head more deeply into his shoulder. As her crying subsided, it was replaced with occasional hiccupping sounds and finally with regular breathing. "Theo, did I hurt you? I'm so sorry, but I was just so upset thinking Ben had followed us and grabbed us—"

Ted stiffened, gently took hold of her shoulders, and locked his gaze onto hers, "You know, Little One, I only just got here and seem to have missed out on what happened before. Could you fill me in about thinking Ben might be following you?"

"It was really stupid on my part, Theo. He came up behind us and I thought it was you and I was going to hug you and then it was him and then we ran."

Ted smoothed her hair back from her sweating forehead, "Honey, you might need to take a breath and slow down a little bit. Where exactly was this?"

"We were standing beside the big tent and he was so close I could feel him. That's why I thought it might be you. He actually didn't do anything, but I ran anyway. I know it was nothing and it makes me feel bad that I acted like such a baby." She took a breath and gave him a brave smile although her bottom lip quivered. "Beth will be as glad as we are to see you. She said our dinner would be ready by the time we got back. She'll like this surprise since she didn't expect you for a while yet. Please don't tell her how dumb I acted. No need for anyone else to know, is there?"

"Honey, you did exactly what we've talked about. I said for you to find a way to get out of uncomfortable places and not to let anyone make you feel bad. You did a nice job of keeping you and Amy safe; and later on, maybe I'll run into Ben and have a talk with him. Don't be sad that you did the right thing, and I think Beth needs to know this. I'll bet she's as proud of you as I am."

With a girl on each side, he let them guide him to where Beth and Emma were waiting. Although he appeared calm, the hard expression in his eyes and the firm set of his jaw revealed the tension seething inside. Scanning the grounds as they made their way, he caught a glimpse of his quarry and paused, "You know, I think I'd better go back and get my gloves from my saddle bags. I'd hate to lose them, if you know what I mean. Let Beth know I'll be there in just a few minutes, okay?" He propelled the girls in the same direction as he veered off.

Ted planted himself directly in front of Ben and stared silently with unwavering animosity. Ben gave a start and began stammering, "I don't know what got into those girls, Ted. I swear I didn't do a thing and they took out like a pair of deer. I hope they've calmed down by now. Maybe I can go talk to them and let them know it was all a mistake. You know I'd never—"

"You bet I know you'd never do anything, that is, unless you thought you'd get away with it. I don't know of anything too low-down for you, and you just proved that by sneaking up on those little girls. How many times do I have to say the same thing until you get the message? This had darned well better be the last time I ever hear your name coming from the lips of scared little girls or so help me, it'll be the last time anyone hears your name again. Do I make myself clear?" Ted's voice was low and intense and his lips were tight and pale as he glared at the man in front of him. At some time in the conversation, Ted had instinctively grasped Ben's collar, and he appeared mildly surprised about his hold. Releasing his grip on the collar, Ted kept his hand on Ben's front while smoothing out the wrinkles he had just squeezed into the material.

Ben's eyes darted left and right to make sure no one was paying attention to his humiliation, and once again began his futile attempt at justification, "There's no need for you to be so doggoned hostile. Ted, you've got it all wrong. I don't know what they told you, but honestly, I just walked up there and they took off. I didn't do a thing to them, no lie."

"Guess what, Ben. I don't want to hear it. There's only one way to figure out if you're lying, and that's to see if your lips move. Personally, I don't have the time nor the inclination to sort out your twisted stories, so I'm telling you to stay away. Stay away from those kids, and stay away from our place. Even if you and Fred are drinking buddies, you'd better not ever show up at the ranch again. The next time you do, I promise you, there'll be marks on your body even worse than those you put on your son's back. Now get out of here and don't foul up the day by being where any of the fine citizens here have to look at your face." He made one final savage thrust against Ben's chest.

Stumbling backwards, Ben adjusted his shirt and moved away with as much dignity as he could muster.

Ted whirled around and swung his fist at the same cottonwood tree where he had comforted the girls earlier. The pain of his blow brought him back into the moment, and he realized the need to compose himself before joining Beth and the others. Sucking on his knuckles as he walked, he felt the grim satisfaction of knowing he did have a powerful right hand swing that could inflict some serious damage. "That little toad better watch it, or I'll come uncorked and he'll be wishing he was back in the swamp where he belongs."

One deep breath and Ted had regained his composure. The unpleasantness temporarily left his mind as he came around the corner and saw Beth watching the crowd for his approach. He had barely come into view when everyone of his group started shouting and waving at him. Beth didn't even make a pretense of being calm as they met. She reached out her hand, "You know, I'm so glad you're here and we're all together. The girls seemed kind of in a turmoil so I let them go ahead and eat. Seems like it settled them down a little bit. Are you hungry? Emma and I decided to wait for you, so I'll fix some plates now." She never looked away from his gaze, and continued her babbling until he reached out to put his finger on her lips.

"Beth, you have no idea how powerful good it is to be here right now. If you don't mind, I think I'll pass on the food for a few minutes until I catch my breath, and then I'll dig in. Right now what I need the most is a tall drink of water and you beside me. How about if we just sit for a spell before we do anything else?" Ted felt the tautness of his shoulders relax as he came into her presence, and he knew he needed a bit more time to get past his previous encounter.

Darlene and Amy had nearly finished their plates; and just as Beth had predicted, food had proven to be an effective restorative. "Ted, this potato salad is scrumptious and you'd better grab one of those sandwiches before they're all gone. Beth made them with tiny biscuits and fresh cucumbers. I've never had anything like them before, but she says the British eat like that all the time. Maybe we'll have to take a boat over there and check it out after I get out of high school. What do you think?"

"Well, I think you've made them sound so good that I'd better have one before you starving girls make short work of them. As to the boat trip to England, I think you three girls need to do that and I'll stay here and make sure you have a home to come back to. Our folks had stories about sea travel that weren't very pretty, so I'm thinking the good old sand under my feet is all I'll ever need." Ted made his way to where Beth was dishing up his dinner, and he softly murmured to her, "I could get in the habit of coming in for dinner and having you there serving my meals."

What he had meant as an endearing declaration of his affection came out wrong. "Oh, could you? And what other jobs would you like me to do for you? Maybe you would like me to stand over a washboard and an ironing board and scrub the floors and—" Her temper flared instantaneously as she heard only the subservient portion of his words rather than the flowery sentiments she was waiting to hear about how sorrowful he had been without her.

This outburst, coupled with the unpleasant scene which he had just experienced, proved overwhelming to Ted. He stood in front of her just like a little boy, unsure about how to get out of his latest fiasco. "Honey, please don't do this. All I meant was that I want to be with you all the time, and I'd be honored if we were sharing the same home. I'm kind of beat right now, so maybe I'll go on over to the blacksmith shop and come back later."

As soon as the words were out of her mouth, Beth had regretted them. In her heart she knew what he meant, but her emotions were so heightened that she had vented without even wanting to. "Ted, I'm sorry for what I said. I've missed you so much that I don't know what to do with myself. Then the first time we're together, I talk to you like that. You know what? I'd like to get in the habit of doing everything for you I possibly can. Please forgive me."

Ted laughed and reached over to pat her on the head, "One thing about it, I'll never have a dull moment with you around," then worried that he might have said something wrong, he hastily added, "and that's a good thing, you know. Let's have a bite of lunch and talk over what's happened since we last met. Maybe I'll catch a little snooze after I eat, and then we can go see the sights. How's that sound?"

"Perfect." Beth's one word answer came just as a little cloud scooted away from the sun, and a burst of sunshine served as their omen of good things to come.

"Ahhh, now that's living. A wonderful meal in the company of four of the finest ladies ever seen. It just couldn't get any better than this." Ted had stretched out in the shade of the tree, resting his head on Beth's lap. As Beth stroked his hair back from his forehead, Emma looked pleased while the girls rolled their eyes and giggled. "It's a pity to waste our time here, but I sincerely feel a nap coming on." Turning to the side so he could catch Beth's eye, he asked, "Do you mind if I take five minutes to let that meal settle before we take in the entertainment?"

Beth gently pushed him off her lap as she stood up, "After you got up and did a full day's work before you got here, I'd certainly think you'd need a bit of rest. I'm going to leave for a few minutes to make myself more comfortable, but I'll be right back. You take all the time you want; and when you're ready, we can have a leisurely afternoon together. After all, that's really the point of the day, not how much we can get done while we're here. See you in a few minutes."

"Some of the neighbors are over there on the north side, and they asked me to come for a little visit. I'll leave right now so as not to bother you. Glad you got here so soon, Ted.

See you later." With that, Emma took her leave and was soon in the midst of lively conversation.

Ted rolled over on his stomach and motioned the girls to him. "After that scare you had this morning, I think we'd better come up with a plan. I'm thinking Ben won't be a problem for you, but better safe than sorry, right?"

Both girls solemnly nodded and lay beside him on the grass. Propping her elbow so she could hold her chin in her hand, Darlene answered, "I've been wondering what to do. I sure don't want to be such a scaredy-cat that I'm always peeking around corners and looking over my shoulder, but I know you told me to trust how my stomach feels. So what's your plan, Theo? You have some kind of magic wand to give us? That'd be neat if we had something so he'd just disappear."

Ted nodded at his little sister and shared his thoughts, "Lena, the neat thing is that you do have something close to a magic wand. You might not know it, but I think you can use it to make him disappear. Want to hear about it?"

"Wow! You bet I do! Amy, we've got power and didn't even know it. Tell us, Ted, tell us before we go absolutely crazy." Darlene had risen up to sit on her hips and bounced up and down with elation. "We're so ready to hear it, aren't we, Amy?"

Ted put his hand on her shoulder in a gentle motion to stop her up and down movements, and then he let it rest there, "Well, I'm glad to see you're ready to take care of yourselves, and this morning's little run-in might be a good reminder that you need to be on the look-out whenever you're around other people. Do you remember that day in Tracy's store when we talked about what you do if you're feeling cornered?" Ted slowly moved his fingers toward his lips as he waited for his sister to recall.

"Phweet!" As quickly as Darlene caught on to his drift,

she too had moved her fingers and made one of the ear-splitting whistles she had learned from Ted. "Oh, I can't believe I forgot about doing that. I was so startled that I guess I didn't take time to think—I just ran. Dumb move on my part."

Ted was quick to turn her shoulders and bring her face directly in front of his, "Hold it, Little One. I don't ever want to hear you say that about yourself. You had a feeling that you needed to get out of there, and the best way in the world is to avoid danger if you have the chance. What we're talking about is those times you might be trapped and not have an escape route. Never feel bad about saving yourself by getting the heck away from trouble. Do you hear what I'm telling you?"

"I guess there is a difference, isn't there? When we ran, we lost him in a hurry, so that did work out all right. We sure didn't hang around to find out what he had in mind, did we, Amy?"

Amy sat transfixed. She didn't know Darlene had learned how to whistle, and when it came blasting out of her friend's mouth, it startled her totally. This happened while she was processing Ted's words about a wand and she still needed time to figure it all out. "That is the loudest sound I've ever heard. How did you get so you could do that? Do you think you could teach me? I'd love to know that little trick."

"Isn't it the neatest thing? Ted taught me so I could whistle up the horses, so I'll teach you now so we can both do it. Knowing how to do it will be our little secret, but trust me, it won't be a secret when we let one of those rip."

Amy gave Ted a big squeeze and brushed her lips across his cheek. "You're our hero, Ted. You really are. And you're right about having something magic in our own two hands. A whistle like that should be enough to keep the bad guys away, or at least let the good guys know to come in a flash."

Amy and Darlene jumped to their feet and had taken two steps before Ted stopped them. "One thing more, girls. Do you suppose it'd be a good idea if you stayed together with so many people around today? It seems like a good way to take care of each other, and then you can tell us about all your adventures when we get back together. Maybe it'd be a good idea if we all agreed on a meeting time so we can plan the rest of our day. What time should we say to wander back here?"

"According to Em, it was close to two when she left, so how about around four? We'll probably be ready to come back by then. Even if we haven't seen everything, it'll be fun to hear what everyone's done. See you later, Theo." With that jaunty farewell, Darlene and Amy joined hands and trotted off to sample the day's offerings.

Ted lay down on his back, pulled his hat over his eyes, and almost immediately was breathing deeply and occasionally snuffling out a snore. As Beth returned, she softly sat down beside him, and then carefully eased down alongside him so she could simply enjoy his presence. Never awakening, Ted turned up on his side facing Beth and reached his arm out to pull her close. She snuggled against him and then remained completely still for fear of disturbing him. Lying beside him, she allowed herself to examine the depth of her feelings for this lanky rancher. As she lay there, Beth heard the rustling of the cottonwoods and felt the gentle breeze as it cooled the sweat which had beaded on her forehead and lips. After much consideration, she admitted to herself that life as she had known it had irrevocably changed. Beth was wise enough to know the change would bring uncertainty, exhilaration, and an intensity of emotion that had been largely absent in her life until now. After the strain of contemplation and the surrender to what she realized was inevitable, Beth felt the tautness of her shoulders gradually diminish, and she entered the same state of total relaxation as Ted.

Emma came back to check on everyone's schedule for the rest of the day, but as she viewed the restful poses of the young bodies, a hint of a smile came over her lips, and she quietly rejoined the neighbors she had just left.

Ted awakened with a start, opened his eyes, and discovered he had been holding Beth while they both slept. Ever so cautiously, he settled back to stare at the beauty beside him. Beth had piled her hair on top of her head in a bun, and several tendrils had escaped to frame her face. The breeze would rise and move the damp curls away from her face; and then as the breeze waned, the curls would once again drape over her sun-tanned skin. He took in the sprinkling of freckles over the bridge of her nose and across her cheeks, and saw for the first time the mole below her right ear.

Although Ted had willed his muscles to total inaction, his unbroken gaze at the woman to whom he was completely committed made her stir. Although she had been hard asleep, Beth jerked awake as she sensed his watching her. "Oh, my soul. I never intended to fall asleep. My intention was to let you get some rest and enjoy being with you. Then you turned over just like you knew I was there; and when you held me, I felt so safe and secure that I guess I just drifted off. Did you have a good rest?" She had turned to face him as she became more wide-awake. "Mine was delicious."

"I'd say this is the best I've ever felt waking up, so it must have been a good nap. On second thought, it might have something to do with the company I'm sleeping with, suppose?" Ted's words and smile brought tears to Beth's eyes; and once again, he felt the terror of a bachelor who's made a big mistake with his words. "I didn't mean anything bad by that, Beth, I just meant I like sleeping with you—no, that's not what I meant at all—." The more he talked, the deeper the hole he dug for himself, and finally he stopped when he realized she hadn't flared up. Actually, it was rather the opposite. Beth let him dither about until he fell silent.

Softly she placed two of her fingers across his mouth, and laid all his fears to rest. "Shush, Theo. I knew what you meant before you even started talking because that's exactly how I feel. You don't have to be so nervous about what you say to me even though I did fly hot this morning. That's not how I usually am; as a matter of fact, that outburst even surprised me. What I had in my heart didn't come out of my lips, and once again, I'm so sorry for that. Please don't feel like you have to walk on eggshells to keep me from getting mad." She snuggled closer, "I like sleeping with you, too, Mr. Soehl."

Ted was astute enough by now to realize his best course of action was no conversation at all. Wordlessly, he pulled Beth closer where they lay for a few minutes in complete harmony. Beth let out a little giggle, and lay still for a few moments until she couldn't contain herself. "Did you know you have an upside down mouth? I've never seen anyone whose mouth turns down when they smile, but yours does. I think it's just the cutest thing I've ever seen."

Once again, Ted entered the confused state. Here he and his woman were sharing one of the most precious times he could imagine, and she bubbled up with a remark about his mouth. How in the world was he supposed to know what was going on in her head? "Well, Beth, I'll tell you that's a family trait. Emma, Elsie, Darlene, and I all got that same look from our mother, so you probably need to know there's a good chance our children don't have a prayer of escaping that mark. Think you can handle that kind of future for your babies?"

"Here we are again, Ted. We haven't been together but twice, and both times we get to talking about what it's going to be like for us when we're together. What's up with that?" Beth sat bolt upright and gazed directly at him as he, too, pushed up to a sitting position. "And yes, I think our babies would be adorable with a cute little smile like that."

"How come our talks never go like I think they will? It was my plan to spend a glorious day with you and then sit down to decide where this thing is headed. Seems to me the right time to decide is now, and I think we both have a pretty good idea of what we want. I'm going to take a chance on putting some of my words out there so you'll know what I've been thinking. And by the way, I don't think I'll ever know what you're thinking, but you seem to do a good job of setting me straight when I'm off track."

They leaned together to laugh at the lightness of the moment, even while realizing the serious discussion that lay ahead of them. "Trust me, Ted, I'm not one to hold back when I feel strongly. The good thing is that I'm not one of those women who brood and pout and suffer in silence while making everyone around them suffer too. What I think will erupt, I'll say it, and then I can move on. That's how I am, and I'm surely not going to make any promises that I'll change since I think that would be false and misleading. What you see is what you get. If that's acceptable, we can go on with the conversation. If not, we both need to know it right now."

Ted's heart thumped inside his chest. "Beth, if 'what I see is what I get,' I'm the luckiest man here today, or anywhere for that matter. I'm not down on my knees right now, but I can get there if that would make this better for you. I'd be honored if you'd be my wife. I've dreamed about finding someone like you, and I'd about given up. I've pretty much decided that living alone is better than settling for someone I don't love. That was before you swept into my life and now I know you're the woman for me. Mama and Papa met and knew they were right for each other, and they had to wait years to get together. I sure hope it doesn't take that long for us, but I probably better wait for your answer before I start rearranging furniture."

"Theodor Soehl, I'd be honored to be your wife. Strange that I'd felt the same way about being alone. I've seen enough unhappy women who felt so desperate to be married that they settled for someone rather than finding the right one. A person can be lonely whether she's single or married, and alone was okay with me. Never did I believe in love at first sight, but that was before the last day of school when Darlene finally got the two of us together. I held myself back so I wouldn't be disappointed if you didn't live up to my dreams, but the more we're together, the more I love you. Yes, I want to marry you."

This time it was Ted's turn to lay his fingers across her lips to silence her. When she stopped talking, he then replaced his fingers with his lips. The kiss they shared sealed their engagement, fueled their desire, and lasted long enough they both drew back breathlessly. "Wow, Beth. I'm thinking that said at least as much as all our words. I think it also told us waiting won't be good for either of us. Are you willing to set a date or do you need more time to make plans?"

Beth snorted, "Ted, I'm going to be honest with you. Ever since we spent Darlene's birthday together, I've been considering what I'd say if you asked, and what date would be appropriate. So, no, I don't need any time to think. We just have to agree and then get everything done."

"Before we go any further on this, Beth, there's something you have to know. I didn't mention it before, and if it makes you uncomfortable, it's your right to turn me down. Darlene is a part of this whole arrangement. Emma is making plans to go back East, and Darlene will stay with me. It's kind of like she's my daughter at the same time she's my sister. I'll understand if you'd rather not have another female in the house. Right now, the two of you are comfortable, but I don't want you to feel forced to take on the role of mother at the same time you become a wife. If you need to turn away, I'll understand. She'll be with me always." Ted knew the best way to avoid misunderstandings was to clarify details at the outset, so he wanted to inform Beth and let her make a decision instead of springing a surprise on her after she had agreed.

Beth never flinched, "Ted, I knew you were a package deal, and it never dawned on me she wouldn't be with us. I thank you for your honesty, and I have to say that spending this summer with Amy's family really let me know what I'm in for. Loving children isn't the whole story, and finding a way to let them become independent while keeping them under control is a kind of balancing act. I'm coming into this situation with open eyes and an open heart, so a ready-made family is not a stumbling block so long as you want to have babies with me. Yes, I'd be honored to make a home with you and Darlene."

Ted hadn't realized it, but he had been holding his breath waiting for her reply. Gently exhaling, he directed the conversation back to the question of timing. "You said you had been thinking of when and where, and so have I. Let's hear some of your ideas."

"School boards are sometimes kind of funny, and I've signed my contract for this next year, so we may have to do some checking with them. It doesn't seem to be such a big deal if a teacher is married anymore, but we'll need to tell them. I had given Christmas vacation a bit of thought. We'd have time to go back to Omaha where my family is so they could meet you and Darlene if we decided to get married there. You'd mentioned that was where your mom and dad started out, so that might be kind of fun. What do you think of that?" As Beth talked, she was carefully scrutinizing Ted's face. Although he worked hard to keep a neutral expression, she noticed how his jaw muscle had bulged several times while she spelled out the Omaha option, so she paused to hear his feedback.

Ted chose his words carefully, "Christmastime and Omaha make sense, especially since it's important your family gets to know me. It's true we'd have a special connection if we started where my parents did so I feel like your plans would be good in the long run for us." He paused, then decided to charge right in and reveal his true feelings, "I guess I really didn't want to wait that long. It seems like we've known each other forever, and we've been waiting for so long to find each other that I was hoping for sooner rather than later. I know I'm being selfish about this, but is there any way we could get married before school starts and then go visit your folks in December? I don't know how I could stand being alone and knowing the woman I love is just over the hill every day at the school. If it's important to you that we wait, I can darned sure make it work even if it means weeks apart."

Throwing her arms around Ted's neck, Beth began crying, "I didn't want to be forward, Ted, so I thought I should say December. What I'd really like to say is this afternoon, but I know that's not possible. Yes, yes, yes. Let's do make August our wedding month. We can come here to Arthur and have the justice of the peace perform the ceremony with as many of your family as want to come and hear it. Then when we go to Omaha, we can go to my church and have the minister bless our union with my family all there. That way not very many people would have to travel, and we'd have a chance to spend a bit of time away from the ranch before calving starts. I can introduce you to my friends, and they can all be jealous of the handsome rancher I'll be spending my life with. What fun."

In his wildest dreams, Ted had never allowed himself the hope of such an immediate date. "I agree that today would be perfect, but we might need to make a few more plans before we jump right in. Emma plans to move into Arthur until she's ready to move to York, so we'll want to help her get settled. Then that'll give you a chance to come over and decide how to make my house into our home. I also want you to have a special ring, so I'll need time to get somewhere for that. I suppose women have stuff to do before a wedding too, even if I don't have a clue what that is. Would a month give you enough time to get ready to be Mrs. Theodor Soehl?"

"Perfect." For the second time in one day, Beth gave the one word answer that summed up how they both felt.

One more long embrace, and they turned toward the events occurring in the park. Holding hands, they had taken only a couple of steps when Emma came bustling up behind them. "Hey, sleepy heads. Did you finally decide to take in the sights while we're here in the city? Glad you're up and at it." She took one look at their faces and continued, "Okay, spill it. You both look like the cat that swallowed the canary so I'm guessing you have some news to share with me. Let's hear it." She had a strong inkling what had transpired in her absence, so she folded her arms and cocked her head to the side as she looked back and forth at the couple. "Which one of you is going to be the one who tells all?"

Ted stepped forward and put his arm around her, "Emma, you're right. We do have news to tell, and you're the first one to hear it. This magnificent lady has agreed to become my wife, and we've set the date. Want to hear it?"

"Oh, my body and soul, Theo, do I want to hear it? What

in the world do you think I asked for if I didn't want to hear it? Sometimes you men are so dense that I can't believe it. Beth, can you do better than that? Don't keep me in suspense any longer."

"Emma, how does August 28th sound to you? It's one month away, and we're hoping that will give you ample time to make arrangements. If that won't work for you, we can set it back further. We thought getting married before school starts would be a good idea. It would make for less upheaval for Darlene and the other students, and besides, we're so excited we don't want to put it off any longer than necessary."

Encircling the two of them in her bony arms, Emma threw her head back and laughed, "I knew this would be a good day if we gave you two kids time enough alone. One month sounds perfect, and the only ones more excited than you will be Darlene and Amy. Can you imagine how they'll like the idea of being related to each other once you're married. Get ready for a flurry of questions and action once those girls hear the news." Emma released them and gave them a searching look. "Surely you're not going to tell me this has to be kept secret, are you? I'd explode if I had to keep this inside me."

"No, Emma, we're ready to tell the world; and even if we weren't, those two girls couldn't keep it secret even if they tried. Let's go tell them so we can celebrate together. Have you seen them anywhere?" Ted had started scanning the crowd to see if he could catch sight of Darlene's auburn hair; and all of a sudden, he spied her. "They're coming this way right now. What time is it anyway?" Looking at his pocket watch, he was amazed to see that it was a few minutes before four o'clock.

"Here we are, just like you said, Theo. We've seen some really neat things, and I'll bet you've got lots to report too.

Do you want to go first or should we?" Darlene was ready to share her reactions to the show since she and Amy had traversed the entire grounds, and she wanted to know if the others had encountered something she had overlooked."

Ted put up his hand, "You know, Little One, I think Beth and I'll start out if that's okay with you girls. Are you girls ready for this?"

Amy and Darlene picked up on the excitement in his voice and the intensity in Beth's eyes, and they nudged each other while exchanging private looks, "Sure, Ted, we're ready for it. Have right at it." They had already decided their favorite part was when they had had their portraits done, and they had giggled about how Ted and Beth probably had theirs done together so they wouldn't have to be apart any longer than necessary. Absolutely certain that Ted was about to tell them this, they stood with their hands on their hips. Darlene tapped her toe impatiently, "Come on, slow poke. We don't have all day, you know."

"Okay, I won't keep you in suspense. While you were gone, we made good use of our time together." Seeing the girls exchanging knowing glances, he grinned and paused, "Oh, well, you probably aren't interested anyway in what a pair of old folks like us have to say. Why don't you fill us in on your afternoon?" Immediately he was overtaken by an onslaught of girls' arms and a chorus of complaints.

"No way, Theo. You know it's not polite to start something and not finish it. You're not too old to have some fun, just as long as you give yourselves some time to recover from the excitement. What did you do? Did you go to the picture place or did you go to the poetry reading? Beth probably had to drag you there, but it looks like you survived it anyway. A little culture won't hurt you, Theo, and you might even decide to go listen to the woman with the screetchy voice who is doing something called 'opera.' She hasn't been here long enough to learn our English words, so it's kind of hard to catch on, but I'll bet you'd go if Beth batted her eyes and asked you nicely. Don't keep us in suspense any longer. Please tell."

Ted nonchalantly shrugged, "Well, since you put it that way, it's only right that you hear about our adventures. As I was saying, we put our time to good use even though we didn't go anywhere. Beth and I decided to invite you to our wedding that will be one month from today. How's that for some action from a pair of old foggies?"

Total silence. Darlene and Amy had the same shocked expression on their faces as their lips made fish-like movements. Never long without words, Darlene recovered the soonest and launched herself at the laughing couple with a barrage of questions and comments. "I can't believe this. Who could have ever imagined? What are you going to wear? Do I get to stand up with you when you say the words? Are you going to kiss her loud in front of everyone? Does this mean Amy and I'll be cousins? Can you still be my teacher even though you'll be my newest sister?" Finally she had to catch her breath, and she wordlessly buried her head in Ted's shoulder while pulling Beth close to her. "The two people I love more than anyone else on earth, and you'll be with me all the time from now on. This is the best ever." Releasing Ted and Beth, Darlene whirled to grab Amy with all her might. "Do you realize we'll be family forever? That means we'll never have to be apart, even when we grow up and move away."

Dancing around and around with each other, the two little girls surrendered themselves completely to the joy of the moment until they were so breathless and dizzy that they collapsed in a heap. All of a sudden, Darlene had a flash of inspiration, "You know what you guys need to do? You need to go over to that booth and have the woman do your picture.

We'll go along and tell her it's because you're going to be married, and she'll do something really special. How about it? Mr. and Mrs. Soehl—oh, I never thought Ted would get a wife, and now he's about to have the best one ever. We'd better go so she doesn't quit before we get there." Running ahead, she and Amy would turn around and run backwards while motioning for the grown-ups to follow, then whirl and skip along before checking once again to see how close Ted and Beth were.

Arriving at the booth, they found the woman finishing a portrait of two red-headed boys who were having a great deal of difficulty sitting still. Darlene started giggling and whispered to Ted, "You know you could have little boys who look just like that, don't you? How fun will it be to have babies in the house just like Amy has?" As soon as the words were out of her mouth, tears gushed down her face.

Ted and Beth were completely taken aback by her sudden display of emotion, and they squatted beside her. "What's the matter, honey?" Beth pulled the sobbing girl into her arms, "Please tell me."

"Will you want me to go somewhere else to live, Beth? I will, you know, so you and Ted can have a real family. I can go with Emma when she moves away, or Alma always tells me I can come live with them. I don't mind, you know, because you'll want your own family just like those little boys there." Standing ramrod straight, she leveled her gaze, gave her bravest smile, and patted Beth's shoulder. "We'll make it all right, won't we, Ted?"

Beth gave Ted a meaningful shake of the head as she lifted her palm towards him to warn him against intruding in the moment, "Darlene, I'm so proud to be asked into your family, but I wouldn't even consider marrying Ted if I thought it would cause heartache for anyone. I truly appreciate what you just said, and that proves to me I want to be a part of your family more than anything." Beth paused and caught Darlene's eye. "I want to ask you something, Darlene. Do you love your kitten Johnny?"

Darlene gave her a puzzled look, not understanding the turn which the conversation had taken, "Of course I do. He's special because I got him first."

"And now, I have another question for you. Do you love your kitten Jitney?"

"Well, sure I do. He's special too, even if he wasn't there first. I still love him lots."

Beth held Darlene and rocked back and forth as if she were a baby in need of comforting, "Honey, that's how it is with you and Ted and me. When you found Jitney to love, it didn't cut your love in half; it doubled it. That's the funny thing about love; the more people you have to love, the more love you have. Ted loved you first in a very special way, and now he loves me in a special way. The good thing to know is that there's room in his heart for both of us, as well as for all the babies that come along. When we get married, the three of us will be a real family, and nothing can ever change that. If you'd decide to go live somewhere else, Ted and I would be very sad."

"Do you mean it, Beth? You really want me to stay? Promise me you mean it."

"Darlene, I promise. Cross my heart and hope to die. Stick a needle in my eye. Isn't that what you say to make a promise that can't ever be broken?"

Darlene grabbed her around the waist and the tears continued, but this time they were for relief and joy rather than the deep sorrow which had overwhelmed her earlier. Rubbing the tears away, she ran over to the artist and commenced talking. Although they were out of earshot, Ted and Beth could tell by Darlene's gestures she was making grand arrangements for their engagement portrait.

Motioning them over, the woman adjusted their stances until she was satisfied, then covered the canvas with bold strokes and delicate shadings while Darlene stood guard over her shoulder. In less than ten minutes, she turned to Darlene and asked, "Does this meet with your approval, young lady? If there's anything you can think of, just let me know."

Darlene went into her usual ritual of concentration. She lowered her brows into a scowl, pursed her bottom lip, and put her hand up to her chin. After a few minutes deliberation, she nodded at the woman who handed her the picture. "This one's on the house, folks. It's not every day I'm part of an engagement celebration. Congratulations, and perhaps by the next time I make my rounds, there'll be another little red-haired baby to draw."

Beth blushed bright red, and Ted let out a huge belly laugh. "You can bet we'll look you up when we need some baby pictures. In all likelihood, that'll be quite a while, so don't get impatient if you don't have a lot of business from us right away. We thank you for this keepsake, ma'am."

About this time, Emma emerged from the tent which was set up as a place for visitors to rest and rejuvenate themselves. "I was hoping I'd run into you folks somewhere close. I must have gotten too much sun today because I've felt kind of puny all afternoon. I hate to do this, but I think I need to get home and put my feet up. Darlene, I know you'd like to stay longer, but do you suppose you could help get stuff loaded so we can head out? I'll make it up to you somehow, I promise."

"Oh, Em, don't think a thing about it. Of course we need to go home if you're feeling poorly. It won't take us but a minute and we can be on our way." Darlene could see the sweat on Emma's upper lip, as well as the pallor under her suntan, so she realized how unwell Emma was.

"Do you want me to come along with you, Em? If you think you need help, let's leave right now." Ted was solicitous about his sister's condition since the entire family knew she simply never was the one ailing. She was the one they relied on to care for others when they were injured or sick, but no one ever felt as if their help were required on her part.

"Land sakes, no, Ted. It'd be plumb silly for you to come home with us. What do you think you'd do when we get there—watch me sleep? I plan to go to bed when I get home, and nothing is going to make me stir until the sun comes up. You stay here and take your honey to the dance. We'll see you in the morning."

"Okay, if you're sure, but you know I'll come if you change your mind. We'll get everything loaded and see what you say by then. Okay?" Ted held out his arm to steady Emma as they made their way to the car. He helped her into the driver's seat and went to pack the picnic basket and supplies.

"Darlene, as hot as it's been today, I think Em probably got overheated, so it'd be a good idea if she'd drink some cool water before she goes to bed. Maybe you can get her a glass after she gets her nightclothes on. I'll be home later."

Big brother and little sister shared a warm embrace before Darlene turned toward the car. "Ted, will you tell me all about the dance when you get home? I'll bet you and Beth have a joyous time. I'm so happy for you and me and all of us. Thanks for telling us so we can be happy together."

In the distance, a soft rumble sounded, and the two of them looked to the southwest where a soft line of puffy clouds had formed on the horizon. "Hmm. As hot as it's been today, that could really be a gullywasher if it comes this way. We need the rain so bad that we'll welcome whatever it takes to get us some moisture. When you get home, you might take time to shut the barn doors if it looks like a storm might hit. Don't worry about the chores. It'll be close to dark by the time you get there, and we've got everything set so we'll get back on track in the morning." Ted fluffed Darlene's hair as he said goodbye, "I love you, Little One, and I'll pay attention so I can tell you everything that happens at the dance. See you in the morning."

"Theo, will the cattle need moved tomorrow again? If they do, let's do it together so you can tell me everything about tonight. How's that sound?" Darlene had started to crawl in the passenger door when this thought hit her, and she had skipped back to where Ted was standing.

As he answered her, Ted had the same business-like tone in his voice that he used when he talked to other adults, "I'm lucky you're such a good ranch hand, Lena. It sure makes my job more pleasant. How about we see if this little cloud scares up some wind so the mills pump. If that happens, we won't have to worry about the water situation for a day or so. If it doesn't, you bet we'll head out together. Thanks for your offer. We can talk in the morning and plan our day's work. You take good care of Emma and get some rest yourself so you're ready at the crack of dawn."

"Now, Ted, do you really think you'll want to jump out of bed and work all day long after you get home late tonight? You might want to be lazy and sleep late, 'specially if you're having sweet dreams about Beth that you don't want interrupted." Darlene and Ted laughed at the idea of him lying in bed once the day had started, and they shared one more quick chuckle.

Ted swatted her behind and sent her toward the car. "Emma's waiting and you've got a bunch of gates ahead of you so you'd better get started. Thanks for being such a good sport when I know you'd like to be here tonight."

"Oh, that's all right. Now that you have Beth, you won't need me as a dancing partner like before. I'll just have to find myself another handsome cowboy to whirl me around the dance floor." Darlene spun a couple of times on her way to the car door before Ted caught her.

"You know what, Little One? The bad news is that you're stuck with me as your dancing partner, no matter what. Let's do a quick spin right here so I get to dance with you before you leave for home." On the grassy slope, brother and sister glided together as they hummed their favorite dance melody. "There now, fancy lady. I thank you for giving me the first dance of the evening. It was a real joy and honor." Ted bent his head down to kiss her hand, then picked her up and carried her to the vehicle. She flung her arms around his neck and giggled as she planted a huge kiss on his cheek.

"Your chariot awaits, Madame. Have a safe journey and we'll meet again." Placing her in the seat, Ted straightened up, snapped a smart salute in her direction, and stood at attention until Emma eased the car out of the lot and turned it east toward the ranch.

Ted's eye on the weather proved accurate. By the time Emma pulled up to the second gate, the wind had come up and was whipping sand in Darlene's eyes as she jumped out. Even though she held tightly to the car door, the wind grabbed it and flung it against the fender. "Oh, gosh, Em, I thought I had a good enough hold it couldn't do that. Wow, this is tough." She leaned into the gale and made her way to the gate post. After struggling with it, she finally turned and shouted to her sister, "Emma, I'm sorry but it just won't budge."

Before the words were even out of her mouth, Emma's strong arm reached around the post and pulled so Darlene could lift the barbed wire latch. She then hurried to the car, drove through, and jumped out to help close the gate. "This isn't going to be much fun if we have to fight this much wind all the way home, is it?" A sharp bolt of lightning split the sky, followed almost immediately by a huge crack of thunder that shook the ground. "Get in right now. I hope we get closer to home before the rain hits."

Usually a conservative driver on the sandhill ruts, this time Emma pushed the limits. She jammed the gas pedal down and the car lurched forward. Fighting to keep it in the trail, Emma sped along as much as conditions allowed. Huge drops pelted the windshield, falling at four or five second intervals at first, and then increasing in speed until they were a steady drumming on the vehicle. Even though the sky was dark and filled with boiling clouds, the constant strikes of lightning illuminated the terrain so much that they could have navigated even if the car lights had failed. Every now and then a crack of lightning would hit so close that the girls would yelp and jump away as if to dodge it. Then the thunder would rumble and boom for what seemed an interminable time.

"Honey, we're just about home. That was the last gate, and now we have that little swale to drive through. Last time we got rain, a huge puddle stood there, so we'll have to hope we can make it without the water drowning out the engine. This car's usually not very good if it gets wet, so here goes nothing." Unfortunately, Emma's prediction about standing water and its effect on the motor were both on target. They chugged about three quarters of the way through when the car sputtered, shuddered, and died. Looking at each other, they shrugged and shook their heads. "Too bad I was right on that one, isn't it? Can you reach our coats, Darlene? I think they're right there in the back seat.'

Darlene turned and stretched into the back seat. "I'm sorry I laughed about bringing our coats, but I'm glad you insisted. Good thing we left Ted's with him, isn't it?" Handing Emma's coat to her and putting on her own, Darlene shivered and asked, "What do we do now, Em? It's cold and dark and I'm scared."

"Honey, if we knew when the storm would be over, we could wait it out. Truth is, this could go on all night, so our best bet is to get out and hoof it for home. We'll grab hands and not let go of each other so it'll be all right." Emma had pushed open her door and realized the water was lapping at the running boards. "Don't be scared, even if the water feels real deep. We drove most of the way through so you won't have to wade very far. I warn you, it's going to be really, really cold so take a deep breath to get ready. I'm going to get out my side and come around to you, so sit still until I get there. When I tell you, jump out and start moving." With that, Emma pushed herself out the door and into the frigid water. Since the water was too deep to step over, she forced each foot forward until she was on the passenger side.

Darlene was quietly crying, but she didn't protest when Emma told her to jump. As she left her seat and plunged her legs into the water, she cried out, "Emma, it's too deep. I can't reach bottom." Just then she felt her feet hit the ground and shouted, "It's okay now. Just don't let go. Promise me you'll hang on." The water was so deep on her short little legs that it came to the top of her thighs, and she worried she might hit a deep hole and slip completely under the water. She also knew she had no choice but to keep moving, so she and Emma slowly made their way out of the deep water.

They trudged ahead, making sure to follow the ruts so they wouldn't get lost. After just a few minutes, Darlene lost her bearings and had no clue where they were. "Emma, I don't think I can go another step. We'll never get home."

Just then sheet lightning lit up the sky and lasted long enough for Darlene to see they had traveled the last half mile leading to the house and indeed were just a few yards from the garden fence. They plodded forward so they could take hold of the wire and follow it to the yard. Reaching the porch, Emma grabbed the door knob and flung open the door. Both fell on the floor and lay there until they caught their breath. Emma was the first to stand up, and she shed her wet coat and threw it beside the door. "Stay there until I light a lamp, Darlene. Then we'll get out of these wet clothes and crawl under the covers. You sleep with me tonight so we can get warmed up."

Darlene's lips were shivering so much she didn't even try to talk. She nodded her head and started peeling off the wet layers, leaving them by the door with Emma's coat. When she finally could talk, she told Emma, "I don't think I'm going to shut the barn door. I think Ted'll understand, don't you?"

"Closing that door now after the storm hit would be like shutting up the chicken house after the coyote had eaten his fill. He'd want you to stay here where you're safe and warm." All of a sudden, Emma's attempt with the kerosene lamp was successful and the room was flooded with warm light. It was as if a transformation had taken place for the two sisters. Home now felt like the familiar haven where they knew they were safe, and they relaxed as they toweled themselves off and put on their night gowns. "Do you want something to eat before we go to bed? I can rustle up some grub if you're hungry."

"No, thanks, Em. I just want to crawl in bed before I fall down. My legs are so shaky I don't know if I can make it down the hallway. That was really a long, scary trip home, wasn't it?"

"I am so proud of you, honey. You were so brave when you crawled in the water, and then you marched on just like a trouper even if you don't like the dark."

Darlene shivered as she recalled the water rising higher and higher on her legs, "You know what, Emma? I'll bet I'm not scared of the dark after tonight. It was actually kind of pretty when the sky would light up all the way across the hills and it sure made it easier to keep going. Good night, Sis. I'll have the bed warm for you when you get there."

"I'm right behind you, Darlene. Guess it was kind of a good thing we headed out when we did. We might have had an even longer walk if we'd have hit deep water sooner. I think we're pretty lucky after all. Night, sweetheart." With that, Emma blew out the lamp and the girls soon drifted off into the hard sleep that follows exertion such as theirs.

Chapter 5

When the morning light awakened Darlene, she slipped out of Emma's bed and tiptoed down the hallway to Ted's room. Seeing he was not still in bed, she hurried to put on her clothes and hustled out to the kitchen to see if he were drinking a cup of coffee. Not finding him there, she stepped outside and took a deep breath of the rain-filled air. After several weeks of hot, dry weather, the landscape looked scrubbed and fresh. She noticed the deep green of the hills and the whiteness of the sand as she walked across the yard toward the barn. Cats poured out of the barn door for their morning bowl of milk, and the dogs stretched and whined when they saw her coming.

Pausing at the barn door, she let her eyes adjust to the darkness and softly spoke, "Ted, are you in here? Nice little rain we had last night, wasn't it?" Stopping so she could hear where he was by the direction of his answer, she was met by silence. When the bucket calves heard her, they started bawling, and she scoffed at them, "You guys aren't that bad off. You act like you're starving, but you're all right. We'll get you some milk pretty quick." Making her way on through the barn so she could let the cows in, she pushed open the sliding door.

So stunned she couldn't make a sound at first, all of a sudden she let out a huge scream. Cheyenne was standing outside the corral with his head hanging over the gate. At first glance she took in the bridle with broken reins dangling from the bit. As she moved closer to open the gate, she noticed he hadn't moved since she first saw him. Then she saw a gaping wire cut that had slashed open his chest and made it difficult for him to walk. Pushing the gate out of his way so he could follow her into the barn, she checked out the saddle for any sign of damage as he slowly hobbled across the corral. She turned him into the box stall, patted his butt on the way by, and lunged out.

Darlene started to cry and ran back toward the house, yelling as she went. She charged into the house and stumbled back to Emma's bedroom, "Em, come quick. Big trouble. No Ted. Riderless horse, Emma, riderless horse." She grabbed Emma's shoulders and shook them back and forth. "You know Mama always said a riderless horse's the worst sign ever. Cheyenne came home but Ted didn't. Cheyenne's cut and Ted's gone and I'm scared. Come quick. We gotta go."

Emma threw back the covers and slid into her trousers, "You get the horses in and I'll tell Fred and Alma. We'll find him, honey, don't you worry." Emma was covering the dread she felt when Darlene had shouted out that traumatic phrase. Every time a riderless horse showed up, it meant a rider in need of help. Perhaps he had been bucked off and was walking back home, could be that the horse had stepped in a hole and fallen on the rider, maybe the horse spooked and jumped out from under the rider. Outcomes ranged from the comic to the tragic, but every situation was scary for those who saw the riderless horse.

"Phweet!" Darlene let out the whistle that Ted had taught her, and in trotted the horses, Boxer at the lead. Although she had never ridden this young horse before, she knew Cheyenne was out of commission so she really had no choice. Haltering him in a hurry, she threw on her blanket and saddle, jerked the cinch tight, and tied him in a stall. She knew Emma would ride Pete and Alma would ride Clipper, so she hurried to get them ready. Cheyenne softly nickered at her when she went into the stall to loosen the cinch so she could pull off Ted's saddle. She lugged it to the saddle rack and shoved it back as far as it would go. Tossing the cinches over the saddle, she hung the saddle blanket so it could dry, and then stepped back. Ted would like how she'd taken good care of his tack when he got home.

By the time she was done, her sisters came running into the barn and slipped the bridles on their horses. Emma swung on Pete, "We'll split up and each ride a pasture on the way to town. Fred's going to town and he'll have someone ride from that direction so we'll meet up somewhere. Be sure to check your cinches and be careful. Stop and listen once in a while so Ted can let us know where he is. It'd be a good idea to look on the trail first, and then branch out in the pasture in case Cheyenne spooked and ran off. That storm was a fierce one last night."

Darlene had mounted Boxer and took a few turns around the corral on him before she headed out, "Alma, I'm glad you stayed here last night so you're here to help. Boxer and I'll probably be the ones to find him, and I'll let out a whistle so you know where we are. See you soon." With that, she kicked Boxer into a high lope and sped along the usual path the Soehls followed when they rode to town.

After a morning of searching, Darlene began to lose confidence that she would be the one to rescue her brother.

She had imagined the scene when she would ride up to find him where he had fallen after Cheyenne had spooked. He probably had a sprained ankle so he couldn't walk, and he would be so grateful she was there. He would say, "Darlene, what're you doing on that horse? I won't have a horse left if you keep taking them out from under me. How about a lift home, Little One?" After an afternoon of searching, Darlene no longer envisioned Ted as joking with her about riding his horse, but she figured maybe he'd have a broken bone and be in a great deal of pain. She'd make him comfortable and signal the others who'd then bring a car and haul him to the doctor while she rode along to comfort him. He'd look at her with grateful eyes, and she'd soothe his brow until Beth could get there.

By the time it was getting dark, Darlene headed back to the ranch. She could hear other riders assembling at the gate beside the barn, and she could tell by the tone of the voices that no one had found Ted. Just then the milk cows bawled, and she realized they hadn't been milked for two days. Wearily she unsaddled and grabbed a milk pail. Neighbors who had come to ride asked her where to put their horses; and when they saw her with the pails, they pitched in and finished the milking and feeding in short order.

The entire group went to the house where Emma had fixed ham sandwiches which they munched in silence. Most of the neighbors lived far enough away that they had decided to stay overnight and resume the search at dawn's light. Some sprawled on the living room floor while others went to the barn and lay down on the straw, using their saddles for pillows. It was a somber collection of friends and neighbors who had very little to say but much in the way of bleak thoughts.

Darlene shook her head when Emma urged her to eat a bite, but Alma pulled her down on her lap and rocked her like a baby. Darlene started to whimper, and Alma stroked her hair, "It's all right, Lena. You've done everything you can for today, and we all need to be strong and ready to put in a full day tomorrow. I'm thinking a bit of food will keep you going. It'd be too bad if you'd need to stay home tomorrow when we head out." With the idea of being left behind, Darlene agreed to a half a sandwich and half a glass of milk. "That'll let you sleep a little so we can take out bright and early, honey. Tomorrow will be better, you'll see."

Alma had come back to visit her family and to attend the gathering in Arthur, otherwise she wouldn't have been on the ranch. She hadn't planned to stay over, but the storm had changed her plans. She and Emma sat up after everyone else had gone to bed, and they were close enough that they could share concerns and gather strength from one another. Having gone through difficulties together, they knew it was good to have family support in tough times.

Fred hadn't ridden a horse to help with the search, but he had rounded up the entire neighborhood. He had contacted those neighbors who lived close by and people in town who were Ted's close friends. Because Fred hadn't heard about Ted's engagement; he hadn't taken the time to inform Beth, so she was oblivious to the drama taking shape on the Soehl ranch. She had spent the day at home remembering the joy from the night before and planning her wedding. It wasn't until everyone came in for supper that they realized the oversight, and Fred had left immediately to go pick her up and bring her back to the ranch. It was nearly midnight when he walked her up to the door.

Emma was dozing in the chair when Beth walked in, and she rose to hold Beth. They cried together, talked about how they couldn't believe it, and discussed when he had headed out for home after the dance.

"Tracy and Ed asked him to stay overnight, but he

thought the storm had let up enough he could zip right home. According to him, he was so keyed up that he'd never get to sleep and would keep everyone up with his rambling. I offered to drive him home, but he didn't want to leave Cheyenne behind either. When I saw he was serious, I insisted we leave the dance before it was over. I finally got him out of there about nine o'clock." Beth stopped as tears welled up, "He kissed me and said, 'I'll be glad when we can go home together,' swung up on Cheyenne and took off. I watched until I couldn't see his outline any longer, and then Amy and I drove home. I wish I'd have made him listen to me then we'd all be sitting here together and he'd be laughing at me for being a Nervous Nelly. I should've stopped him."

"I've got news for you, Sweetie. When a Soehl makes up his mind, I don't think there's a force on earth that can change it. Even though he loves you with all his heart, he still has a super hard head." The two women leaned their foreheads together and laughed at a truth they both recognized. Emma then escorted her to Ted's room. "Here, Beth, you can stay in here until he gets back. He'll be so happy to see you that the rest of us might as well disappear for a day or two. Thanks for coming. See you in the morning."

When Darlene heard sounds coming from the kitchen, she bolted upright in her bed and gazed with shock at the sun peeking above the horizon. "I can't believe I'm still here and the sun's up. Ted needs me and I'm being lazy. This is terrible." Throwing off her bedclothes and tugging on her trousers, she nearly fell down as she tried to put both legs in at once. "Okay, Mama. I know, I know. 'The hurrieder you go, the slower you go.'" Pulling one leg out and leaning back on the bed, she finished her pants, and then couldn't help herself from rushing any longer. Grabbing her blouse, she pulled it over her head as she ran down the hallway.

"You know we don't have time for breakfast, Em. I'll get

the horses saddled and let's go find Theo," she grabbed the doorknob and looked back over her shoulder. "Okay?" She paused and was nearly overcome by the aroma of the platter of bacon sitting on the sideboard and the sizzling of eggs in the cast iron skillet. "I know that's my favorite, but I just don't have time." It finally registered on her consciousness that Beth was sitting at the table, patiently waiting for her to finish.

"The best thing you can do for Ted is take the time for a good breakfast. You might not be close enough to make it back here at noon, so do this for him. He'll need you to be strong for him, don't you think?" Beth handed her a pancake with bacon strips and a hard egg rolled up inside it. "It's hard to slow down long enough to eat, so maybe you can eat this and take one more for your pocket. It might get kind of squishy, but it's better than nothing." As she held out the snack, Darlene hurled herself into Beth's arms for a quick squeeze before running out the door.

Emma laughed, "Sometimes the Soehls are short on words and long on action. Guess this is one of those times." Turning off the stove, she grabbed a rolled-up pancake and prepared to leave the house. "I think some of the guys still might drift in for a bite, so maybe you can look after them. Make yourself at home, Beth. Actually, this is your home now, isn't it? Glad you're here."

In the frontier way of neighbors pitching in, the men had already done the chores by the time Darlene and Emma came out of the house. When all the horses were saddled and the riders had mounted up, they formed a circle to have a strategy session. After much discussion, each person headed out to the same pasture as the day before to resume searching. Since they knew where they had already looked, it appeared to be more efficient if they stayed in the same location to continue the tedious process.

More neighbors had heard what was going on and came to join the search, so it was possible to assign several riders to the same area for more rapid and thorough coverage than before. To the casual eye, sand hill terrain appears uncluttered and stark. Those who had a close acquaintance with the land, however, knew it was deceptively simple. Huge hills were interlaced with washouts of gargantuan proportion, blowouts of constantly shifting sand, and soapweeds clustered in large clumps. With thorny foliage and rose hips, the rosebushes that had bloomed so delicately in June now created a dense ground cover which required a rider to examine each patch closely. This was the daunting task facing the rescuers, and they undertook it with fierce determination.

Totally unable to ride a horse and be comfortable, Fred pursued the job of finding his brother through use of the car. He traversed the route continually so he could be there when Ted was found. Repeating the identical route throughout the day offered ample opportunity for him to replay all the difficult conversations and anger-filled shouting matches that had filled the days since Maria's death. What he saw was not to his liking because he was basically a genial, fun-loving man. The majority of the tensions between the brothers occurred because Ted was the consummate rancher while Fred was the epitome of a natural salesman. One liked to work, one liked to talk, and both were frustrated with the other. Ted was a natural stockman, Fred was a natural mechanic, and both despised the tools which satisfied the other. Ted was a country boy, Fred was a social person, and both questioned the other's approach to life.

As often happens in emotionally-loaded times, Fred made a resolution to keep his temper under control; and with his new resolve, he drove even faster so he could show Ted the new and improved life they would share. After he had burned enough gas that it was necessary to refuel in town on one of his circles, he showed the depth of his determination at the gas pump. This time he didn't stroll inside so he could lean on the counter and talk with the onlookers as usual, but stayed in the car while Ed pumped the handle back and forth to raise the gas into the bubble on top. After the car was full, Fred pulled out his cash, paid Ed at the pump, and drove out to the country again to resume his constant vigil.

By mid-afternoon, Darlene was grateful that Beth had insisted on her eating before she left the house. She and her partner had decided to criss-cross the pasture, and they had covered enough area that she had arrived at the windmill which was in the center of the section. Getting off her horse for the first time all day, Darlene was surprised that she couldn't feel her feet. After sitting in one position for so long, she was slow and stiff when she moved. She stomped one foot and then the other to get the feeling back, led Boxer close so he could drink his fill, and leaned over the lead spout which delivered the water to the tank. "Man, am I glad there's a breeze today," she muttered to no one in particular. Boxer slurped at the water, turned to rub his face on her sleeve, and slobbered all over her. Darlene rubbed his nose and sat down on the rim of the tank. "That feels so good that I'd appreciate a little shove from you so I could take a dip. Probably better not take the time to do that, so I'll just have another drink instead." She dipped her handkerchief into the water and tied it around the back of her neck to relieve the sunburn from the past two days. "Good thing I grabbed this hat of Ted's on the way out this morning. That sun's a bear."

Weary still but somewhat refreshed, Darlene scanned the horizon in all directions. She stood completely still and quit breathing so she didn't interfere with any signals that Ted might be sending her way. Repeating the same pattern in each direction, she slightly shook her head and patted Boxer's neck. "Break time's over, fella. We've got work to do and not a whole lot of day left to get it done. Wouldn't it be a crazy deal if we've spent all day out here and someone found Ted this morning. They'd probably haul him into town just to let Doc take a look at him before they let him come home, and he's probably sitting in the rocking chair at home right now. Even if he is, I think we'll keep on looking, just in case he's waiting to see how long it'll take me to find him." Kicking Boxer in the ribs, she was off again.

Darlene had finished her north and south investigation, and when she and Joe met at the gate, they decided to exchange directions. "I've explored these hills a lot, so maybe it'd be a good thing if we traded and went the other way. I know of a few thickets that are kind of tricky to get to so I'll head to the west corner and trail through there. You never know, he could've kinda lost his way and ended up off the trail and not have known it. Cheyenne had to hit the fence somewhere to get a gash like that, so I want to check out the fence line. You can go back if you want, but I believe I'll take a gander off this way."

Joe had ridden every inch of the thickets, much to his horse's disgust, but he wasn't about to tell Darlene there was no reason to keep looking. "You know this pasture so well that I think that's probably a really good idea. Maybe I'll tag along with you so we're sure not to overlook a thing. Would that be okay with you?"

In reality, Darlene needed someone with her. She had spent nearly two days alone, contemplating all the horrible visions and imaginings a nine year old mind could concoct. As the light started to fade, the realization she would have to go in after yet one more unsuccessful search was about more than she could handle. "Sure, Joe. That'd be a super plan. We can cover more ground with the two of us than I could alone. Let's go." Off the pair went at a deliberate walk so they could continue looking while heading to the corner.

After gouges and scrapes from riding through the locust thorns, she had to admit there was no sign of Ted. "Joe, we'd better get back or they'll have to send out a search party for us. That'd be pretty bad, wouldn't it, if the lookers got lost themselves?" She let out a dry little chuckle that suddenly became a choked-off sob. "Oh, Joe. Whatever do we do now? I'm so scared." She covered her face with her hands and cried like a lonely little girl.

Joe was a burly older man with young daughters of his own. His heart ached as he felt her give in to the same desolation he was feeling. "Now, honey, you know how all-in we are at the end of the day. We've been out here in the heat without taking time to eat or rest; and by the time evening comes, we're spent. After we get back to the house and have a warm meal and take a break, everything will look lots better. Let's go back so we can grain our horses and turn them out to graze a bit this evening. That little horse of yours has heart. He's given you one hundred per cent every inch of the way, and he'll be right there at the gate in the morning, too. We've got to take care of him so he can help us out tomorrow again. Who knows? Maybe someone heard something while we were gone." He reached over and awkwardly patted Darlene's hand, "How about it? Do you think we'd better skedaddle for home?"

Darlene slumped in her saddle and nodded as she laid the rein on Boxer's neck. He took the signal and spun around to face the road home. She snorted to Joe, "I must've been too easy on him if he's got enough energy to be spinning around like that." She rubbed Boxer's mane as she lengthened her hold on the reins. "He's got a magnificent walk—as long as he's headed back to the barn. Watch this, Joe. He'll outwalk your mare now even though he had trouble keeping up with her all day long. Isn't he funny?"

Enjoying the lightened mood, the two riders silently

followed the path which led back home. Occasionally Darlene would hold Boxer in place and give Joe's roan mare a chance to catch up. "I had him figured about right, didn't I, Joe? Guess he saves himself so he's fresh enough to get to the grain first. He's not much for day long speed, but he's a good one for a blazing finish." When they were in sight of the barn, she nudged Boxer into a trot even though the Soehls never ran a horse back to the barn. She wanted in the worst way to hear some good news, but the moment she saw the faces around the corral, she knew it had been another fruitless day for all concerned.

Keeping her face ducked so the guys couldn't see the tears running down her cheeks, she led Boxer into the stall, unsaddled him, and fed him outside so he could eat his grain and then go out to graze.

On her way back to the barn, she heard a familiar nicker from the shadows and hurried out to stroke Cheyenne. Before she left, she had doctored his wound with some of Ted's potion for wire cuts. As she had examined it closely, she saw that it wasn't as deep as she had originally thought. Although the flesh was torn across his entire chest, none of the muscle was hanging below the wound. The belladonna and mineral oil which Ted kept mixed up and handy in the barn would help with the pain and keep scarring to a minimum. Rubbing the big black's forehead, she turned toward the barn. "Wait here, big fella. I'll get some grain and rub you while you munch on it. It'll be all right if you just take it easy for a few days. Then we'll be back at our old habits before you know it." As if he understood her, Cheyenne stood patiently until she returned with his portion of grain. As he ate, she applied the medicine liberally and then brushed him until his coat was clean. By the time they were both done, they were ready to turn in for the night. She popped him on the rump as he maneuvered his body around and out the gate. Although it was painful, he slowly made his way to the grassy side hill and put his head down to graze.

Darlene pushed all her breath out in a big puff and trudged across the yard to the house to get caught up on everyone's reports. As she walked into the kitchen, people murmured to her and she gave a half-hearted wave to everyone.

Beth had been watching for her and met her with a warm washcloth. "Here, honey, you just stand there and relax for a minute. I've got your plate ready, and when you're done, we'll go lie down together. I'll tell you everything that happened so you won't miss a thing."

Bone weary and sad, Darlene nodded and did as she was told. Beth handed her a plate with the little tomato and cucumber sandwiches which were her favorites, along with a cold drumstick. Silently she cleaned her plate, handed it to Beth, and wordlessly drank a full glass of milk. Rubbing her milk moustache on her sleeve, she made no protest as Beth propelled her down the hallway.

Darlene loosened her belt, unhooked the buttons, and shimmied out of her trousers. Flopping down on the bed, she covered her eyes with the crook of her arm. "It's bad, isn't it, Beth? You know Ted wouldn't stay away this long if he could help it. I get so scared when I hear those coyotes howling, and I'm so worried about him. Why does it have to be this hard?" She turned over, buried her face in the pillow, and softly cried herself to sleep.

Beth crawled in beside her, cradled her body, and cried right along with her. Neither one moved much throughout the night, and when the dawn broke, they sat up at the same time and grinned at each other. "One good thing I'd say, Darlene, is that at least you don't snore very loudly. You didn't keep me awake more than half the night."

"I hate to be the one who tells you this, Beth, but you make those funny little snorty sounds every time you turn over on your back. You'd get really wrapped up until I'd poke you with my elbow and tell you to turn over. Then I could get a few minutes' sleep again before you were right back at it. I'm lucky I had any shut-eye at all. It's a good thing I'm such a strong person because this might get the best of someone who isn't." Darlene's natural good humor showed itself after a good night's sleep, and she found relief as she often did by joking and laughing, even though she was hurting inside.

"I smell bacon again, Darlene, so I think I'll get out there and help so you and Em can get ready to ride again. I have a good feeling about today, and I think more of Fred's crowd plans to come and help. Most of them like cars better than horses, but they'll do what they can. The more we have helping, the sooner we'll get our news." Beth had straightened her clothes, twisted her hair into a bun, and was tying on an apron by the time Darlene appeared for her pancake sandwich.

"Hi, Sis," she greeted Emma as she hastily gobbled about half her food. Darlene had a huge mouthful of milk ready to swallow when all of a sudden she shot milk across the table and onto the floor.

"What in the world? Are you all right, Lena? What's the matter?" Beth had rushed over to the table and was leaning over Darlene's shoulder. She had a cloth and was wiping up the spill as she patted the little girl. Then she followed the direction of Darlene's gaze and sucked in a gasp of air. Ben Reichers, standing at the door just ready to knock, smiled and pushed his way in. "Did you need to see someone, Mr. Reichers? I think Fred is still at his house if he isn't at the shop with the rest of his cronies. You're free to go find him." She delivered this message with the finality that her students knew very well. Once Miss Edgars used that tone, there was no room for further discussion.

Ben knew what he'd been told, so he tipped his hat and graciously replied, "Well, thanks, ma'am. I was hoping I'd find him before he took out. When a tragedy like this happens in the neighborhood, it's important that we all pull together. I'll just make my way there and see how I can help out. Darlene, it's always good to see you and my prayers are with you and your entire family." With that, he marched down the steps, fully aware of the eyes on his back.

"Oh, he's such a snake. I hate him. I know it's evil and wicked to hate someone, but I do hate him, Beth. He's so goody-goody and I know darned good and well that he and Ted hated each other and he comes here acting like he's our best friend. Man, he makes my blood boil." With that, Darlene stomped out of the house toward the barn. All she wanted was to saddle up and ride out as fast as Boxer would go.

Beth could see that the little sorrel had better be ready to make tracks when they left the corral, but she was secretly glad to see Darlene's flash of temper. Trying to be brave and strong, she had absorbed all the tension of Ted's absence without allowing herself to release the emotions she was experiencing. Beth knew that Darlene's outburst of anger was a surge of pent-up feelings, so she had hung back and not responded to any of the sentiments Darlene had expressed. Later on they could have a philosophical discussion of hatred; but for now, it was enough for Beth that Darlene had spoken her mind. Besides, Beth agreed with Darlene's assessment of Ben.

Trying to retrace Ted and Cheyenne's path was complicated by the heavy rain which had washed out all signs they could use for tracking. One clue they were trying to hash out was where the big black had run into a barbed wire fence. Since the majority of the pastures Ted rode through were winter range without any cattle, all the gates but one had been draped back on the fence and left open all summer. That perhaps meant an accident had happened closer to town by the closed gate, but a spooked horse will often lunge ahead oblivious of his surroundings while running in blind panic. The riders could come to no agreement as to where to focus their efforts, so they decided to switch pastures and ride one which they hadn't yet covered. Sometimes a fresh eye lends new perspective to surroundings, so the volunteers traded assignments and left the ranch.

By now, the entire community had heard about Ted's being missing, so riders from the far reaches of the county assembled to help look. As Rod Kramer put it when introducing himself to Darlene, "Even if we don't know Ted and your family, you're still one of ours. No one deserts a neighbor at a time like this. We'll find him, little lady, don't you worry." He had placed his huge hand on her bony shoulder, winked at her, and put his hat back on his head. Genuine prairie friends tended to be unfailingly polite and considerate, quick to lend a hand and quick to disappear when the thanks were being handed out.

"Appreciate it, Mr. Kramer. You riding with Joe and me today?" Darlene was ready to take on a new pasture since she was certain they had covered every inch of the last one. She swung up on her saddle, patted her horse's neck, and told him, "You need to give me all you've got today, Boxer. We've got to find Ted, no matter what." Kicking her heels into his side, she whirled and left the lot at a quick trot.

Trailing behind her, the two men took advantage of their privacy to trade what each one knew. The version of when Ted left town, how the horse came home, and what had been done so far was pretty much the same for both of them. Rod knew Fred had stopped in town this morning to pick up the undertaker since he felt certain it would be a bad outcome. Joe told how a bunch of Fred's buddies had come the night before and were drinking and carousing most of the night. "If you want to know what I think, they're a pretty seedy crew. I'll tell you this much—I sure wouldn't want my women folks around that bunch after they've been in the sauce." They exchanged looks of agreement and broke into a lope to catch up with Darlene.

The new undertaker, Tom Wilson, had reached out to shake Fred's hand when he came out to the car. "This is a tough time for you and your family, Fred. I'm glad you asked me to come along, and let's just hope I'll be riding along as a friend and not in a business capacity."

"That'd be nice, all right, but after two days in this heat, I can't imagine he'll make it. If he got hurt, it must be so bad he can't flag anyone down, so I've pretty much resigned myself to the fact he's gone. I appreciate you being with me in case we need to take care of anything. Most of all, I hope our sisters aren't the ones to stumble on to him, 'specially Darlene. That'd be too much to expect a little girl to go through, even one as tough-minded as she tries to be."

Tom, who had moved to the area from Gothenburg, was fascinated with the prairie way of life. "I grew up in town, and I always thought our Pony Express Station was the neatest place ever. I'd go hang out there and play like I was one of the guys whipping and slashing to get the mail through. I never had a real horse, but I could sure gallop a hole in the wind on my favorite branch. Mom'd let me take it in my bedroom, and I'd tie him to my bedpost. What you guys do around here is the real thing, and I think I'd like to get myself a real horse. It looks like fun."

Fred shrugged and leveled with Tom, "I hate horses. When I was a little boy, that was the only way we could get around. It seemed like they knew I didn't like them, so they'd act up and run away with me. The one pony I did kind of get along with must have figured out he was in charge, and he ran under Mom's clothesline and whapped me right off. I had a mark for weeks, and all the kids teased me that it looked like someone tried to hang me." Fred rubbed his neck as if he could still feel the shame of the mark which had disappeared long ago.

"Is it easier to drive a team than ride a saddle horse? At least you wouldn't be so close to them." Tom was genuinely surprised to hear that anyone who had a chance to be around horses didn't want anything to do with them. "I always wanted to hold those long reins."

Fred laughed, "Just one word of advice for you, Tom. When you're driving a team, you hold lines. When you're riding a horse, you hold reins. Don't want you making one of those slipups when you get to talking to the teamsters. They're kind of a picky bunch when someone from the outside tries to fit in."

"Thanks for keeping me from embarrassing myself on that, at least. For what looks like a simple way of life, there's sure a lot I don't know." Tom laughed as he remembered several of his own bloopers. "What's the story on your brother? He must like horses or he wouldn't have been out for a ride on a stormy night like that."

"Of course, brother Ted was a whiz with any animal, but almost a wonder worker with horses. When we were little, he would cry when the day was over cause he'd have to leave the barn. Seems funny that two guys raised the same could be so different, doesn't it? Now I'm driving a car back and forth trying to figure out what happened. We all know what a hand Ted was with a horse, so no one can believe he got dumped. He broke his own colts and made sure they were foolproof before he called them finished. Every horse he started was good enough to be a world beater, and

Cheyenne was no different. To tell the truth, I got kinda tired hearing of what a wonder horse he was." Driving along the road that ran along the fence to the south of the horse route, Fred pointed out different home places as he and Tom traveled the hills.

Both men settled back into the upholstery and withdrew into their private thoughts as Fred eased the car up the hills to resume the search. Pulling up to a gate that led to the pasture, Fred glanced at his passenger, "Mind opening this so we can pull in here? We call this the Carter place, and from here on, the gates are open. To me, that means the horse probably ran into some wire around here so I'd like to take a look. When I was a kid, the folks would always tell us this was halfway; and if we could last till we got here, they'd stop and let us run around here while they watered the horses. The Carters had a cellar over here where the old house stood, and that draw over there is where Ted and I would slide while the folks checked the load and readjusted the harness straps. If I remember right, there was a kind of overhang where the water had carved a hole like a cave under the bank. We'd hide there and the folks would pretend they didn't know where we were so we'd sneak out and scare them. They'd jump and yell, and we'd go laughing back to the wagon. Dad would hoist us over his shoulder and say, 'Mama, I've got two sacks of taters here. Where do you want them?' She'd tell him, 'Just toss them in the back,' and he'd softly let us down to the blanket she always laid on the boards for us. Times like that were good."

While he talked, Fred strolled up the draw to show Tom the overhang. "Too bad, Tom. Looks like it finally got so weak the whole top caved in. Must've been the rain that made it let go." Kicking clumps of grass aside, Fred dropped to his knees, "I remember Ted saying this would have been the perfect place to hide from the Indians. He'd scrunch back against the wall in a little ball. Honestly, the way he could kinda fade into the background made it seem like he probably could be safe there."

Staring more closely at the mound of sand, he let out a mournful moan and started scratching at the sand. "No, Ted. Not here, not where you always said you'd be safe." Digging frantically at the scrap of material he had seen peeking out of the ground, Fred flung dirt backwards until he had uncovered three fingers. He jumped up and bolted away from his find. Retching violently, he sobbed and covered his eyes, "If you hadn't been so bull-headed about riding that stupid horse home, you never would've stopped here." With that, Fred dropped to his knees and lay down beside the mound which covered his brother's body. "All I ever wanted was to be as good as you, Ted. You were always the smart one, and I never did anything right. I've changed, but now you'll never know. How can I run a ranch without you, Ted? You can't leave me like this."

Tom let him go through all his expressions of grief and stepped forward only when Fred had finally regained his breath and sat quietly stroking the exposed fingers. "Fred, I'm sorry it worked out like this, but now I'm going to need some help out here to remove Ted's body, and we'd better let everyone know he's been found. Let's go to town so I can get my own vehicle, and we'll get someone to drive you back home. When we get the body dug out, I'll take him right to town. After three days, there's no way we can have any kind of viewing or service. We'll have to bury him immediately, so you've got to buck up and tell me what arrangements you want to make. Do you hear me?"

Tom's words and strong grasp brought Fred out of his shock and back to the reality of the moment. "Oh, Tom, yeah. I know we'd want him in Ogallala with the rest of the family. What do we do about that? Can you take care of it? I can't even think what I need to do next, let alone make any plans." He gave a sad little grin, "I guess you think you're ready for anything, but it's a different story when it's right in front of you, isn't it?"

"Let me handle everything on this end, Fred. Let's get back to town and find someone to drive you back home where you belong." Tom guided the stumbling man to the passenger side where he slid in and covered his face. Fred never looked up all the way to town, and never made a sound other than an occasional grunt as if he'd been slugged in the stomach hard enough to knock the wind out of him.

Tom pulled up in front of Ed and Tracy's store. They came running out when they saw Fred's car, then abruptly stopped as they saw Fred slumped over. Tom waved Ed over where they held an animated conversation, then Ed nodded and stepped to Tracy's side where he spoke earnestly to her as Tom made his way to his undertaker's establishment. At that point, Tracy pulled the door shut behind her, locked up the store, and climbed in the back seat. Ed slid in the driver's seat, pulled the car into gear, and hit the gas.

Tom, who was standing beside his own car as Ed drove closer, waved him to a stop. "Whenever you come to a new pasture, you'd better stop and be sure they know it's time to end the search. Be sure to tell them all to go to the Soehl headquarters instead of coming to help me. I don't want anyone there when we pull him out. It'll be a grim sight they'd be better off not seeing." He reached inside the window to tap Ed's shoulder, "Thanks, Ed. Tracy, you'll be a lifesaver to the whole outfit. Glad you could help out."

With that, Ed gunned the car out of town, followed closely by Tom and his helper who had loaded gloves, shovels, and tarps to help them with their business.

The Dolphs were good enough friends with the Soehl family that they could sit in silence as long as Fred wanted.

When he took a breath and looked over at Ed, the dam burst. "Oh, you guys. I can't believe this. I was just showing Tom where we played when we were kids, and I happened to see a corner of his shirt sleeve. What in the world would have made him stop there, do you suppose? If the storm got really bad and he needed to get out of it, that hole probably would have made sense to him. Maybe Cheyenne was standing there when it caved in, and it scared him so bad he just ran blind. The lightning was so bad that night it made me duck every time it hit, and I was sitting in my car. I can't even imagine how bad it must have been out there with him riding across those hills." Fred closed his eyes and shuddered.

"At least we have some kind of an answer now. It's a terrible tragedy, but somehow it's better knowing a hard truth than never finding out. I feel so sorry for your family after all they've been through. Your folks never had it easy from the very first they got here, but they kept putting one foot in front of the other. Maria and Ernest were so good together. I was so glad when they got the new house built so they had some room, and then Ernest died. Maria kept going but she was never the same after that. What workers. You come from good stock, Fred." Tracy patted his arm. "I guess if there's any good here, it's that Maria didn't have to know about this. I was worried that losing Harry would do her in, but she just worked that much harder and loved you kids that much deeper. It's sad to have to go through this, and I imagine it'll be hard to have to say good bye without seeing him for one last time."

Fred sat up a bit straighter, "That's what I dread having to tell the girls most of all. I know it's that way, but I still wish we could have him at the house for one more night." Looking up at the hills, he saw riders combing the blowouts. "We'd better let them know, and maybe they can head home and gather up everyone on the way. Toot the horn and we'll wave them over here."

As the riders heard the tinny sound, they trotted down the hill and loped over to the fence. Ed crawled out and delivered the news, gesturing back west where Ted had been discovered, and then motioning east where the riders were to gather. As the riders turned back toward the ranch, Ed crawled in. "They saw Darlene in the next pasture, so maybe we can find her and be the ones to tell her. Otherwise she might head back to the Carter place, no matter what anyone else tells her." He sighed, "This'll be tough."

Driving over the rough trail, the three occupants were lost in their own thoughts, most of which dealt with the future of the Soehl ranch. Fred knew he was in over his head, and the Dolphs held the same opinion. Although each person was intensely sad at the loss of Ted, looming ahead were the immediate actions and decisions that would be key to the saving or destroying of Ernest and Maria's legacy.

"Oh, look. Over there riding down the catsteps. See that sorrel horse? I think that's Darlene. Honk at her and I'll wave her over here." Tracy was the first to spot her, and she hung out the window and signaled Darlene to the fence. "After three days out here, she must be exhausted, but I'll bet it never crossed her mind to stay home."

Once they had picked their way down the hillside, Darlene had kicked Boxer into an easy lope and made her way to the fence. She swung off, wrapped the reins around the post, and climbed through the barbed wire. "Did you find him? Is he okay? Take me where he is so I can talk to him." She began babbling the minute she got to the car as if the only truth that could exist was the one she told. Grabbing Tracy who stood by the car, Darlene insisted, "Tell me where you found him. We've looked so hard that I can't believe he's okay. This is such good news."

All of a sudden, Darlene stopped in mid-sentence as she

felt Tracy's hot tears drop on the back of her hand. Looking up and recognizing the awful reality in Tracy's eyes, Darlene collapsed beside the car. "No, Tracy, no," as all the emotions of the past days came surging forth.

Her hurt and sorrow flooded over as she lashed out in anger. "Fred, why didn't you do something? All you did was drive this stupid car back and forth when Ted needed you. If you'd jumped on a horse and gotten out there with the rest of us, he'd be here today." Jerking at the car door, she shouted at Ed, "Take me to him right now. I've got to be with him."

When she sensed the hesitation on his part, she slammed the door shut and bolted for the fence. "I don't need any of you. I'll just jump on Boxer and he'll take me to Ted."

As she bent to climb back through the fence, Fred caught up to her and pinned her arms to her side. He held her firmly until she stopped struggling and wilted into him. Stroking her hair and brushing her cheek with his lips, he murmured, "I know, Darlene, I know. The only time he ever needed me and I let him down."

"Fred, I'm sorry. Now will you just please take me to Ted? I have to see him." Darlene pushed against her brother and turned back to the car as she pleaded with him.

Shaking his head, Fred grasped her arm. "Darlene, we can't. After three days in this terrible heat, Tom told us there's no way we can ever see Ted again." He paused to let her process his words. "I knew we'd want him buried in Ogallala with the folks and Harry, so Tom was going to take him there as soon as they recovered his body. All we can do now is go back home. Let's get in and Ed can take us there."

Standing ramrod straight, Darlene nodded her head, "I understand, Fred, and I know we need to be home. You guys go ahead in the car, and Boxer and I'll meet you there. It wouldn't be right to leave my horse out here in the hot sun, so I'll take him home and turn him out." With that, she slid through the fence, unwound the reins, and pulled herself up. Turning Boxer's head toward home, Darlene glanced back and motioned Fred and the Dolphs to follow the trail to the ranch.

Watching as her lone figure receded, Tracy struggled to maintain her composure, "That is one special little girl, and it makes my heart ache to see her hurting so." Climbing into the car, she nudged Ed, "Let's get a move on so we're there when she gets home. I can't believe how helpless I feel, but I know I need to be there."

Ed continued the journey, stopping as he saw riders and giving them information and directions. By the time they pulled in the yard, most of the riders had arrived and were mingling in front of the house where they gathered after they did the chores. Looking around, he whispered to Tracy, "Maybe you ought to check out the barn. I don't see Darlene anywhere, and she's had time to get back by now."

Tracy moved around the back of the car as Ed escorted Fred into the house where Emma, Alma, and other family and friends had gathered. Peering into the darkness of the barn, she could see Darlene's saddle and bridle. She moved on past the box stalls and slid the door open so she could look out. Boxer, who had just finished rolling in the white sand of the corral, pushed himself up onto his front feet, gathered his back legs under him, stood up, shook, and ambled out of the corral.

Closing the door behind her, Tracy retraced her steps to the box stalls and stopped as she heard a shuffle in the nearest one. His black form obscured by the shadows, Cheyenne stood at the front of the stall with his head down. "Hey, old guy, how's that cut? I heard it was a nasty one." The soothing sounds of Tracy's words made him turn to look at her. As he lifted his head, Tracy caught sight of

Darlene tucked in the corner of the stall, knees sticking up, arms clasped around them, and forehead plastered against her trousers.

"Honey, can I come in?" Tracy paused at the gate and waited for an answer. When she saw the negligible nod of Darlene's head, Tracy made her way to the corner and sank down in a similar pose. They sat there in silence until Darlene shifted her weight and leaned against Tracy. At that point, she put her arms around the little girl and they rocked gently together.

Sobbing softly, Darlene asked, "What's going to happen to me? Emma's going away and I was going to live with Beth and Ted. I don't have anyone left, and I don't have anywhere to go. Seems like this is the only place I belong." She took a deep breath, punctuated with the jerky breathing that accompanies deep crying, and gave a little smile, "Did you know that Ted and I had a sadness barrel? When Mama was sick, we decided we'd come here to the barn to that spot when we needed to get away. It seemed right for us to have a place to feel bad together. Now he's gone, and I'm all alone. At least when Mama died, we had each other. Now I've got nothing."

Tracy held the little girl until her cries faded into little snuffles. "You'll never be all alone so long as we're around, Darlene. We'll always be here for you."

Hugging Tracy, Darlene took a deep breath, squared her shoulders, stood up as straight as she could, and started for the door. "We'd better head to the house so we don't keep everyone waiting. It was sure nice that so many people came and helped out, wasn't it?"

"Sweetie, Ted was a man who had all kinds of friends, and everyone knew your folks were always there if anyone ever needed help. You come from a good family, Darlene, and you're one special girl." With that, Tracy smoothed

Darlene's hair back from her face, tipped her chin up to give her a soft kiss on the forehead, and they slowly made their way to the house.

Neighbors who were gathered in small groups, discussing what they knew and guessing at what would come next, parted to let Darlene and Tracy through to the house. Men would tip their hats and murmur, "Sorry" as they moved aside and took out their handkerchiefs to wipe their eyes.

All the sisters and the remaining brother had congregated in the front room where they were discussing arrangements. Even though Ted's body could not be brought back home, they had decided to have a memorial service for him. Emma looked up to see Darlene come in, and rushed over to her. Grasping each other, the two sisters rocked together as tears coursed down their cheeks. Silently, they finally faced the reality that they had refused to consider for the past three days. "Honey, we were thinking we could get some of Ted's stuff that meant a lot to him and lay it out. Then anyone who wanted to could talk about him. What do you think of that?"

Darlene nodded and reached out for Ted's work hat, "Wouldn't be right if we left this out, would it? He only took it off to go to bed or go to town." Stroking the brim, she gently laid the battered hat on the middle of the table. "Do you want me to run out to the barn and get that headstall he was working on? It's not quite done, but it's sure fancy."

Alma asked, "Would you mind if I came along? I always liked going into his tack room, and I haven't been there for a spell." The two sisters joined hands and trudged across the yard to retrieve the leatherwork.

"Hard as it is, I guess we'd better get the Bible out here and do the writing. Now that we're all together, this seems like the right time to get that done. I'll get it out of Mama's room." Going down the hall, Emma turned in, opened the drawer, and returned with the book clasped tightly against her.

Turning to Beth who had been standing silently in the background, Emma continued, "Beth, when we got home that night in the storm, Darlene was worried about her picture so she put it inside her shirt and brought it in. When we unrolled it, we found the one of you and Ted inside hers, so we laid them on the dresser to dry out. Things have been so crazy since then that I forgot to mention it to you until now. Would it be all right if we'd put it in a frame and set it on the table, too? It's up to you."

"I'd be honored if you'd like to use it. Thanks for asking." Beth recalled the joy of sitting with Ted and laughing about the little red-headed boys they expected in their future, and she found herself unable to speak further. Nodding her head, she closed her eyes and pursed her lips to hold in the pain.

Darlene and Alma returned with the headstall, silver conchos, and Tater. "Seems like we need a hound if we're talking about Ted. Darned seldom he went anywhere without one. Besides, Tater helped Mama towards the end too." Alma arranged the items on the table as Darlene gave the signal to Tater, and he lay down quietly on the rug. She smiled ruefully, "You know, this would have been one more reason for Mama to hate August. First Harry and now Ted."

Fred was the first to break silence as he cleared his throat and addressed his sisters, "We really don't have enough room for everyone to come in here, so how about moving the table outside? If anyone wants to speak about Ted, it'd be easier for us all to hear. What do you think?"

"Let's do that. People have been so good to us, and his friends need a chance to say what's in their hearts. Good idea, Fred. " Alma gathered up the pieces of Ted's life as several of the men hauled the heavy oak table out to the yard, and the sisters soon had the table set up just right. Along with his hat, leatherwork, and picture, Emma's bouquet of daisies sat in the center beside the family Bible.

As a respectful silence fell over the crowd, Fred began the service. "You folks have been here in many of our sorrowful times, and we want you to know how much it means to us. I see lots of familiar faces who were here with us to mourn when we lost Papa, then Mama, and now Ted. We were raised to be God-fearing folk, so if you'd like to join with us while we recite the 121st Psalm, we'd sure like that a lot. Ted's voice was always strong in the part about lifting his eyes to the hills, so it seems fitting to say these words one last time for him."

"Ich hebe meine augen auf zu den bergen, von welchen mir Hulfe kommt." As Fred began with the first few syllables, soon an entire chorus of voices completed the verse. Many of the settlers were of German origin, and the familiar words of the psalm echoed across the yard as they recalled saying them first for Ernest and Maria, and now for Ted. The somberness of the ritual combined with the tragic end of Ted lent an oppressive air to the gathering.

Trader Keith stepped forward and cleared his throat, "I just want to say that Ted was as honest as the day is long. His word was good, and his handshake was final. In all the horse-trading we did, there was never a time that a horse was less than he said or a price that was more than it should have been. I'll miss him." With that, he turned aside and made his way to the back of the crowd to regain his composure.

After the first testimony to Ted's character, it was as if the floodgates opened and anecdotes flowed easily and often. Stories of his ability with stock, his good humor, and his dedication to family and ranch were plenteous and moving. The afternoon was punctuated with laughter, tears, and regret as they bid farewell to one of their own.

When the stories subsided and onlookers were standing in silence and engaged in their own thoughts, Fred stepped forward. "There's no way we can thank you enough for what you've done these past three days. You left your homes and came as soon as you heard Ted was missing, and you've given all you had to help out. As everyone goes home, I hope you'll be careful and travel safely. The way our family closes these services is to write in the Bible, and after a word of prayer from Reverend Stotts, Emma will write Ted's death date of July 28, 1925. We'd like you to have a bite with us before you head out, and once again, thanks for being here for us."

After the prayer, Emma opened the family Bible to the middle where Maria had started recording the events of the Soehl family, and she finalized Theodor Soehl's entry. Nodding at Darlene who stood beside her, Emma closed the Bible and handed it to Darlene. "How about taking this inside? We'll clear the table and put out the food for our friends."

With a quick hug of her big sister, Darlene reached out for the book and returned it to the top of the dresser in Maria's room. Gently putting the Bible down, she leaned her head against the wooden front and let the tears slide down her cheeks. Now she knew it was over. After a few minutes, she composed herself, wiped her nose on her sleeve, and slowly made her way out to the kitchen where she stood silently and looked out at the crowd.

Leaning against the door jamb, she gradually became aware of another presence in the kitchen. Turning her head toward the stove, she saw Ben who had slipped inside while she was in the back room. Standing beside the stove, he held up his hand in a signal for quiet as he gave her a conspiratorial smile and slowly began to make his way toward the door. "Lena— I know that was Ted's pet name for you, and I like to think I can use it too. I hope we can get beyond that misunderstanding in town last Saturday. When Ted and I talked that day, I explained that all I wanted to do was be a good neighbor and friend. I don't know if he told you, but he thanked me and said he appreciated my interest in you." Moving closer, Ben was relieved that Darlene didn't make a run for it. Instead, she dropped her head as her eyes filled with tears, and she shyly put her hand up to her face. Ben hadn't noticed that Darlene had the habit of biting her fingernails, but as she slid her fingers into her mouth, he put his arms out as if to embrace her.

All of a sudden, she blasted out the loudest whistle that she had ever delivered, and instantly the room was bustling with activity. Tracy and Beth burst into the room, and they held Darlene between them. "What's going on, Darlene? What ever possessed you to do that? It almost scared me to death." As Emma questioned her sister, Beth turned around to see where Darlene was pointing.

"You! I might have known. Is there anything too low down for you, Ben? After what Ted told you in town, I'd think you'd know better than to pull something like this. Who do you think you are, anyway? Just because her big brother is gone doesn't mean she's at your mercy." As Beth spoke, her voice became louder and stronger. "I swear no one is safe around you, no matter what or where, and I think it would be best if you never showed your face here again."

By this time, Fred had barged into the kitchen and heard Beth's harangue. "Now wait just a darned minute, young lady. You may have been Ted's woman, but you need to remember your place. You may be upset, but there's no need for you to take it out on my friend." With that, he crossed the kitchen and flung his arm around Ben's shoulder. "I'll be the one who decides who stays and who goes, and I say he's welcome here any time he wants."

Emma interrupted Fred with her suggestion, "You know, I think it'd be a good idea if we let Darlene fill us in about why she whistled us all in here. Go ahead, honey."

Feeling everyone's eyes on her, Darlene dropped her eyes to the floor and shook her head.

"See there, folks, it was all a misunderstanding. Beth, no hard feelings. I know you're overwrought and said some things you didn't mean, but I can sure let that go. After all, we're in this together." Ben felt the shift in momentum after Fred had vouched for him, and he was feeling invincible. After Darlene shut down in front of everyone, his sense of relief was huge.

Tracy had slipped in behind Emma and pulled Darlene to the side where they held a whispered conversation. Standing upright, she held up her hand in Ben's direction, "Not so fast, Ben. Darlene decided she has something to say." Stepping aside so Darlene could move in front of her and yet lean against her, Tracy continued, "Anytime you're ready, Darlene."

"When I came out of the bedroom, I stopped here for a minute to get ready to talk to everyone. That's when I noticed that Ben was hiding here in the kitchen. Just like he always does, he tried to get close enough to touch me, and he was telling all kind of lies while he headed for me. He said Ted thanked him for being interested in me and that Ted asked him to look after me. I know Ted wouldn't say anything like that because he had said I was never to be alone with Ben. We talked on Saturday about how scared Amy and I were when Ben sneaked up on us, and Ted had told me that anytime I needed to be safe from Ben, all I had to do was whistle and get someone's attention. That's just what I did, and now he stands there and acts like he's the good guy when we all know he's a low down dirty liar."

Emma and Fred jumped in at the same time, but with

totally different responses. "How dare you say something like that, Darlene? You always did have a big imagination, and it's sad to say, but I think Ted must have filled your head with all kinds of nonsense. I always knew there was bad blood between him and Ben, but I never realized he had poisoned your head with it. I truly think you'd better apologize to Ben for all those nasty things you made up. We'll talk about this later, but for right now, you tell him you're sorry."

Whirling around to face Fred, Emma was the first to take him to task, "Fred Soehl, what in the world is the matter with you? Your little sister told us this man was making unnatural advances to her and you defend him? How can you live with yourself? This is the most unbelievable thing I've ever heard, and if anyone needs to apologize, it's you for not believing family, and then Ben for all he has put our little sister through."

Ben stood looking back and forth at Fred and Emma wondering who would prevail, and he was startled to hear a totally new voice enter the fray. "You know, this might be a little hard to sort out since Ted isn't here to give his version, but maybe I can help out a bit on that score. I had just gotten to town Saturday afternoon and was wandering through the park when I saw Ted. I wanted to talk to him so I went in his direction but had a heck of a time catching up. He was quite a ways in front of me when all of a sudden, he stopped in his tracks and reached out to grab someone. As I got closer, I could see it was Ben, and I can tell you the gist of their conversation. Actually it was pretty one-sided because Ted was so mad that he didn't lose any time spelling it all out for Ben." Trader Keith put his hand on Darlene's shoulder and gave Ben an unblinking gaze.

"Just because you say Ted was mad and blew up at Ben, that wasn't anything new for him. Ben told me many times that Ted would pick up the mail and jump all over him for no reason at all. You haven't convinced me that this was anything but a quarrel between two men who didn't like each other." Fred discounted Trader's version in his determination to clear Ben's name.

"Well, Fred, that may be, but I'll tell you exactly what Ted had to say, and then you can judge for yourself if he asked Ben to look after Darlene. As I recall, these were his exact words, 'I don't know of anything too low-down for you, and you just proved that by sneaking up on those little girls. How many times do I have to say the same thing until you get the message? This had darned well better be the last time I ever hear your name coming from the lips of scared little girls or so help me, it'll be the last time anyone hears your name again.' Then Ben started whining again, and Ted gave him pretty specific orders. 'Personally, I don't have the time nor the inclination to sort out your twisted stories, so I'm telling you to stay away. Stay away from those kids, and stay away from our place.' To me it was clear that Ted didn't trust Ben around little girls, and to me that's serious stuff. Just telling you what I heard."

It was Fred's turn to speak, and he found himself in a particularly difficult position. Although he had never admitted his suspicions to anyone, he had seen some questionable conduct on Ben's part. Fred didn't doubt the truth of some of the accusations against his good friend, but if he turned against Ben, it was like Ted was still in charge, even from the grave. Nothing bad had really happened to Darlene or Amy, so he didn't feel inclined to give up a friend just because they were a pair of hysterical little girls. Looking around the room, he chose his favorite strategy— avoidance. "I don't think this is the best time to be discussing something like this. Emotions are running high, and we're all worn out from the strain of the last three days. We're here to honor

Ted's memory, so let's keep that in mind and we'll deal with this later." With that, he linked his arm through Ben's and started toward the door.

"No, Fred, I don't think that's any kind of answer. This needs taken care of. It's pretty clear you're taking Ben's side, and that doesn't look good. We might as well hash out what happens next so we can all make plans," Alma, usually quiet and easy-going, spoke up with an unaccustomed firmness. "I can't feel comfortable leaving Darlene if I know Ben is free to come and go, especially now that this is all out in the open."

Fred erupted in the same way as he had when Ted had questioned any of his decisions. "All right. If you all want to know what happens next, I can tell this much. It's galled me that I'm the oldest and my wife and I had to live in that little house while Ted and the rest of you stayed in the big house. Mama's been gone over a year, and you've kept that bedroom of hers like it's some kind of a shrine. I think that's a waste of good space, and as soon as we can, Ruth and I'll be moving into the big house. Since all the family's here, I'm telling you to get whatever you want out of the house because it's mine from now on. And you know what, all of my friends are welcome in my home, no matter what you say. Any questions?"

"Yes, I do have a question for you. Are you planning on Emma and Darlene staying with you since that's been their home all along, or do they have to move out?" Alma didn't back down from his bluster and pushed him to declare his intentions.

Fred realized his image in the neighborhood was at stake, so he lightened his tone, "Of course they can stay. I'm not saying I'm moving anyone out so we can move in, I'm just saying we're going to change a few things. Since I'm the only brother Darlene has left, it would seem right for her to live with Ruth and me. I know my duty and I'll do what I have to, so no one has to worry about her even if it'll cost more to have her living with us. Don't know but maybe you girls can chip in some to help out with the finances."

The crowd gave a collective gasp at what his words revealed. The coldness which he revealed when speaking of taking Darlene in as his duty was overshadowed by his open grab for cash. Even for Fred, that was a crass, money-grubbing remark.

Darlene had buried her face in Emma's dress and grasped Alma's outstretched hand. "How can this be happening? Emma's going back East and you're headed to California and I'm all alone. She sunk to the floor and sobbed as she covered her face.

Chapter 6

All of a sudden, she felt herself lifted in strong arms and held in a man's grip. She looked up to see that Ed had picked her up as Tracy stepped forward and announced to the crowd. "I promised Darlene that she didn't have a thing to worry about as long as Ed and I are here, so it looks to me like she's coming to live with us. We need a daughter and she needs a home so that's settled; settled so long as Darlene agrees. What do you say, honey? Would you like to come live with us?"

Through her tears, Darlene nodded her head, "Would you take me in, Tracy? That'd be the best thing ever. I promise I'll help out and not be a burden. I'm a good worker and I can help earn my keep."

"Sweetheart, it's an honor for Ed and me to have a girl to call our own. If you want to live with us, you don't have to earn your keep, all you have to do is be a little girl and let us love you." Tracy choked back her tears and stroked Darlene's head as it lay on Ed's shoulder.

Emma stepped up to the Dolphs and made her own offer,

"You know there's no way I would just go off and leave Darlene. If you want to reconsider, I'll stay around here so she and I can live together. We can get along just fine. I had made my plans before we lost Ted, and I'll stay here as long as she needs me."

Patting her arm, Tracy reassured her, "Em, you've given up so much for your family that it's time for you to get back to your own life. I know you came home because you wanted to be with your mother, and you stayed to help out as long as you were needed. You go ahead with your plans and we'll be delighted to have you come back and visit as often as you can. While you're gone, you can write back and forth to keep up with each other. That way you'll both have something to look forward to."

Turning to Fred, Tracy continued, "How about us coming back in a week? That way, Emma and Darlene will have time to pack up what they want to take, and we'll come to help them move. We'll be back next Tuesday if that works for everyone."

Fred was taken aback at the sudden turn of events, but he realized agreement at this point might be his best course of action. "Well, I guess it's a good thing we talked it over and got that settled. We've been on pins and needles for at least three days, so the best thing might be for our family to all to get a good night's rest and meet here tomorrow. Then we can all figure out how to split up the folks' stuff and move on with our lives."

As he and Ben moved through the clustered people in the kitchen, Ben stopped to flash a triumphant grin at Beth, and they continued to the yard where Fred stopped to address those still remaining. "This was a painful time for all of us, and now we have to figure out what to do next. Thanks for being good neighbors, and if you'd like to join us down at the little house, I might have a few refreshments there to help you on your way home."

The sisters heard his words and silently shook their heads at his callous disregard for propriety. "Darlene was right—Mama wouldn't have liked this August at all." Alma reached out to embrace the Dolphs. "Later on after we get settled in California, maybe we can find a way for Darlene to come stay with us. Until then, I won't have a moment's worry about her since I'll know she is safe and loved. There's no way we can ever repay you for your kindness."

Since Fred had picked up Beth at her home, she needed to catch a ride home with a neighbor who was ready to leave. She held Darlene in her arms as she prepared to leave. "Honey, I've decided I can't stay around here without Ted. I still can't believe he's gone, but I know I wouldn't have a moment's peace if I had to worry about staying away from Ben every moment. I've decided to go back to Omaha and get a job where my brother can help me get settled. I'd love it if you wanted to come live with me in the city, but it might be too much right now for you to leave everything and everyone you know. Remember my offer is always open. I didn't say anything earlier since you had enough to sort out, but all you have to do is let me know and I'll come get you.

Darlene grabbed on to Beth and held on as if she would never let go. "Thanks for asking, Beth, but for right now, I think my place is here with the Dolphs. Ted would be happy that you're getting away from Ben, and you're lucky to have a brother who wants to help out." Drying her tears, Darlene pulled back and put on a brave smile, "You know what, Beth? I've decided I want to be a teacher just like you. Maybe someday we can teach in the same school. Wouldn't that be the best ever?"

"Darlene, I'd consider it a fine honor to work with you. How about us writing to each other so we can keep in touch? Deal?"

"Deal." Darlene stuck out her hand the way she had seen Ted do so often. "Let's shake on it. That's like a promise, you know, so we can't ever break it."

The two solemnly shook hands, fell together for one last embrace, and both turned away. Darlene waved as long as Beth was in sight, and then turned to talk to those neighbors who had quietly done the chores before leaving for their homes.

When everyone was finally gone, Emma and Darlene sprawled in the kitchen chairs, "You know, Darlene, this is the last time this'll be our home. After we divide up the pieces out of our past and move on, it'll be Fred's house. When I think of how excited Mama was when we got to move in here from that soddy with the crumbling walls, it makes me glad she isn't around to see what has happened to our family. I remember how she brought in a big load of quilts and set them down in the middle of the kitchen floor. She looked around and said, 'Is good. Is good to have a big family and a big house to hold it. Papa, when we get old, we can sit on the porch in our rocking chairs and do nothing.' Papa just laughed at the thought of Mama sitting still because she never could just sit and do nothing. Even when she sat and rocked, she would take out her mending or needlework."

"I wish I'd had a chance to know Papa, Em. Everyone says Ted was a lot like him, but now they're both gone. What is your favorite memory of all? You've got the best stories and remember so much that happened before I ever came along. Tell me one I've never heard before, please?" Darlene was intent on gathering as many fragments of the past as she could before she left her old life behind.

Emma took some time to consider before giving her answer, and Darlene sat patiently. When she saw a small smile creep about Em's upside down mouth, she sat up expectantly. Emma chuckled as she described a particularly powerful moment out of the past. "Papa was such a shrewd trader, but sometimes he came home with stuff that didn't make much sense to us. We'd tease him about being a soft touch to anyone who had junk they wanted to unload, but sure enough, he'd always find someone who wanted just what he had brought home. You can imagine how we'd all rush out to see him when he'd been gone for a while, and how excited we were to see what he brought home this time. He'd been gone to Ogallala for several days picking up fencing supplies, and we crawled all over that wagon when he pulled in. Usually he'd hold up his 'treasures' as he called them and laugh right along with us when we'd make fun of his trades. This time, he just shook his head when we asked and told us to run to the garden and bring Mama out.

She was picking beans and finished the row she was on before taking the pails of beans to the house and then making her way to the wagon. 'Maria, today is the same day as when we first met in the old country, and I have something special for you.' Of course the kids jumped up and down and were so impatient that he shushed us so she could hear his words. 'For you I have this gift,' and he handed her the most beautiful white soft kid leather gloves. 'When we go to town, you will be the finest lady there.'

Mama was completely dumfounded, and she just stood there holding the gloves. Papa was like a little boy wanting approval 'Do they fit? Aren't they the softest things you've ever touched? Do you like them? Are you going to try them on?'

She held out her dirt-covered hands and shook her head. 'To ruin them would not be good. They are so beautiful that I want to keep them nice forever. Emma, take these inside so I can be clean when I put on my fine new lady gloves.'

I could see Papa swell up with pride with the way she

knew what he was saying with his gift, and then he gave out his booming laugh and said, 'Maria, the new gloves are good for town, and this will be good for home. Hope it's the right size for you.'

He reached under the seat and pulled out a huge cast iron skillet. 'Frying chicken for a big family takes a big pan, and this one looked like it might work.' Papa handed it over the side to Mama, and that was when the tears rolled down her cheeks. 'I'm sorry, Maria. I didn't mean to disappoint you. I'll take it and trade it off the next time I go on a trip.'

'Oh, Ernest, never would I let you take this away. How could I have been so lucky that time so long ago when we were so young? You're such a good man and so kind to me. Every time I cook in this skillet, you will be right there with me.'

Papa climbed down and right there in front of all of us kids, he put his arms around Mama and they actually kissed! We'd never seen that before, and we just stood there with our mouths open. Papa lifted his head and told us, 'Better close up before the flies fill you up.' That brought us out of our silence and we hooted and hollered until he shooed us out of the way. He and Mama walked into the house with their arms around each other, and we had the good sense to leave them alone."

"That's the big skillet we still use, isn't it? Mama had to use two hands to lift it onto the stove, and she never would let us wash it. She'd wave us aside and say, 'This I can finish now.' She'd clean it, wipe it dry, and rub softly over the top of it as she put it away. Funny how I saw that so many times and didn't know the story behind it. Papa must've been fun to know. If I ever get married, I hope I find someone who'll be good to me."

"Honey, when you're older and it's time, you'll find a man who's right for you. Just don't get in a hurry. Married is for life and that can be a long time, especially if you settle for the wrong one."

After Emma had finished her story, she tidied the kitchen as she always did before going to bed, much to the mystification of Darlene. "Why do you take the time to put all that stuff away when we're just going to get it out in the morning, Em?" She watched as Emma emptied the coffee pot and wiped it out before bending down to place it on the bottom shelf. "Why can't you just leave it there and grab it in the morning? Seems like a lot of extra work to me."

Continuing to clear the clean coffee cups off the counter so she could wipe it down and finally hang the dishcloth over the oven handle, Emma smiled as she answered, "You know, honey, I used to say the selfsame thing to Mama. We'd all be bone tired and ready to hit the hay, but she always had to putter in the kitchen so it was spotless before she could rest. She'd say, 'No old mess for a new day' and make sure everything was in its place. It didn't matter that she'd be up in a few hours to start the stove, make the coffee, and cook huge meals for all of us. It's something I do because she did it, and also because I like to end a day with everything in its place."

Darlene laughed, "I think I'm a little bit like that. When I stayed with Amy, she jumped out of bed, dressed, and ran down the stairs. When she noticed I wasn't right behind her, she came back up and couldn't believe I was making the bed. 'You don't need to do that, Darlene. After all, the next time we get back here, we'll unmake it so why bother?' Even if I didn't have a good answer for her, Mama had insisted that we make the bed before we ever left the room, and that's the only way it feels right to me. Walking in and finding the quilt all smooth gives me a soft feeling in my tummy so I try to make my bed every day. When we were looking for Ted, I didn't take the time, and it felt all wrong when I got ready for bed. Funny how you get used to things being the same, and when they're different, it's kind of upsetting."

"Lots of things in our life will be different now, Darlene, and if we let them upset us, we'll be in a sad state. We're both going to a new place and a new life, so I guess we'd better get ready for change. Think how Mama and Papa came here to a completely strange land and made a new life. If they could do it way back then, I'm sure we can do it now." The sisters walked down the hallway as they chatted.

Darlene laughed, "Oh, boy. Think of all their hard times, and yet all Mama ever talked about was how good she had it. At least we have don't have to hitch up the mules to take us to town like they did. Man, this has been a long day and I'll be glad to flop down on my bed." She paused at her doorway. "Guess we'd better enjoy sleeping here 'cause soon it'll be all over." Darlene shimmied out of her clothes and tugged her nightgown over her head. "This used to fit me just fine, but seems like I've outgrown it. Kinda like I've outgrown this place and have to find somewhere with room for me. For darned sure it isn't with Fred and Ruth and all their friends."

"Maybe when we're all more adjusted, we can get back together and make different arrangements. Fred has a lot on his mind right now, but later he might want to mend some fences."

Darlene snorted, "Fat chance. He's never been too big on the whole fencing business, so I'm not holding my breath for that. Besides, there's not a big enough room in the whole world for me to stay with them. Could you believe how he stood up for Ben even if everyone there knew what a sneak and liar he is? Why would he go against his own family for someone like that? It's like I really only had one brother anyway. Since Ted's gone, I'm gone too. It's just lucky Tracy and Ed were here today; otherwise, who knows what would have happened to me?"

Emma reached out to tousle her little sister's hair, "You'd be with me and you'd be just fine. Now we both need to get some rest so we're ready to make arrangements for what we do next. Good night, Little One. Love you."

"Love you, too, Sis. See you in the morning bright and early since we have those darned chores to do. Probably won't see Fred out there in the barn anytime soon. Wonder how he'll handle things when we're all gone and he's the only one here? He won't even know how much to feed the bucket calves or which stall the horses belong in. Maybe it's a good thing I won't be here to see how bad it gets." With that, Darlene wiped a tear from her eye and flopped down on her bed. "Maybe I can take one of Mama's quilts to Tracy's when I move in with them. That'd make it feel like I had a little bit of home with me."

Emma slowly made her way to her bedroom, pausing to step into Maria's room. Fred was right about how the room had remained largely unchanged, but that had come about not from a desire to form a shrine to Maria but more to cling to the familiar in a world filled with change. Her children sensed a closeness to her as they entered the room which had held her both in life and finally in death. Emma knew this would be the last time to experience the serenity of the untouched room, so she gazed one more time in an attempt to fix the scene in her mind.

Fluffed up and sitting on top of Maria's final appliquéd quilt with whimsical flowers on each block were the white on white embroidered pillow cases which Darlene liked so much. The dresser scarf was more original handiwork with its open squares and tiny, even stitches. Maria had always insisted on placing the family Bible precisely on the center of the dresser, and that was where Darlene had replaced it after they finished Ted's entry. Simple white curtains fluttered in the breeze, and the rag rug under the bed finished the simple furnishings.

Emma gingerly rubbed the simple pine headboard with curlicues carved in each corner which Ernest had brought all the way from Omaha. Peeking out from under the bed were Maria's fancy black dress shoes that had been largely unused most of the time while they lived on the ranch. Often Maria would pick them up and softly stroke them with a faraway look. When Darlene had asked what good they were since she never got to wear them, Maria had smiled at her little girl, "Sometimes the good is from the memories, and these take me to a time long ago. I was tiny, your father was tall and handsome, and we were good together. I don't see shoes; I see long slow walks and quick dances. I see my mother polishing them so I could be ready to go to church with the family. I see our wedding in Omaha and the beginning of our life together. Even if I don't use them now, my head takes me to where I've been."

The newest piece in the room was Ted and Beth's framed picture that had been the center of the memory table. As Beth left, Emma had handed it to her, but Beth declined, "I'd like Darlene to keep that if she wants it. It was her idea, and it seems right to let her have it." Darlene had clutched it tightly and run into Maria's room to set it on the end of the dresser where it now stood.

As she continued to her own room, Emma realized that sleep would be elusive with all the thoughts racing through her mind, but she also knew that Darlene had one ear cocked for the squeak of her bedsprings. Pulling on her night clothes, she turned out the light, sat down on the edge of the bed, and then stretched out to her full length.

Right as her head touched the pillow, she heard Darlene's drowsy voice, "See you in the morning, Em," and Emma smiled as she sent back a soft reply.

When morning came, it was as Darlene had predicted.

The girls had finished breakfast and all the chores before Fred made his appearance on the porch. "Good morning, ladies. I was going over some business and lost track of the time, otherwise I'd have been here sooner to help out. Guess I'll have to keep a little bit different schedule than what I've been used to. Good thing I have everything pretty well under control in the shop so I can look after the livestock now." All three of them stood awkwardly until he broke the silence.

Looking at his sisters, he cleared his throat as he waved them both closer. "You know that yesterday all our feelings were running pretty strong, what with the bad news and all; and I hope you aren't upset by anything that was said. We're still family and I don't want any hard feelings. Darlene, I hope you know I'd be willing for you to stay here with Ruth and me. Of course you could keep your room and we'd do our duty by you. Emma, too, you're welcome to stay as long as you'd like.

Emma was the first to reply, "Fred, that's mighty nice of you, but I think it'll be better if I go ahead with my plans. I'll help get everything out of your way so you and Ruth can move in, but then I'll be on my way. Thanks for the offer, though."

"I wouldn't want to disappoint Tracy and Ed, so I'll probably go ahead and move in with them." Darlene was deeply torn between wanting to stay with the familiar and wanting to get as far away as possible since nothing about home would ever be the same without Ted. "When Alma and everyone else gets here, we'll decide who gets what. It seems funny to think about taking Mama's stuff, even if she is gone."

Fred gave an impatient shake of his head, "Well, I'll feel better when everything's out of there. It's just a bunch of old stuff that needs moved out anyway, so why don't you girls take whatever you want and I'll get rid of anything you leave behind. The same goes for Ted's stuff. I can't imagine what you'd keep of his, but get what you want and then I'll finish up when you're done."

Totally unaware of how cold his words sounded, Fred continued, "If there's anything in the barn you might want, it needs cleaned out too so you might want to check there before you quit. I'll be at the house if you need me for anything." Turning his back to his sisters, he stepped off the porch in the direction of his house.

"Before you go, Fred, there is one thing I've been wondering about." As Emma spoke, he reversed direction and faced her once more. "Sometime we'll need to figure out how we're going to settle up the estate. While you and Ted were running it, some of us lived here and had a say in what went on, but now that he's gone and you'll be the only one here, it'd probably be a good idea to decide what we want to do with everything. Do you suppose we might want to have a talk about that when we're all together?"

Immediately, Fred became hostile. "What is the big deal now? I don't get how this is any different than it was a few days ago. No one seemed concerned about who was doing what as long as Ted was here. All of a sudden he's gone and we need to settle up? What's the matter? Don't you trust me? Just exactly what do you want to talk about anyway? Maybe you can spit it out right now so I have some idea what's eating at you." The longer he talked, the louder he became, and the closer he had come. With his last word, he was shaking his finger in Emma's face.

Emma had seen this side of her brother many times, and she was not shaken by his attempt to intimidate. "Right now, I'd have to say nothing's eating at me, but that might not always be the case. I don't know that all of us girls are going to walk away and give you everything that Mama and Papa worked so hard to put together. Every one of us did our part while we were growing up, and we were glad to. Now that we're all going our separate ways, it seems like this is something we need to think about. Mama's will was pretty specific that we all shared equally, so let's decide how we can make that happen."

As she talked, Emma reached out and gently pushed his hand aside, "And, Fred, your hand in my face isn't going to make this go away, so best not do that again."

As always, when someone called his bluff, Fred shriveled up and lost his bluster, "I'm sorry, Em, but I've spent my whole life trying to measure up to Ted, and even if he's gone, I still have to justify myself. What would you have done if it would've been the other way around? Would you be trying to push him around like this?" As he talked, his anger emerged once again, "I doubt it, but that's neither here nor there. Here I'm willing to stay here and make this ranch work, and that's what I get—a bunch of nasty sisters who won't even give me a break. You bet we can talk this over, and you tell those sisters of yours that I'm not about to give up without a fight." He stomped off the porch and never looked back on his way home.

"Wow, Em, I was scared there when he came yelling at you. That's the way he'd act whenever Ted would want to talk to him, and I didn't like that either." Darlene dropped her head on Emma's shoulder and choked back her tears. "Why's he like that?"

Emma took a deep breath before undertaking an answer, "Ever since he was a little boy, he was jealous of Ted. No matter what they did, Fred always felt like the folks played favorites with Ted, and maybe they did a little bit. Ted was born to be a rancher, and he was a natural at it. Fred was born to be something other than this, but no one really could ever figure out what it was.

What made it worse was that his little brother could do

anything he set his mind to. Fred would try something once or twice; and he'd quit if it didn't come easy. He got into the habit of blaming everyone else for his misery and that's where he is today. Not a pleasant place for him, but I'm not about to back down from his temper tantrums. He knows better than to try to push me, and I'm not the only sister who's on to his little game."

Just then Alma drove up with the other sisters, and after greeting one another, they migrated toward the house. Emma served some of the cinnamon rolls sent over earlier by the neighbors and put on a pot of coffee to boil while the other six girls found their places around the table. Amid jostling and good-natured kidding, each one was aware of the imminent change that lay before them. The oak table had been a mute witness to the saga of the Soehl family, from its first small beginnings to the increasing family size and the amassing of several sections with wet valleys to its current crisis.

Maria's minimum goal to have a section for each child had been met long ago, and her shrewdness in land purchases had resulted in a large spread that was totally debt free. Even when she had borrowed from the bank for a new chunk of land, she made certain to pay off the mortgage when the next calf crop was sold. While they waited until October when they marketed, Maria found other ways to improve their cash flow. The family had a reputation for hard work, based on the massive amounts of cream they marketed as well as the huge numbers of eggs, chickens, and turkeys they sold.

All the sisters seated in the kitchen had begun working as soon as they were big enough to carry an egg basket to the hen house. From there they moved to milking, feeding the bucket calves, and herding the turkeys. Long hours in the hayfield had been tiresome yet provided a strong sense of satisfaction. This was the background they shared, and it was a tie that remained even when each one would leave the ranch to take up a different occupation.

Some had married like Alma, some had gone on to work as Emma was ready to do, and others were just recently out of high school and considering their next step. While Ted had been the main resident of Maria's house, the sisters had felt comfortable landing back at home base as needed. When they would come home, they would fit comfortably into the rhythm of the ranch, each one pitching in as needed.

Since they had heard Fred's declared intention to take over the house and run things his way, each one knew this would never be a haven to which they would return. Sitting in companionable silence, they enjoyed being together at home for one last time.

"Fred made it loud and clear that he wants this house cleaned out, so the first thing we need to do is figure out how we're going to work together and end up on good terms with one another," Alma was the first to broach the reason they had gathered, and her remark set the tone for the days ahead. "Does anyone have an idea as to how we can split up what's here?" She looked around the kitchen where Maria had set her indelible stamp, just as she had in each of the rooms which Ernest had designed and built for her.

Clara offered an opinion that she felt would make for fairness, "How about if we go room by room, and have one person start out. Then we take turns saying what we want in that room until we've divided it all. When we go to the next room, a different person gets to start, and we keep taking turns until we've made our way through the whole house." Looking around for approval, she listened carefully as the others offered refinements to her idea.

"If we don't get to change the order until we go to a different room, the same person will get to pick first each time. How about going through one way, and then reversing the order so the last one to pick is the first one the next time? Then we can keep rotating who starts a new round until we all have first chance on what is left?" Usually soft-spoken and agreeable to what the older girls suggested, Millie spoke up softly and seemed apologetic about offering her own thoughts.

Emma reached out to pull a curl behind Millie's ear and patted her on the arm, "I like that idea, Millie. Then everyone has an equal chance. Let's draw straws to see who starts out, and then we'll keep track of whose turn it is. Maybe it'd be a good idea if someone kept a list so we can always go back and check to see who chose what." Millie ducked her head to the side and gave a grateful look to her big sister.

Reaching into the cupboard where Maria had kept the writing supplies, Alma drew out a piece of paper and pencil. "Anyone volunteering? I'll do it unless someone else really wants to." With that, she pushed back the cup and saucer and made seven columns. "While I'm doing this, someone can get some straws so we're ready to get started. Do we have anything that obviously should go to one of us? I know Elsie bought Mama that fancy set of cups after graduating from cosmetology school. Remember how excited Mama was when she actually had fine china for her coffee instead of blue speckled enamel cups that burned her hands? I don't think stuff like that should be in the draw but should go home with the giver.

Elsie smiled at the memory of how thrilled she was to be able to buy something delicate for Maria and also at how Maria wordlessly caressed the cups, tears flowing gently down her cheeks. "Thanks for saying that, Alma. It meant a lot to me when I could do something special for Mama, so having those cups will feel good to me."

Gradually all the gifts in the kitchen had been catalogued,

and it was time to divide Maria's household belongings. Alma drew the longest straw and made her choice of the kitchen table. Since she was the only one with a family, everyone agreed with her choice. "Would it be okay if we'd just throw in the chairs too? I'd hate to see the set split up, so I'd vote to give the whole thing to Alma," Clara glanced at each sister who nodded her agreement with the proposal.

"I really appreciate this, girls, and I'll take myself out of the circle for the next couple of rounds," Alma stroked the table top and wiped her eyes as she spoke.

As they completed the rounds, the sisters alternately laughed and cried at some of the choices. As they would pick an item, they usually shared the reason for their picks. Some were of childhood joy as they drank from a special cup, others were hilarious mishaps that had ended well in spite of all kinds of dangerous youthful energy, and yet others were of poignant memories of family dinners in happier times.

When Darlene's turn came, she tentatively asked for the huge skillet, "That is, unless you want it, Emma. You said it's a part of your favorite memory about Mama and Papa. I'd never take it if you want it." Looking across at her sister, she reached out so they could lace fingers.

"I don't think I need to drag something like that to the city. Doubt that I'll be frying chicken for a threshing crew anytime soon, so it'll be enough that I know where it'll be. When you have your own family, you can invite us all over and show us how good of a cook you are." Emma's reassurance gave Darlene a boost and yet a moment of embarrassment as everyone chimed in about how many children she'd be chasing around and cooking for. She'd been in the middle of these moments enough to know the best answer was often a grin and silence. Soon they resumed selecting items and were done in the kitchen.

"I want you to know I don't plan on taking the furniture

until the end of the week when you girls are moving out," Alma directed her comments to Darlene and Emma. Hearing this, those who would be living close by agreed they would come back later to pick up their portion, and those who lived in the eastern part of the state asked if they could remove their belongings when they were ready to go back home.

Emma reassured those who had come from a distance, "Of course we'd expect you to take your things when you leave. You heard Fred, whatever's left when we're done will probably get tossed out anyway, so please feel free to take whatever is yours. It'll be hard to see the house empty, but maybe we all need to so we know there's no turning back. Darlene and I can make it work, can't we?"

"You bet we can, Em. We're a darned good team if I do say so myself," Darlene put on a brave front even though she was feeling a bit shaky about the next phase of her life. "If we're done here, let's go on to Mama's room. There's some stuff in there I'll bet we all think is pretty special."

With that, they moved down the hall and into the bright airy room where Maria had breathed her last.

Softly shuffling so everyone could fit in, all fell silent as they surrounded the perfectly made bed covered with Maria's handiwork. A few of the sisters reached out to touch the material, almost as if they were in touch with the very fabric of their lives. When they were breathing more easily, Alma broke the silence. "I just want to say that it's not my turn to pick first in this room, but I hope someone can take this furniture. We all know the story of how Papa kept the headboard from scratches on the train by wrapping it in all the quilts and coats of the whole family. The funny thing is that even when we were cold, we never let on. He'd look around and see us shivering and squeeze us close to him until we'd warmed up, then he'd say, 'Soon the cold goes and the warm home stays.' He was in his shirtsleeves all the way, even though it was in the fall when the nights really got cold; but he never asked us to do something he wouldn't do. It'd be a pity if no one had room and Fred just threw it out on the scrap heap."

They nodded their heads in agreement, and one by one, each mentioned why the headboard wasn't a piece they could take. Some lived too far and didn't have a way to haul it home, others lived in tiny temporary quarters and couldn't see themselves trying to move it several times, while others already had furnished their homes with bedsteads. Millie spoke up with her suggestion, "Since Darlene will be living closer than the rest of us, how about asking the Dolphs if they have room for it? Then even if Darlene goes on to school or moves away, they could keep it and use it until she has a place for it." Each of the sisters murmured assent and turned to see Darlene's reaction.

At first she was completely taken aback because her thought processes were those of a little girl without a roof to call her own, and the next moment she had the opportunity to still be surrounded by a big part of her past as she moved on. "We can sure ask Tracy if she'd be willing to put this in her house. I don't know if she has room, but I'd really like it if I could sleep in the folks' bed when I go away."

That part settled, they took to parceling out the smaller items. When it was all over, they realized Maria's foresight even in death. Each daughter chose and held tightly to handmade quilts, pillowcases, dresser scarves, and doilies that she had created specifically for each one. Although of little monetary value, each was a treasure deeply cherished.

Darlene had held her breath each time a choice was made, and then slowly let it out when the white on white pillowcases still remained. When it was finally her turn, her outburst amused the entire room, "I get the whites! I'm the luckiest girl ever because I got the best even if I had to wait."

Her sentiment was similar to what each sister had felt when a particularly special piece was still available even after all the others had had their turns.

Many times they all knew about an association with an item for one particular person, and they made sure she ended up with it. That was how Emma became the proud possessor of the soft white gloves which had been Maria's prized possession. They were lying in her top dresser drawer, wrapped in the original fine tissue paper that Ernest had so proudly chosen. "Remember when Papa brought these home? He was so proud of himself, and Mama acted like he gave her the moon. They were so cute, just like a pair of giggling kids who were courting."

"Why did he waste his money like that? For all the time she had them, she never got to wear them even once. He could've gotten her a dress or a locket or even a ring, so why'd he pick out something so useless? He should've known she'd never get to use them." Darlene had been pondering this question since Emma's describing her favorite memory. "That doesn't make any sense to me."

Emma smiled pensively at her little sister, "If you ever heard Mama tell about how they first met, you know how Papa always loved her hands. When he got home that day, it was almost like they both were kids again in the old country. He never did see her as old, and she never did see him as wrinkled, even if everyone else did. Sometimes when people buy special gifts, it's not so much spending money as it is saving memories. They were good together, and we're lucky for what they gave all of us."

"I know that and I didn't mean to be mean," Darlene paused when she heard the words bump up together, "but you know what I mean." Immediately lapsing into giggles, her sisters joined her laughter as they all appreciated the break in the difficult process. "Em, I'm glad you have those, even if you'll never probably wear them either. It feels right knowing you're taking good care of something that mattered so much to Mama."

Darlene could scarcely contain her excitement since it was her turn to choose again, and Mama's petite black shoes still peeked out from under the bed. "I pick these shoes," she said, reaching to pick them up, "and I'll bet I'm the only one they fit." As she hoisted them in a kind of celebratory gesture, the fine buttonhole hook fell out of the right shoe. "What's this? Why would Mama store a crochet hook in a shoe? Maybe it just fell in there without her knowing it."

Puzzled at the wave of laughter, she watched quizzically as Alma signaled her to slip on one of the shoes. After she had it on, Alma directed her, "Now why don't you go ahead and close it."

As Darlene fumbled with the tiny buttons, she became frustrated with her inability to fasten them. "These are so darned little that it'd take me till noon to be ready to leave the house. No wonder Mama left these here and wore something else."

Alma patted her curls and placed the hook across her palm, "Now try this, Little One. You might find it easier to latch those buttons with a bit of help from this 'crochet' hook." She held Darlene's hand to show her how to run the hook for the first couple of buttons, and then let go as soon as Darlene had the knack of it. "Little easier with that, isn't it?"

Darlene slipped on the other shoe and continued using the fastener. "Since I have these on, I might as well wear them around the house." Tottering on the heels, she took a few tentative steps around the bedroom. "You know, it's not as easy as it looks to wear these things. Good thing I have them so I'll be practiced by the time I have my own high heeled shoes."

That was the final item in Maria's room, so they moved on to Ted's room. Typical of a bachelor, it held few nonessential items. Neatly arranged on the dresser and in the middle just as he had left them sat his hair brush, shaving mug and brush, and a pile of what he had called his "seed coins."

He had noticed Darlene's puzzled expression when she first heard him use that term, so he proceeded to explain. "You know how you have to have seeds to plant in the ground when you want something to grow? Well, it's pretty much the same with money. It takes money to make money, and Papa was really good at that. These are the coins he had in his pocket when he died, so I've always kept them so his luck would be with me." He had placed them in her hand and went on, "So far, they've done a fair job for me."

Everyone had teased Ted about the few superstitions he'd admit to, and he'd laugh right along with them. Then he'd go right back to doing those very same things, like never putting a hat on the bed, or tossing spilled salt over his left shoulder, or hanging horseshoes in his tack room with the two ends on top so the luck wouldn't run out. He was famous for scanning the sky and making weather predictions. He always had dogs around, so when he told Darlene to look at the sundog, she checked each hound to see if he had a new yellow one. He had laughed and pointed to the western sky, "Do you see that little blip to the side of the sun? The one that looks like a chunk of a rainbow with a yellow cast? That's called a sundog, and it says a change is coming, usually cooler with some kind of moisture."

"How did you find that out, Ted? I've never read anything like that in my books at school, so who told you?" Darlene was fascinated with his knowledge, especially after his prediction had come true the next day. "I wish I knew as much as you do. Every time you look at the sky and say something, it's pretty much true. I don't get it."

It hadn't dawned on Ted how much she paid attention to his forecasts, and he appealed to her observation skills, "Lena, it's just a matter of watching for patterns around you. By the time you've seen the kinds of skimpy gray clouds that are usually around a sundog and you notice that the next day generally brings a weather change, it just makes sense to connect the two things. Same thing with the sky. Papa always said, 'Red sky at night; sailors' delight. Red sky at morning; sailors take warning.' We were right smack in the center of the sandhills, so that didn't make much sense to me, but what I did notice was that first of all came the red sky, and then came the wind. Makes a difference if it's red at dawn or dusk too. My guess is that sailors watched the sky so they'd know if they were heading into a storm or not. Even if we're not in a boat, it helps to know if a big blow is on the way, so I tried to learn what each sign meant."

"Like last week when that big black cloud rumbled over, you told me to head for cover before the hail hit. When I asked you how you knew, you laughed and pointed to those weird looking clouds. Before I even had time to ask you more, that freezing cold wind hit and we both ran for the cellar. Man, did it look tough when we came out. Those trees we had around the buildings looked like it was the dead of winter, even though it was June. And those poor animals. Dead birds and rabbits everywhere and huge welts on the horses and cattle that were outside. Your colt ran through the barbed wire fence and you had to destroy him because he was hurt so bad."

Darlene shuddered as she recalled the shot after Ted had sent her to the house while he did the only thing he could do for the little sorrel colt. "So you're telling me the funny greenish-bluishgrayish clouds that swirl around in a storm mean hail, and you'd better head for cover if a blast of cold air comes? Anything else?"

Ted had been intrigued by her question since he had seldom considered how he knew what he knew. Most of the time he operated from his sense of knowing what was needed rather than wondering how he got his knowledge. "I haven't seen it very many times, but if one of those spring storms has swirly black clouds, pay attention to what they do. If they just tumble and spin and go on, it may be rain and thunder; but if some of those swirls come down and look like spinning tails, that means to get to the cellar too. Best not wait around to see if my guess is right, best to be safe in that hole in the ground. Storms like that can flatten everything in their paths so don't take chances, especially when a pattern lets you know what's up before it happens."

All that conversation played in Darlene's mind as she absently fingered the coins on the dresser, and she barely heard the others as they chose from Ted's things. All of a sudden she remembered the contents of his pocket which the undertaker had delivered to the Soehls. "Wait a minute, you guys. Remember when Tom handed us the envelope with Ted's stuff in it? I think I laid it on my dresser when I went into Mama's room to get the Bible. I'll run and get it." With that, she clattered down the hall in her high heels and noisily returned, clutching it to her. "Here it is. Bet I can tell you what's in it without looking. He never went anywhere without his knife so it'll be in there, and he probably had a little money since he never wanted anyone else to pay his way. Don't know if there'd be anything else."

Alma gently reached out to her sister. "Honey, why don't you open it so we can see what's there. I'll bet you called it just about right."

Opening the package, Darlene carefully dumped its contents on the dresser. First the knife came tumbling out, then the coins, and then a small object tumbled out and fell on the floor. They all backed up and felt around on the wooden floor until Millie called out, "Here it is. I found it under the bed."

Pulling the cover aside, she lifted her hand with the object held tight. As she gradually opened her fingers, they could all see a delicate gold ring lying on her palm. "Oh, no. Poor Beth. He never got to give it to her. Where do you suppose he got it?" As they surged around her, each sister felt an overwhelming sense of sorrow for things that would never be.

"Can't you just imagine how pleased he was with himself when he thought of how excited she'd be? Pretty much like Papa was every time he brought something special home for his sweetheart." Emma went back in time remembering how her father had acted whenever he came home after a trading expedition. "They were so much alike. You'd look at them and think they were really fierce big guys. Then when you'd get to know them, you'd realize they were just little boys living in great big bodies. What softies they both were." Almost as an afterthought, she added, "And now they're both gone. That's hard to believe."

"What are we going to do with this ring? Even if it makes her really sad, I think Beth needs to have it. If she doesn't want to keep it, she can do something with it later. How about if we set it aside for her?" Clara had seen the anguish in Beth's eyes, but she also believed this ring couldn't go to anyone else. "Maybe we can send it to her after she's had a chance to figure out what she's doing next. Okay with everyone?"

The entire group nodded and made little sounds of agreement as they handed it to Emma. "I'll look after it and see she gets it. It'll make her cry, but she's going to be crying most of the time anyway." With that, she pushed it deep into her pocket and turned back to the rest of Ted's pieces. "I've kind of lost track of whose turn it is to pick, but someone surely knows."

Elsie chose the brush, a seemingly natural choice since she was in hairdresser school; and Eva took the mug and brush. She jokingly said it would come in handy once she had found a husband to go with it, and that left the coins and the knife.

"Let's give Darlene those things. If she hadn't remembered what Tom gave us, we wouldn't have even known they were here. She spent the most time with Ted lately, so it makes sense for her get them." Clara was one who voiced a sentiment agreeable to everyone there, and they handed Darlene her share of Ted's belongings.

"You know what, you guys? I'm going to put this money in a safe place and let it be my seed money just like it was for Ted. It'll be fun to see how much it grows from now until I'm old like he was." When her sisters started laughing at her description of him, she continued, "I don't mean old exactly, more like done with having fun." Once again, their laughter let her know the words weren't quite right yet, "Maybe I mean when I'm done being a little kid."

Clara tapped her on the arm as she praised her way with words, "One thing I'll bet is that when you're done being a little kid, you'll probably be a teacher. You have a way with words and you never give up until you're satisfied you've got them just right. It'll be fun to see how much that seed money grows then. I think it's a super idea to hand it over to you." Unspoken was the fact that Darlene had endured more difficulty than most young girls, beginning with the long drawn out illness of Maria, Ted's untimely death, and finally the loss of her home. Although her sisters couldn't erase any of the pain, they did what they could to ease her transition into completely new territory.

"One question I have is who's taking the Bible? If we

leave it here, Fred might toss it out like so much trash so we'd better decide that right now." Alma ordinarily was easy-going and smoothed over disagreements, but Fred's behavior the day before had been too much even for her good-nature.

Ted had always joked with her about how he knew she'd been pushed too far. "Yeah, Sis, when I see that jaw get all locked up and your chin sits there and doesn't move, I know we might as well save our air. No one gets anywhere with you when you get to that point."

Darlene had never heard that tone from Alma before, so she took a good look at her sister. All of a sudden, she realized what Ted had meant when he talked about someone locking a jaw. As she recalled Fred's behavior from the day before, Alma's profile subtly altered, her chin jutted out ever so slightly, and the space below her ear twitched as she clenched her teeth together.

"Well, how about Emma taking it for safe-keeping with the understanding that it really belongs to all of us. Hopefully we won't need to write in any more sad days for quite a while; but when we do, we can get together and take care of it." Alma had helped avoid bitterness over who would hold the family's most valuable possession, and they all appreciated settling what could have been a difficult issue. "Guess that makes Emma the keeper of our family history, that is, if she's willing to take it on."

Emma was moved by the offer to let her hold on to the family Bible since it was the remaining connection with all that had gone before. "You bet I'll be glad to be the Bible's keeper." She chuckled and added, "Just might not be the best idea right now to ask me to be my brother's keeper. Maybe that can come later after some of these wounds have healed, but for the time being, I'd say we're pretty much all the family that's left. Fred decided to throw in with his cronies instead of with us, so that's the way it is now. Maybe he'll change his mind later, but we've all got to move on with our lives." She heaved a sigh and announced, "I think we've sorted out everything in the house, so if anyone wants or needs anything from the shop or barn, we might as well saunter in that direction and get it over with."

Taking one last look as if to capture an image of the house while still intact, they exited the door and took off in the direction of the shop. They were a few steps away when Fred appeared at its door. "Just wondering why you're headed out here. I'd think it'd be enough for you to strip everything out of the house without thinking you've got the run of the whole place. I've furnished this shop and I'm staking claim to what's inside here. Don't think you girls need a bunch of tools and equipment for anything so you might as well not bother stopping here." With that pronouncement, he spread his legs and folded his arms defiantly across his chest.

"We understand you've put together quite a shop here, Fred, and it's easy to see you'd like to keep it for yourself. I guess it crossed my mind to wonder how much money you spent on all those tools and equipment. As I recall, everything in there was paid for by the ranch account and not your personal money. Was there something I didn't know about or are you maybe bulling your way because you know you're on shaky ground?" Emma had spent so much time at the ranch toward the end that Maria had turned all the accounts over to her. Riled up as he had her, she wasn't about to let him push them around.

Emma's remark took Fred completely by surprise. Since he had natural mechanical abilities, this was the one place he felt comfortable. "What does that have to do with anything? I can't believe how you're all acting like I'm the bad guy and you're in charge of the world." As he spouted off to them, the entire group had come close enough that they brushed past him even as he blustered. Forced to step aside and then to follow them inside, he clearly recognized his disadvantage. "Really, girls, we can probably settle this pretty easy. Don't imagine you have much of a need for wrenches or tools or the other stuff here, but take your time looking around."

Sitting in the shop at the moment were the two items of which he was most proud—the touring car and the tractor. Never once did it dawn on him that he'd have to give up either, but as he saw them gathering around the auto, he had a sinking feeling that drove his remarks. "Remember when we all decided the ranch needed a car? We've all used it at one time or another, so it would seem to me like that is a part of the operation. Don't know, but sure seems like it to me."

No one was in a hurry to answer him, so it was as if his words hung there with no response. When a voice from the back did begin, he was amazed at the direction of the conversation. "You know, Fred, you're right. We did have a family meeting and came to the conclusion that a car would be a big help to us all. No doubt about that part of what you said. Seems like we may have a bit of a problem with where you said it's a part of the whole operation. That might have been the case when we were all involved with what went on here, but you've made it crystal clear that you're the one completely in charge. No matter what, you staked your claim to independence yesterday when you threw in your lot with that low-down chum of yours and cut us all out. Now I guess you get the benefit of being the one who makes the decisions about the ranch, but we're the ones who hold the pocketbook. Kind of a dilemma for you, I'd say."

Emma's voice was soft yet firm. "Now if you want this car to stay here, you can pony up the cash and call it yours. If not, it becomes a part of the total assets, and probably the majority has the say about who uses it and when. Maybe you'd like a bit of time to think it over, so we're headed to the barn to see if there's anything we want from there. Feel free to join us if you'd like."

With that, the group swooped out just as they entered, as a united group intent on the division of property. Fred was totally at a loss as to what he should do. No way he wanted in the middle of that bee's nest, but he did need to know what would be left when it was all over. "I'll take you up on that offer to tag along, Em. As I see it, there's no need for anyone to be hard to get along with, and I'm sorry if you misunderstood anything I said. After all, as one of the oldest, I've been part of this all along. No way I'd turn my back on you after all we've been through together."

Fred revealed an interesting aspect of his personality with his words. Because his main concern was being part of the group, being excluded from his own family circle truly bothered him. He had surrounded himself with guys who used him to bankroll their entertainment at the expense of his relationships with his sisters. Now that he lacked his usual support system, his main focus at this point was to worm himself back into his sisters' good graces. In many ways, he resembled a puppy trying to get in good with an older impatient dog. He smiled, joked, and made it a point to exchange a friendly expression or gesture with what turned out to be a rather unresponsive audience. The longer he went, the more desperate he felt, and the more insistent he became.

As the barn door slid open, they took a moment for their eyes to adjust to the darkness, and while they waited, familiar odors of timothy hay and old leather imbued with years of horse sweat drifted toward them. Each person was affected differently, but most felt a wave of nostalgia for times gone by. Soehl offspring worked outside as soon as they could, and the first opportunity seemed to come in the barn where they would accompany the others to do the chores. As they sat and played with the cats, they clamored for a chance to milk their first cow and feed the bucket calves. Once they began, it quickly dawned on the new chore person that this was a permanent assignment, not just a temporary escapade. Although the work was hard and the hours long, being old enough to work alongside the family held its unique reward.

Harnesses still hung on pegs on the south wall as they had since Ernest and Maria had built the barn. Horse collars, hames, single trees, double trees, work horse bridles, snaffle bits—all were arrayed in their accustomed places on braces on the wall beyond the door. Riding equipment wasn't visible as it was inside the tack room which Ted had organized into a work area.

As they entered it, the familiar smell of neat's-foot oil and new leather were a fresh reminder of their loss. Ted loved the world of horseflesh, all the way from tiny foals to massive work horses. He was a great believer that horses were much like people; all appeared the same but each one was unique. He took the time to observe them so he could figure out which rig would work the best for each horse and then put together a huge collection of bridles and bits. Some had blinders for spooky horses, some had snaffles, and some had mouthpieces with combinations of rollers and broken mouthpieces. Each one hung neatly on a peg with reins draped so they hung at exactly the same length. The scrap barrel was about half full of left over pieces he would use for repairing reins and lines, and he had built a set of cubby holes deep enough to hold the sides of leather he kept on hand for tooling and repair.

This was one place Fred didn't even bother entering because he didn't care what was there and had plans for whatever the girls decided to leave behind. There'd be time enough when he was rid of them to take stock so he waited outside beside the harness area. It seemed to him that they took forever inside the room, so he looked around and took a seat. The wooden barrel was close enough that he could lean it back against the wall and take it easy, so that was where they found him when they emerged, carrying their choices.

Darlene was the last one out, and she stopped abruptly when she saw him sitting there. She grabbed Emma's sleeve and whispered something to her, then walked past him without a word. He had seen her tense up when she caught sight of him, but he chalked it up to her having a tough day. Little did he realize his seat of choice was the selfsame "sadness barrel" that Ted and Darlene had used to get through any dark days they encountered.

Fred noticed that all of the sisters had carried out one of Ted's bits as they exited the tack room on their way to the saddle racks so that seriously depleted the inventory he had assumed was his. Darlene folded her arms over her saddle as she waited for the others to assemble. One by one they touched their choices, with Emma claiming Mama's saddle, Alma Papa's saddle, and the others waved away their choices as they had no need for that type of equipment in the lives they were leading. Darlene had watched closely and spoke up as they finished, "Does anyone want Ted's saddle? If you don't, maybe I'll take it so I've got one to ride when I'm done being a little kid."

The sisters broke into laughter as Clara praised Darlene, "Nice job of remembering not to call the rest of us old, Darlene. You're quick on your feet. I don't know about anyone else, but I'd sure feel good knowing you'd take good care of his saddle. That just seems right to me." Looking around to assess the others, she continued, "Looks like you get the nod, Girl."

Puzzled because he didn't find Darlene's words a bit

amusing and angry to see his trading stock vanishing out the door, Fred lashed out, "Now that you've cleaned out all the good stuff and made it plain you expect me to get along on leftovers, I hope you're satisfied. All I ever wanted was someone on this place to like me as much as you did Ted, but not a one of you would give me half a chance. I'm just glad it's finally out in the open, and you don't have to pretend any more."

When he went into a pout and a rage, over the past years everyone had formed the habit of letting him spout off and never confronted him in an attempt to keep the peace. Now the entire dynamic of the family had changed, but he was a bit slow in realizing it. Thinking he could make them feel guilty, he charged on. "You know what, I don't even care anymore. Every one of you made darned sure to grab one of his bridles to take home, and for what? Just so you'd have something of his to shove in the back of a closet? That seems pretty spiteful to me, but I'm not surprised because I'm used to this kind of treatment."

As he glowered at his sisters, an amazing thing happened; they glowered right back. Rather than dropping their eyes and saying, "Sorry, Fred," as he had expected, they returned unblinking, direct looks to him and let their open contempt show.

"I don't even know where to start, Fred. First of all, you shove us out and then try to make it sound like we're the ones pushing you around. Then you're jealous that we want some little keepsake of Ted to take with us. Then you try that old trick of playing on our sympathies as the little boy who was always left out. Guess what? This is a new game and those old tired ways won't get you very far with us. We 'cleaned out all the good stuff' as you put it because you said you'd throw away whatever we didn't take. You got what you wanted, so quit whining about it. I don't know why you're in such an uproar out here in the barn anyhow. You never wanted to set foot here before so I must be missing something."

At the same time the words came out of Emma's mouth, it dawned on her what she had overlooked. "Oh, Fred. It always comes down to the money, doesn't it? There's probably a pretty good market for the gear we're holding, and you see dollar signs walking right out the barn and down the road. That's it, isn't it?"

Caught in a trap of his own making, Fred was stuck. He truly didn't want to be on the outside, yet he did need as much as possible left on the ranch so he could finance his expensive habits. Ernest and Maria had occasionally enjoyed card parties with the neighbors, but no wagers ever rode on the outcome of the hands. Fred loved the thrill of holding cards and the possibility of hitting it big, and easily enough he had found a group of card sharks willing to indulge his dreams. Forgetting Ernest's admonishment, "Never risk what you can't do without," Fred had gambling debts needing immediate attention. Caught between wanting acceptance from his family and the pressing demands he faced, he changed tactics.

"Now, Em, don't you think that's pretty harsh thing for a sister to say? I don't want this kind of disagreement to be what we remember about today. How about us just letting this all drop and trying to get back to where we were when Mama was here. I don't think she'd like this at all, do you?"

Emma stood beside Ted's saddle, hands on her hips, "Nice try, Fred, but when you talk about what Mama would have wanted, it reminds me of the time when you were a little boy and you left the grain bin open. Your pony got in and ate all night, and then later when he foundered, you threw yourself on the ground and threw a regular tantrum. As I recall, you were mad that everyone else still had a horse and you didn't have anything left. Never mind that you were the one who made the mess, you still blamed it on us and never once faced up to your part in it. This plays out about the same with you stirring up a situation that put us all on edge, and then you want us to feel like the ones in the wrong. Not this time, brother. You're on your own."

This was a new order for him to work through, so he let his conciliatory pose drop and shrugged, "Suit yourself, Em. I can see you've turned them all against me so I'm not even going to try to talk sense into them. One week from now, every one of you will have taken the last thing off this place you'll ever get a hold of, so I guess you'd better get serious about scrounging all around. Maybe you want to divide up the hens too so you have a little bit of egg money to squeeze by on. Don't come crying to me when you can't make it on your own. I've done everything I can to get along, but you're just too darned bull-headed to listen to reason." With that, he shoved off the barrel, kicked a gray cat out of the way, and stomped back to the shop.

After a silence during which each sister came to grips with what had transpired, Darlene broke the tension, "Well, I guess he knew what he was doing when he sat down on that sadness barrel of ours. He seemed mighty down in the mouth." She walked over to comfort her kitten Johnny and had a totally new thought. "If he's going to be so mean about what we leave behind, I'd better gather up Johnny and Jitney. I can't leave them behind."

Just then Cheyenne shuffled into the barn and nickered for his grain. Rubbing the big black's forehead and feeling the tears slide down her cheeks, she had a bigger concern. "Who'll take care of you, feller? I don't see how I can ask Tracy and Ed to take you in too. They live in town and don't even have a place for a big dog, let alone a horse." She buried her face in his mane as her sisters stood in silence.

"Honey, everything usually sorts itself out the way it's supposed to. How about us getting back to the house for a bite of food? Maybe we just need to take a break and time to figure out what we all do next. We've got tons of stuff to move and I think we all need to think about the best way for us to get everything done." Alma gently pulled Darlene's head from the horse over to her own shoulder and caressed her just like the mother she was desperately missing. "Let's go to the house, okay?"

Darlene nodded and wiped the tears away, "I guess we might as well. I'm not hungry but no need to stay here any longer either. Feels like a long time since we started this whole mess, doesn't it? I'll be glad to get back to the house where at least it's cool."

Wordless as they considered their private thoughts, the sisters made their way to the house. Emma waved them to the chairs around the table, "I thought it might be too hot to cook today so I fried up a little bit of bacon early this morning before you got here." With that she opened the icebox and brought out a heaping plate of meat which she set in the middle of the table. "You know the heat this summer has been good for one thing and that's the early tomatoes we've been having. I thought a nice bacon and tomato sandwich would hit the spot, so just help yourself to whatever you want." While she was talking, she continued to fill the table. "Here are some biscuits that did turn out pretty good, if I do say so myself, and enough slicers that we can all eat our fill. Later on you might like some strawberry shortcake to top it all off."

The Soehl tradition was to make do with seasonal foods, and the height of summer brought out several of their favorite foods. Once they started, cucumbers and onions sliced together in vinegar were a staple with each meal until frost; and other garden crops such as string beans and corn were filling and abundant. Finding ways to use the oven sparingly had yielded unique dishes, such as the shortcake Emma had provided. When her first strawberry patch took hold, Maria had devised drenching dinner biscuits with sweetened berries swimming in bright red juice and drowned with fresh cream. The girls savored the simple fare, not realizing they were dining on fine food which would fetch a premium in other locales.

As they ate, jokes and memories made up their noontime conversation, and finally the talk turned to Fred and the future of the ranch. "I don't know about anyone else, but I can't see how he can make it work," Alma offered as a way to lead into a conversation which they all dreaded. "He never did really like the ranch, but it seemed like he just kind of faded away from the whole operation once Mama took to her sick bed. If Ted hadn't taken care of everything, it's hard to say what would have happened around here. Now he's got to run it all alone, and who knows how long he can hold on. I don't want to sound greedy, but if he loses the ranch, we all lose."

"You know, I'm not sure it was Mama's being gone that made him act like that. It seemed to me he changed when that crew started hanging out here at the ranch. You know the guys I mean, the ones who drifted in when the word got out he was an easy mark. At least before that he went outside to work everyday." Elsie outlined what they had observed during the past months. "You know how he's always wanted people to like him? Seems like his idea of impressing the guys was to flash money around so they'd take him seriously, and he fell in with a pretty questionable lot lately."

Clara pushed her chair back and stood up, "Now I don't feel right talking about Fred when he's not here to defend himself. If we're a family, we need to find a way to get back together instead of making bad remarks about him. We don't know what all he's been through either." Putting her dishes in the sink, she rinsed and dried her hands. "Matter of fact, I'm going to go talk with him right now," and she made her way out the door as the sisters sat in silence.

Mystified, Elsie looked around at the others. "Now where did that come from? She's heard all the nasty things he's had to say lately, so I don't understand what she's getting at. Does this make sense to anyone?"

"Remember how she came back a few days early for Chautauqua? You haven't been around here lately like she has, so there's no way you'd know she's sweet on one of the dandies Fred calls his friends. Roy is a guy who's so smooth that he's in solid with Fred, and he's made a point of charming Clara while she's been here." Emma hesitated before continuing, "Could be wrong, but I think he likes the idea of her having a regular paycheck. Now that she's teaching in Lincoln, I'll be surprised if he hangs around here very long when she goes back."

Millie had remained largely silent throughout most of the discussion, and now she tentatively spoke up, "She's right about one thing, though. Even if it seems like Fred hasn't tried to get along with us, he's basically a good-hearted guy. I'm afraid that our family will never get back together if we leave without making some kind of peace this time. Eva and I are planning to stay in the little house in town until we finish high school, and I'd like it if we could still drop in here. The way it is right now, it'd be tough to come back."

No one spoke for a time as each mulled over the situation, and finally Alma broke the silence, "It's never good when a family has a blow up. Who's to blame won't matter when it's all said and done if we leave the way things are now. Losing Ted was tough, but there's no need for us to lose Fred in the process, even if he is acting like a real jerk right now.

Maybe he feels backed into a corner and doesn't know what else to do. The truth of the matter for me is this—I'm so put out right now that I need some time to get to where I can at least be civil to him." She patted Millie's arm, "Thanks for speaking up. You sounded a lot like Mama just now. If she'd seen this mess, I know she wouldn't just walk away and leave it be. I'll make an effort to mend some fences before I go home."

Torn between their disgust and their dread of totally broken family ties, the sisters contemplated their options and decided to approach Fred. Agreeing with Alma that waiting until evening would give everyone a chance to calm down, they settled in to spend a relaxing afternoon together.

After naps and quiet talks, they took up the job of organizing their moves. Getting Millie and Eva's things moved to Arthur wouldn't be difficult, so they decided to start with that load. If they were careful about how they packed everything, it would take only one trip to finish that part of the relocation.

"It's so stifling that I don't exactly relish the idea of filling the car right now. How about if we pile our stuff in the corner of the kitchen so we're ready in the morning? That'll give us a chance to double check before we head out." Eva grabbed Millie's arm and they were off.

Clara had come back to the house while they were planning, so she and Elsie agreed they could take the majority of their items in Elsie's car. "Since Emma will be going east like we do, we might be able to put our extras in with her load. That'd sure help us out. If nothing else, we can go back to York later on."

"Dolphs will be here on Tuesday for Darlene's stuff, so I guess that pretty much leaves me to make a plan." Emma stood with her hands on her hips. "Seems to make sense that we'd use the ranch car to move my stuff. Fred is right that we agreed to use it around the ranch, and I'm not suggesting I keep it in York. Don't know if he'll want to; but if Fred helps me move, he could bring it back here. My idea is that it's available if any one of us needs it later on, but he can use it the rest of the time. What do you think?"

The plan basically left intact the arrangements with which they were all comfortable, so no one had a problem with her suggestion. That was one item on their discussion agenda with Fred, and they sat around talking about what else they wanted to bring up.

"You know, it made me sad when he talked about tossing out anything we left behind, but there's more here to think about. We've all spoken for the stuff we want, but what's the story on the livestock? Ted was the one who put together the horse herd by buying the best breeding stock he could find and making them into good horses. Does Fred automatically get ownership of all the horses just because he's still here? I'll bet you he sees dollar signs running out there in the pasture, and it won't be long before he finds a way to turn a profit off Ted's work." Since Alma was just two years younger than Fred, she knew very well how his mind worked. "It'll really set him off if we bring it up, but I don't think it's fair that he can just do whatever he wants."

Darlene spoke up next, "I don't think he cares about the cattle either. He hasn't even gone out to check the wells to see if they have water. Ted was the one who always looked after them; and now that he's gone, what's going to happen to the cows and calves? I hope they don't all die."

"We have quite a list of things to talk about this evening. Let's hope we can get through it without a big blowup, but it has to be done, no matter how it turns out." Emma had written the sisters' concerns as they talked, and she laid the paper on the kitchen table. "Maybe we'll do the chores first so Fred can figure out what needs done at the barn, and then we'll come back here to eat. After we're finished, we'll just have to barge in and see where it all ends up."

At five o'clock, Clara volunteered to go get Fred, and no one argued with her. Her light step and flushed cheeks as she hurried down the porch steps reinforced Alma's belief in Clara's new love interest. "Hope he plays square with her, but that's not the feeling I have when I'm around him. He's just a bit too smooth for my liking." Ironically, Alma could see the potential pitfalls that lay ahead for Clara, perhaps because it closely resembling the disastrous circumstances of her own marriage.

Everyone had changed into work clothes so they could help with the chores. Even though most of the girls had left home and moved into town, not a one of them had forgotten how to milk a cow. As they grabbed the one-legged stools tucked into the braces beside the door, it was as if they were holding fast to a bit of their youth.

Early and late, whoever was home had always assembled at the barn to milk the cows and feed whatever animals were being kept up. Doing the chores together made them go faster, and dividing the chores by special interests made good sense. When a few cows remained to be milked, someone would start feeding the horses, others the calves, and still others would gather eggs. One of the women would have stayed in the house to fix supper so they all finished at about the same time.

Maria was as comfortable working outside as she was inside, and her entire family had been raised to help each other no matter what. Because the women helped wherever needed, the men did the same. The boys learned to cook when young, and they were also quick to clean up when meals were over. When they assumed responsibility for the ranch work, Fred and Ted had spent most of their time away from the house looking after details, but they had still lent a hand when possible.

As Fred and the girls gathered for evening chore time, much of the earlier tension fell away as they assumed their customary roles. Gradually they began to laugh and joke and found themselves thoroughly enjoying their time together. Reaching the house at the same time, they took turns washing and then helped put the food on the table. Supper consisted of fried beef steak, mashed potatoes, and a thick white gravy made by adding flour and milk to the hot grease and crumbs in the huge cast iron skillet. Garden produce rounded out the meal with cucumbers, tomatoes, and green onions, along with hot green beans laced with strips of bacon. Fred's wife joined them just as they were ready to sit down to eat.

Alma had volunteered to stay inside because she wanted to fix a special meal for everyone; and by the time she served her special fried bread, they all agreed she had accomplished her goal. "Wow, Sis. If you cooked for me every day, I'd be too big to waddle through the door," Elsie leaned her head back against Alma who was standing behind her at the time. "This is what I'll remember when I think of our family sitting down together. I'm stuffed."

"Oh, I'm sorry to hear that, Elsie. Does that mean you don't want any apple dumplings for dessert? I remembered that was your favorite so I whipped up some. If you don't eat them this time, I guess you'll have to come out to California so I can make you some." Alma had purposely slid in her announcement about moving away with them all at the table. This way she could get the surprise over all at once and avoid the heart-to-heart talks she so dreaded.

"Whoa there, girl. What do you mean by that?" Elsie was the first to respond. "I thought you and James planned to lease that school section close to town and get your own spread started. Wasn't he going to work at the hardware store and haul freight to Ogallala? When did this happen?"

James was notorious for jumping from one venture to another as soon as the newness wore off. He'd been employed at nearly every available job in the county, as well as in surrounding communities. When a new whim would hit, he'd make huge brags to Alma about how this was the time he'd really make it big and he'd be back for the family as soon as he got settled in. She was so loyal to him that she never complained about anything even though the whole family realized how hard it was for her to get by.

Maria and Ted had sent in all kinds of produce to her whenever anyone made a trip to town, and they made sure she got her share of the calf check. The problem was that James had it timed so he was always back home when the cash rolled in, and she couldn't tell him no. The result was that the money slipped through his fingers, and they lived from hand to mouth most of the time.

The sisters had privately discussed how long James had been gone this time, and they had secretly hoped he'd stay away. Alma would work long and hard while he was gone; and just as she had a nest egg built up, back he'd come. No one ever said a word to her, but they believed she'd be better off without him. The biggest problem was that he was a charmer, and she truly cared for the guy. She had two children she loved deeply, and she didn't want them to grow up without a father, even one as unreliable as he.

"Last week he ran into a friend who's working in a huge freight business in Los Angeles. They can't find enough help out there so they're paying really good wages. He's going to take the train this week end, and the kids and I'll drive out as soon as I get things taken care of here. Even if I can't take all my stuff, it'll be good to be settled where James can earn good pay. I guess people have tons of money out there so it's easy for a man to make a lot of money."

Alma spoke emphatically to convince them of the wisdom of the move, and perhaps also to convince herself this would be the time her husband would provide for his family. "I thought I might ask Eva and Millie if I could leave the table and chairs in the family house in Arthur until I get settled. When I know for sure I have room, the kids and I can come back to get whatever we left behind. How's that sound?"

Millie was quick with her answer, "Alma, you know we'd love to help out, so we'll be glad to use them until you come back. With just the two of us there now, we'll have plenty of room for your stuff. I think it'd be easier to drive all that way with two little kids if they weren't packed in like sardines, so feel free to leave any other extras with us. As a matter of fact, we'll move it in the morning, and you can bring the kids by to see how it looks." She jumped up and gave Alma a big hug, "I hate to have you go, but it sounds like James has a good job lined up."

The rest of the family had regained its composure to the point they could offer her good wishes and promises of visits after she was settled. "One nice thing is that you can probably leave all your winter coats here since I hear it stays nice there most of the time. I'll bet you have a beautiful flower garden and a big strawberry patch once you're settled in. It'll be fun to come visit you in your new home." Clara was aware of James' track record, but she still wanted to support Alma, especially since she suspected the family would have similar reservations about her upcoming plans with Roy. He had made his interest in her very clear and had promised to relocate in Lincoln to be close to her.

Alma served her luscious dessert with whipped cream, and the kitchen was filled momentarily with silence and delectable odors. Their habit of passing dirty dishes to the person sitting closest to the counter cleared the table in short order, and they sat savoring what appeared to be their final meal together for the foreseeable future.

Reluctant to upset the companionship into which the family had settled for the moment, Emma knew it was time for a frank discussion of how the Soehls would operate from now on.

"Thanks, Alma. That's a meal I'll bet we remember for a long time, and thanks to everyone for pitching in to get the chores done in record time. Quite an outstanding crew, I'd have to say."

She paused for a long breath, and the quiet in the room indicated that everyone knew what was next. "After tomorrow, everything will be different. Not only how the house and barn look, but everything we've ever known will change. We'll be going our separate ways to build our own lives now, and we'd better take advantage of this family gathering to talk through anything we have on our minds. Up until now, we've all pitched in to keep the family ranch going. Mama and Papa left us in a good place with all the land paid off and a nice herd of cattle. We've all done our share, but now we're going away and Fred will be the only one here. That's the bare bones of it all, and we've got lots to decide about. Anyone care to start?"

Fred shifted in his chair so he could scan the faces around the table. Each time he made eye contact, he smiled and nodded in a rather conspiratorial way. He ended up with about an even split of friendly responses and noncommittal returned nods. Having assessed their moods, he felt confident this might turn out better than he had feared earlier in the day. "I just want to let you know I'm sorry if anything I said over the past few days upset anyone. Family means the world to me; and no matter where we all end up, that'll never change. We've all been through some really tough times lately, and I might not have handled things right. I hope we can put that behind us and end on a happier note."

Looking around the table but seeing no one was comfortable beginning the discussion, Emma reached into her pocket, unfolded the list, and looked at Fred. "I wrote down a few questions that came up while we were talking this afternoon, so here goes. After that little tiff in the shop this morning, we talked over who should get the car, and here's one idea we came up with. Since we bought it for all of us, it seems like we should be able to use it when we need it. Other than that, we're in agreement that the car stays here on the ranch in your hands. Okay with you?"

"Absolutely. If anyone ever needs it, all you've got to do is let me know. We can darned sure work together like family should," Fred felt the tension ease from his shoulders as the discussion started out on such pleasant terms. "I promise I'll keep it in prime condition."

The sisters had no doubt he would do just as he said. Machinery was his domain and the car a particular favorite, so he would be as good as his word. It was almost as if they all let out a collective sigh upon sensing the easy camaraderie in the room.

"Good enough, Fred. Thanks for making this workable," Emma knew the really tough questions still lay ahead, so she made a point of encouraging him to keep the peace as long as possible. "Seems like there are a couple of livestock issues we'll have to tear right into, so here goes. Ted was the one who did all the horse business, using his own time and money. Now that he's gone, what's your plan for the horse herd?"

Fred's shoulders squared up again as he felt the familiar tension tighten in his stomach. "Since you girls have already talked over most of this, maybe it'd just be easier if you tell me what I need to know. Don't know why you wouldn't have come and gotten me so we could all be in on it, but what's done is done. Let me hear it."

"Whoa, Fred. Remember we're just trying to sort out what we need to do. We aren't ganging up on you, and we darned sure don't have all the answers. Why don't you help us sort it out?" Emma chose her words carefully to achieve a balance between standing up to Fred's bullying and encouraging him to cooperate. "Tell us what you think would be fair."

"You all know that horses aren't my cup of tea, so I suppose I do need to decide how many I need to keep around. I'd rather take a beating than have to ride a horse all day long, but I suppose they're kind of a necessary evil. Driving a tractor beats hitching up a team any day, but once in a while real deep snow and clogged fuel lines might call for a back-up plan. Given that, I'd think it'd be smart to keep a couple of saddle horses and one team. Otherwise, they won't do me any good so I'd think we could sell most of them." Talking about selling the horse herd was a bitter pill for Fred to swallow. He had already made plans for the sale, but he had hoped the sisters wouldn't think about it this soon. "Sounds like we're pretty much in agreement with this too."

Darlene sat quietly while tears ran down both cheeks. She discreetly wiped them away, but not before Alma noticed, "Honey, I know this is hard for you, but it's something that's got to be done."

"Ted gave me Cheyenne, and I want to keep him, but I can't take him with me because I'll be living in town. Boxer's such a good little horse that I hate to think of him going to a bad home, but I guess that's just the way it has to be." Her sisters had become so accustomed to treating her like one of the grown-ups that seeing her vulnerable, wretched form perched on the edge of the chair brought tears to all their eyes. Since they were all headed away from the ranching scene, not one of them could take either or both horses for her. Her devastation was complete.

Fred decided this was the time to take charge of the group, so he cleared his throat and announced, "If that's what you want to do, I'll stop and see Trader Keith sometime and ask him to come out and have a look. I'll dicker with him and let you know what he offers."

In a perverse way, he was enjoying his power to inflict pain. It didn't matter to him that his nine year old sister was on the receiving end because she represented every one of the girls who had set themselves up in opposition to him. He wanted them all to have a measure of misery so they'd get a taste of how much they'd hurt him. No way he was going to offer to keep those two geldings around. The one would fetch good money, and Cheyenne didn't have any lasting injuries. Down the road they would go. "I know Ted would want you to have them, Darlene, and I wish there was a way to make it work. I promise you I'd do it for you if I could."

Instantly, Darlene recalled Maria's warning about Promisers Big and knew she had just heard one. There was no reason Fred couldn't keep the horses, but she knew it wasn't going to happen. Darlene had heard enough of the arguments between her brothers that she could recognize the tone of anger and resentment that came when Fred didn't get his own way. She didn't know what had upset him so much, but she knew the signs in spite of his apparent amiability. "That's okay, Fred. Don't worry about it." Even though she was hurting deeply, there was no way she'd reveal it to him.

"Thanks for offering to take care of the sale for us, Fred. Do you have any idea when Trader might come out here? He always wanted some of Ted's horses so I'll be surprised if he puts it off for long. If he comes while some of us are here, one of us will be glad to join in the bargaining. That way you won't have to find each one of us and repeat the same conversation several times." Emma had realized what Fred was trying to do, so she grasped control again in a way that made it clear they wouldn't be ignored.

Darlene was watching him out of the corner of her eye, and she saw the telltale warning of a flush beginning just above his collar. Every time he lost control, that was the first sign of his distress no matter how he tried to conceal it. "I don't know what Trader's plans are, but I'll be sure to let you know if he decides to show up. We should be able to work out something with him. Anything else on your list?"

"As a matter of fact, there is, Ted. We need to figure out what kind of arrangements will work out fairly for all of us when it comes to the land and the cattle. We know we each own a share of the land since Mama made sure to tell us which section we would inherit. The same's true of the cow herd since it's a part of the estate that the folks left all of us. All of us sisters may be leaving, but we're not walking away from everything." Emma was also aware of the indications which appeared when Fred approached his flash point, and she noticed the flush had crept up to cover his entire face. "We want it to be fair to you so you can make a living, and also to us so we get our fair share. Do you have any ideas how we can make this work?"

"Your fair share? What do you think makes up your fair share? I'll be here doing all the work, and you'll be off doing whatever you want and still taking a cut from me? I'd think you'd be ashamed of yourselves for even suggesting such a thing. If you want to stay around and pull calves and dig post holes and everything else that goes into ranching, be my guest. Otherwise, I don't see why you think you have a dime coming, and I darned sure don't want to work my fingers to the bone just so you can hit it rich."

By the time he had finished, his face verged on being purple and he had lunged out of his chair. Standing at the door, he shouted, "I should have known you'd pull something like this after you tried to soften me up with food and talk about family and all that bull."

Before he could bolt out the door, Alma had planted herself in the opening so he came to an abrupt halt as he turned to stomp out. "Fred, this is one time you're not throwing your fit and marching off. I'd suggest you calm down and come back to the table. We're not pulling anything and you know it, but we're equal shareholders in this place who have something to say about it. Now sit down and help us figure out how you can make a living here and still treat us fairly." Taking his arm, she firmly turned him back to the table, "Let's finish clearing the table and get down to business." With that, she gave him time to regain his composure and relieved the tension that had filled the room.

After Clara had washed off the table and they sat down again, Elsie broke the silence. "We're not asking you to buy our land or lease our sections, Fred. In return for your using them, it seems like we would be entitled to a share of the calf check. Let's find a figure we can all live with." Checking out Fred's reaction, she saw that his color was back to normal and noticed that he had leaned forward to be a part of the circle. "Let's start with a number for the sake of discussion. If you took half the calf money and we split the other half, how would that work out?"

"That sounds pretty skimpy to me. How about if I take out the expenses before we split the calf check? Then I wouldn't be the one who had to pay for everything, do everything, and then just get half of the money. I think I could live with that." Looking very pleased with himself, he leaned back and put his arm around Ruth.

"I could see that you'd like that arrangement, but it seems to me we've already pitched in to pay our share of the expenses if we let you use our land and our share of the cattle without asking for lease price." Emma had expected a counter offer somewhat like this, so she was ready to remind him of their part in the operation. "One half might seem like you're losing a half, but you might want to remember that you've never had the whole check anyway. As a matter of fact, no one ever got close to half before, so you'd actually be getting quite a bit more that what you're used to."

By now, Fred had both fists on the table and was giving Emma a cold stare. "That may be, but do you know how hard I'm going to have to work now? Now that Ted's gone, I'll have to do it all by myself. Now how fair is that? You expect me to take on his work and not get his share? That's a sorry state of affairs."

"Ted did it all by himself, Fred. If he could do it, why can't you?" Still smarting from how he had hurt her over the horse deal, Darlene had spoken the truth they all knew in a small, firm voice.

Furious that she had called him to task on how little he had been involved, Fred shoved away from the table and toppled his chair behind him. "Tell you what. Since you all know so much, just sit here and hash it all out without me. When you're done, send someone to tell me what I'm supposed to do. If you think I'm going to sit here and be railroaded by you and then say thanks for the mistreatment, you've got another think a-coming. If you know what's good for you, you won't try to stop me this time." He jerked Ruth's chair back and grabbed her by the hand, "Come on. We don't have to put up with this kind of abuse from anyone, let alone family."

In the aftermath of their exit, the sisters sat quietly for a time, then Alma picked up his chair, shoved it under the table, and straightened the other. "So much for a calm talk. We might as well set down our conditions on paper and deliver it to him. If he won't stick around to settle it, I guess we can." Turning to Emma, she encouraged her, "You have a knack for getting to the heart of the matter, so how about being the secretary today? Besides, it'll be good practice for when you have a career of your own."

"Works for me." Emma's direct reply conveyed her determination to finalize the points of the day, with or without Fred's input. "Where are we all on the share of the calf check? Half for him and half for us sound okay?" She established eye contact with each sister to check for reactions. Noticing Clara's discomfort, she asked her point blank, "What do you think about this? If you have a problem with it, you need to tell us right now. You might feel bad about having to stand up to Fred; but if we don't do it, there's a good possibility we'll end up with nothing. I'd feel bad if that happened."

Clara shifted uncomfortably and let out a huge sigh, "It's just so hard to feel like I have to choose sides. I know Fred's said some unfortunate things, but he's the only brother we have left. Do we really have to do this right now? How about letting it slide and taking care of it later? He'd have time to cool off and maybe see it our way. I'd sure like that better."

"So would I—if I thought we had a snowball's chance in you know where of that happening." The sisters laughed at Emma's remark and indicated their agreement with her sentiment. "The only thing we'd gain by doing this later is avoiding the clash right now. He's not about to agree with anything we suggest, so I say let's put it on paper so there's no doubt where we stand. If we decide this is what we want, I'll write it down, we can sign it, and I'll take it to him in the morning." With that, Emma wrote up the original suggestion and handed it around the table so the sisters could read and sign it.

As Darlene woke to the familiar smell of bacon and biscuits the next morning, she grabbed her chore clothes before remembering that Fred was now responsible for the work. She put on clean work clothes so she could help load the car for Millie and Eva before sauntering out to the kitchen. "Oh, man, Em, there's not a better smell in the world to wake up to. You're the best ever."

With that, Darlene filled her plate with bacon, eggs, and cinnamon rolls. "You know, Em, I've been thinking. Do you suppose it's about time for me to start drinking coffee? All you grown-ups do, so I've been wondering how old I need to be before I can have a cup of coffee. What do you think?"

"I think you need to grab a cup right now and fill it about half full. No time like the present for you to get started being all grown-up, I always say," Emma watched with amusement as Darlene filled her cup, set it on the table, and sat down with her arm over the back of the chair.

Bringing the cup up to her mouth, she blew across the brown liquid once before taking a cautious sip. Spewing the coffee into her hand, she wiped it on her pants and then shook her head, "Yipe! Why didn't you tell me it would be that hot and that bad? Yuck! I can't imagine why you old people sit around and act like you really like that terrible stuff. I'm sticking with my cold milk from now on." Dumping the rest of the coffee down the sink, she filled the cup and sipped it quickly, "I darned sure needed to get rid of that rotten taste. Does all coffee taste like that or did you just do a bad job of cooking it?" She ducked and giggled as Emma threw a dishtowel at her head. "I can't believe anything that smells so good could taste so bad."

Emma sank down in the chair beside her and gave her a quick hug, "I always wondered that myself, but I kept at it until I could choke it down. Now I have to admit I really like it, so maybe you can get used to anything if you try hard enough."

As the other girls straggled out of the bedrooms, Darlene looked out the window and caught sight of a cloud of dust on the road. "Do you suppose that's Alma coming back? She didn't think she could get here very early because she had to get the kids up and fed before she could leave. James doesn't like to do that, and she's so softhearted that she puts up with his nonsense. I won't ever put up with stupid stuff like that from some guy, I'll tell you that right now."

"Careful, girl. Mama always said 'Never say never' and that's pretty good advice. Lots of times people do stuff they bragged they'd never do, and that can be embarrassing. Better to not make brags so you don't have to eat your words." Emma privately agreed with Darlene but knew Maria would have offered the same words of caution.

Darlene shrugged, "Okay. I'll keep my mouth shut while I'm not putting up with stupid stuff. Is that better?"

Emma tousled her hair and gave a hearty laugh, "That's the best plan I've ever heard, Honey. The less you have to say, the less people know about your business."

All of a sudden, Darlene hooted, "No wonder there was so much dust; it was two cars." Running out of the house hollering and waving, she reached the cars just as they pulled in the yard. "What in the world are you doing here? It's only Saturday and I didn't think you were coming until Tuesday." She jerked open the door and pulled Tracy out to give her a squeeze. "I'm so happy to see you." Stopping so abruptly that Tracy bumped into her, she turned around, "Is anything wrong? Did you change your mind about me coming to live with you? I hope not, but I'll understand if you did."

"Honey, no, nothing like that." Tracy was quick to reassure her, "We just got some of the best news you could ever imagine, and I didn't want to wait a minute longer to tell you. We were working on this when we were here, but we couldn't say anything until it was a done deal. Now it is, so hang on to your hat." Pausing to be sure she had Darlene's full attention, she made her big announcement,

"We're moving."

Shocked into silence, Darlene simply stood and stared. By the time she recovered to the point she could talk, all kinds of scenarios flashed through her mind. "What does that mean? How far are we going?" Running out of questions, in desperation she pleaded, "Will you just please tell me?"

Tracy appreciated the enthusiasm and related completely to Darlene's anxiety, "We closed on a deal with Ben to basically switch places. He wanted to get to town, and we've been looking for a country place for a long time. This way we can both keep doing what we know how to do but change our locations. We wanted to add some land so we could have our own cows, and he was tired of that kind of work." She saw the amazement in Darlene's eyes and laughed, "For once you're speechless. What do you think about it?"

The wheels had spun very rapidly for Darlene, and nearly everything she was thinking came tumbling out, "I'll still be living in the country and not having to leave Amy and going to the same school and Ben and Robert will be gone. What do you think I think about it? I can't imagine anything any better. This is the best news ever." She danced around Tracy, hugged Ed, and ran back to Tracy, "Just one thing I've got to know. Will you have room for any of my animals?" Waiting anxiously for Tracy's answer, she started jumping up and down with excitement when Tracy nodded yes.

No sooner had she had time to process this thrill than she looked up to see the driver of the other car approaching. "Trader Keith. What in the world brings you out here today? I'm surprised to see you, but I've got the most wonderful news." Quickly she glanced at Tracy to see if she could tell him. Tracy smiled, and Darlene blurted out, "We're moving to Reichers and they're moving to town. What do you think of that?"

Trader reached out and softly placed his huge hand on her shoulder, "I don't think I've ever driven into a yard and had so many questions fired at me. I just got out of the car and it's not easy for me to think that fast. Slow down and start where you want me to start. What's your first question?"

"What do you think of us moving to Ben's place and him moving to town?" That was the most recent query so she started with it.

"I'm glad for everyone involved. Dolphs have been looking for a place for so long I wondered if they'd ever find one that suited them. Ben's been wanting out from under that place ever since he had to come home and help out, and I didn't know if it'd work for him either. Then you throw in the fact that you're staying in your home neighborhood where you've always lived, and it couldn't be any more perfect. That's what I think about all of that. Okay, help me out here. What's the next thing you wanted to know?"

"I'm surprised to see you here today since you were just here a few days ago. Usually it's a long time between your visits, but this is a great way for me to start out the morning. Did you wake up and decide it's a good day for a drive and that's how you ended up here?"

Trader pursed his lips and waited a moment before answering, "After the memorial service, Fred asked me if I was interested in buying any horses, and I darned sure didn't want Ted's string to get away from me. I'm here because he asked me to drop in."

Once again, Darlene's mind was engaged before Trader had even finished. "So this is a horse trading trip, you might say. I'll run get Em and let her know you're here." With that she was off to the house at a full run, shouting her sister's name loud and often.

"What in the world is up with you, Darlene? I had hold of that mirror Eva wanted to take home, and I nearly dropped it when you bellered out my name. Maybe you can fill me in as soon as you catch your breath."

"Trader's here and Dolphs are moving to Ben's place and Fred lied and I get to keep my horses after all." Able to reduce a complicated situation to its basics, she relayed the essence of the morning to her sister in quick, breathless gasps.

Emma immediately stopped where she was and stooped so she was at eye level, "Wait a minute. That's a mouthful of news and some of it's a little hard to follow. I get the part about Dolphs and you moving to the Reicher place, and I can't imagine anything any better. I also get the part about Trader being here since I can look out in the yard and see him. Why did you say Fred lied? Even though we had that sorry blow-up last night, I don't think you should talk about him like that. Try to remember he still is your brother."

With an exasperated expression on her face and a hand on her hip, Darlene shrugged, "Okay, Em. You're probably right. I maybe shouldn't have said that Fred lied, but on the day of Ted's service, Fred told Trader he wanted to sell the horse herd." She stopped to give Emma time to think about their earlier conversation. "If I heard it right yesterday, Fred acted like it was a mystery to him if Trader would decide to show up or not. That seems a little bit like a lie to me, even if he is my brother."

Where Fred's face went red when he was agitated, Emma's went white. When Darlene saw the color change, she edged her way over towards Tracy. "I think this'd be a good time to ask Tracy if Tater can come along with us. I never dreamed there'd be a chance he could come too."

Emma barely took the time to acknowledge Darlene as

she took out toward Fred's house. Just then he came strolling up from his house. "Looks like quite a bit of action here this morning already." He nonchalantly nodded at Emma who had stopped in his path, "Mornin' to you, Em. I got a little late start on the chores this morning so I hoped some of you girls could take pity on me and help out. I was just headed to the house to find out." Although he had hoped all the unpleasantries of the previous evening would disappear, he knew his sister well enough to know her pale color was not a good sign for him.

"Fred, it seems Trader's here because you told him there'd be business for him with Ted's horses." Emma had the reputation of being unfailingly courteous, no matter what, so this direct, rather cool greeting conveyed much more than the simple words themselves contained.

Fred had a momentary sense of panic that he had been caught in his own web of deceit, but then he fell back on old habits. "Oh, Em, I meant to mention that to you but it just slipped my mind. Even though I hadn't talked to you girls the day of Ted's service, I knew the fair thing would be to sell the horses and split the money. Sure a good thing Trader got here before anyone had to leave, don't you think?"

Emma simply stood and looked him in the eye, revealing no emotion at all. Her silence continued until he was so uncomfortable that he jumped in with running set of comments.

"Don't know why the Dolphs are here today. I thought they planned to wait till Tuesday to pick up Darlene's stuff and move her out, but I sure want to go talk to them. Then we can all head to the barn and give Trader a chance to look over the herd. Then we'll get down to serious horse trading."

Still no response from his sister, so Fred waved to Ed and Tracy and ambled over to their car. "Good to see you folks today, even if it's sooner than I expected. If this's a neighborly call, I'm darned certain glad to see you. If it's because you need some help at anything, we'll all be glad to lend a hand after all you've done for us lately." Extending his hand to Ed and tipping his hat to Tracy, he waited for their reply.

Tracy beamed at the chance to share their good news, "We're so excited about what's happening for us, and we wanted Darlene to be one of the first ones to hear it from us. We've traded places with Ben, so his family will move to town and we'll move out here. This swap makes both outfits feel like we've gotten the best end of the bargain, so it must be good all around."

By the time she was finished, Fred had processed all parts of this new development. First of all he was sad that Ben was moving out of the neighborhood. They shared a common mentality and love for the good life that he would miss, but the good news was that he could go visit his friend in town so that made up for his disappointment. Almost immediately he recalled his needling of Darlene when they were talking about the horse deal. Why'd he have to lip off and make that big shot promise she could have those two horses? There was no way on earth that should have ever happened, and now two of the horses that would have fetched the highest prices would be standing around her pasture instead of lining his pockets with serious cash.

"Welcome to the neighborhood! I can't imagine how lucky we are to have you joining us. It'll be good to run into you at our country post office and store instead of having to wait until we get to town. I didn't have a clue this was even in the works, so I'm excited for everyone concerned. You know, this relieves me about Darlene moving out. Of course I hate to see her go, but I was so worried about her having to live in town and change schools that I about made myself sick thinking of it. She's one lucky little girl."

Trader had finished talking with Emma and joined the conversation in time to hear Fred's remark about Darlene's luck. "I'll say she's lucky. The only thing that bothered me about buying Ted's horses was that I felt like a heel taking those two from her. Now that I hear Dolphs will have room for them and that you promised them to her, I'm good with this deal." He looked expectantly at Fred who waved toward the barn, and the whole group moved in that direction.

Darlene had run on ahead to wait for them, and as they slip open the barn door, she let out the piercing whistle that had become her trademark. "Trader, hurry up so you can watch Boxer. Once he hears that, he's on the move. Isn't it neat that Ted taught Cheyenne and him that and then showed me? It's kind of like he's with me every time I do it." She made her remarks in the matter-of-fact way children speak the truth, and she continued to watch the horses running into the corral while the grown-ups turned aside to conceal their awkwardness. "Cheyenne's usually at the head of the bunch, and it won't be long before he takes over again with as fast as he's healing."

By the time she was finished, a huge milling herd of horses of all sizes and ages had converged in the corral. Work horses, saddle horses, brood mares, colts, and one lone mule circled and stomped. They would come to the door to check on their chances for grain, and then move away disgustedly when they didn't get a hand-out. "They're such grain hogs we can catch them anywhere. All we have to do is shake a bit of oats and they come on the run. Kinda handy but you have to pay attention or they might step on you if you're not careful." Darlene had climbed up the bridge plank fence and swung one leg over the top while she rested her other foot on the second board from the bottom. Secure on her perch, she waited for Trader to join her.

"Can you give me a run-down on what we have here?

Looks like you're the one who knows what's going on in the horse world," Trader had slid both feet on the bottom plank so he and Darlene stood as equals on the fence.

She nodded and then motioned to Fred, "He said he wanted a team and a couple of saddle horses out of here, so I suppose we'd better ask him if he has an idea of the ones to cut off." She waved to Fred and Emma who made their way up the fence also.

Trader turned to Fred, "Do you want to pen up your keepers so I can get an idea of what's on the block? Probably need to sort them off so we don't have any misunderstandings."

Fred cleared his throat and looked at Darlene, "Do you remember the team Ted used the most last winter? They'd probably be the ones I'd want." Embarrassed that he didn't have a clue which team to pick and that he had to ask the little sister he had treated so badly for advice made for a difficult moment for him. "I've kinda lost touch with the horse end of the operation lately."

"Flash and Fancy were the ones he worked most of the time last winter, but if I were you, I'd probably pick that set of black mares over there by the fence. Guess it's up to you." Darlene offered the input Fred had requested, but the minute her suggestion went against his first inclination, he immediately rejected it.

"I said I wanted the ones he worked last winter, so Flash and Fancy it is. I appreciate your pointing out those other horses, but it'd be dumb not to take the ones he worked the most. Let's shove them in the west pen, and while we're out there, we might as well slide off those other two horses I'll keep so I have them if I ever have to ride. Those two brown geldings over there look gentle enough to me." Fred crossed the corral and opened the gate so Trader could ease the four out of the pen.

"Now I need to know which ones are broke, which mares are bred, and how many of the young horses have been started. Darlene, would you come over here and tell me what you know?" Trader knew how much time she had spent with Ted; so, unlike Fred, he trusted her judgment completely. "Sounds like you think that team of blacks is pretty solid if I heard you right."

By then she was at Trader's side and out of Fred's ear-shot. "I told the truth when I said he worked Flash and Fancy last winter, and I also know he said they're a pair of knot heads that won't pull their own weight. These blacks are really gentle and voice broke. The taller one with the little white fleck above her eye is Dawn, and the one with no markings at all is Dusk. They're half sisters out of that Percheron he got out of Iowa, and should last for quite a while since they're just 5 year olds.

While Trader kept a mental tally, she told him the status of every horse in the pen. By the time she was done, he knew what to offer so he could make a profit and still give the family a fair price. "Just between you and me, Darlene, how about giving me a shot at Cheyenne and Boxer? They'd round out this deal just fine." He was pleased that the horses would be staying with her, but he and she had an easy way of teasing one another.

"Shucks, Trader. I'd like to unload them but couldn't do that to a friend like you. Thanks for offering to take them off my hands, though. I appreciate knowing you're looking after me like that." The two of them laughed as they trudged through the sand to where Fred and Emma were waiting for them.

As they reached the middle of the corral, Trader put out his arm and stopped Darlene. "You know, I've got to ask you this. What in the world was Ted doing with that mule? There isn't a jack around here to breed a mare to, so I know he didn't raise him. Whenever I asked him about it, he'd just laugh and tell me, 'Jaspar's my secret weapon.' How about sharing that secret with me? I'd really like to know. "

"I will, Trader, but first I want to tell you why I loved having Jaspar around. You know that Mama was strict about how we talked, boys and all. Whenever Ted and I sorted horses, it seemed like that mule was always in the way. I'd rear back and yell over at Ted, 'Get your ass out of here' and he'd just about double over laughing at me. Then he'd look over his shoulder to see if anyone else heard it, and he'd warn me, 'Missy, you'd better not do that where those others can hear it. If you do, we'll both be in big trouble.' That's the only time he'd let me say something like that, kinda like our little secret."

Trader had leaned over, slapped his knee, and finally recovered his breath, "That sounds just like that rascal. Trust me, that secret's safe with me, but I don't think I'll ever be able to look at Jaspar and not bust out laughing." He wiped his eyes and went on, "Now about that secret weapon deal. Want to let me in on that?"

Darlene grinned at him, "You know how you always asked Ted how in the world he got those work horse colts so nice to work with? For a while he fought them around and pulled and tugged until one day he said, 'Must be a way to get this done with less wear and tear on me. Think I'll go visit the livery stable.' When he got back, he came to the house to get me so I could see his newest bargain. When I walked in the barn, ole Jaspar let out that bawling bray of his and I just about wet my pants. When Ted quit laughing, he introduced me to that mule, 'Lena, I want you to meet my latest labor saving device, Jaspar.' The next morning he haltered Jaspar and a work horse colt, tied their halter ropes together, and turned them loose. We didn't know what to expect, so we leaned on the fence to we could watch the fun.

Old Jaspar went on about his business like always, and that colt had no choice but to go along. He'd plant his feet, fight his head, and then lunge forward to get some relief; then try it all over again. All the while Jaspar didn't miss a lick. He went and got a drink, ate his fill of hay, and then strolled around the pen like he was sightseeing. At first the colt fought him pretty good, but after he lost the tug of war a few times, he marched along like a real gentleman. The show was over for then, and Ted couldn't wait for night to see how much the colt had learned. When he unhaltered Jaspar and turned him loose, the colt tried to move once; but when Ted pulled on his nose, the colt stood as quiet as a mouse. Ted gave me that big grin of his while he put his arm around the colt and petted him, 'This is how a thinking man does his work, courtesy of wonderworker Jaspar.' And now you know Ted's secret weapon."

"What were you two laughing about over there?" Emma looked quizzically at the two of them. "Looked like you were having quite a bit of fun for a while there. Anything we need to know about?"

Bursting into laughter as they exchanged knowing glances, Trader and Darlene answered in unison, "Nope." Trader continued, "Darlene's quite a comedian sometimes. Must come from being out here alone so much that she spends all her words once she's got an audience."

Darlene recognized the signs of adults getting ready to transact business, and she decided to make her escape rather than stand around while they haggled. "I need to check with Tracy about when we can take my stuff to our new house. Fred, you did say you wanted me to have Cheyenne and Boxer, didn't you? If that's still all right with you, I'll see what she and Ed think about me taking them. I thought I might take Tater along too, unless you want to keep him here."

Fred looked directly at her as he summoned up his most sincere tone, "Sis, you know I promised I'd make it work if I could, so I'll darned sure keep my word. No need for me to keep that hound since I'm not a coyote hunter nor a dog fancier. Maybe we can even work in some talk with Trader here about a pack of hounds that are up for grabs."

"Thanks, Fred. I better check all this out with Dolphs before I get all excited." Darlene sprinted out of the corral, through the barn, and to the house to visit with her new guardians.

She found Ed busy carrying Millie and Eva's bundles out to the Soehl car. After a group discussion, they had agreed to load Alma's table and chairs first, then tuck in as many items as they could before driving to Arthur to unload. "I don't know if there'd be room for one more thing as packed as the car is now." Ed came back after his last trip to tell them it was full, "If you want me to, I'll follow you to town and help you put this in your house; and then we can be back here this afternoon to finish with your stuff. Tracy and I could bring out another load of our stuff to take to our new place so we can do our moving at the same time. We already left some of our things over there this morning before we came here."

Tracy looked up to see Darlene and motioned her inside, "Oh, look, here's my new girl. Did you get all the horsetrading done out there? I don't see the others so they're probably still nickel and diming each other. We're a lot more fun in here."

"It's just dull talk now, nothing to do with the horses so I left. You're already taking me in, and I'm so happy to be going with you that I can't believe how lucky I am. I know Mama always told me to say thank you and not to ask for more when people do something nice for me, but I've just got to ask. Will you have room for me and all my animals, too, now that we'll be in the country? If you and Ed don't want to bother with them, I'll understand."

Tracy hugged Darlene, "How about filling me in on all your animals? Right up front, I'd say I'd be reluctant if you have a baby skunk or a porcupine, but otherwise, we're probably open to almost everything else."

"Oh, Tracy, you know me better than that," Darlene giggled and continued, "It's kind of a long list, so here goes. Cheyenne and Boxer are my two horses, Johnny and Jitney are my two cats, Tater is my dog, and that's all. I don't rightly think of any of the milk cows as my favorites, and I'll be glad to leave those nasty turkey gobblers as far away as possible. Guess that's about it."

"I don't even need to check with Ed to see if this is okay since I know we'll have room for the horses out in the pasture. Ben didn't like working with livestock so he'd gotten rid of most of his before we even started talking about a trade, so the barn and the fences will need a bit of fixing. We plan to have milk cows and some stock cows, so we'll be super glad you can help out with your horses. Barns need cats and dogs, so I'd say your animals will fit right in. Thanks for sharing them with us." Tracy had hardly finished when she felt herself in a choke hold as Darlene flung her arms around her and squeezed with all her might. "I just hope I don't run out of breath before we get moved."

Darlene realized she was holding tight and quickly let go, "Oh, Tracy, I hope I didn't hurt you. I was just so excited that I guess I kinda lost control. Sorry about that," she apologized while fluffing Tracy's shirt where she had grasped so tight.

"Honey, that's probably one of the best reasons to lose control I've ever heard. Happiness seems to be kind of short-lived around here so you'd best hang on to it when you get it." Tracy took Darlene by the hand, "Let's go out and let

Ed know the good news. He'll be glad to hear those cats are coming along. When he walked into the barn, he said it smelled like mice had been living there for a long time. Don't let on I told you, but he's not very comfortable around mice."

Darlene gasped, "Do you mean he's afraid of mice? A big guy who runs a black smith shop afraid of a little gray mouse? Johnny and Jitney are the best mousers we have on the place, so they'll be the best news he's had today. I promise I won't tease him about mice. I know how I hate it when someone gets into my head and then makes fun of me. That's not a nice thing to do."

"I knew I could trust you to do the right thing so that's why I told you. We can take care of any mouse situation that comes up and not bother him with it. The good thing is that I feel the same way about snakes, and Ed's good about getting rid of them so I don't have to. I'm glad we're adding you to our team, Honey. This'll work out just fine." Tracy and Darlene found Ed tying down the chairs for the trip to town.

"I was about to come and get you, Tracy. We might as well go home and start on our next load. When these girls get to town, they can let us know and we'll help them unload. Are you done here for now?" He stood up and slid his arm around Tracy's waist on one side and around Darlene's on the other.

"Before we go, Darlene wanted to ask you about bringing some of her animals when she moves in with us. Maybe you can listen and give her your answer so she won't have to wonder."

Ed turned to face the little girl, "Why, of course. Get started anytime you're ready."

"Well, I'm really attached to my horses, Cheyenne and Boxer. Ted gave them to me and I think they're fine animals we can use to do cattle work. Then I have two fine cats,

Johnny and Jitney, the best mousers I've ever seen so they're good to have in a barn. I have a dog named Potatoes because he reminds me of mashed potatoes but I shortened it to Tater and that's what he answers to. He is a coyote hound but really doesn't know it since he always tags me around and doesn't chase anything or get in any kind of mischief. And that's what I'd like to bring along if it's all right with you, Sir."

"Hold it. We need to get something straight before we go any further. Your mother taught you wonderful manners, and I like being around polite young ladies; but if you're going to move in with us, you'll need to call me something besides 'Sir.' I know I'm not your father, but I'm not a stranger either. Have you given any thought to what you'd feel comfortable calling Tracy and me?"

Darlene had given this topic much thought, and she was surprised that he had realized the need to sort out labels and relationships. "Yes, Sir—I mean, yes, I have. How would you feel if I called you Uncle Ed? I don't have anyone else close enough to call uncle, and that could be a special name for you that I'd like to say. Then I could say Aunt Tracy too, and that'd feel real good to me."

"Yes, indeed, little lady. I like the sound of that. Now back to the animal question. From your descriptions, they all are fine animals that would be very welcome to come live with us. Plan on moving them when we come to take you home with us next Tuesday. Anything else we need to hash out before Tracy and I get back to town so we can get this move done as quick as possible?"

"No, S—no, Uncle Ed. I think that just about covers everything I had in mind right now. Oh, wait a minute. There is something else. When we were sorting out Mama's things, the girls wanted me to take the bedstead and headboard that Papa brought. It's pretty big, so I need to ask about bringing that along too. I've not been in the house over there, so I don't know what it's like inside. Maybe you need to look at it the next time you go and let me know later.

"Actually, Darlene, we had been talking about that very same thing. We didn't have another bed in our Arthur house, so we'll need one in your room. It's big enough that the bed should fit, so we'll plan to move the bed on Monday so you can sleep in it Tuesday when the move's final."

"Oh, I'm so relieved. I was worried we'd have to leave it here, and Fred said he's pitching anything we don't get out of here. That's a big worry off my mind. Thanks, Uncle Ed and Aunt Tracy. See you when you get back." Stepping back, she waved as they climbed into their car and turned toward town.

By then Trader, Fred, and Emma appeared on the porch. "Come on in for a cup of coffee, Trader. I might even scare up a cinnamon roll too," Emma passed into the house followed by the two men.

"Oh, darn. I forgot I needed to do the chores." Fred belatedly remembered that the chores would wait until he did them, and he was quick to look around for some help. "Millie, do you suppose you and Eva could get started milking the cows and I'll come as soon as we're done here?"

The two girls paused at the door, "We'd help out, Fred, but Ed and Tracy are waiting in town to help us unload so we'd better get a move on." Hustling out the door, they left a disappointed Fred still trying to find someone to impose on. Just then Clara came down the hall with a load of her own which she situated in the corner of the kitchen.

"Say, Clara. I need a favor. I haven't had time to do the milking yet, and I need some help. How about going down to my house to let Roy know I could use him at the barn. That is, unless you've got something else really pressing to do." Fred watched as Clara's face turned pink and she smoothed her hair. "If you're not busy, I suppose you could help us chore so we have it done before noon."

Clara turned and smiled, "I'll be glad to do that for you, Fred. Those cows and calves don't seem to like it when they get off schedule. I'm close enough to being done with my packing that I sure can lend a hand in the barn. I'll be right back." With that remark delivered over her shoulder, she took off and practically ran all the way around the curve.

Trader and Emma exchanged glances which Fred picked up on, "So what's that all about? I just asked my sister to help, and she was kind enough to pitch in—which is more than anyone else around here is willing to do." Then he gave a knowing grin, "Nothing wrong with helping young love, is there?"

Emma gave a cynical, slow answer, "Nothing at all, unless you've got motives that aren't on the up and up. She's pretty gullible and you know that. I just hope that Roy fella knows how to treat someone that trusting. If she gets hurt, Fred, it's on your head. That's all I'm going to say."

"Well, that's a relief. You kept it short and sweet and only managed to threaten me once in that conversation. That might be a record." Then he laughed to show he was joking with her, but both Emma and Trader simply sat and looked at him.

"Okay, then. Are we done with all our business? You take the horses in the corral and I'll throw in that pack of hounds. I don't really care what you do with them, even if you have to knock them in the head. At least they'll be out from under my feet." Fred made a kicking motion to show how annoying he thought they were.

Trader shifted in his chair, "You know, Fred, usually when I'm done with a trade, I like it when both of us walk away thinking we got the best end of the deal. This time I can't leave here without letting you know that every rancher around has been asking if there's a chance they could get hold of some of Ted's hounds. Trust me, I won't be knocking them in the head; and I won't be hanging on to 'em very long either."

Fred glowered at Trader, "I don't think that's a neighborly way to act, Trader. You took advantage of me and the girls when you agreed to take those hounds for nothing. I'd think you'd be ashamed of yourself."

"Fred, you know better than to act like that. You're the man who opened his mouth so you're the man who has to live with it. Don't try to finagle a different deal by bringing in us sisters. That's not the way we do business." Emma knew the family had lost money on the dog transaction, but she thoroughly enjoyed seeing Fred realize he had thrown away perfectly good, valuable trading stock.

Darlene burst in the kitchen as they finished their coffee and rolls. "Trader, are you going to want to do something with that stallion of Ted's that he called Sport? He's over in that pasture away from the mares and colts so we completely forgot about him. Just thought I'd better catch you before you leave if you want to look him over. I could go along and help you catch him if you want to."

A pleased smile spread over Fred's face as he realized he had a chance to redeem the cash he had lost on the hound deal. "I'm not sure we want to let him go, Trader. He's sired some of the best colts on the place, so it'd take a pretty penny to get me to sell him." Fred leaned back to let Trader stew about this new development.

"Fred, you're right. It would make sense for you to keep that horse. He's got good bloodlines and throws fine colts. Probably you'll enjoy having a stallion like him around." Then Trader leaned back to watch Fred squirm.

Emma leaned forward, "Both of you quit it right now. Fred, you know darned good and well you're not about to put up with a stallion. You don't have any mares left and wouldn't find it much fun to have a crop of colts every year to break anyway. Trader, don't try that coy business on me. I know your mouth's watering at the chance to get a hold of that horse, so you and Lena go look and then you can come back and shoot us a respectable deal. How's that sound? In the meantime, Fred can go milk his cows and I'll get dinner started."

Trader scooted his chair back from the table, clapped his hat on his head, and laughed, "Emma, I like how you cut to the heart of the matter. You might think about going partners with me—we'd be an awesome team." Turning to the door, he waved Darlene out ahead of him and they went to the barn to saddle their horses.

Two miles away from the barn, they came to a barbed wire gate. "Trader, this is as far as we dare go with our saddle horses. If Sport finds another horse in his pasture, he'll whip him bad. All I have to do is whistle and he'll come running." She let out a blast that made Trader stick his finger in his ear and wiggle it around. "Sport's such a grain hog it's easy to catch him. I put some oats and a halter in my bags so we can nab him when he shows up. I'll let you catch him because Ted made me promise not to mess with him even if he is good-natured. He said it's not a good idea to trust a stud horse."

Trader nodded as he reached out to take the halter and grain, "Your brother was a wise men, Darlene. Some folks forget they're what they're working with when it comes to stallions, and that's how they get hurt. Better cautious than all crumpled up."

"I haven't told you the funnest thing about Sport. When he was a colt, his mother didn't give much milk so Ted kept them behind the barn so he could grain them. Then he broke him to drink milk out of a bucket just like the calves. From then on, Sport always tried to sneak in the corral where we set down the buckets of milk and slurp up his fill. Do you think it's funny to have a bucket horse?"

Darlene and Trader shared a good laugh as Sport popped up on the horizon.

Seeing the saddle horses, he blared out a challenge and came flying up to the fence. Prancing and pawing the ground, he arched his neck and flared his nostrils. Making several small circles as if he were leaving and then suddenly reversing to run at the fence and swerve at the last minute, he showed his abilities in a fine manner. Satisfied that he couldn't grab hold of the neck of either horse to clamp down hard and shake it like a puppy, Sport relaxed and fixed his attention on Darlene and Trader. He stepped to the fence and accepted the grain from Trader's outstretched hand.

"Wow. This is one magnificent animal, Darlene." Trader admired the antics which the stallion had performed while running free; but once the halter slipped over his head, Sport dropped his head and behaved like an old broke saddle horse. "Ted darned sure put his mark on him, didn't he? This horse acts better than most people's kids." With that he slipped the halter off and let the horse free so he could run back over the hill to resume his grazing.

"Why'd you turn him loose, Trader? Don't you want him? I thought you'd really like him." Darlene was amazed at what she had just witnessed. She crawled up on her saddle and waited.

Trader swung on and chuckled, "You bet I want him, Darlene, but there are a couple of reasons I decided to leave him here. First of all, I don't have a place I'd feel comfortable putting a horse like that right now. I've got to figure out what'll work out the best when I take him. The second reason is that Fred's sitting back there expecting me to beg to buy the horse. I've got to be nonchalant and make him think he needs me more than I need him." Smiling at his friend, he continued, "I wouldn't give away the secrets of the trade if you weren't Ted's right hand man, or girl— oh, you know what I mean."

"Yeah, I get it. You want him scared he'll end up with Sport and not have a clue what to do with him so you'll let him stew in his own juices for a bit." Darlene giggled at how panicked Fred would be if he felt a dollar slip through his fingers. "He's a funny guy. In some ways he's so tight he squeaks, and in other ways he throws money around like it's nothing. It's like he wants his buddies to think he's a real big shot, so that's when the dollars fly. If he's around family, it's Katie Bar the Door because he'll grab anything that's not bolted down and never pay a dime if he can help it. Ted always just laughed and said sometime it'd catch up with him. Don't know how that can happen the way things are right now."

Darlene and Trader made their way back to the house, and she jumped off the horses and offered to unsaddle. By the time Trader had walked the length of the barn, Fred had crossed the yard and met him at the door. "Well, how about that horse? Ted was as high on him as any horse he ever owned. Don't think I ever heard him say a cranky word about him which is darned sure more than I can say about some of his other horses. He's pretty high powered, but I might see my way fit to let him go."

"Aw, Fred, I don't know. He meant a lot to Ted so you'll probably want to hang on to him. You know how it is when a guy raises a horse from a colt. That horse might be a real nag in someone else's eyes, but it's hard sometimes for an owner to see the true picture. Sport's nice enough, all right, but I don't exactly have a place for him right now and I'd hate to shell out a huge number of dollars on what I'd call an iffy proposition."

Fred gulped at this unexpected turn of the conversation, and he made a mighty effort to convince Trader that this was an affordable and desirable horse. By the time he was done, Fred had talked himself into a pittance compared to what Trader had been willing to give for the horse, and he also agreed to pasture Sport until Trader could have a pen ready for him by fall. "Shake on it then, Trader. I know a deal's done once we put our palms together."

"You drive a hard bargain, Fred. I don't know what I was thinking when I agreed to your terms, but I might be able to break even if I really get out there and beat the bushes to find buyers. I'd like to say it's been a pleasure doing business with you, but that'd be a stretch of the imagination. If you can have those horses in tomorrow morning, I'll come and drive them to my place, and then I'll be back to get my stud horse probably by early September."

Trader directed his next remark to Darlene, "How would you feel about moving those horses with me early in the morning? We can do it before it gets hot, and I'll give you a ride back home when we're done. That way you can ride one of my horses, and I can haul you and your saddle later."

"I'd like that a lot, Trader. I really don't have much to do here, and it'll feel good to be horseback again. What time do you want to leave? I can be ready anytime." Darlene was excited at the thought of spending a day outside and leaving the tension of the home place behind.

Trader mused before answering, "I'll be here by six if that's okay with you."

"Perfect. And plan on a bite of breakfast before you and Darlene head out. Six o'clock it is," Emma entered the conversation as the three of them approached the house. "I'll fix something to hold you till you're finished, and then you'll be here about supper time too. I'll enjoy having you."

Trader paused before accepting. He understood prairie

hospitality and the generous nature of most of the Soehl family. He recognized Fred's traits as being more attuned to self-serving purposes than most of the others, but Trader was a man who accepted all comers as they were and didn't waste any time on regrets. "Never found a place I felt more at home, Emma. You and your mama put on a fine spread that warms an old bachelor's heart. I'll plan on supper here and then haul the hounds in the car rather than making them run all the way home. Who knows how many I'd lose if they jumped an old coyote's trail. See you all in the morning."

With his exit, each of the three sought a private place. Fred went to his house to chat with Ruth and Roy, Darlene curled up in the wicker rocker on the porch, and Emma cleaned the kitchen and began preparing supper. It had been a grueling day for each one, even if for widely different reasons. Fred had seen his dream of total horse profits evaporate, Darlene had seen the dispersion of Ted's pride and joy, and Emma had seen the very core of Fred's selfishness. They were tired.

When chore time rolled around, Fred made it very apparent it was time to milk. He banged the pails together, called the cows into the corral, and yelled at the bucket calves. Darlene and Emma had already gone to their room to pack their belongings, so they remained in the house in spite of his obvious but unspoken invitation. "Do you think Fred will ever like living on the ranch, Em? Right now it seems like he hates everything he has to do." Darlene sat on Mama's bed while Emma finished up by gathering her quilt and the family Bible.

"Honey, some people enjoy being miserable. They're not happy unless they're unhappy, and he might be one of them. If he didn't like it before, I don't know why he'd like it now that he's in charge. Before he bragged about being the oldest and yelled about wanting to make decisions, but deep down, he's afraid to decide anything. It's easier to let someone else and then complain. Now he's got no one to blame and I think he's scared." Emma had studied the situation and she could feel pity for Fred who was in an inescapable bind even if she knew he was responsible for his own difficulty. "The good thing is that we won't hear about it all the time like we have been doing. It'll be easier for us to be gone, for a while at least, until he figures out what he's doing."

Darlene pondered Emma's remark, "I never thought I'd be moving away before I was grown up, but it does feel right. Once in a while I wonder if I should stay here, being's Fred is my brother, but then I get that jumpy feeling in my stomach that I really don't like. Mama said she'll always be my mother, even if she's gone; and it helps me to remember Ted'll always be my brother, even if he's gone too. When I live with Aunt Tracy and Uncle Ed, I can just think about that and still have my family even if I don't live with my real family any more. You're still my sister even if you'll be a long ways away, so I'm okay with moving out."

"Sweetie, you bet I'll always be your sister, and thinking about you will make it seem like I'm not so all alone when I to go to a new place. People usually leave home when they're grown up, but you're heading out sooner than most. I feel like I can leave since I know Ed and Tracy will take good care of you; then after you graduate, maybe we can live together in the city. How's that sound?" Emma sat down beside Darlene and they leaned heads together.

Darlene took her time before answering, "Can I wait and see if I want to move to the city before I say 'yes' or 'no?' Right now, it's hard for me to imagine being old," once again she quickly changed her wording, "I mean, it's hard for me to imagine being all grown up."

"Absolutely the right thing to say, Lena. And you don't

have to worry about saying 'old' in front of me. You're nine and I'm seventeen years older than you, so it's okay to use that word. Sometimes it's exactly what I feel." Emma's heart went out to her little sister who was working so hard to be reasonable and mature in her decision-making. It hardly seemed right that so many tragedies and complications had landed in her lap, but she never once backed away from the harsh realities of her life as she absorbed whatever life brought her way.

Darlene shrugged and shoved herself up from the bed, "What's for supper, Em? I'm starved." With the quick focus of youth, she was into the moment and beyond her previous concerns.

After supper, Darlene cleared her dishes and announced, "I'm headed out to the barn to see my cats. Catch you later."

Emma had noticed how quiet Darlene had been during supper, so she gave her a bit of time before following her out to the barn. As she peered inside, she could see Darlene perched on the sadness barrel, cuddling Jitney.

Emma waited until Darlene sensed her, then joined her. "Sounds like Jitney's pretty happy you strolled out to visit with him. He's purring so hard he might strain his innards if he's not careful." Stroking the cat's fur, Emma asked, "You all right, Honey?"

Softly, Darlene let out a muffled sob and turned her head into Emma, "It's just so hard to get along without Ted. With everything that's happened around here, it's like no one even notices he's gone. His bedroom's empty, there's only one harness left on the wall, and I only see empty pegs when I look inside the tack room. Tomorrow Trader will come and we'll get rid of his horses and hounds, and then what's left of Ted? Everything he ever cared about'll be gone, and it's kind of like he never even was. We're the only ones who know how good he was with a horse or how funny he could be, and once we leave, all sign of Ted will disappear. How can a man spend his whole life working that hard and have it not amount to anything right after he dies? It doesn't seem right."

"Lena, do you remember how hard it was the first few days after Mama died? We all walked around feeling mighty lost and worried what we'd do. Then little by little, the hurt got smaller and we found out we could go on with our lives. Do you remember that?" Emma had leaned against the wall beside the barrel as she talked. "It seemed wrong that a strong woman like Mama was so weak and helpless at the end. Then when she died, I thought the same thing—we're the only ones who really knew her; and when we're gone, everything about her would disappear."

Darlene sat up a bit straighter, "Funny, isn't it? I didn't even think about that when she died, probably because I thought we'd all stick together. It hurt when she died, but all of us that knew her were still close enough that it was sorta like she was still around even though she was gone."

"That's exactly what I'm talking about, Darlene. Mama's been gone over a year now, but has she disappeared? I still find her when I'm in the kitchen fixing some dish she concocted or on the porch listening to a meadow lark sing in the morning or working hard enough the sweat runs in my eyes like it always did into hers. It's the same way with Ted. Even though we might be leaving where he spent most of his time, we'll still take him with us. What do you think will remind you of him once you're not living here anymore?"

Darlene thought for a moment and smiled, "When I hear the snow crunch, I'll hear him tell me it's too cold for man or beast out here. Or when I see a bird that looks like she has a broken wing running through the grass, then I'll go the opposite direction and find her nest with the four little speckled eggs just like he showed me." Warming up to the idea of how much of Ted remained within her, she brightened up and continued, "Every time I see a cow with a calf starting to be born, I can look to see if his toes are up or down so I know if it's coming right or backwards. When I smell bread baking, I'll remember how he liked the heel slathered with fresh butter. I'll never break a promise, and I'll always tell the truth. Is that what you mean?"

"That's exactly what I mean. It doesn't matter where you live because Ted will always live in your heart. Then when you have children, you'll teach them what he taught you, and he'll be with them too. Even though Ted died, he's still very much alive inside you. I hope you can hold on to that, because you're going to have some days when you just feel like crying, and that's okay too. We don't get over the hurt all at once; but little by little, it gets so it isn't as painful. Ted was a big part of you, and it's only natural to be sad when you lose someone like him."

Darlene sat up and pulled her arm across her eyes to dry them, "You know what I'd like to do? I'd like to take this sadness barrel with me to Dolphs. Maybe they'd let me set it out in the barn and I could go there if I need to. He and I agreed to go there when we felt bad, and it'd help if I could take this along."

"There's no reason on this earth you shouldn't have that barrel, Darlene, so let's take it to the house right now and have it handy. Ed and Tracy will understand once we tell them why you want it." Emma hoisted the barrel on one end, and Darlene grasped the other. Together they carried it up and set it on the porch against the wall. "That's a job well done. I'm thinking it's time for us to get ready for bed, especially since you'll need to be up early to help Trader drive the horse herd to his place."

With that, the sisters intertwined arms and turned to the door. As they tried to go through the opening at the same time, their hips hit the jamb and they came to an abrupt halt. Giggling, Darlene stepped back and bowed deeply, "After you, my dear."

Emma tipped her head to reply, "Thank you kindly, Miss. I appreciate your fine manners."

By morning, Darlene had pushed her concern about Ted being forgotten to the back of her mind and had moved on to the excitement of a new adventure.

Chapter 7

She bounded out of bed, hurriedly dressed, and skipped down the hall to the kitchen where Emma had a huge platter of pancakes waiting. "I just love the morning, Em, don't you? It's so fun to wake up and hear the birds chattering outside and then smell bacon and coffee—even if it does taste yucky. I'll have a bite and then run out to the barn so I'm saddled by the time Trader gets here. It'd be fun to ride Boxer, but it's even better that he and Cheyenne get to stay with me. Guess I'll use Pete today 'cause he doesn't get crazy when we have to run horses."

Chattering all the while she filled her plate and doused the cakes with syrup, she glanced up at Emma's face and instantly voiced her concern. "What's the matter, Em? Are you feeling all right? You look kinda peaked. Do you need to go back to bed?

Emma let a small smile come forth as she shook her head, "Thanks for looking after me, Hon, but I'm all right. You know I'd been gone for a while before Mama got sick, and when I came home, I slipped right back into the old routine.

Riding and cooking and doing everything the way we used to reminded me of how much I had missed being outside when I was in town, and that's what I'm going back to. You mentioned how solid Pete is, and I fell in love with him while we were looking for Ted. It makes me sad to think of all I'm leaving behind, and at the same time it makes me excited to think of the new things I'll run into. Crazy, isn't it?"

"It's that same way with me. I think this will be a really fun ride with Trader today, but then I remember we're driving Ted's horses away, and that's tough to think about. I'm sorry you can't take Pete with you, but that might be a little bit hard." Darlene put her plate in the sink and hugged Emma.

Emma started laughing at the thought of getting a horse all the way across the state, "I'd have to get him to the railroad so they could ship him for me, and I don't think Pete's got a hankering to see the city sights. You know, Darlene, I'll bet Pete would rather be out here than standing in that tiny yard beside my house. I won't have time to ride him, so he'd probably be pretty lonesome, too. I truly think it's best that he stays here even if it makes me sad to think of it."

"I promise I'll make this a fun ride for him. What do you want to bet me that those old geldings will take out across the meadow on a high run? They always act like colts when they get out of the corral and stick their tails in the air. Pete and I'll have to get around them and turn them a different direction than they usually go, so we'll be flying. When we get them settled down and headed the right way, Pete'll drop his head and walk along like an old plug. Aren't horses funny? They're all different; but if you pay attention, you can usually figure out what they'll do next. I guess that's why I like them so much. Whatever they do seems to make a lot of sense, especially if you try to look at things the way they do."

"Honey, it's that way with nearly every person in the world. If you'll try to get out of your skin and into theirs, you've got a pretty good chance of figuring out what makes them tick. If you always stay in your own little world and insist on your own way, you might just make your life harder than it has to be. If you'll try to figure out people just like you do your horses, you'll get along just fine."

Torn between her desire to resume her own activities in the city and guilt about abandoning her little sister, Emma worked at reinforcing family values every chance she had. "You're good at figuring out what makes people tick, and you need to trust your own instincts. Listen to what your heart tells you, no matter what, and you'll do just fine."

Darlene grabbed a pancake, sprinkled sugar on it before rolling it, smashed it together, and tucked it into her pocket. "Gotta go, Em. Right now my heart's telling me to keep my stomach happy, so this'll come in handy later on today. See you tonight." She tore out the door so she could be ready when Trader pulled up.

"Steady, old boy. We're about to take a long ride this fine morning, so you'd better have a bite of grain before we go. You can munch while I get you ready." Darlene haltered Pete, tied him in the stall, and began to work with the brush and curry comb. She had thrown on the saddle and was pulling the latigo when she heard Trader drive in the yard. Patting the big gelding and pushing him over to the side, she headed back out into the corral to catch Spike for Trader.

Sliding the door open, Trader hollered in the barn, "Anyone else here yet or is it just you cats?" Ducking as Darlene pitched a round piece of dried horse manure at him, he put on an air of injured pride, "Is that road apple the thanks I get for taking you on a wonderful trip? I expected much more than that from you."

"If you want more, Trader, I've still got lots more right here in front of me. Is that what you had in mind?" Darlene pulled back her arm as if she were ready to lob some more pieces in his direction, "Just trying to please, you understand." Dropping her arm, she laughed, "Truce, Trader, okay? I thought you might want to ride Spike so I've got him right here. Ted liked him because he's a big stout guy that never gets tired. He can go all day and still be prancing by the time we hit the barn at night. Sound okay to you?"

Trader strolled to the door and reached out for the halter rope, "You know I trust your judgment on this deal, 'specially if this was a horse Ted liked to ride. I'll throw my saddle on and we can get on the way before it gets scorching hot. Probably have quite a run at first, wouldn't you guess?"

"That's what I told Em at breakfast. These horses will test our air right out of the corral, and then they'll settle down after they get their run out. How about if I get out ahead so I can turn them before they make it all the way to the south end of the meadow? They're used to going east, so it might take a while before we can convince them to head the other way. How's that sound?" Darlene led Pete outside and crawled on.

Trader was done saddling Spike, and he motioned at her to get situated beyond the gate.

"Go on down there where you want to be and whistle when you're ready for me to open the gate. Then we both better have our hats cranked down and our behinds deep in the saddle. Ready for this?"

"Ready, Trader. I'll let out a blast as soon as I'm set." She dug her heels into Pete, trotted to the curve, and reined him in as she sent her signal.

Trader unlatched the gate and swung it wide open. Just as they predicted, the horse herd bolted past him and thundered down the lane. Darlene and Pete lunged out at the leaders as they neared, and her whooping and hollering forced them to veer away. She stayed abreast of the two lead roans and pressured them to continue turning away. Trader followed behind and headed off the stragglers that cut behind her. Soon the whole valley was filled with dust and pounding hooves as the entire mass curved toward the unfamiliar gate.

Gradually the herd slowed from a wide open run to an easy lope to a gentle trot before settling into a brisk walk. Occasionally one renegade would take a run at another with teeth bared and ears pinned back to his head, only to be answered by a swift kick on the way by as the victim dodged to the side. Both would once again fall in line where they would revert to their easy pace.

By the time Trader and Darlene had trailed the herd through two gates, it was as if they were all one cohesive unit. The horses had found the ruts of the sandhill road and took their direction from that, occasionally pausing to grab a bite of grass on their way by. Stopping to give the horses some breathing room, the riders sat easy in their saddles, arms crossed over the saddle horns with reins held loosely in their left hands. "I think there's a tank around this next corner so we might as well plan on them taking a little break. I won't mind one myself by then either. How about you?" Trader glanced at Darlene to get her reaction.

Nodding vigorously, she yawned right then. "Man, am I ever ready for it. It's been a nice morning, but it'll feel good to crawl off and walk around a little. I've got one of Em's pancakes in my pocket we can split, and that water will taste darned good with it. Glad those horses figured out where to go so we don't have to work quite as hard now."

"You're always one to plan ahead, aren't you? I traveled with Ted enough to know he took pretty good care of his stomach, too, so I grabbed a little bit on the way out of the house this morning. How do you think these licorice sticks will work with your pancake sandwich? I'd say quite nicely."

Darlene giggled at his last statement which he had delivered in a British accent. "You're so funny, Trader. I'm really lucky to have you as a friend. I don't think I could stand it if anyone else was taking Ted's horses. You know how he wanted them to have good homes so I think you'll be careful about who you sell them to. It'd be so wrong if they ended up with someone who'd treat them mean, but I know you'll do what's right."

"That's a mighty kind compliment you just paid me, Darlene. Ted was the finest horseman I ever had the privilege of knowing, and I promise you I'll look after these animals. I never dreamed I'd have a chance at this many of his good horses, and I take it as an honor to be the one looking after them. The ones I sell will go to good homes, and lots of them will stay right with me, especially the young mares. Maybe we'll have time at my place so you can fill me in about all of them. Would you do that for me?"

"Trader, I'm glad you asked. Some of them are green broke and just need some wet saddle blankets to make good horses. It'd be a pity if you got disgusted with them and didn't give them a chance. I can tell you which ones are full brothers and sisters, and that'll help you know which ones you want to keep in your broodmare band and which ones to sell. Every now and then Ted would come home with a new horse he bought from someone else, and I never could figure out why he needed to buy one when he had so many at home. One day I asked why he spent money like that, and he said, 'Spending money for good stock never costs; it pays.' Course, I didn't have a clue what that means, but I liked the sound of it anyway." Darlene cocked her head to wait for Trader's reaction.

He took his time, and then looked her in the eye, "Beats me how Ted got so smart and never went anywhere to do it. He stayed right at home and figured out what lots of people go to school to learn. It doesn't matter if a person is thinking about cattle or horses, his rule holds true. Even though he had to come up with money to give to another person, in the long run, he improved his herd so they were worth more. It might have taken some time to happen, but he ended up with the finest animals in this part of the country. He wasn't cheap or so prideful he couldn't admit anyone else had good stock, so when he saw a good horse, he went after it. He was quite a guy."

Ambling up to move the horses along, Darlene squeezed her eyes tight to keep the tears away. "He sure was, Trader. He sure was. I miss him a whole bunch."

Sure she wasn't watching, Trader quickly wiped his cheek, "I know what you mean. It's tough when someone like that goes away too soon." Kicking his horse into a trot, he called back over his shoulder, "Let's make our way to the windmill before all the horses get done and wander off. Meet you there."

Darlene stayed behind to hustle up the stragglers, then hauled Pete around behind the tank so she could reach the lead pipe. She leapt off the saddle and wriggled inside the tower. Stretching her full length along the pipe, she cupped both her hands over the end and caught water as it gushed out. Drinking deep and long, she slaked her thirst and shinnied back so she could stand up. Reaching into her pocket, she pulled out the rolled up pancake and held it up so Trader could see it. "It's a little smooshed but not too bad. Do you want to split it in half?"

"Nah, go ahead. You brought it so I'll trust you to take care of it."

Laughing, Darlene told him, "You must not have been

from a very big family. Any time two of us had to split up something, Mama would have one of us divide it and the other got to pick first. That'll probably work here too." Reaching into her pocket, she pulled out Ted's knife. "No need to worry, Trader. After I found out it was mine, I washed it up real good so I could use it. It'll be like Ted's here helping us out." She opened the longest blade, set the pancake on top of the nearest hedge post, and cut it in two. "Glad he kept the blade sharp. It went through that just like nothing." Wiping the blade on her pants, she folded it, being careful her fingers were not where the blade would fold back in.

"Looks like these are exactly the same size, so I'll take this one closest to me. Thanks much, Darlene. It'll help us to get this drive finished in good time, even if the horses decide to take their time. They seem pretty content to wander along right now as long as they can get a mouthful of grass every now and then. We'll be home long before I would have guessed, mostly because you turned them so soon and saved us a bunch of time back there on your home meadow."

Finishing with the main course, both of them returned for another massive drink of water. "We can probably move on now, even if we get thirsty after eating the licorice. Bet there'll be another well along the way, and it's nice we have a breeze to cool us off and keep a stream of water pumping so we can have something to drink." Darlene wiped her hands on her trousers and bounced back into the saddle. "Feels good to be here again. I was getting a little bit tired before we stopped, but now I'm ready to go."

"Me, too. Sometimes a little break makes the job easier, doesn't it?"

Darlene broke into an easy trot and moved the herd back together. Chirping and yipping to get their attention, she turned them away from the meadow and back toward the trail they were to follow. "One thing I've been wondering about, Trader. You drove over this morning, and after we get these horses to your place, what do we do then? If we ride back to my place, it'll probably be after dark when we get there, and then you still have horses that need moved. What do you have in mind to get all your stuff back to your house?"

"I was kind of puzzled by that myself, Darlene, but when I saw your sister this morning, she offered to come down and get us. All we have to do is drive the horses to my home, unsaddle, and then ride back in comfort. How's that sound to you?"

Darlene turned in her saddle to beam one of her biggest smiles, "Wow. That's the best news I've had today. It's so darned hot that I really didn't know if the horses could turn around and go right back, and I knew I didn't want to. I imagine Emma will be there by the time we are, and I'll also bet she has some scrumptious food ready for us when we get home. You're truly a thinking man, Trader, and I'm glad to be traveling with the likes of you."

"Don't guess I'm brave enough to ask for more detail about what you mean by 'the likes of you,' but I will say that sounds just like something that Ted would have said. Funny how much you're like him and yet so much different at the same time." Trader tipped his hat to Darlene and they continued riding in silence, mulling over their private thoughts.

Miles later, as they came to a sharp bend in the road, he alerted her to the next challenge that lay ahead of them. "These horses won't know it, but they'll have to swerve sharp to the left as soon as they round that curve. My horse lane starts there and leads to a set of corrals where we'll do some sorting. When we get there, you can tell me what Ted had planned for them and how he has them broke. It'll mean I can do a better job with them."

"Where do you want me to go? Would it be better if I came to the back and you could push them when the time's right? That's okay with me, or you can give me orders and I'll do what you say. Either way works for me." Darlene was standing in her stirrups and turning to the rear to hear Trader's reply.

He waved her on while giving instructions, "You've been out in front all day, so they're pretty used to answering to you. If you'll get out ahead of them, there's a big cottonwood tree right where they need to turn, so dash up there and you'll be ready for them."

She kicked Pete into his easy, ground-eating lope and found the lone tree just as he had said. Murmuring to her horse, she eased him into a slow walk, whirled him around, and was in place by the time the lead horses appeared. "Yii, yii, yii, boys. Find a hole and move on over." Darlene and Pete eased the herd down the lane and into the holding pens where they milled and churned up a tremendous cloud of dust.

"Nice job, girl. This has been one fine ride, I'd have to say. Do you want to take a break now or are you ready to sort out these animals?" Trader patted her on the back as he pushed the last horse in and leaned over to latch the wooden gate. "Might be a good idea to let them calm down before we go in and start riling them up again. Don't know about you, but I'm ready for another swig of water and maybe a few steps on the ground to loosen up my old joints."

The pair of them swung off and looped their reins around the top pole as they sought the shade of the shed on their way to the well. "Now this is luxury, my dear. Have a look at this." Trader had wrapped a wire around one leg of the tower and suspended a tin dipper from it. "How about a deep drink from one of my best mugs? Can't think of anything that's finer than a draught of blue splash after a long day in the saddle." With that, he unhooked the dipper, caught a full measure, and handed it to Darlene.

"Oh, that's one of the finest treats I think I've ever tasted. Funny how something so simple as a drink of water can be so good, isn't it? Guess when you do without something you get to know how special it really is." Darlene emptied the cup, wiped her mouth on her sleeve, and handed it to her friend. "I'll always remember today, Trader. Getting to help move Ted's horses and see where they'll be calms my mind and makes giving them up a whole lot easier. Thanks for letting me come along."

Trader took his time before answering, partly because he was at a loss for words, and partly because he was choked up with the reminder of all he had lost. "I'm the one who needs to thank you. If you hadn't been so willing to pitch in and make this work, it would have been a darned sight harder to move this herd. I couldn't have done it by myself, and I don't know any man who could have done as well as you. I hope you consider me your friend, Darlene, and if there's ever a time I can help, all you have to do is let me know. That means anytime you need a horse or a favor or a friend, I hope I'm the one you think of."

Solemnly, Darlene extended her hand, "Let's shake on it. Ted always said that meant a promise you could never break, no matter what." He took her hand and bowed slightly as they clinched their previous words. "Guess you're stuck with me now, Trader."

Chuckling, he said, "Don't know if you know what you're in for, but I do promise I'll look after you any way I can." Looking back at the road they had just covered, he continued, "I'll bet that cloud of dust means Emma's on her way. We'd better not let her catch us sitting around or we'll both be in a world of hurt. Jump on and I'll let you into the corral to cut out some of the colts. We'll turn them out together so they can explore without the whole herd charging along. Might keep them from hitting the barbed wire, especially if they keep coming back here where the big herd is."

Darlene softly moved Pete among the horses while she edged the younger horses closer to the gate. When she would get about three or four singled out, she'd call, "Out," and Trader would release those few. After she had moved through four different times, she motioned him over. "What do you want next? We could cut out the work horses, and I can tell you which ones pull together and which ones need broke to harness. That'd make us a bit more room so the others will sort easier."

"Sounds like a plan, ma'am. Head right back in there and send out the big boys." Trader stood with his hand on the gate, ready to swing it as the draft horses appeared. Not much later, she pulled up and he hollered, "Is that it? Looks like it to me."

"Yep. Everything in here's been saddled at least once, and some of them are pretty well broke. We could split them up so you know which ones are ready to go and which ones will take the most work. Some of these are brood mares, and they've all been broke to ride. You might not care about that right now, but if one comes up empty, you can sell her as a riding horse later on. Seems like we can handle these horses since we got those others out of our way."

Trader moved over to the gate between two pens and unlatched the gate. "Let's put the green broke ones in here so I can get to work with them. I'll keep them up and get a feel for what they know."

Darlene resumed her quiet way of slipping the horses out of the herd. Groups of two or three that tended to hang together in the pasture would move in unison, and she eased them to the gate. Before long, she once again stood up in her stirrups and signaled she was done. "This worked out pretty easy, so now all we have left is the broke ones. What do you want to do with them?"

"It might be a good idea if we'd halter them and tie them up so I get them straight. There are lots of roans and sorrels in here, so it'd sure help me get a handle on what I've got."

Darlene crawled off her horse and wrapped the reins loosely around a post. "Sure enough, Trader. I'll feel better if you know all about them. Are your halters handy?"

"I'm on my way to the barn to get them. Good thing I keep extra tack on hand for trading. I'll need everything I've got on hand." Trader walked to his barn and stepped out the door to greet Emma who had appeared in the drive. "Come on in, Emma. We've just got a little more sorting left, and we'll be ready to head out. You're welcome to join us in the corral."

Emma stepped up to join him, "Thanks for asking Darlene to come along on this. She needed to see where Ted's horses went so she could be done with that part of her life. I'd imagine she was pretty handy to have along, too."

"I'm glad she was with me. She has a knack with horses and knows so much about all of them that I'm in good shape with these. I'll tell you what I told her—if you ever need anything, let me know. Ted was a good friend to me, and I respect your family so please don't hesitate to ask." Handing the halters to Emma, he continued, "Guess you might as well make yourself useful. We're going to catch the broke horses so Darlene can fill me in on what she knows."

As they emerged from the barn, Darlene hugged Emma, "Glad you're here, Em. We had a good trip here and this is all we have left to do. We've already turned out some of the horses and they seem to be pretty happy. Course it didn't hurt they had a long trip and were ready to put their heads down and graze. We might as well start right here."

With that, the haltering and discussing began. By the

time they had captured each animal and discussed its breeding and habits, Trader had gained a wealth of information about the horses. "Just one question, Darlene. Are you sure you didn't want to send Boxer and Cheyenne here to me? Now that you've seen how nice it is, maybe you'd like to reconsider." Trader made his joking offer as the three of them stood in the shade of the barn and looked over their day's work.

"Good of you to offer, Trader, but you might be overloaded if you had to work with two more horses. How about it if I do you a favor and hang on to them so you're not swamped? Just looking out for your interests, you understand."

He laughed and turned to the barn. "I know when I'm licked, so I give up. You sounded just like Ted right then, and I know he'd be proud of you." Patting her on the back, he continued, "Never forget I'm in your corner, Darlene."

"Likewise, Trader. I'll help you any way I can." Shaking hands, they walked through the dusty barn. "Funny how barns all smell the same, isn't it? I think that may be my favorite smell of all time." Then catching herself, she quickly added, "Right after Emma's apple dumplings, of course."

All three of them laughed as they emerged into the sunlight. The events of the day had consumed many hours, and the sun was far in the western sky. "We'd better head back or it'll be well after midnight before I get back here again. Ladies, after you." Trader opened the doors so the girls could crawl in, he scooted under the steering wheel, and they were off.

In spite of the bumpy road and intense August afternoon heat, Darlene fell asleep in the back seat. When they pulled up in front of the Soehl house, she roused and rubbed her eyes.

"Well, Sleeping Beauty, I thought maybe you were going to snooze the entire night away. You know I plan to haul my new dogs there on my way home, so you might have been underneath a whole pack of hounds and ended up back at my house again. Glad you're among the living once again." Trader pulled the seat forward for Darlene, and she slowly emerged from the car.

"That was a nice little nap, and now I'm ready for some chow. Bet Emma has something special for us. Let's check it out."

Trader stood beside the car, "You know, maybe I'd ought to gather up the hounds and head back home. I've got quite a bit to do once I get to my place."

"That wouldn't be neighborly at all, Trader." Emma beckoned him to the house, "You've got to eat sometime, and it won't take you that long to fill your gullet. When you're done, we'll all help you get loaded and out of here. Now I don't want to hear any more of that nonsense." She entered the house without waiting for his reply.

"You knew better than that, didn't you? No way anyone ever leaves at mealtime if Emma has anything to say about it. Besides, she's making the most of these last few days when she'll be around home and spending time with people she won't see for quite a spell. Best just mind your manners and do as the woman says." Darlene skipped up the steps and paused to wait for him. "Coming, Slowpoke?"

A blast of heavenly odors hit them as they entered the kitchen. Not only had Emma baked the apple dumplings Darlene loved, she had baked Swiss steak so it was simmering and hot by the time they returned. Fresh loaves of bread and tantalizing warm cinnamon rolls rested on the counter, promising a fine dining experience .

"Go ahead and get washed up. I had everything pretty well ready so we can just sit down and dig right in. Hope you brought good appetites with you so I don't have a bunch of leftovers." With that, Emma proceeded to place the steaming bowls in front of them. White fluffy mounds of mashed potatoes, fresh beans with slices of bacon floating on the surface, and piping hot Swiss steak swimming in a garden tomato sauce were accompanied by a huge bowl of sliced cucumbers with onions dowsed in vinegar and sugar. "Oh, I forgot." Emma hurried back to find the fresh butter and strawberry jam she had preserved earlier in the summer. "That about does it. If you're still hungry when you're finished, not much I can do about it." With that, she sat down and the meal commenced.

"Oh, no. Do you remember I have to drive home and do chores yet? I don't know how I could possibly squeeze in another morsel," Trader moaned and leaned back to take the pressure off as he rubbed his stomach appreciatively. "Emma, if you ever want to come back for a working vacation, feel free to call me and come be my cook for a week or two. I'd be so big I couldn't crawl on a horse, but, man, would I be happy."

Emma laughed and patted him on the shoulder as she removed his plate and replaced it with a walnut-covered cinnamon roll sticky with caramel sauce made from fresh cream and brown sugar. "Just think of this as my farewell gift to you. Won't have many chances to sit down at a meal together from now on out. Kinda of sad to think of it, but kind of fun to think of city life for a while again."

Darlene covered her face, but then she looked up with a big smile for her sister, "Em, I'll be sorry you're not around, but I'm still glad for you. Maybe sometime I can come visit and you'll show me all around. I've never been much of anywhere, but I have big plans for when I graduate."

"Let's make our plans right now that you'll come see me in May when you're done with school. We can do some shopping and sightseeing before you have to leave. I'm already looking forward to our big outing." Emma pulled Darlene's head over to her shoulder and gave her a big squeeze.

Trader stood up and pushed the chair under the table. "Thanks a million for all your help, Darlene. You did a man's job today getting those horses to my place without any problems. You're looking a bit sleepy, even if you did take that great big nap on the way home, so I'll be shoving off. I saw the hounds sleeping in their pen beside the barn, so I'll pick them up and be on my way."

Darlene jumped up and met him at the door, "I'd better go along so you get them all and leave Tater. He's so darned friendly that he'll want to jump in with all the others." She gave a little shudder, "I have to say I'm glad to stay home this trip, Trader. I can just imagine all those hounds jumping around and slobbering all over. Doesn't sound like a fun trip home to me."

They had reached the enclosure where the hounds were sleeping, and one by one, the dogs were loaded and Trader slammed the door shut. Going around to the driver's side, he slid in, hung his elbow out the window, and looked at Darlene. "I have a feeling you might be right about this ride. Maybe they'll be back asleep before long."

With that, he pulled the car into gear, eased off on the clutch, and was off. Darlene ran to the porch and shouted in at Emma, "Come quick, Em. You've got to see this.

Trader pulled out of the yard with hounds hanging out of each window, tongues hanging out as they looked back and forth. All of a sudden, one hound apparently sighted a movement in the far end of the meadow, and they all piled out the windows, yelping and sprinting. Trader screeched to a halt, jumped out and yelled at the top of his lungs. Realizing the futility of calling them off, he leaned against the car so he could enjoy the chase. Ted's favorite dog, Jumbo, led them on the coyote's trail, and the rest of the pack held a position slightly behind him. As they neared the coyote, Jumbo grabbed him and the two of them tumbled along the lake bed. Fannie, the kill dog, jumped in for a throat hold at precisely the same time Jumbo rolled to his feet. The two hounds collided, the coyote made a run for it in the rushes, and the entire pack of hounds circled and surged in a vain attempt to find the trail.

Finally the hounds eased up in their search and heard Darlene's whistle calling them off the hunt. Trader waited for them beside the car and signaled them to load up. When he had shut the door on the final hound, he shouted back to the house. "That should take the run out of them until I can get home. Glad to know the signal to call them off. See you guys later." With that, he resumed his journey, slobbering dogs and all.

With arms around each other's waist, Darlene and Emma were glad the action-packed day had finally ended.

With the dawn of the next day, Darlene jumped up and ran to the kitchen where she found her sister cooking breakfast. With the bacon sizzling and the French toast nearly done, Emma was ready to put food on the table to serve her sister for the last time in a long time. They both knew this was the day life as they had known it would change forever. The Dolphs would load the bedstead, as well as Darlene's smaller items and move over the hill to the Carmen Post Office. Emma and Fred would pile all Emma's possessions in the car so Emma could make a new life in York. The girls were silent in their nostalgia as each realized they would seldom, if ever, wake up in the same house and share meals as family.

"I think this might be the best batch of bread you've ever baked, Em. It's a good thing you taught me Mama's recipe so I can make it sometimes too. It's kind of crazy how you just dump flour in until you think it's about right, and sure enough, it is. Don't know when I'll get that good, but at least I know a little about it."

Emma patted her on the shoulder, "Tracy is a great cook, and I know she loves to bake bread so she'll get you in practice. It'll be fun for me to come visit sometime and eat some of your rolls. You can always come to York to see me too, you know."

Quietly, they poured syrup, cut the toast, and cleaned their plates. Emma had one last cup of coffee before she sighed and scooted her chair back. "Guess we might as well get at it, Lena. No sense putting it off any longer." With that, she cleaned the kitchen one last time, and started carrying boxes out of her room. Darlene lent her a hand, and soon the room was stripped of all Emma's marks.

"I thought Dolphs might be here already, but this gives me a chance to get all my animals ready too. Think I'll head out to the barn so I can feed Johnny and Jitney before we go. Not sure exactly what the plan is for Boxer and Cheyenne, but I'll find out when they get here." Darlene was still talking back over her shoulder as she opened the door and bumped into Tracy. "Oh, I'm so sorry, Tracy. I didn't know you were there. Are you all right?" Darlene was embarrassed and concerned at the same time.

"I'm fine. It'd take more than that to give me any trouble. But I am glad I caught you here since there have been a few changes in our plans." Seeing Darlene's frightened look, she hastily offered comfort. "No, nothing bad at all. Actually, it's pretty good news the way I look at it. Fred decided he doesn't have time to do morning and night chores, so he offered to sell the milk cows to us. Right now seems like an easy time to move them since you can use your horse and get everything to our place at the same time. How about that?"

Darlene and Emma were both taken aback by the news, but not totally shocked. They had noticed how Fred found it difficult to be tied down by chores that needed done at regular times, especially the milking and separating. Selling cream had provided income for the Soehl family from the time they first moved out here, but Fred was always ready to innovate, especially if it meant less work for him.

"Well, the place belongs to Fred now, so he can do what he wants with the milk cows. Just wondering when you're planning to settle up with him on this deal." Emma casually queried Tracy about the details to determine the best way to approach Fred. Offering to share money was never an action that came easily to him, and it appeared this might be one more of his schemes to sell family assets and keep the cash all to himself. If there were a way to stop the money from making its way into his pocket, perhaps she could minimize his resentment at having to give the girls a share.

Tracy had picked up on Fred's desire to do the trade on the sly, and she had decided it was a family affair that was none of her business. She realized her plans would reveal his plans, but moving the livestock with Darlene's help required informing other family members of the situation. "He asked if he could come over later on today and pick up the money, but it makes sense to me to pay him right now. That way there's no confusion about who owns what."

Fred had hurried out of his house to intercept the Dolphs; but seeing he was too late, he plastered on a smile as he bustled up the steps. "Haven't seen you girls lately to fill you in on my plans, but I decided to sell the milk cows and calves to Tracy and Ed. It's hard for me to keep up with all the chores and get my work done, so I think this'll be better all around. One less problem on my plate sounds mighty good to me."

"Darlene, do you want to saddle up your horse now so

we can get a move on? It's still nice and cool, and once we get you on the way, we can load up your stuff and still be there to open the gates for you." Tracy had felt the tension between the brother and sister, so taking Darlene to the barn seemed like a wise move.

"Sure, Aunt Tracy." That was the first time Darlene had tried out the new title, and it fit just fine. "These old milk cows take their time, no matter how much I try to push them. I'll bet the calves run and buck at first, but then they'll settle down and go with the herd. This means Cheyenne can probably make the trip without hurting too much. Might seem like it takes forever, but we'll be home when we're done."

The two went chatting to the barn, and Emma stood without a word and looked at Fred.

"What? Don't give me that look of yours. It's not like I was trying to be sneaky about anything; I just hadn't found the opportunity to tell you yet." Fred jumped into the silence and offered justification for what was basically a plan gone wrong. He indeed had tried to be sneaky and hoped he could pull it off. The last few nights had been hard on his pocketbook as he had suffered serious losses at card games. Not only that, but the prospect of rising early every morning to do the chores after a night of carousing was too much for him to consider. If he could sell the cows, pocket the money, and be rid of tedious daily chores, he'd be ranching on his own terms.

"Oh, really, Fred? And when did you plan to let us know? If you found it hard to talk to us when we're here, do you suppose it might slip your mind when everyone is gone? No matter. What's nice about this is that Ed can pay you while I'm here, and I'll see to it that the girls all get their share. That way you'll know it's done and not have to bother with it. Now, did you want to bring the car up here so we can get loaded out? I think everything's gone except Darlene's and my stuff, and Dolphs will take hers this morning. Maybe we can get my things loaded and go most of the way today. Then you can probably make it home by tomorrow night after we unload." Emma stood her ground and gave Fred a look that made him feel like a little boy caught in the midst of a huge lie.

He smiled and, as always, put forth the effort to be back in her good graces. Fred was basically a good man, but he had never grown past the self-centered desires of a little boy. Easily influenced by others, he went along with whatever the crowd wanted. He knew the right thing to do; doing it was the hard part. Men of convenient morals such as he are always easy prey for manipulators and users, and he was currently surrounded by a flock of vultures intent on living the good life with him and through him. Fred would laugh and write off another man's gambling debt, but seldom received the same courtesy. His need to increase his cash flow had led to the cow debacle, and Emma's discovery now meant he had only one-seventh as much as before.

"Now, Emma, you know I just want to get along. We'll split the money, of course. Now I'll bring the car so we can get loaded and on our way."

Emma was so accustomed to his behavior that she didn't even waste any energy on anger; instead, she simply nodded at him and turned back to the house. After Fred had moved Emma, he would then haul the table and chairs to the Arthur house where Alma planned to leave them for the time being. Emptying the kitchen of the table would remove the final vestige of family. Every major decision, such as land purchases, house construction, cattle acquisition, and the myriad minor issues of ranching had occurred after lengthy discussions at the table. These were often accompanied by a strong pot of coffee, much fervent conversation, and finally a course of action which they all agreed to pursue.

Fred was relieved that, in two days' time, he wouldn't have to answer to anyone else. With the sisters gone, Ruth and he would finally be in charge. No one to notice what time he got up or went to bed, no one to keep track of how many late night visitors he entertained, no one to give sly little digs about work not done, no more irritating sisters to poke their noses into his business. He was ready to be done with everything from the past.

He did feel a twinge about the distribution of the estate, but only because he had wanted to avoid a confrontation while attaining more of the assets. No one would find him all sorrowful about the scattering of family to all different points. None too soon in his opinion.

All the livestock was ready for moving, so Darlene tied her horse in the barn and slowly emerged into the sunlight. Taking in the sight of the shimmering pond with blackbirds raising a cacophony of sound as they sat on the reeds and cattails, glancing up at the hills that rose majestically behind the barn, hearing the faint cluck of the hens as they scratched beside the shop, and seeing once again the shadings of green as the meadow ended and the hills began, she savored the familiar. Knowing she would never again be a part of this landscape, she spent her final time absorbing her surroundings. Counting each of the five steps up the porch, she dragged her feet all the way into the kitchen to tell Emma good by.

Surprised at not finding her close to the door, Darlene peered into the dim kitchen pantry and felt, more than heard, a soft sobbing sound. When she rounded the corner, Emma hastily wiped her eyes and turned to grab Darlene fiercely. "I don't want you to remember our last day together like this so I'd planned on being really strong, but then I found Mama's work shoes tucked under this shelf. They've been here since she went to the doctor the first time, and I guess I kind of unraveled when I caught sight of them."

Darlene grasped her sister with a strong grip and then pulled back, "Why do those shoes make you so sad, Em? You were the strong one while we went through all Mama's pretty quilts and other stuff, and now you cry. Why's that?"

"Remember when Mama told you it's not really the shoes but the memories? I remember when we were living in the first soddy that Papa built. It lasted pretty good, but one spring the snows laid in big drifts against the walls, and then it seemed like the rains would never let up. All that moisture raised the water in the meadow so it was level with the floor. As if that weren't enough, the soddy walls started to crumble while the water just kept getting higher and higher. Papa had left the house early in the morning to hitch up a team to a slip to see if he could get some kind of a ditch so the water wouldn't come in any further." Emma softly stroked the worn leather as she reminisced.

He hollered orders at us on his way out, "Get everything valuable up high. Maybe we can save some of this stuff. I'll be back as soon as I can." We scurried around and lugged the trunk with sugar and flour to the kitchen and all of us got it on top of the table. Then we turned around to see what Mama had saved. We couldn't imagine what in the world was in her head. Her dearest treasures—the family Bible and all her shoes—sat perched high on top of the trunk. Yes, I said her shoes. Later on, I figured out that back then it was hard to come by a new pair of shoes so that was what she grabbed.

Can you imagine what Papa thought when he came back in and saw her shoes? He came barging in, took one long look, and finally started talking to Mama like the two of them were the only people on earth, "Ah, Maria. It is a hard place I've brought you to. It's pleased I am that your good shoes are kept." Then he stroked her face, "Our next house will have a special place for your shoes, one where they will be neat and safe. For now, I think we all had better get blankets and go for higher ground. We'll let the water do what it will do and then we'll see."

Sitting on the hill as the water kept rising was hard for Mama and Papa, but of course we kids had a fun time romping around and then wrapping in the blankets to hide from each other. After a few hours, we could see the water was level and when it started dropping, Papa said we'd better go see how bad it was. He went in first and let out that huge laugh of his, "Mama, you need to see this."

She waded inside and found all our valuables high and dry. Actually, just barely high enough since the water line was clear up to the bottom of the table top. The table was dry enough that there was no damage. "Now I can work with dry feet when it's time to build again."

That was all she said, but later on Papa joked with her about what she had saved from the water. "It's good you didn't have to choose between your children and your shoes. That would have been a hard choice, wouldn't it, Mama?"

She shushed him with soft swat on the arm. "Oh, Ernest, how you do talk." Then they leaned against each other for a bit before they stepped back to decide what to do next.

Emma held Darlene while she mused, "Papa was as good as his word, and that's why he always built shoe shelves for her." She wiped the tears away and gave Darlene a long, solemn look. "We're from good stock, Little One. Never forget it, no matter what."

"I won't forget, Em, I won't. I promise I'll remember." Darlene crossed her heart as she made her vow.

With that, Emma squared her shoulders and led Darlene out onto the porch where they were covered with sunshine. "Go be happy, Darlene. I'll be in touch."

As Emma returned to the empty house, Darlene leaned her forehead against one of the porch supports and let out a plaintive sigh. Seeing the marks on the post reminded her of one of the family traditions which had started when she was much younger. As the youngest of the brood, she always wanted to be at least as big as the biggest, so Maria and Ted finally hatched a plan so she could keep track of how much she had grown since the last time they checked.

Darlene remembered when Maria had had Ted stand with his back to the post, "Theodor, you know to stand up straight and tall. Now be still so I can write."

As she stretched vainly to reach above his head, Ted threw back his head and laughed at his tiny mother. "Mama, just because you're mighty doesn't mean you're tall. How about if we give you a little lift?" With that, he strode into the kitchen, returned with a solid wooden chair which he set in front of the pillar, grasped her by the waist and whirled her around before depositing her on the chair.

Maria readjusted her skirt and hair before tapping him gently on the head with her pencil. "Theo, you may be a strong man, but you're still my little boy. Don't forget that. I'm still big enough to take care of you. Now stand still."

"Mama, trust me. I'm not about to forget who's the boss around here." He backed up to the post and stood stock still with a mock serious face while she marked his height. "Is it okay if I move now?"

Once again, she tapped his head with the pencil before nodding at him, "And don't try any funny stuff with me, either, young man."

"Oh, like this?" Whisking her off the chair, he whirled her around three times before sliding her into the vacant chair. Ducking as she swung at him, he jumped off the porch and stood out of her reach while she sputtered and then broke out in waves of laughter.

"Lena, whatever am I to do with that man? He's all so full of jokes," Maria pulled herself up to her full height and motioned Darlene to move in place at the post. Holding the pencil firmly on the top of her head, Maria began marking Darlene's place. "Now it's your turn, Little One. Soon you'll be up and up and up until I have to stand on tiptoes to see your eyes."

At first, Darlene had Maria check every week, and she was hugely disappointed to turn around and find no progress. "Mama, how long is this going to take?" Letting out a big groan, Darlene plopped down in the rocking chair on the porch after one of her disappointments. "What can I do to make this happen really, really fast?"

Maria made her way to the chair, lifted her onto her lap, and held the little girl so determined to hurry up and grow. "Honey, grown-up is forever. Sit on my lap here where my baby belongs." Darlene snuggled against her; and together, they wordlessly shared the rhythm of the creaking rocking chair.

For a time, Darlene was distracted by other pursuits, so the measuring stopped for several months. Then one morning, she leaned against the same post while waiting for Ted so they could go move cattle. "Hurry up, slowpoke. It'll be noon before we even make it to the barn."

Bursting out of the door, all of a sudden Ted skidded to a stop and called out to Maria. "Mama, come quick. I've got something to show you. You're not going to believe this."

Reacting to the excitement in his voice, Maria forcefully shoved aside the screen door to ask, "What's happening? What's there for me to see?"

"And me, too, Theo. You've got to show me too. What are we going to see?" Hopping from one foot to the other, Darlene wrapped both her tiny hands around one of his huge hands and literally shook with excitement. She tingled with anticipation of the glorious unknown sight promised by her big brother. "What's there to see?"

"You, Little One, you. That's what I want Mama to see," Ted picked up his little sister and placed her solidly against the post. "Look how she shot up. Won't be long before she catches up with me."

Maria squinted at her daughter and then scooted her to the side so she could check on the original mark. "I can't believe this. Let's get a pencil so Lena can see how she's shooting up to the sky." She ruffled Darlene's hair before continuing, "Won't be long before you outgrow both of us at this rate."

Ted made a great flourish of drawing the newest line, and then he pulled Darlene straight towards him before twirling her around to face the post. "There you go, Little One. You're on your way to great things, and I can't wait to see where you end up."

Choking back a sob as the images flashed through her mind, Darlene hurriedly smoothed her eyes with the back of her hand so no one would see her crying and think she was scared to leave home.

As she thought about it, everyone who had made this feel like home was gone: Maria, Theo, Emma, all the sisters. She slid down the post and hunched over, arms wrapped around her knees. Sitting there in the shelter of the porch, she recalled stories of Ernest and the olden days that Maria and Ted had recounted time and time again. Flashes of past family moments flooded over her and filled her with a melancholy so deep that her breath came in short gasps that made her ribs hurt. "Oh, Mama. Oh, Theo. Oh, no. How can this be?" And the sobs wracked her tiny body as she huddled alone on the porch.

Almost as if the crying had served to release the sorrow she had never voiced, it also appeared to release a new-found strength and perspective. Gradually regaining her composure, she sat up straight and took a deep breath. Unwinding her arms and pushing herself upright, she stood beside the pillar and stroked the growth marks as she looked around with clear eyes. "It's a good thing I hurried up and grew fast like I did so I'm not a baby anymore."

Striding to the steps, Darlene paused and turned for a final look at the house that had been home for her entire nine years. "It's time to get on with my life now. Theo, I'll take good care of Boxer and Cheyenne. Mama, I'll be a good girl when I live with the Dolphs. I promise."

With that, she turned toward the rising sun, trotted to the barn to crawl on her horse, and set out for her new home.

Printed in the United States
202975BV00001B/76-105/P

9 781432 722258